Oliver Twist

CHARLES DICKENS

**An
Adapted
Classic**

GLOBE FEARON
Pearson Learning Group

Cover design: Jules Perlmutter
Cover and text illustrations: Don Schlegel

ISBN 1-556-75001-3
Printed in the United States of America

7 8 9 10 11 12   05 04 03

1-800-321-3106
www.pearsonlearning.com

About the Author

Charles Dickens was born in Portsmouth, England, in 1812. He grew up in a large family with little money. As an author, he drew on his childhood experiences with poverty and neglect. His writings show sympathy for the poor and abused and criticize the selfish and cruel.

At the age of 12, Charles was forced to leave school in order to work in a shoe-blacking factory, first to help support his family and then simply to feed himself. When his father was sent to debtor's prison, young Charles lived on his own in a shabby attic room, scared and hungry.

This experience, which lasted about four months, was a "secret agony" to Dickens, who rarely spoke of it in later years. But it had an effect on his life. It made him work hard to achieve success.

As a young man, Dickens worked as a newspaper reporter. But by the time *Oliver Twist* was published in serial format between 1837 and 1839, Dickens had already achieved considerable success as an author. The novel, along with *David Copperfield, A Tale of Two Cities*, and *Great Expectations*, established Dickens as one of the greatest authors of English literature.

Adapter's Note

This adaptation maintains the style and flavor of Dickens' novel. No events important to the plot have been omitted. To make the story easier to understand, standard American spellings are used and certain long passages have been abridged. Meanings that may be vague to young readers have been clarified, vocabulary has been simplified, and some dialogue has been expanded.

Preface

In the late 1830s, when Dickens was writing *Oliver Twist*, England was in the midst of industrialization, which led to great changes in the way people lived and worked. Small farms were turned into large estates and many peasants lost their land. Work that had once been done by hand was now performed by machines. More and more people were forced to leave rural fields to work in urban factories. In cities such as London, life was harsh and unrewarding for the working class. Wages were low. Workdays were long. Few factory workers could read or write. A shortage of housing led to overcrowding and disease. The homeless of all ages were forced to live in workhouses, much like the one in which Oliver Twist was born.

Crime flourished in these miserable conditions. In *Oliver Twist*, Dickens portrayed robbers and murderers realistically, with none of the charm romantic novels of the time gave them. In the preface to the third edition of *Oliver Twist*, Dickens wrote: "I saw no reason, when I wrote this book, why the very dregs of life, so long as their speech did not offend the ear, should not serve the purpose of a moral....I wished to show in little Oliver the principle of good surviving through every adverse circumstance and triumphing at last." To show the villains in *Oliver Twist* "as they really are," said Dickens, was a "service to society."

If *Oliver Twist* were a color, it would be gray. It is basically a gloomy tale, a novel about miserable people living in hard times. But it is also a story of hope. It was written by a man who had wealth but never forgot the pain of poverty; a man who used the best weapon he had—his pen—to make his contemporaries aware of the squalid life around them; a man who lived the rags-to-riches story that is the core of *Oliver Twist*.

CONTENTS

CHARACTERS IN THE STORY

Oliver Twist, an orphan lad, born in a workhouse

Mr. Bumble, the puffed up parish beadle

Mrs. Mann, matron of the branch workhouse

Mr. Limbkins, chairman of the poorhouse Board

Mr. Sowerberry, a parochial undertaker, to whom Oliver is apprenticed

Charlotte, the Sowerberrys' maid

Noah Claypole, a charity-boy employed by Sowerberry

John Dawkins, the "Artful Dodger," a young thief

Fagin, master of the crime school

Charley Bates, another young thief

Nancy, a member of Fagin's band, devoted to Bill Sikes

Mr. Brownlow, a refined old gentleman

Mrs. Bedwin, his housekeeper

Mr. Grimwig, Mr. Brownlow's friend

Bill Sikes, a robber, associated with Fagin

Bull's-eye, Bill Sikes' faithful dog

Toby Crackit, another crook

Monks, a "mystery man"

Mrs. Corney, matron of the workhouse; later Mrs. Bumble

Mrs. Maylie, a wealthy and cultured lady

Rose Maylie, her beautiful young ward

Harry Maylie, handsome and talented son of Mrs. Maylie

Doctor Losberne, their family physician

Sally
Annie } old pauper women in the workhouse
Martha

Part 1
Oliver Meets the Underworld

1   *A Life for a Life*

"Let me see the child, and die."

The frail, young mother spoke in a weak voice as she raised her pale face feebly from the pillow. In great fear, she had listened to the sounds of her baby's struggles for breath. When she heard at last his lusty cry, her strongest desire was to see him and hold him in her arms, in spite of her own weakness and sad plight.

And in many ways it was a sad plight for her newborn son. He was at the mercy of one of those wretched "homes," called workhouses, which were supposed to provide proper care for the unfortunate English poor of long ago. But we should be thankful that our hero and his mother could be given *some* attention. For, had she not been discovered lying by the roadside the night before, cold and exhausted, probably her child never would have succeeded in drawing his first breath.

In that case, his first adventure would have been his last; and this story could be concluded here.

The young mother had two attendants: a parish doctor, whose services were obtained by contract, and a very poor old nurse. She was half-drunk most of the time, because she frequently sipped the contents of a bottle that could be hidden when necessary in the pocket of her dress.

2

When his mother spoke the words with which this chapter begins, the crying child was lying on a little flock mattress, and the doctor was sitting with his face toward the fire, warming his hands. The faint plea of the mother aroused him. He stepped to the head of her rude bed and, with more kindness than might have been expected of him, said, "Oh! You must not talk about dying yet."

"Lor' bless her dear heart, no!" added the old nurse, from a corner of the room, hastily returning the bottle to its hiding place.

But the patient only shook her head and stretched out her hands toward the child.

The surgeon placed it in her arms. With cold, white lips, she kissed it lovingly on its forehead. Then she gazed wildly around, shuddered, fell back—and died. The surgeon and the nurse worked over her, but her blood had stopped flowing forever.

"It's all over, Mrs. Thingummy!" said the doctor at last.

"Ah, poor dear, so it is!" agreed the nurse, replacing in the gin bottle the cork that had fallen out on the pillow as she stooped to take up the child. "Poor dear!"

"You needn't mind sending up to me if the child cries too much, nurse," said the surgeon, slowly pulling on his gloves. "It probably *will* be troublesome. If so, give it a little porridge."

Then he put on his hat and, pausing by the bedside on his way to the door, added, "She was a good-looking girl, too. Where did she come from?"

"She was brought here last night by the overseer's order," replied the old woman. "She was found lying in the street. She must have walked some distance, for her shoes were worn to pieces. But nobody knows who she is, where she came from, or where she was going."

The doctor leaned over the cold body and, shaking his head as he lifted and examined the left hand, said, "The old story: unmarried mother, unknown father—Well, good night!"

The medical gentleman then left for dinner. The nurse, having once more applied her lips to her bottle, sat down before the fire with the child and proceeded to dress it.

In his blanket, Oliver might have been the child of a nobleman or a beggar. It would have been hard for anyone to make a guess as to his proper place in society. But now, wrapped in the old calico robes, grown yellow in the same service, he was labeled and ticketed, and thus given his proper place at once: He was a parish child—the orphan of a poorhouse—to be humbled and half-starved—cuffed and kicked through the world—despised by all and pitied by none.

Oliver's cries were strong. But, if he could have known that he was an orphan, left to the tender mercies of church-wardens and overseers, perhaps he would have cried even more loudly.

2 Workhouse Clutches

For the next eight or ten months, Oliver lived as best he could without a mother's love and care, and in spite of all kinds of ill-treatment.

But Oliver did not become healthy, for he was not given the nourishment that his tender age required. And, when officers of the parish and the poorhouse learned of his serious condition, they decided to do the "right" thing by Oliver. So they agreed that he should be "farmed." That is, they planned to send him to a branch-workhouse about three miles away. There, for only a few pennies per week, they could be "sure" that he would be "properly" cared for, along with twenty or more other unfortunate juvenile "offenders" against the poor laws.

The branch-poorhouse was in the charge of an elderly female who was very stingy. Out of each shamefully small weekly payment per "culprit," she managed to save the greater share for herself. She was very careful not to overfeed the children or spend too much for their clothes. In fact, so great was her "wisdom" and experience in caring for children, that she knew *almost* how little food was required to keep them barely alive. But all experimenters make mistakes; and death can occur at any age. So, who could blame her if, occasionally, one of her brood failed to live just one more day? Was he not removed from this world because of a weak constitution? Did he not fall into the fire, or smother or scald himself to death, or otherwise come to an early end because of pure accident or disobedience?

But Oliver Twist outlived some of his fellows. And his ninth birthday found him pale, thin, and stunted in growth. No doubt his strong spirit, his will to live, rather than the spare diet offered him, made it possible now for him to "celebrate" his ninth birthday. But even on that great day he had been wicked enough to say that he was hungry; and two other bold young gentlemen committed the same crime. Hence, Mrs. Mann, the good lady of the house, gave the three a sound thrashing and locked them in the coal cellar. There Oliver's birthday might have been gaily celebrated for many long hours, had not the arrival of an unexpected visitor interfered.

Mrs. Mann happened to look out of the window and was startled at the sight of Mr. Bumble, the beadle [a workhouse officer] trying to undo the wicket of the garden gate. Excitedly, she thrust out her head and called to him, in mock delight, "Goodness gracious! Is that *you*, Mr. Bumble, sir?"

Quickly turning to Susan, a maid, she ordered her to "take Oliver and them two brats upstairs and wash 'em directly."

Then, in sweeter tones, she called again to her visitor, "My heart alive, Mr. Bumble, how glad I am to see you, *surely!*"

The fat and angry overseer did not respond kindly to the openhearted greeting. Instead, he shook the little wicket violently and then gave it a vicious, official kick.

Quickly noting that the three boys had been removed from the coal cellar, Mrs. Mann ran out of the house toward Mr. Bumble. She called to him in the kindest terms she could muster, offered false excuses, and begged him to go in with her. He reminded her of his exalted position and her lowly place. But she persisted in making him feel just as important as he thought he was; and he slowly relaxed.

"Well, well, Mrs. Mann," the beadle said, at last, "it may be as you say. Lead the way in, for I have come on business."

After Mrs. Mann had ushered him into a small parlor and had placed a comfortable chair at his disposal, she deposited his cocked hat and his cane on a table with proper care. As he mopped his perspiring forehead, he looked calmly and proudly at his hat and cane—and actually *smiled*.

Then, with captivating sweetness, Mrs. Mann observed, "Now don't be offended at what I'm a-going to say. You've had a long walk, you know, or I wouldn't mention it. Now, will you take a leetle drop of somethink, Mr. Bumble?"

"Not a drop. Not a drop," said Mr. Bumble, waving his right hand in a dignified, easy manner.

But Mrs. Mann did not find it too difficult to persuade him to take just "a *leetle* drop, with water and a lump of sugar"; and he drank to her health.

"And now about business," said Mr. Bumble, taking out a leather pocketbook. "The child that was half-baptized Oliver Twist is nine year old today."

"Bless him!" put in Mrs. Mann, inflaming her left eye with a corner of her apron.

Then Mr. Bumble explained that rewards offered, up to twenty pounds, and "supernat'ral exertions on the part of his parish" had failed to bring forth any information concerning Oliver's father and mother.

Mrs. Mann expressed her astonishment, then added, "How comes he to have any name at all, then?"

With great pride, the beadle replied, "I inwented it."

"*You*, Mr. Bumble!"

"*I*, Mrs. Mann. We name our fo'ndlings in alphabetical order. The last was a S—Swubble, I named him. This was a T—Twist, I named *him*. The next one as comes will be Unwin and the next Vilkins. I have got names ready-made to the end of the alphabet, and all the way through it again."

"Why, you're quite a literary character, sir!" exclaimed Mrs. Mann, beaming.

The beadle was pleased at the compliment and said, "Well, well, perhaps I may be, Mrs. Mann." Then he finished his drink and added, "Oliver being now too old to remain here, the board have decided to have him back into the house. I have come myself to take him there. So let me see him at once."

"I'll fetch him directly," said Mrs. Mann, leaving the room. When she examined him and observed that most of the dirt had been hastily scrubbed from his face and hands, she returned to the little parlor with him, ordering him to make a bow to the gentleman.

Before Oliver could show too much joy at the prospect of leaving Mrs. Mann's establishment, as announced by Mr. Bumble, he saw her shake her fist at him from behind the beadle's chair, and inquired, "Will *she* go with me?"

"No, she can't," replied Mr. Bumble. "But she'll come and see you sometimes."

Then, aided by hunger and the memory of recent ill-treatment, poor Oliver managed to force a few tears into his eyes. Mrs. Mann gave him many embraces and something much more welcome: a piece of bread and butter. She thus impressed the beadle with her "motherliness" and provided some guarantee that Oliver should not appear to be too hungry when he returned to the workhouse where he was born.

As Mr. Bumble led him away from the wretched home, Oliver felt suddenly alone, realizing that his little companions in misery, left behind, were the only friends he had ever known. And poor Oliver burst into an agony of childish grief as the cottage gate closed after him. But there was no choice. So he started out on the long and weary walk with Mr. Bumble.

Oliver had not been within the walls of the workhouse a quarter of an hour, when Mr. Bumble told him that the board had said he was to appear before it at once.

Not understanding clearly what a live board was, Oliver was rather startled by this announcement and was not quite certain whether he should laugh or cry. He had no time to think about the matter, however, for Mr. Bumble gave him a tap on the head with his cane to wake him up, and another on the back to make him lively. He then conducted him into a large white-washed room where eight or ten fat gentlemen were sitting around a table. At one end of the table, in an armchair slightly higher than the rest, sat a particularly fat gentleman with a very round, red face.

"Bow to the board," said Bumble. Oliver brushed away two or three tears and, seeing no board but the table, fortunately bowed to that.

"What's your name, boy?" asked the gentleman in the high chair.

Oliver trembled at the sight of so many gentlemen. And the beadle gave him another tap behind, which made him cry. When the poor boy did answer in a hesitating voice, a gentleman in a white vest said he was a fool, which was a strange way of raising his spirits and putting him at ease.

"Boy," said the gentleman in the high chair, "listen to me. You know you're an orphan, I suppose?"

"What's *that*, sir?" inquired poor Oliver.

"The boy *is* a fool. I thought he was," said the gentleman in the white waistcoat.

"Hush!" said the gentleman who had spoken first. "You know you've got no father or mother, and that you were brought up by the parish, don't you?"

"Yes, sir," replied Oliver, weeping bitterly.

"What are you crying for?" inquired the gentleman in the white vest.

"I hope you say your prayers every night," said another gentleman in a gruff voice, "and pray for the people who feed you and take care of you—like a Christian."

"Yes, sir," stammered the boy. The gentleman who spoke last was unknowingly right. It would have been very like a Christian, and a marvelously good Christian, too, had Oliver prayed for the people who fed and took care of him. But he hadn't, because nobody had taught him how.

"Well! You have come here to be educated and taught a useful trade," said the red-faced gentleman in the high chair.

"So you'll begin to pull the fibers from old rope tomorrow morning at six o'clock," added the surly one in the white waistcoat. "We'll sell that hemp for sealing cracks and stopping leaks in boats."

Oliver bowed low, by direction of the beadle, and was then hurried away to a large ward. There, on a rough, hard bed, he sobbed himself to sleep—What a noble illustration of the tender laws of England! They let the paupers go to sleep!

Poor Oliver! He little dreamed, as he lay sleeping, that the board had that very day made a decision which would greatly affect all his future fortunes. But they had. And this was it:

The members of this board considered themselves very wise men. And when they turned their attention to the poorhouse, they found out at once what ordinary folks would never have "discovered"—the poor people "liked" it! It was a place of public "entertainment" for the poorer classes; a tavern where there was nothing to pay; a public breakfast, dinner, tea, and supper all the year round; a place of "all play" and no work. "'Oho!" said the board, looking very wise. "*We* are the fellows to set this to rights. We'll stop it all, in no time."

So they established the rule that all poor people should have the choice (for the board would compel nobody, not they) of being starved by a gradual process in the house, or by a quick way out of it. With this in view, they contracted with the waterworks for an unlimited supply of water; and with a salesman to supply, at certain times, small quantities of oatmeal; and issued three meals of thin gruel a day, with an onion twice a week, and half a roll on Sundays. They "kindly" undertook to divorce poor married people. Then, instead of compelling a man to support his family, as they had previously done, they took his family away from him!

There is no saying how many applicants for relief, in those last two groups, might have started up in all classes of society, had relief not been coupled with the workhouse. But the board had provided for this difficulty: The assistance was bound up with the poorhouse and the gruel; and that frightened people.

For the first six months after Oliver Twist was returned, the system was in full operation. It was rather expensive at first, because of the increase in the undertaker's bill, and the necessity of making smaller the loose clothes of all the paupers, to fit their shrunken forms, after dieting a week or two on thin gruel. But the *number* of workhouse inmates became thin, as well as the paupers. So the gentlemen of the board were delighted.

The room in which the boys were fed was a large stone hall, with a huge copper kettle at one end. Out of it the master, dressed in an apron for the purpose, and assisted by one or two women, ladled the gruel at mealtimes. Of this weak mixture, each boy had one serving in a small bowl, and no more—except on, occasions of great public rejoicing, when he had two ounces and a quarter of bread besides! The bowls never seemed to require washing. The boys polished them with their spoons. And when they had performed this operation (which never took very long, the spoons being nearly as large as the bowls), they would sit staring at the big kettle with eager eyes, as if they could have devoured the very bricks which supported it.

Boys usually have excellent appetites. Hence, Oliver Twist and his companions suffered the tortures of slow starvation for three months. At last they became wild with hunger. Indeed, one boy, who was tall for his age and hadn't been used to that sort of thing (for his father had kept a small cookshop), hinted darkly to his companions. He declared that, unless he had an extra basin of gruel per day, he was afraid he might some night happen to eat the boy that slept next to him, who happened to be a very weak and very small young fellow. So a council was held.

Lots were cast to decide who should walk up to the master after supper that evening *and ask for more;* and it fell to Oliver Twist.

The evening arrived and the boys took their places. The master, in his cook's uniform, stationed himself at the copper. His pauper assistants ranged themselves behind him. The gruel was served; and a long grace was said. The watery meal disappeared. The boys whispered to each other and winked at Oliver, while his close neighbors nudged him. Child as he was, he was desperate with hunger and reckless with misery. He arose from the table. Then, advancing to the master, basin and spoon in hand, he said, somewhat surprised and alarmed at his own boldness,

"Please, sir, I want some more!"

The master was a fat, healthy man; but he turned very pale with anger. He gazed in blank astonishment upon the small rebel for some seconds and then clung for support

to the copper kettle. His assistants were paralyzed with wonder; the boys with fear.

"What!" exclaimed the master at length, in a faint voice.

"Please, sir," replied Oliver, "*I want some more!*"

The master aimed a quick blow at Oliver's head with the ladle, caught him in his arms, and shrieked for the beadle.

The board was sitting in solemn session, when Mr. Bumble rushed into the room in great excitement and, addressing the gentleman in the high chair, exclaimed,

"Mr. Limbkins, sir—I beg your pardon, sir!—Oliver Twist *has asked for more!*"

There was a general start. A look of horror appeared on every face.

"For more!" said Mr. Limbkins. "Compose yourself, Bumble, and answer me distinctly. Do I understand that he asked for *more,* after eating his full share?"

"He did, sir," replied Bumble.

"That boy will be hung," said the gentleman in the white vest. "I *know* that boy will be hung."

Nobody contradicted the gentleman's opinion. A lively discussion took place. Oliver was ordered into instant confinement; and a bill was next morning posted on the outside of the gate, offering a reward of five pounds to anybody who would take Oliver Twist off the hands of the parish. In other words, five pounds *and* Oliver Twist were offered to any man or woman who wanted an apprentice to any trade, business, or calling.

Said the gentleman in the white waistcoat, as he knocked at the gate and read the bill next morning: "I never was more convinced of anything in my life than I am that Oliver Twist will come to be hung."

3 *How Much for Oliver?*

For a week after his "crime" of asking for more, Oliver remained a close prisoner in a dark and solitary room. He cried bitterly all day. When the long, dismal night came on, he spread his little hands before his eyes to shut out the darkness and, crouching in the corner, tried to sleep. He often awoke with a start and a tremble, drawing himself close to the wall, as if even its cold, hard surface were a protection in the gloom and loneliness which surrounded him.

The weather was cold, and, for exercise, Oliver was allowed to wash his face every morning under the pump, in a stone yard. His overseer was Mr. Bumble, who, to prevent the boy from catching cold, caused a tingling sensation to run through Oliver's body by repeated applications of the cane. As for society, he was carried every other day into the hall where the boys dined and there sociably flogged as a public warning and example. And, for religious "comfort," he was kicked into the same apartment every evening at prayer time. There he was permitted to listen to, and console his mind with, a general prayer by the boys. That prayer contained a special new clause, inserted by authority of the board, in which the young paupers begged to be made good, virtuous, contented, and obedient. Es-

15

pecially they asked to be guarded from the "sins" and "vices" of Oliver Twist.

It chanced one morning, while Oliver's affairs were in this state, that Mr. Gamfield, chimney sweep, went his way down High Street. He was deeply concerned about how to pay his overdue rent, for which his landlord had become rather pressing. Mr. Gamfield's most hopeful estimate of his finances could not raise them within five pounds of the desired amount. He was, by turns, forcing his brains and beating his donkey, when, passing the workhouse, he saw the bill on the gate.

"Wo-o!" said Mr. Gamfield to the donkey.

The donkey was wondering, probably, whether he was to be fed a cabbage stalk or two when Mr. Gamfield had disposed of the two sacks of soot with which the little cart was laden. So, without noticing the command, he jogged onward.

Mr. Gamfield growled fiercely at the donkey and, running forward, bestowed a blow on its head. Then, catching hold of the bridle, he gave the beast's jaw a sharp wrench and turned him around. Another blow on the head followed, just to stun the animal until his master came back again. Then Mr. Gamfield walked up to the gate to read the bill.

The gentleman wearing the white waistcoat was standing at the gate with his hands behind him. Having witnessed the little dispute between Mr. Gamfield and the donkey, he smiled brightly when the former came up to read the bill. For he saw at once that the rough-looking man was exactly the sort of master Oliver Twist needed. Mr. Gamfield smiled, too, as he read the poster. Five pounds was just the sum he had been wishing for. And, knowing all about the poorhouse meals, he was sure that the boy would be a nice, *small* pattern: the very size for register stoves. So he spelled the bill through again. Then, touching his fur cap as a sign of respect, Mr. Gamfield spoke to the gentleman in the white vest:

"This here boy, sir, wot the parish wants to 'prentis," the bargain hunter began.

"Ay, my man," said the fine gentleman, with a condescending smile. "What of him?"

"If the parish would like him to learn a right pleasant trade, sir, in a good 'spectable chimbley-sweepin' b'isness," continued Mr. Gamfield, "I wants a 'prentis, and I am ready to take him."

"Walk in," said the gentleman in the white waistcoat.

"It's a nasty trade," said Mr. Limbkins, when Gamfield had again stated his wish.

"Young boys have been smothered in chimneys before now," added another gentleman.

"That's acause they damped the straw afore they lit it in the chimbley to make 'em come down ag'in," said Gamfield. "That's all smoke and no blaze. Vereas, smoke ain't o' no use at all in making a boy come down, for it only sinds him to sleep, and that's wot he likes. Boys is wery obstinit and wery lazy, gen'l'men, and there's nothink like a good hot blaze to make 'em come down vith a run. It's humane too, gen'l'men, acause, even if they've stuck in the chimbley, roasting their feet makes 'em struggle to free theirselves."

The gentleman in the white vest appeared very much amused by this explanation, but his mirth was speedily checked by a look from Mr. Limbkins. The board then proceeded to converse among themselves for a few minutes.

At length the whispering ceased; and the members of the board, having resumed their seats and their solemnity, Mr. Limbkins said:

"We have considered your proposition, and we don't approve of it."

As Mr. Gamfield did happen to have the slight repu-
tation of bruising three or four boys to death already, it
occurred to him that the board had, perhaps, taken it into
their heads that this report ought to influence their proceedings. It was very unlike their general mode of doing
business, if they had. But still, as he had no particular wish
to revive the rumor, he twisted his cap in his hands and
walked slowly from the table.

"So you won't let me have him, gen'l'men?" whined
Mr. Gamfield, pausing near the door.

"No," replied Mr. Limbkins, "at least, as it's a nasty
business, we think you ought to take something less than
the premium we offered."

Mr. Gamfield's face brightened, as, with a quick step,
he returned to the table and asked,

"What'll you give, gen'l'men? Come! Don't be too hard
on a poor man. What'll you give?"

"I should say three pound ten was plenty," said Mr.
Limbkins.

"Ten shillings too much!" declared the gentleman in
the white vest.

"Come!" said Gamfield. "Say four pound, gen'l'men,
and you've got rid on him for good and all. There!"

"Three pound ten," repeated Mr. Limbkins, firmly.

"You're desperate hard upon me, gen'l'men," said
Gamfield, wavering.

"Pooh! pooh! nonsense!" exclaimed the gentleman in
the white vest. "He'd be cheap with *nothing,* as a premium.
Take him, you silly fellow! He's just the boy for you. He
wants the stick, now and then. It'll do him good. And his
board needn't come very expensive, for he hasn't been *over-*
fed since he was born. Ha! ha! ha!"

Mr. Gamfield looked doubtfully at the faces around the
table. Then, observing a smile on each of them, he gradually
broke into a smile himself. The bargain was made. Mr.
Bumble was at once instructed that Oliver Twist and his

papers were to be placed before the magistrate, for signature and approval, that very afternoon.

Then little Oliver, greatly surprised, was for the moment released from bondage and ordered to put himself into a clean shirt. He had hardly performed this very unusual gymnastic act, when Mr. Bumble brought him a basin of gruel and the holiday allowance of two ounces and a quarter of bread. At the tremendous sight, Oliver began to cry very piteously. He feared that the board must have determined to kill him for some useful purpose, or they never would have begun to fatten him up in that way.

"Don't make your eyes red, Oliver, but eat your food and be thankful," said Mr. Bumble, in a tone of high superiority. "You're a-going to be made a 'prentice of, Oliver."

"A *'prentice, sir!*" exclaimed the child, trembling.

"Yes, Oliver," said Mr. Bumble. "The kind and blessed gentlemen, which is so many parents to you, Oliver, are a-going to set you up in life and make a man of you, although the expense to the parish is three pound ten!— *Three pound ten,* Oliver!—And all for a naughty orphan which nobody can't love."

As Mr. Bumble paused to take breath, the tears rolled down the poor boy's face.

"Come," said Mr. Bumble, somewhat kindly, for it was gratifying to his feelings to observe the effect his fine speech had produced. "Come, Oliver! Wipe your eyes with the cuffs of your jacket and don't cry into your gruel. *That's a very foolish action, Oliver.*" It certainly was, for there was quite enough water in it already.

On their way to the magistrate, Mr. Bumble instructed Oliver that all he would have to do would be to look very happy and say, when the gentleman asked him if he wanted to be apprenticed, that he should like it very much indeed. Oliver promised to obey, because Mr. Bumble threw in a gentle hint that, if he failed in either particular, there was no telling what would be done to him. When they arrived at the office, he was shut up in a little room by himself and ordered by Mr. Bumble to stay there until he came back to fetch him.

There the boy remained, his heart beating rapidly, for half an hour. Then Mr. Bumble thrust in his head and said aloud:

"Now, Oliver, my dear, come to the gentlemen." As Mr. Bumble spoke, he put on a grim and threatening look, and added, in a low voice, "Mind what I told you, you young rascal!"

Oliver stared innocently into Mr. Bumble's face at this somewhat contradictory style of address. But the beadle prevented his offering any remark in return, by leading him at once into a large room. Behind a desk sat two old gentlemen with powdered hair. Mr. Limbkins was standing in front of the desk on one side; and Mr. Gamfield, with a partially washed face, on the other; while two or three bluff-looking men, in top boots, were lounging about.

One old gentleman, wearing spectacles, gradually dozed off over a small sheet of official notes. Then there was a short pause, after Oliver had been stationed by Mr. Bumble in front of the desk.

"This is the boy, your worship," said Mr. Bumble.

The other old gentleman, who was reading a newspaper, raised his head for a moment and pulled the sleeve of the gentleman wearing spectacles. Then the latter woke up.

"Oh, is this the boy?" he inquired.

"This is him, sir," replied Mr. Bumble. "Bow to the magistrate, my dear."

Oliver roused himself and made his best bow.

"Well," said the old gentleman, "I suppose he's fond of chimney sweeping?"

"He dotes on it, your worship," replied Bumble, giving Oliver a sly pinch to intimate that he had better not say he didn't.

"And this man that's to be his master—you, sir—you'll treat him well and feed him, and do all that sort of thing, will you?" asked the old gentleman.

"When I says I will, I means I will," replied Mr. Gamfield, doggedly.

"You're a rough speaker, my friend, but you look like an honest, openhearted man," said the magistrate, turning his spectacles in the direction of the candidate for Oliver's premium, whose villainous countenance was a regular stamped receipt for cruelty. But the magistrate was half blind and half childish, so he couldn't reasonably be expected to observe what other people did.

"I hope I am, sir," said Mr. Gamfield, with an ugly leer.

"I have no doubt you are, my friend," replied the old gentleman, fixing his spectacles more firmly on his nose, and looking about him for the inkstand.

It was the critical moment of Oliver's fate. If the inkstand had been where the old gentleman thought it was, he would have dipped his pen into it and signed the contract, and Oliver would have been straightway hurried off. But, as it chanced to be immediately under his nose, he looked everywhere else for it, without finding it. And, happening to glance straight before him, he beheld the pale and terrified face of Oliver Twist. Despite all the warning looks and pinches of Bumble, the boy was regarding the repulsive face of his future master with an expression of mingled horror and fear.

The old gentleman stopped, laid down his pen, and looked from Oliver to Mr. Limbkins.

"My boy!" said the magistrate, leaning over the desk. Oliver started at the sound, for the words were kindly said; and strange sounds frighten one. He trembled violently and burst into tears.

"My boy!" repeated the high official. "You look pale and alarmed. What is the matter?"

"Stand a little away from him, Beadle," said the other

magistrate, laying aside the paper and leaning forward with an expression of interest. "Now, boy, tell us what's the matter. Don't be afraid."

Oliver fell on his knees and, clasping his hands together, begged that they would order him back to the dark room—so that they would starve him—beat him—kill him, if they pleased—rather than send him away with that dreadful man.

"Well!" said Mr. Bumble, raising his hands and eyes most solemnly. "Well! of all the artful and scheming orphans that ever I've seen, Oliver, *you* are one of the most bare-facedest."

"Hold your tongue, Beadle!" said the second old gentleman.

"I beg your worship's pardon," said Mr. Bumble, unable to believe his ears. "Did your worship speak to me?"

"Yes! Hold your tongue."

Mr. Bumble was amazed. A beadle was ordered to hold his tongue! A moral revolution!

The old gentleman in the tortoiseshell spectacles looked at his companion, who nodded.

"We refuse to approve these agreements," said the other gentleman, tossing aside the papers as he spoke.

"I hope," stammered Mr. Limbkins, "I hope the magistrates will not form the opinion that the authorities have been guilty of any improper conduct, on the unsupported evidence of a mere child."

"The magistrates are not called upon to pronounce any opinion on the matter," said the second old gentleman sharply. "Take the boy back to the workhouse and treat him kindly. He seems to want it."

The next morning, the public was once more informed that Oliver Twist was "To Let," and that five pounds would be paid to anybody who would take possession of him.

4 *A Way Out*

Mr. Bumble had been sent forth by the poorhouse board to find a master for Oliver. On his way back to the workhouse to report no success, he met Mr. Sowerberry, the parish undertaker.

"I have taken the measure of the two women that died last night, Mr. Bumble," said the undertaker, smiling.

"You'll make your fortune, Mr. Sowerberry," said the beadle, as he thrust his thumb and forefinger into the undertaker's snuffbox, which was a well-designed model of a coffin.

"Think so?" asked the undertaker. "The prices allowed by the board are very small, Mr. Bumble."

"So are the coffins," replied the beadle, with as much of a laugh as a great official ought to indulge in.

Mr. Sowerberry was much tickled at that remark. It made him laugh a long time. "Well, well, Mr. Bumble," he said at last, "there's no denying that. Because of the new system of feeding, the coffins are something narrower and more shallow than they used to be. But we must have *some* profit, Mr. Bumble. Well-seasoned timber is expensive, sir, and all the iron handles come by canal from Birmingham."

"Yes, yes," said Mr. Bumble, "every trade has its drawbacks. A fair profit is, of course, allowable."

24

"Of course, naturally," replied the undertaker. "And if I don't get a profit upon this or that particular article, why, I make it up in the long run, you see!" Then he laughed at his own joke.

"Just so," said Mr. Bumble, smiling with care.

"Though I must say," continued the undertaker, "one very great *dis*advantage is that all the stout people go off the quickest. Those who have seen better days, and have paid rates for many years, are the first to sink when they come into the house. And, indeed, Mr. Bumble, three or four inches over one's calculation makes a great hole in the profits, especially when one has a family to provide for, sir."

Mr. Bumble now thought it advisable to change the subject, and, as Oliver Twist was uppermost in his mind, he spoke of him:

"By the by, you don't know anybody who wants a boy, do you? A parish 'prentis, who is at present a deadweight around the parochial throat? Liberal terms, Mr. Sowerberry, liberal terms!" As Mr. Bumble spoke, he raised his cane to the bill above him and gave three distinct raps upon the words "five pounds."

"Why!" exclaimed the undertaker, taking Mr. Bumble by the gilt-edged lapel of his official coat, "that's just the very thing I wanted to speak to you about. You know—dear me, what a very beautiful button this is, Mr. Bumble! I never noticed it before."

"Yes, I think it is rather pretty," said the beadle, glancing proudly downward at the large brass buttons which decorated his coat. "The die is the same as the parochial seal—the Good Samaritan healing the sick and bruised man. The board presented it to me on New Year's morning, Mr. Sowerberry. I put it on for the first time to attend the inquest on that *very thin* tradesman who died in a doorway at midnight."

"I recollect," said the undertaker. "The jury decided: 'Died from exposure to the cold and want of the common necessaries of life.' Didn't they?"

Mr. Bumble nodded. Then:

"Well, what about the boy?" he asked, determined to drive a bargain.

"Oh!" replied the undertaker. "Why, you know, Mr. Bumble, I pay a good deal toward the poor's rates."

"Hem!" said Mr. Bumble. "Well?"

"Well," replied the undertaker, "I was thinking that if I pay so much toward 'em, I've a right to get as much out of 'em as I can, Mr. Bumble; and think I'll take the boy myself."

Mr. Bumble grasped the undertaker by the arm and led him into the building. Mr. Sowerberry was closeted with the board for five minutes. It was arranged that Oliver should go to him that evening.

Little Oliver was taken before "the gentlemen" that evening and informed that he was to go, that night, as general house lad to a coffin maker's. If he complained, he would be sent to sea, there to be drowned or knocked on the head, as the case might be. He showed so little emotion that they pronounced him a hardened young rascal and ordered Mr. Bumble to remove him at once.

Poor Oliver's luggage was soon put into his hand. All of it was wrapped in a small brown-paper parcel. Then he pulled his cap over his eyes. And, once more attaching himself to Mr. Bumble's coat cuff, he was led away to a new scene of suffering.

For some time, Mr. Bumble drew Oliver along, without notice or remark; for the beadle carried his head very erect, as a beadle always should. It was a windy day, and little Oliver was almost completely covered by the skirts of Mr. Bumble's coat as they blew open. As Oliver and the beadle drew near to their destination, however, Mr. Bumble thought it wise to look down and see that the boy was in good order for inspection by his new master. He did so with a becoming air of gracious consideration.

"Oliver!" said Mr. Bumble.

"Yes, sir," piped Oliver, in a shaky voice.

"Pull that cap off your eyes and hold up your head, sir."

Oliver did so at once and passed the back of his unoccupied hand briskly across his eyes. They were wet with tears when he looked up at his guide. As Mr. Bumble gazed sternly upon him, tears rolled down Oliver's cheeks. The little boy made a strong effort to stop them, but was unsuccessful. Withdrawing his other hand from Mr. Bumble's, Oliver covered his face with both and wept until the tears trickled out from between his chin and bony fingers.

"Well!" exclaimed Mr. Bumble, stopping short and darting an angry look at his little charge. "Well! Of *all* the ungratefullest and worst-disposed boys as ever I see, Oliver, you are the—"

"No, no, sir," sobbed Oliver, clinging to the hand which held the well-known cane. "No, *no*, sir, I will be good indeed; indeed, *indeed* I will, sir! I am a very little boy, sir, and it is so—so—"

"What?" inquired Mr. Bumble in amazement.

"So *lonely*, sir!" cried the child. "Everybody hates me. Oh! sir, don't, *don't* be cross to me!" The child beat his hand upon his heart and looked in his companion's face with tears of real agony.

Mr. Bumble regarded Oliver's piteous and helpless look with some astonishment. Then, bidding Oliver dry his eyes and be good, and once more taking the boy's hand, he walked on with him in silence.

The undertaker, who had just put up the shutters of his shop, was making some entries in his daybook by the light of a dismal candle, when Mr. Bumble entered.

"Aha!" said the undertaker, looking up from the book, and pausing in the middle of a word. "Is that you, Bumble?"

"No one else, Mr. Sowerberry," replied the beadle. "Here! I've brought the boy." Oliver made a bow.

"Oh! *that's* the boy, is it?" said the undertaker, raising the candle above his head to get a better view of Oliver. "*Mrs.* Sowerberry, will you have the goodness to come here a moment, my dear?"

Mrs. Sowerberry came in from a little room behind the shop. She was a short, thin, squeezed-up woman, with a vixenish countenance.

"My dear," said Mr. Sowerberry, "this is the boy from the workhouse that I told you of." Oliver bowed again.

"Dear me!" said the undertaker's wife. "He's very small."

"Why, he is rather small," replied Mr. Bumble, looking at Oliver as if it were his fault that he was no bigger. "He *is* small. There's no denying it. But he'll grow, Mrs. Sowerberry—he'll grow."

"Ah! I dare say he will," replied the lady pettishly, "on *our* victuals and drink. I see no saving in parish children, not I. They always cost more to keep than they're worth. However, men always think they know best. There! Get downstairs, little bag o' bones!" With this command, the undertaker's wife opened a side door and pushed Oliver down a steep flight of stairs into a damp, dark stone cell. It was next to the coal cellar and was called the "kitchen." An untidy girl, in shoes worn down at the heels and blue worsted stockings very much out of repair, was sitting in the room.

"Here, Charlotte," said Mrs. Sowerberry, who had followed Oliver down, "give this boy some of the cold bits that were put by for Trip. He hasn't come home since morning, so he may go without 'em. I dare say the boy isn't too dainty to eat 'em, are you, boy?"

Oliver Twist clutched at the scraps that the dog had neglected, tearing them apart with all the ferocity of one who was dying from hunger.

"Well," said the undertaker's wife, when Oliver had finished eating, which activity she had watched with fearful thoughts of his future appetite, "have you done?"

As nothing was left within his reach, Oliver replied in the affirmative.

"Then come with me!" ordered Mrs. Sowerberry, taking up a dim and dirty lamp, and leading the way upstairs. "Your bed's under the counter. You don't mind sleeping among the coffins, I suppose? But it doesn't much matter whether you do or don't, for you can't sleep anywhere else. Come; don't keep me here all night!"

Oliver lingered no longer, but meekly followed his new mistress.

5 *Death Takes No Holiday*

Oliver was rudely awakened in the morning by a loud kicking at the outside of the shop door. He hurriedly put on his clothes, while still only half awake. In the dull light of the early day, he could see the outlines of an unfinished coffin on trestles in the center of the shop. That dismal long box, which looked so deathlike, gave him the "cold shivers" now, just as it did when he lay down on his flock mattress under the counter the night before. And it still haunted Oliver, making him wonder again whether some frightful form would slowly rear its head to drive him mad with terror. All the elm boards, cut and ready to be put together to make more coffins, were still standing grimly at attention against one wall. The air was still stuffy and seemed to be tainted with the smell of coffins.

As the loud kicking noise continued and became more violent, the frightened boy remembered what he had said to himself before he finally fell asleep:

"I wish I were dead and buried in that coffin!"

A very short time, which seemed long to Oliver, had passed before he stumbled to the door and began to unfasten the chain. It was then that the kicking ceased and he heard a voice shouting, "Open the door, will yer?"

"I will, directly, sir," replied Oliver, turning the key.

"I suppose yer the new boy, ain't yer?" said the voice through the keyhole.

"Yes, sir," replied Oliver.

"How old are yer?" inquired the voice.

"Ten, sir," replied Oliver.

"Then I'll whop yer when I get in," said the voice. "You just see if I don't, that's all, my workus brat!" And, having made this pleasant promise, Oliver's visitor began to whistle.

Oliver drew back the bolts with a trembling hand, and opened the door.

He saw nobody outside but a charity boy sitting on a post and eating a slice of bread and butter. Recognizing the stranger's uniform, Oliver knew that he was a poor boy who attended a free school, because his parents could not afford to send him to the pay school conducted by the parish.

"I beg your pardon, sir," said Oliver, seeing that no other intruder made his appearance, "did you knock?"

"I *kicked*," replied the charity boy.

"Do you want a coffin, sir?" inquired Oliver, innocently.

At this the charity boy looked very fierce and said that Oliver would want one before long, if he joked with his superiors in that way.

"Yer don't know who I am, I suppose, Workus?" asked the charity boy, descending from the top of the post, meanwhile.

"No, sir," replied Oliver.

"I'm Mr. Noah Claypole," said the charity boy, "and you're under me. Take down the shutters, yer idle young ruffian!" So saying, Mr. Claypole kicked Oliver, and entered the shop with a dignified air. He was a large-headed, small-eyed youth, of clumsy build and heavy features.

Oliver took down the shutters. He broke a pane of glass

in his efforts to stagger away, beneath the weight of the first shutter, to a small court at the side of the house. Noah assured him that "he'd catch it," and condescended to help him. Mr. and Mrs. Sowerberry appeared a little later, and Oliver really "caught it," as Noah had predicted.

Then, as he followed that young gentleman down the stairs to breakfast, poor Oliver felt most miserable.

"Come near the fire, Noah," said Charlotte. "I saved a nice little bit of bacon for you from master's breakfast. Oliver, shut that door at Mister Noah's back and take them bits that I've put out on the cover of the breadpan. There's your tea. Take it away to that box and drink it there. Make haste, for they'll want you to mind the shop. D'ye hear?"

Then Oliver Twist sat shivering on the box in the coldest corner of the room, eating the stale pieces which had been specially reserved for him.

Noah was not a workhouse orphan. No chance-child was he, for he could trace his family history all the way back to his parents, who lived close by. His mother was a washerwoman, and his father a drunken soldier, discharged with a wooden leg and a very small pension. The shopboys in the neighborhood had long been in the habit of branding Noah, in the public streets, with nicknames such as "leathers" and "charity"; and Noah had endured them without reply. But, now that fortune had cast in his way a nameless orphan, at whom even the meanest persons could point the finger of scorn, he abused him with interest and delight.

One evening, after Oliver had been at the undertaker's about three weeks or a month, Mr. and Mrs. Sowerberry—the shop being shut—were eating supper in the little back parlor. Mr. Sowerberry, after several cautious glances at his wife, said,

"My dear—" He was going to say more; but when Mrs. Sowerberry looked up with a frown, he stopped short.

"Well," said Mrs. Sowerberry, sharply.

"Nothing, my dear, nothing," said Mr. Sowerberry.

"Ugh, you brute!" exclaimed Mrs. Sowerberry.

"Not at all, my dear," said Mr. Sowerberry, humbly. "I was only going to say—"

"Oh, don't tell me what you were going to say!" interrupted Mrs. Sowerberry. "I am nobody. I don't want to intrude upon your secrets." As Mrs. Sowerberry said this, she gave a hysterical laugh, which threatened violent consequences.

"But my dear," said Sowerberry, "I want to ask your advice."

"No, no, don't ask mine." replied Mrs. Sowerberry, in an affected manner. "Ask somebody else's." Another hysterical laugh followed, which frightened Mr. Sowerberry very much. So he began to beg, as a special favor, to be allowed to say what his sweet wife was most curious to hear. After a long argument, the permission was granted.

"It's only about young Twist, my dear," ventured the undertaker. "A very good-looking boy, that, my dear."

"He need be, for he eats enough!" snapped the lady.

"There's an expression of sorrow in his face, my dear," resumed Mr. Sowerberry, "which is very interesting. He would make a delightful funeral attendant, my love. I don't mean a regular helper to attend grown-up people, my dear, but only for children's affairs. It would be very new to have a mute in proportion, my dear."

Mrs. Sowerberry was much struck by this clever idea; but it would have lowered her dignity to have said so. Hence, she merely inquired sharply why such a simple suggestion had not occurred to her husband before. Mr. Sowerberry rightly regarded this as an acceptance of his proposition. It was speedily determined, therefore, that Oliver should be at once initiated into the mysteries of the trade; and that he should accompany his master on the very next occasion when his services were required.

The occasion was not long in coming. Half an hour after breakfast next morning, Mr. Bumble entered the shop. Supporting his cane against the counter, he drew forth his large leather pocketbook, from which he selected a small scrap of paper, which he handed over to Sowerberry.

"Aha!" said the undertaker, glancing over it with a lively countenance, "an order for a coffin, eh?"

"For a coffin first, and a parochial funeral afterward," replied Mr. Bumble, fastening the strap of his pocketbook.

"Bayton," said the undertaker, looking from the scrap of paper to Mr. Bumble. "I never heard the name before."

Bumble shook his head, as he replied, "Obstinate people, Mr. Sowerberry, very obstinate. Proud, too, I'm afraid, sir."

"Proud, eh?" exclaimed Mr. Sowerberry with a sneer. "Come, that's too much."

"We only heard of the family the night before last," said the beadle. "A woman who lodges in the same house applied to the parochial committee for them to send the parochial surgeon to see a woman as was very bad. He had gone out to dinner; but his 'prentice (which is a very clever lad) sent 'em some medicine in a blacking bottle, off-hand."

"Ah, there's promptness," said the undertaker.

"Promptness, indeed!" replied the beadle. "But what's the result? What's the ungrateful behavior of these rebels, sir? Why, the husband sends back word that the medicine won't suit his wife's complaint, and says she sha'n't take it, sir!"

Mr. Bumble was so angry that he struck the counter sharply with his cane.

"Well," said the undertaker, "I ne—ver—did—"

"Never did, sir!" exclaimed the beadle. "No, nor nobody never did. But, now she's dead, we've got to bury her; and that's the direction. And the sooner it's done, the better."

Thus saying, Mr. Bumble put on his cocked hat wrong

side first, in a fever of parochial excitement, and flounced out of the shop.

"Why, he was so angry, Oliver, that he forgot even to ask about you!" said Mr. Sowerberry, looking after the beadle as he strode down the street.

"Yes, sir," replied Oliver, who had carefully kept himself out of sight, during the interview; and who was shaking from head to foot at the mere recollection of the sound of Mr. Bumble's voice.

"Well," said Mr. Sowerberry, taking up his hat, "the sooner this job is done, the better. Noah, look after the shop. Oliver, put on your cap and come with me." Oliver obeyed, and followed his master on his professional mission.

There was neither knocker nor bell handle at the open door where Oliver and his master stopped. So, groping cautiously through the dark passage, and bidding Oliver keep close to him and not be afraid, the undertaker mounted to the top of the first flight of stairs. Stumbling against a door on the landing, he rapped at it with his knuckles.

It was opened by a young girl of thirteen or fourteen. The undertaker at once saw enough of what the room contained to know it was the apartment to which he had been directed. He stepped in. Oliver followed him.

There was no fire in the room; but a man was crouching over the empty stove. An old woman had drawn a low stool to the cold hearth and was sitting beside him. There were some ragged children in another corner. And, in a small space opposite the door, there lay upon the ground something covered with an old blanket. Oliver shuddered.

The face of the man at the stove was thin and very pale. His hair and beard were grizzly; his eyes were bloodshot. The old woman's face was wrinkled. Her two remaining teeth extended over her lower lip; and her eyes were bright and piercing. Oliver was afraid to look long at either her or the man.

"Nobody shall go near her," said the man, starting up fiercely, as the undertaker approached the covered form. "Keep back! Keep back, if you've a life to lose!"

"Nonsense, my good man," said the undertaker, who was pretty well used to misery in all its shapes.

"I tell you," said the man, clenching his hands and stamping furiously on the floor, "I tell you I won't have her put into the ground. She couldn't rest there. The worms would worry her—not eat her—she is so worn away."

The undertaker offered no reply to this raving; but, producing a tape from his pocket, knelt down for a moment by the side of the body.

"Ah!" said the grieving man, bursting into tears and kneeling at the feet of the dead woman, "kneel down, kneel down—kneel around her, every one of you, and mark my words! I say she was *starved* to death. I never knew how bad she was, till the fever came upon her; and then her bones were starting through the skin. She died in the dark—in the dark! I begged for her in the streets, and they sent me to prison. When I came back, she was dying; and all the blood in my heart has dried up, for they starved her to death. I swear it before the God that saw it! *They starved her!*" He twined his hands in his hair and, with a loud scream, rolled upon the floor. His eyes stared, and foam covered his lips.

The terrified children cried bitterly. But the old woman, who had been as quiet as if she were wholly deaf to all that passed, frightened them into silence. Having untied the cravat of the man who still lay on the ground, she tottered toward the undertaker.

"She was my daughter," said the old woman, nodding her head in the direction of the corpse, and looking more horrible than even the presence of death. "Lord, Lord!— Well, it is strange that I who gave birth to her should be alive now, and she lying there: so cold and stiff!"

As the wretched old mother mumbled in her crazy manner, the undertaker turned to go away.

"Stop, stop!" said the old woman in a loud whisper. "Will she be buried tomorrow, or next day, or tonight? I laid her out; and I must walk, you know. Send me a large cloak: a good warm one, for it is bitter cold. We should have cake and wine, too, before we go! Never mind; send some bread—only a loaf of bread and a cup of water. Shall we have some bread, dear?" she said eagerly, catching at the undertaker's coat, as he once more moved toward the door.

"Yes, yes," said the undertaker, "of course. Anything you like!" He disengaged himself from the old woman's grasp and, drawing Oliver after him, hurried away.

In the morning, Mr. Bumble personally delivered to the family a little bread and a piece of cheese. Later in the day, Oliver and his master returned to the miserable abode to perform their professional duties. Mr. Bumble had already arrived with four men from the workhouse who were to act as bearers. Old black cloaks were thrown over the rags worn by the old woman and the man. And the bare coffin, having been closed, was hoisted on the shoulders of the pallbearers and carried into the street.

"Now, you must put your best leg foremost, old lady!"

whispered Sowerberry in the old woman's ear. "We are rather late; and it won't do to keep the preacher waiting. Move on, my men, as quick as you like!"

The bearers moved on under their light burden; and the two mourners kept as near them as they could. Mr. Bumble and Sowerberry walked at a good pace in front. Oliver, whose legs were not so long as his master's, ran by the side.

There was not so great a necessity for hurrying as Mr. Sowerberry had anticipated, however. For, when the procession reached the obscure corner of the churchyard where the paupers were buried, the preacher had not yet arrived. The clerk, who was sitting by the vestry-room fire, in the little chapel, did not expect him for an hour or more. So they placed the coffin on the brink of the grave; and the two mourners waited patiently in the damp clay, while a cold rain drizzled down. Mr. Sowerberry and Bumble, being personal friends of the clerk's, sat by the fire with him, to wait.

More than an hour later, the minister appeared. After reading as much of the burial service as he could in four minutes, he promptly walked away.

"Now, Bill!" said Sowerberry to the gravedigger. "Fill up!"

It was no very difficult task; for the grave was so full of coffins already, that the new one was within a few feet of the surface. The gravedigger quickly filled the open space, stamped the clay lightly with his feet, shouldered his spade, and left.

"Come, my good fellow!" said Bumble, tapping the grieving man on the back. "They want to shut up the yard."

That mourner, who had never once moved since he had knelt by the graveside, now raised his head, stared at the beadle, walked forward a few paces, and fell down in a swoon. They threw a can of cold water over him. Then, when he came to, they took him safely out of the church-yard, locked the gate, and departed.

"Well, Oliver," said Sowerberry, as they walked home, "how do you like it?"

"Pretty well, thank you, sir," replied Oliver, with considerable hesitation. "Not very much, sir."

"Ah, you'll get used to it in time, Oliver," Sowerberry promised.

⑥ *Counterattack*

"Workus, how's your mother?" asked Noah Claypole, tauntingly, and with an ugly sneer, one day, long after Oliver had become officially apprenticed to Mr. Sowerberry.

"She's dead," replied Oliver, "and don't you say anything about her to me!"

Oliver's anger showed itself in the color that came in his face; and he breathed quickly. He always carried in his heart a deep love for the mother he had never known. His secret thoughts and imaginary pictures of her often strengthened him in his suffering. Noah did not understand this, and now wrongly guessed that Oliver's twitching face was a sign of fear, and that he was about to cry for *that* reason. For Mr. Claypole had bullied the little fellow in every possible manner during the past months. He was bitterly jealous of Oliver, who often led the funeral processions, carrying a black stick and wearing a hatband that reached down to his knees, to the great and tearful admiration of all the mothers who saw him. And, so that Oliver should gain more professional experience, Mr. Sowerberry took him along to assist in most of his mournful expeditions for grown-ups.

Neither Charlotte nor Mrs. Sowerberry was present while the two young men were feasting in the kitchen on a cheap piece of mutton. But both ladies, who also hated Oliver, would have enjoyed the show, which had been in progress for some time. Noah, with his feet on the table-cloth, was playing the leading part, pulling Oliver's hair, twisting his ears, calling him all kinds of ugly names, or promising to be present at his hanging.

"What did she die of, Workus?" inquired Noah, determined to develop his new attack, observing that he had struck a tender spot.

"Of a broken heart, some of our old nurses told me," replied Oliver. "I think I know what it must be like to die of that!"

Noah laughed heartily as a tear rolled down Oliver's cheek. "What's set you a-sniveling now?" he asked, scornfully.

"Not *you*," replied Oliver, hastily brushing the tear away. "Don't think it!"

"Oh, not me, eh!" sneered Noah.

"No, not you," Oliver insisted sharply. "That's enough. Don't say anything more to me about her. You'd better not!"

"Better not!" exclaimed Noah. "Well! Workus, don't be impudent. Your *mother*, too! She was a nice 'un, she was. Oh, Lor'!" And Noah curled up his small red nose.

"Yer know, Workus," continued Noah, made bold by Oliver's short silence, and speaking in a jeering tone: "It can't be helped now; and of course yer couldn't help it *then*. But yer must know, Workus, yer mother was a regular right-down bad 'un."

"What did you say?" Oliver challenged, looking up very quickly.

"A regular right-down bad 'un, Workus," replied Noah, coolly. "And it's a great deal better that she died when she did, or else she'd have been hard laboring in Bridewell—you know: women's prison—or transported, or *hung;* which is more likely than either, isn't it?"

Crimson with fury, Oliver jumped up; overthrew the chair and table; seized Noah by the throat; and shook him, in the violence of his rage, till the bully's teeth chattered in his head. Then, collecting his whole force into one heavy blow, he knocked Noah to the ground.

"He'll murder me!" blabbered Noah. "Charlotte! Missis! Here's the new boy a-murdering of me! Help! Help! Oliver's gone mad! Char—*lotte*!"

Noah's shouts were answered by a loud scream from Charlotte, and a louder one from Mrs. Sowerberry.

"Oh, you little wretch!" screamed Charlotte, rushing in and seizing Oliver with her utmost force, which was about equal to that of a moderately strong man. "Oh, you little un-grate-ful, mur-de-rous, hor-rid villain!" And between syllables, Charlotte gave Oliver blow after blow, and screamed for the benefit of society.

In the midst of the battle, Mrs. Sowerberry plunged into the kitchen and helped hold him with one hand, while she scratched his face with the other. In this favorable situation, Noah arose and pummeled Oliver in the back.

When they were all worn out, and could tear and beat no longer, they dragged Oliver, courageously struggling and shouting, into the dust cellar, and there locked him up. Then Mrs. Sowerberry sank into a chair and burst out crying.

"Bless her, she's going off!" said Charlotte. "A glass of water, Noah, dear. Make haste!"

"Oh!—Charlotte," gasped Mrs. Sowerberry, shocked by the cold water that Noah had poured over her head. "What—a—mercy we have not all—been murdered in our beds!"

"Ah! mercy indeed, ma'am," was the reply. "I only hope this'll teach master not to have any more of these dreadful creatures that are born to be murders and robbers. Poor Noah! He was all but killed, ma'am, when I come in."

"What's to be done now!" exclaimed Mrs. Sowerberry. "Your master's not at home. That awful boy will kick that door down in ten minutes."

"Dear, dear! I don't know, ma'am," said Charlotte, "unless we send for the police officers."

"Or the millingtary," suggested Mr. Claypole.

"No, no," said Mrs. Sowerberry, coming to her senses. "Run to Mr. Bumble, Noah, and tell him to come here at once. Run!"

And Noah ran as fast as he could, never stopping for a deep breath until he reached the workhouse gate.

7 Oliver Breaks the Traces

"Why, what's the matter with the boy!" exclaimed the old pauper who, having been aroused by Mr. Claypole's cries and loud knocking at the wicket, hurriedly opened the gate and stared with surprise at the frightened boy.

"Mr. Bumble! Mr. Bumble!" cried Noah, in tones so loud that they not only caught the ear of Mr. Bumble himself, who happened to be nearby, but alarmed him so much that he rushed into the yard without his cocked hat.

"Oh, Mr. Bumble, sir!" said Noah. "Oliver, sir—Oliver has—"

"What? What?" inquired Mr. Bumble with a gleam of pleasure in his cruel eyes. "Not run away! He hasn't run away, has he, Noah?"

"No, sir, no. Not run away, sir, but he's turned vicious," replied Noah. "He tried to murder me, sir, and then he tried to murder Charlotte, and then missis. Oh! what dreadful pain it is! Such agony, please, sir!" And here, Noah twisted his body into many eellike positions, thereby giving Mr. Bumble to understand that he had received severe internal injury.

When Noah saw that the news practically paralyzed Mr. Bumble, he bewailed his dreadful wounds ten times louder than before. And when he observed a gentleman in

47

a white waistcoat crossing the yard, he acted more wildly than ever, in order to attract the notice and arouse the anger of that gentleman.

The gentleman's notice was very soon attracted; for he had not walked three paces, when he turned angrily around and inquired what "that young cur" was howling for.

"It's a poor boy from the free school, sir," replied Mr. Bumble, "who has been nearly murdered—all but murdered, sir—by young Twist."

"By Jove!" exclaimed the gentleman in the white vest, stopping short. "I knew it! I had a strange feeling from the very first that that young savage would come to be hung!"

"He has likewise attempted, sir, to murder the female servant," said Mr. Bumble, with a face of ashy paleness.

"And his missis," put in Mr. Claypole.

"And his master, too, I think you said, Noah?" added Mr. Bumble

"No! he's out, or Twist would have murdered him," replied Noah. "He said he wanted to."

"Ah! Said he wanted to, did he, my boy?" inquired the gentleman in the white waistcoat.

"Yes, sir," replied Noah. "And please, sir, missis wants to know whether Mr. Bumble can spare time to step up there, directly, and flog him—'cause master's out."

"Certainly, my boy, certainly," said the gentleman in the white vest, smiling, and patting Noah's head, which was about three inches higher than his own. "You're a very good boy. Here's a penny for you. Bumble, step up to Sowerberry's with your cane, and see what's best to be done. Don't spare him, Bumble."

"I will not, sir," said the beadle.

"Tell Sowerberry not to spare him either. They'll never do anything with him without stripes and bruises," said the gentleman in the white waistcoat.

"I'll take care, sir," promised the beadle. And Mr.

Bumble and Noah Claypole hurried away to the undertaker's shop.

Here the situation had not improved. Sowerberry had not yet returned; and Oliver continued his kicking at the cellar door. The accounts of his ferocity, as related by Mrs. Sowerberry and Charlotte, were so startling that Mr. Bumble judged it wise to parley before opening the door. With this in view, he gave a kick at the outside, by way of introduction; and then, applying his mouth to the keyhole, said, in a deep and impressive tone:

"Oliver!"

"Come, you let me out!" cried Oliver, from the inside.

"Do you know this here voice, Oliver?" said Bumble.

"Yes," answered Oliver.

"Ain't you afraid of it, sir? Ain't you a-trembling while I speak, sir?" Mr. Bumble asked hopefully, for the kicking had ceased.

"No!" declared Oliver, boldly.

"Oh, Mr. Bumble, he must be mad," said Mrs. Sowerberry. "No boy in half his senses could venture to speak so to you."

"It's not madness, ma'am," replied Mr. Bumble, after a few moments of deep thought. "It's *meat*."

"What?" exclaimed Mrs. Sowerberry.

"Meat, ma'am, meat," replied Bumble, sternly. "You've overfed him, ma'am. You've raised a artificial soul and spirit in him, ma'am, unbecoming a person of his condition. The board, Mrs. Sowerberry, who are practical men, will tell you so. What have paupers to do with soul or spirit? It's quite enough that we let 'em have live bodies. If you had kept the boy on gruel, ma'am, this would never have happened."

"Dear, dear!" cried Mrs. Sowerberry, piously raising her eyes to the kitchen ceiling. "This comes of being liberal!"

"Ah!" said Mr. Bumble, when the lady brought her

eyes down to earth again. "The only thing that can be done now, that I know of, is to leave him in the cellar for a day or so, till he's a little starved down. Then take him out and keep him on gruel all through his apprenticeship. He comes of a bad family, Mrs. Sowerberry."

At this point, Oliver, hearing just enough to know that some new reference was being made to his mother, resumed kicking more violently than ever. Then Sowerberry returned. Oliver's offense having been explained to him, with additions that the ladies thought would arouse his ire, he unlocked the cellar door in a twinkling and dragged his rebellious apprentice out by the collar.

Oliver's clothes had been torn in the beating he had received; his face was bruised and scratched; and his hair was scattered over his forehead. The angry flush had not disappeared, however; and, when he was pulled out of his prison, he scowled fearlessly on Noah.

"Now, you are a nice young fellow, ain't you?" Sowerberry began, giving Oliver a shake and a box on the ear.

"He called my mother names," replied Oliver.

"Well, and what if he did, you little ungrateful wretch?" put in Mrs. Sowerberry. "She deserved what he said, and worse."

"She didn't," declared Oliver.

"She did," said Mrs. Sowerberry.

"It's a lie!" Oliver shouted.

Mrs. Sowerberry burst into tears.

Her flood of tears left Mr. Sowerberry no choice. If he had hesitated to punish Oliver most severely, he would have been called a brute and an unnatural husband. So he at once gave Oliver a good beating that satisfied even Mrs. Sowerberry, and made Mr. Bumble's application of the parochial cane unnecessary.

For the rest of the day, Oliver was shut in the back kitchen, with nothing to eat but a slice of bread. And, at night, Mrs. Sowerberry, after making shameful remarks outside the door about Oliver's mother, looked into the room. Then amidst the jeers of Noah and Charlotte, the cruel woman ordered him upstairs to his gloomy room.

Alone in the silence of the ugly workshop, the poor lad gave way to the feelings which the day's treatment might have aroused in any child. He had listened bravely to mean taunts and had borne the lash without a cry, for he felt a kind of pride which would have kept back a shriek to the last. But now, unseen and unheard, he fell upon his knees and, hiding his face in his hands, wept bitter tears.

Oliver remained thus for a long time. The candle was burning low when he arose to his feet. Then, after gazing cautiously around him and listening carefully, he gently loosened the fastenings of the door and looked abroad.

It was a cold, dark night. The stars seemed to be farther from the earth than the boy had ever seen them before. There was no wind; and the shadows of the trees looked deathlike in their stillness. He softly closed the door again.

Aided by the last flickering rays of the dying candle-light, he had tied up in a large handkerchief his few remaining articles of clothing. Now he sat down upon a bench to wait for morning.

With the first ray of light that peeped through the crevices in the shutters, Oliver arose and again unbarred the door. After one timid look around—one moment's hesitation—he had closed it behind him and was soon in the open street.

At first uncertain which way to go, the lad remembered having seen wagons toiling up a hill. He took the same route. Arriving at a footpath across the fields (which he knew would lead him out again into the road), he struck into it at a quick pace.

Along this same footpath, Oliver also remembered that he had trotted beside Mr. Bumble from the farm to the workhouse. His way lay directly in front of the cottage. His heart then beat quickly; and he half resolved to turn back. He had come a long way, though, and should lose a great deal of time by returning. Besides, it was so early that there was very little chance of his being seen. So he hurried on.

The runaway boy reached the house. He stopped and peeped into the garden. A child was weeding one of the small sections. Oliver recognized him as one of his former companions and felt very glad to see him. They had been beaten, half-starved, and shut up together, many a time. The early visitor tapped softly at the gate.

"Hush, Dick!" said Oliver, as the younger boy ran to the gate and thrust a thin arm between the rails to greet him. "Is anyone up?"

"Nobody but me," replied the child.

"You mustn't say you saw me, Dick," whispered Oliver. "I am running away! They beat and ill-use me, Dick; and I am going to seek my fortune, far away. I don't know where. How pale you are!"

"I heard the doctor tell them I was dying," explained the child, with a faint smile. "I am very glad to see you, dear friend; but don't stop, don't stop!"

"Yes, yes, I will, to say good-bye to you," declared Oliver. "But I shall see you again, Dick. I know I shall! You will be well and happy!"

"I hope so," ventured Dick. "After I am dead, but not before. I know the doctor must be right, Oliver, because I dream so much of heaven and angels and kind faces that I never see when I am awake. Kiss me," added the child, climbing up the low gate and flinging his little arms around Oliver's neck. "Good-bye, dear! God bless you!"

That blessing for himself alone was the first that Oliver had ever heard; and he remembered it all through his troubles and sufferings in later years.

8 _Beggarman, Thief_

"Please, kind sir, may I sit here on this stone and rest awhile? I am so very, very tired and footsore."

The lone traveler made this plea to an old man who had just collected a tollgate fee from a rich gentleman in a fine carriage that was drawn by two well-groomed horses. The old attendant looked at the dusty, forlorn figure before him, for a moment or two, took his pipe from his mouth, and spoke to Oliver kindly. "Aye, and that ye may, my lad. Whativer is your name, and whither be ye a-goin'?"

'Thank you, sir, very much, sir," Oliver replied, sitting down with a sigh of relief and placing his little bundle by his side. "My—my name, sir, is Oliver Twist, sir; but please, _please_ don't ever tell them that you saw me. They will beat me to death if they find me, sir!"

The turnpike man stooped down and looked more closely at Oliver and, placing a friendly hand on the poor boy's head, said, "Now, now, that's a pretty to-do. But don't ye be one bit affeered. This missis and me can keep a quiet tongue when we've a mind to. Be ya a-goin' far?"

"Oh, yes, kind sir; far, ever so far, to get away from _them_!" replied Oliver. "This is the third day of my tramp. And, by the milestones, I must have walked about thirty-five miles, leaving almost as many more for me to travel before reaching London."

"A long journey indeed, a-foot in the cold," said the gatekeeper. "Have ye food, young 'un?"

"I had a crust of bread and a penny when I started out, sir," Oliver answered, as bravely as he could, trying to control the hunger pains that felt like big knots inside him at the mention of food. "In some villages, beggars are put to jail. Farmers' wives send great dogs to chase me away. And—and—"

"Yes! That's just it! And ye shall come in here this minute!" called out an old lady, who, busy at her mending in the front room of the little house, had heard everything through the open door. She came out and took Oliver by the hand. "Come with me. Bring your bundle. For shame, pappy! Ye would keep the starvin' lad out here forever and offer him nothin'! And our own dear, shipwrecked grandson this very minute likely a-walkin' barefoot and hungry—God knows where!—Come, laddie, I will find some bread and cheese for ye, and we will have a cup o' tea together, and ye can tell me all about everything."

As Oliver dragged his aching feet along, led by the kind old lady, she raised her apron to her eyes and dried the tears that came forth, as she thought of his poor condition and wondered when she would ever hear again of their shipwrecked grandson.

When Oliver left the little home of the only human beings who had befriended him thus far on his long trek, kind farewells were said. Even after he had gone some distance on the road, and had stopped several times to wave good-bye, he would hear the old lady reminding him to keep his feet dry and try to find shelter at night. Gratitude filled his heart. His step was lighter, for he was refreshed in body and in spirit. And he felt that he could never forget that there were at least a few warmhearted, friendly folks in his world of suffering.

Early on the seventh morning after he had left his native place, Oliver limped slowly into the little town of Barnet. He sat, with bleeding feet and covered with dust, upon a doorstep. His whole body ached, and he was very, very lonesome.

Soon the shutters of little houses were opened; the window blinds were drawn up; and people began passing to and fro. But no one paid any attention to him. He had no heart to beg. So there he sat.

Oliver had been crouching on the step for some time when he noticed that a boy, who had passed him carelessly several minutes before, had come back and was now staring at him from the opposite side of the way. The newcomer remained in the same attitude of close observation so long that Oliver boldly returned his steady look. Then the stranger crossed over and, walking up to Oliver, said,

"Hullo, my covey! What's the row?"

Oliver decided that his questioner was about his own age, but one of the queerest-looking boys that he had ever seen. He was an untidy, snub-nosed, flat-browed, common-faced youth who had all the airs and manners of a man. He was short, with bowlegs, and little, sharp, ugly eyes. His hat was stuck on his head so lightly that it threatened to fall off every moment—and would have done so, if the owner had not had a knack of every now and then giving his head a sudden twitch, which brought the hat back to its proper place again. He wore a man's coat, which reached nearly to his heels. He had turned the cuffs back, halfway up his arms. His hands were thrust into the pockets of his corduroy trousers.

"I am very hungry and tired," replied Oliver. "I have been walking these seven days."

"Walking for sivin days!" said the young gentleman. "Oh, I see. Beak's orders, eh? But," he added, noticing Oliver's look of surprise, "I suppose you don't known what a beak is, my flash com-pan-i-on."

Oliver said that he always supposed it was a bird's mouth.

"My eyes, how green!" exclaimed the stranger. "Why, a beak's a mag'strate. And when you walk by a beak's order, it's not straight forerd, but always a-going up, and nivir a-coming down ag'in. But come! You want grub and shall have it. I'm at low-watermark myself; but, *as* far *as* it goes, I'll fork out. Up with you on your pins. There! Now then! Hurry!"

Assisting Oliver to rise, the young gentleman took him to a nearby shop, where he bought Oliver some cooked ham and a little bread.

"Going to London?" the young man asked, when Oliver had finished his breakfast.

"Yes."

"Got any lodgings?"

"No."

"Money?"

"No."

Oliver's new acquaintance merely whistled in reply.

"Do you live in London?" inquired Oliver.

"Yes, I do when I'm at home," replied the boy. "I suppose you want some place to sleep in tonight, don't you?"

"I do indeed," answered Oliver. "I have not slept under a roof since I left the country."

"Don't fret your eyelids on that score," said the young man. "I've got to be in London tonight. And I know a 'spectable old gen'l'man as lives there, wot'll give you lodging for nothink, and never ask for the change—that is, if any gen'l'-man he knows interduces you. And don't he know *me?* Oh, no! Not in the least!" Then he laughed, and Oliver wondered why.

This unexpected offer of shelter was too tempting to be resisted. And there followed a more confidential dialogue, from which Oliver learned that his new friend's name was Jack Dawkins; that he was a special favorite of the elderly gentleman before mentioned; and that he was better known as "The Artful Dodger."

Young Dawkins objected to their entering London before nightfall, and so it was nearly eleven o'clock when they reached the turnpike at Islington, on the edge of the great city of London. With Oliver trying to follow closely, the Dodger then hurried through many little winding streets and alleys, at last reaching the high point of a narrow, sloping, and muddy street with filthy odors. Oliver noticed that there were many small shops and taverns, or public houses, along the way, as well as little groups of dingy houses, from which drunken men and women came and went.

Oliver was considering whether he hadn't better run away, when they reached the bottom of the hill. But his guide, catching him by the arm, pushed open the door of a house near Field Lane and, pulling him into the dark passage, closed the door behind them.

"Now, then!" cried a voice from below stairs, in reply to a whistle from the Dodger.

"Plummy and slam!" was his reply.

This seemed to be the correct watchword; for the feeble light of a candle gleamed on the wall at the far end of the passage, and a man's face peeped out.

"There's two of you," said the man, thrusting the candle farther out and shading his eyes with his hand. "Who's t'other one?"

"A new pal," replied Jack Dawkins, pushing Oliver forward.

"Where did he come from?"

"Greenland!—Is Fagin upstairs?"

"Yes; he's a-sorting' the wipes. Up with you!" The candle was then drawn back, and the face disappeared.

Oliver, groping his way with one hand, while the other was firmly grasped by his companion, ascended with much difficulty the dark and broken stairs. Then the Dodger threw open the door of a back room and drew Oliver in after him.

The walls and ceiling were black with age and dirt. There was a deal table before the fire, upon which were a candle, stuck in a ginger-beer bottle; two or three pewter pots; and a loaf and a plate. In a frying pan on the fire, some sausages were cooking. Standing over them, with a toasting fork in his hand, was a shriveled old man, whose villainous-looking, ugly face was almost hidden by matted red hair. He was dressed in a greasy flannel gown, with his throat bare. He seemed to be dividing his attention between the frying pan and a clotheshorse, over which a great number of silk handkerchiefs were hanging. Several rough beds made of old sacks were huddled side by side on the floor. Seated around the table were four or five boys, none older than Dodger. They all crowded around their associate as he whispered a few words to the old man. Then they turned and grinned at Oliver. So did the old man himself, toasting fork in hand.

"This is him, Fagin," said Jack Dawkins. "My friend, Oliver Twist."

Still grinning through his heavy beard, Fagin bowed to Oliver and took him by the hand, saying he hoped he should have the honor of his intimate acquaintance. Upon this, the young gentlemen with the pipes came around him and shook both his hands very hard—especially the one in which he held his little bundle.

"We are very glad to see you, Oliver, very," said old
Fagin. "Dodger, take off the sausages and draw a tub near
the fire for Oliver. Ah, you're a-staring at the pocket-handkerchiefs! eh, my dear! There are a good many of 'em out,

ready for the wash. That's all, Oliver, that's all. Ha! ha! ha!"

The latter part of this speech was hailed by a boisterous shout from all the hopeful pupils of the merry old gentleman. Then they ate supper.

After Oliver ate his share, Fagin mixed him a strange hot drink, telling him he must take it quickly, because another gentleman wanted the tumbler. Oliver did as he was directed.

Immediately afterward, he felt himself being gently lifted onto one of the sacks; and then he sank into a deep sleep.

⑨ *Fagin's School of Tricks*

Oliver was aroused late next morning by sounds made by Fagin, who was boiling some coffee in a saucepan and whistling softly as he stirred the brew with an iron spoon. He would stop and listen whenever there was the least noise below; and, when he had satisfied himself that no one was coming up, would go on, whistling and stirring again. Oliver was not fully awake.

When the coffee was done, Fagin turned toward Oliver and called him by his name. Pretending to be asleep, the lad did not answer.

Fagin then opened a trapdoor and drew forth a small box that he placed carefully on the table. His eyes glistened as he raised the lid. Then, dragging an old chair to the table, he sat down and took from the box a beautiful gold watch, sparkling with jewels.

"Aha!" said the trick master, distorting his features with a hideous grin. "Clever gang! Staunch to the last! Never told the old parson where they were. Never peached upon old Fagin!—And why should they? It wouldn't have loosened the knot. No, no, no! Fine fellows! Fine fellows!"

With these and other mumbled reflections, Fagin returned the watch to its place of safety. At least a half dozen more were removed from the box and examined with equal pleasure, as were rings, brooches, bracelets, and other costly articles of jewelry. Soon the keeper of the treasure leaned back in his chair and muttered:

"What a fine thing capital punishment is! Dead men never repent; dead men never bring awkward stories to light. Yes, it's a fine thing for the trade! Five of 'em strung up in a row, and none left to play booty, or turn white-livered!"

As the bearded one uttered these words, his glittering, dark eyes glimpsed Oliver's face. The boy's eyes were fixed on his in curiosity; and the old man then realized that he had been observed. He slammed down the lid of the box; and, grasping a bread knife which was on the table, jumped up in anger. He trembled very much; and Oliver, seeing the knife quiver in the air, turned pale with fright.

"What's that?" demanded Fagin. "What do you watch me for? Why are you awake? What have you seen? Speak out, boy! Quick—quick! for your life!"

"I—wasn't able to—sleep longer, sir," answered Oliver meekly. "I am—very sorry if I—have disturbed you, sir."

"You were not awake an hour age?" queried the old man, scowling horribly at the boy.

"No! No, indeed!" Oliver assured him.

"Are you sure?" cried Fagin, with a fiercer look than before.

"Upon my word—I was not, sir," replied Oliver, earnestly.

"Tush, tush, my dear!" said Fagin, suddenly resuming his old manner, and playing with the knife a little, before he laid it down, as if to make Oliver believe that he had caught it up in fun. "Of course I know that, my dear. I only tried to frighten you. Ha! ha! You're a brave boy, Oliver!" And Fagin rubbed his hands and chuckled, but glanced uneasily at the box.

"Did you see any of these pretty things, my dear?" asked the old one, laying his hand upon his box.

"Yes, sir," replied Oliver truthfully.

"Ah!" said Fagin, turning rather pale. "They—they're mine, Oliver: my little property. All I have to live upon, in my old age. The folks call me a miser, my dear. Only a miser, that's all."

Oliver thought the old gentleman certainly must be a miser to live in such a dirty place, with so many watches, but concluded that perhaps his fondness for the Dodger and the other boys cost him a good deal of money. Then the puzzled lad asked if he might get up.

"Certainly, my dear, certainly," replied Fagin. "Stay! There's a pitcher of water in the corner by the door. Bring it here. I'll give you a basin to wash in, my dear."

Oliver walked across the room and stooped for an instant to raise the pitcher. When he turned his head, the box was gone.

He had scarcely washed himself and emptied the basin out the window, at the old man's direction, when the Dodger returned with the lively youth Oliver had seen on the previous night. He was now formally introduced as Charley Bates. The four sat down to their breakfast, consisting of Fagan's pan of coffee, and some hot rolls and ham that the Dodger has brought home in the crown of his hat.

"Well," said the master, glancing slyly at Oliver, but speaking to the Dodger, "I hope you've been at work this morning, my dears?"

"Hard," replied the Dodger.

"As nails," added Charley Bates.

"Good boys, good boys!" exclaimed the teacher of tricks. "What have *you* got, Dodger?"

"A couple of pocketbooks."

"Lined?" inquired the old man, eagerly.

"Pretty well," the Dodger answered, producing two pocketbooks: one green, and one red.

"Not heavy as they might be," grumbled Fagin, after examining them carefully, "but very neat and nicely made. Good workman, ain't he, Oliver?"

"Indeed, sir," replied Oliver, innocently. And then, to his surprise, Mr. Charley Bates laughed uproariously.

"And what have *you* got, Charley, my dear?" inquired the master.

"Wipes," answered the boy, producing four pocket-handkerchiefs.

"Well," said Fagin, inspecting them closely, "they're very good ones, very. You haven't marked them well, though, Charley; so we'll teach Oliver how to pick the marks out with a needle. Shall us, Oliver, eh? Ha! ha! ha!"

"If you please, yes, sir," agreed Oliver.

"You'd like to be able to make pocket-handkerchiefs as easy as Charley Bates does, wouldn't you, my dear?" asked the old man.

"Very much, indeed, if you'll teach me, sir," replied Oliver.

Young Bates then burst into another laugh, which caused him to choke almost to death on his coffee.

"He is so jolly *green*!" exclaimed Charley, after he had recovered, as an apology to the company for his impolite behavior.

The Dodger smoothed Oliver's hair over his eyes and said he'd know better, by and by. Then the old gentleman, observing Oliver's color mounting, changed the subject by asking the other boys whether there had been much of a crowd at the execution that morning. This puzzled the "green" lad still more; for it was plain from the replies of the two "workers" that they had been present. And Oliver then naturally wondered how they could possibly have found time to be so very industrious.

After breakfast, Fagin and his two helpers played another uncommon trick game. The jolly old teacher placed a snuffbox in one pocket of his trousers, a notecase in the other, and a watch in his vest pocket, with a guard chain around his neck. He then stuck a mock-diamond pin in his shirt and buttoned his coat tightly. And, after putting his spectacle case and handkerchief into their proper pockets, the master trotted up and down the room with a walking stick, imitating the way some gentlemen strut about the streets.

Sometimes he stopped at the fireplace, and sometimes at the door, pretending that he was staring into shop windows. At such moments, he would often look around him, for fear of thieves, slapping all his pockets in turn to be sure that he hadn't lost anything. Oliver laughed till the tears ran down his face. The other boys followed their master closely, getting out of his sight nimbly whenever he turned around. At last, the Dodger trod upon his toes, or ran upon his boot accidentally, while Charley Bates stumbled against him from behind. And in that instant they took from him his snuffbox, notecase, watch guard, chain, shirtpin, handkerchief—even the spectacle case. If the old gentleman felt a hand at one of his pockets, he cried out where it was. Then the experiment began all over again.

After this game had been played many times, a couple of young ladies called to see the young gentlemen. The guests, known as Bet and Nancy, wore a good deal of hair, carelessly arranged, and were rather untidy about their shoes and stockings. The ladies were not exactly pretty, perhaps; but they had much color in their faces, and looked quite stout and hearty. Being extremely free and sociable in their manners, Oliver thought they were very nice, indeed.

These visitors remained a long time. Drinks were served, because one of the young ladies complained of a coldness in her inside; and the conversation became very jolly. Finally, Charley Bates suggested that it was time to "pad the hoof." This, Oliver thought, must be French for going out; for the Dodger, Charley, and the two young ladies soon left together, having been kindly furnished some spending money by the friendly old man.

"There, my dear," declared Fagin. "That's a pleasant life, isn't it? They have gone out for the day."

"Have they finished work, sir?" inquired Oliver.

"Yes," replied Fagin, "that is, unless they should unexpectedly come across some while they are out. Make 'em your models, my dear," he added, tapping the fire shovel on the hearth to give force to his words. "Do everything they bid you and take their advice in all matters—especially the Dodger's, my dear. He'll be a great man himself and will make you one, too, if you pattern after him. Is my handkerchief hanging from my pocket, my dear?"

"Yes, sir," said Oliver.

"Try to take it out without my feeling it, as you saw them do, when we were at play this morning."

Oliver held up the bottom of the pocket with one hand, as he had seen the Dodger hold it, and drew the handkerchief lightly out of it with the other.

"Is it gone?" asked Fagin.

"Here it is, sir," Oliver announced, showing it in his hand.

"You're a clever boy, my dear," said the playful old teacher, patting Oliver on the head approvingly. "I never saw a sharper lad. Here's a shilling for you! If you go on in this way, you'll be the greatest man of the time. And now come here, and I'll show you how to take the marks out of the handkerchiefs."

Oliver wondered what picking the old gentleman's pocket in play had to do with his chances of being a great man. But, thinking that the trick master must know best, he followed him quietly to the table and was soon deeply absorbed in his new study.

10 *Stop, Thief!*

For many days Oliver remained in Fagin's room, picking the marks out of numerous pocket-handkerchiefs that were brought home, and sometimes taking part in the handkerchief trick game. Then he had a great desire for fresh air and often begged his old master to allow him to go out with his two companions to work.

Besides, Oliver had seen the strict side of Fagin's character. Whenever the Dodger or Charley Bates came home at night empty-handed, he would roughly lecture them on the penalties of idle and lazy habits; and would convince them of the necessity of an active life by sending them to bed hungry. On one occasion, indeed, he even knocked them down a flight of stairs.

Finally, one morning, Oliver obtained the permission he wanted. There had been no handkerchiefs to work upon for two days; and the meals had been rather slight. Perhaps these were the reasons why old Fagin at last told Oliver he might go out, guided and guarded by Charley Bates and the Dodger.

The three boys started out, with Oliver between the other two. The innocent lad wondered where they were going and what branch of work he would be taught first.

Their pace was very lazy; and Oliver soon began to

think his companions were going to deceive their master, by not going to work at all. The Dodger had a habit, too, of pulling the caps from the heads of small boys and tossing them away. And Charles Bates freely helped himself to apples and onions from the stalls along the sidewalks. Oliver was on the point of turning back, when he observed a very mysterious change of behavior on the part of the Dodger.

They were just leaving a narrow court near the open square in Clerkenwell, which is still called "The Green," when the Dodger suddenly stopped; and, laying a finger on his lips, drew his companions back again, with the greatest caution.

"What's the matter?" demanded Oliver.

"Hush!" replied the Dodger. "Do you see that old cove at the bookstall?"

"The old gentleman over the way?" asked Oliver. "Yes."

"He'll do," said the Dodger.

"A *prime* plant," observed Master Charley Bates.

Oliver looked from one to the other, with the greatest surprise; but he was not permitted to speak; for the two boys walked stealthily across the road and slunk close behind the old gentleman. Oliver walked a few paces after them; then stood still, looking on in silent amazement.

The old gentleman was a very respectable-looking personage, with powdered hair and gold spectacles. He was dressed in a bottle-green coat with a black velvet collar, wore white trousers, and carried a smart bamboo cane under his arm. He had taken up a book from the stall and was steadily reading, as if he were in his armchair at home. It was plain that he saw nothing but the book itself, which he was reading with great interest.

Oliver was horrified to see the Dodger plunge his hand into the old gentleman's pocket and pull out a handkerchief, which he handed to Charley Bates. Then both ran around the corner at full speed.

In an instant the whole mystery of the handkerchiefs, the watches, the jewels, and the trick master cleared in Oliver's mind. He stood for a moment in terror. Then, not knowing what else to do, he ran away as fast as he could lay his feet to the ground.

This was all done in a minute. As soon as Oliver began to run, the old gentleman, putting his hand to his pocket and missing his handkerchief, turned quickly. Seeing the boy running away at such a rapid pace, he very naturally thought Oliver was the thief. Shouting "Stop thief!" with all his might, the gentleman then started after him, book in hand.

But the booklover was not the only one who raised the hue-and-cry. The Dodger and Charley, unwilling to attract public attention by running down the open street, had merely retired into the very first doorway around the corner. But they no sooner heard the cry and saw Oliver running, than they issued forth promptly; and, shouting "Stop thief!" too, joined in the pursuit like good citizens.

"Stop thief! Stop thief!" The cry was soon taken up by a hundred voices, as the crowd quickly grew in size to chase the wretched, breathless Oliver, who was now panting with exhaustion. They gained upon him every instant, hailing his decreasing strength with still louder shouts: *"Stop thief!"*

Stopped at last! A clever blow. And Oliver was down upon the pavement. The crowd eagerly gathered around him: each newcomer jostling and struggling with the others to catch a glimpse.—"Stand aside!"—"Give him a little air!"—"Nonsense! he don't deserve it." "Where's the gentleman?"—"Make room there for the gentleman!"—"Is this the boy, sir?"—"Yes."

Oliver, covered with mud and dust, and bleeding from the mouth, looked wildly around upon the many faces that surrounded him, when the old gentleman was officiously pushed into the circle by the foremost of the pursuers.

"Yes," said the gentleman, "I am afraid it is the boy."

"Afraid!" murmured the crowd. "That's a good 'un!"

"Poor fellow!" said the gentleman. "He has hurt himself."

"*I* did that, sir," said a great lubberly fellow, stepping forward, "and I cut my knuckle ag'in' his mouth. I stopped him, sir."

The fellow touched his hat with a grin, expecting something for his pains. But the old gentleman, eyeing him with an expression of dislike, looked anxiously around, as if he would run away himself.

Then a police officer stepped forward and seized Oliver by the collar.

"Come, get up," commanded the officer, roughly.

"It—it wasn't me, indeed, sir! Indeed—it was two other boys," gasped Oliver, pleadingly. "They—are here somewhere."

"Oh, no, they ain't," said the officer, as if he knew. But it was true: The Dodger and Charley Bates had disappeared. "Come, get up!"

"Don't hurt him," begged the old gentleman.

"Oh, no, I won't hurt him," replied the officer, tearing Oliver's jacket half off his back. "Come, I know you; it won't do! Will you stand upon your legs, you young devil?"

Oliver could scarcely stand, but made a shift to raise himself to his feet, and was at once lugged along the streets by the officer who held him by his jacket collar. The gentleman walked along by the officer's side. And as many of the crowd as could do so kept a little ahead, staring back at Oliver from time to time. The boys in the procession shouted as if a great victory had been won.

11 *Mr. Fang's Fangs*

The mob had the satisfaction of following Oliver through only two or three streets, and down a place called Mutton Hill, before he was led into the backyard of a police station. It was notorious for dispensing make-believe justice to many unfortunate victims in the district. Here those in the lead met a stout man with a bunch of whiskers on his face, and a bunch of keys in his hand.

"What's the matter now?" asked he, carelessly.

"A young fogle hunter," replied the officer who had Oliver in charge, as he pushed him roughly forward.

"Are you the party that's been robbed, sir?" inquired the man with the keys, addressing the booklover.

"Yes, I am," replied the old gentleman, "but I am not sure that this boy actually took the handkerchief. I—I would rather not press the case."

"Must go before the magistrate now, sir," declared the turnkey. "His worship will be disengaged in half a minute. Now, young gallows!" he commanded, as he unlocked a door which led into a stone cell. Here Oliver was searched and, nothing dangerous being found upon him, locked up. The dark little cell was very dirty on that morning, for it had been occupied by six drunken people during the weekend.

The old gentleman looked almost as sad as Oliver when the key grated in the lock. He turned with a sigh to the book that had been the innocent cause of all this disturbance.

"There is something in that boy's face," said he to himself, as he walked slowly away, deep in thought, "something that touches and interests me. *Can* he be innocent? He looked like—by the by!" exclaimed the old gentleman, halting very abruptly, and staring up into the sky. "Bless my soul! Where have I seen something like that look before?"

After musing for some minutes, the booklover walked into a back anteroom. There, retiring into a corner, he tried to remember many faces that he had not seen for years. "No," said he, shaking his head, "it must be imagination. I can recall no countenance of which that boy's features bear a trace." So the puzzled gentleman heaved a sigh over the recollections he had awakened and buried them again in the pages of the musty book.

He was aroused by a touch on the shoulder and a request from the man with the keys to follow him into the office. Then he closed his book hastily and was at once ushered into the imposing presence of the famous Mr. Fang.

The office was a front parlor, with a paneled wall. Mr. Fang sat behind a bar at the upper end. On one side of the door was a wooden pen in which poor little Oliver already had been deposited, trembling very much at the awfulness of the scene.

Mr. Fang was a lean, stiff-necked, middle-sized man, with only a little hair on the back and sides of his head. His face was stern and much flushed with drink.

The old gentleman bowed respectfully and, advancing to the magistrate's desk, handed him a card, saying, "That is my name and address, sir." He then withdrew a pace or

two; and politely waited to be questioned, while Mr. Fang was reading something unpleasant about himself in a newspaper. Such critical articles were published frequently.

"Who are you?" demanded Mr. Fang.

The old gentleman pointed, with some surprise, to his card.

"Officer!" Mr. Fang called, rudely tossing the card aside with the newspaper. "Who is this fellow?"

"My name, sir," said the elderly one, speaking like a gentleman, "is Brownlow. Permit *me* to inquire the name of the magistrate who offers an unprovoked insult to a respectable person, under the protection of the bench." Mr. Brownlow then looked around the office as if in search of some person who would give him the required information.

"Officer!" shouted Mr. Fang. "What's this fellow charged with?"

"He's not charged at all, your worship," replied the officer. "He appears against this boy, your worship."

His worship knew that quite well; but it was a good excuse for annoyance, and a safe one.

"Appears against the boy, does he?" inquired Fang, surveying Mr. Brownlow from head to foot with a sneer. "Swear him!"

"Before I am sworn, I beg to say one word," ventured Mr. Brownlow, "and that is, that I really never, without this experience, could have believed—"

"Hold your tongue, sir!" commanded Mr. Fang.

"I will not, sir!" replied the old gentleman.

"Hold your tongue this instant, or I'll have you turned out of the office!" cried Mr. Fang. "You're an insolent fellow. How dare you bully a magistrate!"

"What!" exclaimed Mr. Brownlow, reddening.

"Swear this person!" shouted Mr. Fang to the clerk. "I'll not hear another word. Swear him!"

Mr. Brownlow's anger was now aroused. But, thinking that he might injure the boy by giving vent to it, he suppressed his feelings and submitted to be sworn in at once.

"Now," said Fang, "what's the charge against this boy? What have you got to say, sir?"

"I was standing at a bookstall—" Mr. Brownlow began.

"Silence, sir!" order Mr. Fang. "Policeman! Where's the policeman? Here, swear this officer. Now, sir, what *is* this?"

The policeman, with regulation respect, made his official report.

"Are there any witnesses?" inquired Mr. Fang.

"None, your worship," the officer answered, timidly.
Mr. Fang sat in silence for several minutes. Then,
quickly turning to Mr. Brownlow in great anger, roared,
"Do you mean to state your charge, man, or do you
not? You have been sworn. If you stand there, refusing to
give evidence, I'll punish you for disrespect to the bench."

In spite of many interruptions and repeated insults,
Mr. Brownlow managed to state his case. He explained that,
in the surprise of the moment, he had run after the boy
because he saw him running away. And he begged that
the magistrate would deal as leniently with the prisoner as
the law would allow.

"He has been hurt already," said the kind gentleman.
"And I fear," he concluded, looking toward the boy, "I really
fear that he is ill."

"Oh! yes, I dare say!" said Mr. Fang, with a sneer.
"Come, none of your tricks here, you young vagabond!
What's your name?"

Oliver tried to reply, but his tongue failed him. He was
deadly pale; and the whole place seemed to be revolving.

"What's your name, you hardened scoundrel?" demanded Mr. Fang. "Officer, what's his name?"

This was addressed to a bluff old fellow in a striped
waistcoat, who was standing by the rail. He bent over Oliver
and repeated the inquiry, but found him really too ill to
understand the question. Then, knowing that failure to
reply would only anger the magistrate still more, and add
to the severity of his sentence, he decided to try a guess:

"He says his name's Tom White, your worship," said
the kindhearted officer.

"Oh, he won't speak out, won't he?" shouted Fang.
"Very well, very well! Where does he live?"

"Where he can, your worship." replied the officer,
again pretending to hear Oliver's answer.

"Has he any parents?" inquired the magistrate.

"He says they died in his infancy, your worship," replied the officer, to whom that was an old story.

At this point, Oliver raised his head; and, looking around with imploring eyes, begged for a drink of water.

"Stuff and nonsense!" cried Mr. Fang. "Don't try to make a fool of me."

"I think he really *is* ill, your worship," insisted the officer.

"I know better!" snapped Mr. Fang.

"Take care of him, officer," said the old gentleman, raising his hands in alarm. "He'll fall down."

"Stand away, officer," commanded Fang. "Let him fall, if he likes!"

Then Oliver promptly fainted and fell to the floor. The men in the office looked at each other, but no one dared to stir.

"I knew he was shamming," said Fang, as if he now had real proof of the fact. "Let him lie there. He'll soon be tired of that."

"How do you propose to deal with the case, sir?" inquired the clerk, in a low voice.

"Without further delay," replied Mr. Fang. "He stands sentenced to three months—hard labor, of course. Clear the office!"

The door was opened, and a couple of men were preparing to carry the insensible boy to his cell. Just then, an elderly man of decent but poor appearance rushed hastily into the office and approached the bench.

"Stop, stop! Don't take him away! For heaven's sake—wait a moment!" pleaded the newcomer, breathless with haste.

Mr. Fang was furious at seeing an unbidden guest enter in such a disorderly manner.

"What *is* this? Who is this? Turn this man out. Clear the office!" cried Mr. Fang.

"I *will* speak!" insisted the man. "I will *not* be turned out. I saw it all. I keep the bookstall. I demand to be sworn. Mr. Fang, you must hear me, sir!"

The intruder's manner was determined; and the matter was growing rather too serious to be hushed up.

"Swear the man," growled Mr. Fang, with ill grace. "Now, sir, what have you got to say?"

"This," said the bookseller. "I saw three boys—two others and the prisoner here—loitering on the opposite side of the way, while this gentleman was reading. The robbery was committed by one of the other two boys. *I saw it done;* and I saw that this boy here was perfectly amazed and stupefied by it." Having by this time recovered a little breath, the worthy bookstall keeper proceeded to relate all the details of the theft.

"Why didn't you come here before?" grumbled Fang, after a pause.

"I had no one to tend the shop," replied the bookseller. "Everybody who could have helped me had joined in the pursuit. I could get nobody till five minutes ago; and I've run here all the way."

"Brownlow was reading, was he?" inquired Fang, after another pause.

"Yes; the very book he has in his hand now."

"Oh, *that* book, eh?" said Fang. "Is it paid for?"

"No—it is not," replied the bookseller, with a smile.

"Dear me, I had forgotten all about it!" exclaimed Mr. Brownlow, innocently.

"A nice person to prefer a charge against a poor boy!" snapped Fang, with a comical effort to look merciful. "Sir, you have obtained possession of that book under very suspicious circumstances; and you may consider yourself very fortunate in that the owner will not prosecute. Let this be a lesson to you, my man, or the law will overtake you yet! The boy is discharged.—Clear the office!"

Oliver, dazed, then tottered toward the yard.

At this point, Mr. Brownlow was almost bursting with the rage he had kept down so long.

"Clear the office!" shouted the magistrate. "Officers, do you hear? *Clear the office!*"

The order was obeyed; and the raging Mr. Brownlow was ushered out, with the book in one hand, and his bamboo cane in the other. When he reached the yard, his anger vanished, for little Oliver Twist lay quivering on the pavement. He was deathly pale.

"Poor boy, poor boy!" said Mr. Brownlow, bending over him. "Call a coach, somebody, pray. Directly!"

A coach was obtained; and, after Oliver had been carefully laid on one seat, the booklover entered and sat on the other.

"May I accompany you?" inquired the bookstall keeper, looking in.

"Bless me, yes, my dear sir," replied Mr. Brownlow, quickly. "I forgot you. Dear, dear! I have this trouble-making book still! Jump in. See the poor lad! There's no time to lose."

Then the bookseller sat beside his good friend, and away they drove.

Part 2

Sunlight to Shadow

1 *As in a Looking Glass*

Ill as he was, poor Oliver Twist could not know that the coach rattled along over some of the ground that he had trod, many weeks ago, after first meeting the Dodger. At length, the patient but weary horses were grateful for a brief rest when they were stopped before a neat house, in a quiet, shady street near Pentonville. Here, a bed was quickly prepared, and Mr. Brownlow had his young charge carefully and comfortably placed in it. Then the coach carried the bookseller back to his shop.

But Oliver remained insensible to all the goodness of his new friends. The sun rose and set many times; and still the boy lay at the mercy of the dry and wasting heat of fever.

Weak and thin, he awoke one day from a long and troubled dream. Feebly raising himself in the bed, with his head resting on his trembling arm, he looked anxiously around.

"What room is this? Where have I been brought to?" asked Oliver. "This is not the place I went to sleep in."

He uttered these words in a feeble voice, but they were overheard at once. The bed curtain was hastily drawn back, and a motherly old lady, neatly dressed, arose from an armchair close by, in which she had been sitting at needlework.

"Hush, my dear," said the old lady, softly. "You must be quiet. You have been very, very ill. Lie down again;

there's a dear!" With those words, she gently placed Oliver's head upon the pillow. Then, smoothing back his hair from his forehead, she looked at him so kindly and lovingly that he could not help placing his thin little hand in hers.

"Save us!" said the old lady, with tears in her eyes. "What a grateful little dear it is. Pretty creatur'! How would his mother feel if she had sat by him as I have, and could see him now!"

"Perhaps she does see me," whispered Oliver, folding his hands together. "Perhaps she *has* sat by me. I almost feel as if she had."

"That was the fever, my dear," said the old lady, mildly.

"I suppose it was," replied Oliver, "because heaven is a long way off; and they are too happy there to come down to the bedside of a poor boy. But if she knew I was ill, she must have pitied me, even there; for she was very ill herself before she died. She can't know anything about me, though," added Oliver, after a moment's silence. "If she had seen me hurt, it would have made her sorrowful; and her face has always looked sweet and happy, when I have dreamed of her."

The old lady made no reply to this; but, wiping her eyes first, and her spectacles afterward, brought a cool drink for Oliver. Then, patting him on the cheek, she told him again that he must lie very quiet.

So Oliver kept very still. He was anxious to obey his kind attendant in all things. Besides, he was completely exhausted with what he had already said. He soon fell into a gentle doze, from which he was awakened by the light of a candle. And soon he saw a gentleman with a very large and loud-ticking gold watch in his hand. He felt Oliver's pulse and nodded as if pleased.

"You *are* a great deal better, are you not, my boy?" inquired the gentleman.

"Yes, thank you, sir," replied Oliver.

But the doctor missed his guess when he suggested that the sick lad was both hungry and sleepy; for the patient decided otherwise—and *he* certainly should have known.

So, instead of taking another chance, but looking just as wise as before, the doctor *asked* the boy whether he was thirsty.

"Yes, sir, rather thirsty," answered Oliver.

"Just as I expected, Mrs. Bedwin," said the doctor.

"It's very natural that he should be thirsty. You may give him a little tea, ma'am, and some dry toast without any butter. Don't keep him too warm, ma'am; but be careful that you don't let him be too cold—Will you have the goodness?"

The old lady bowed quickly and left the bedside. Soon she returned with a tray. And the doctor, after tasting the tea and expressing a partial approval of it, hurried away, his boots creaking in a very important manner as he went downstairs.

Oliver dozed off again, soon after this. When he awoke, it was nearly twelve o'clock. Mrs. Bedwin tenderly bade him good-night, shortly afterward, and left him in charge of a fat old woman who had just come in, bringing with her, in a little bundle, a small prayer book and a large nightcap. Putting the latter on her head and the former on the table, she told Oliver that she had come to sit up with him. Then she drew her chair close to the fire and went off into a series of short naps, broken often with many tumblings forward and moans and chokings.

And thus the night crept slowly on. Oliver lay awake for some time, counting the little circles of light which the reflection of the light shade threw upon the ceiling; or tracing with his weary eyes the pattern of the wallpaper. The darkness and the deep stillness of the room were very solemn. And the boy thought that death had been hovering there for many days and nights, and might yet fill it with gloom. So he turned his face upon the pillow and fervently prayed to heaven.

Gradually he fell into that deep, peaceful sleep which ease from recent suffering brings.

It had been bright day for hours when Oliver next opened his eyes. He felt cheerful and happy. The crisis of the disease was safely past. He belonged to the world again.

Three days later, he was able to sit in an easy chair, well propped up with pillows. As he was still too weak to walk, Mrs. Bedwin had him carried downstairs into the housekeeper's own little room. There, by the fireside, the good old lady sat herself down, too, and, being in a state of considerable delight at seeing Oliver so much better, forthwith began to cry most violently.

"Never mind me, my dear," she managed to say. "I'm only having a regular good cry. There; it's all over now, and I'm quite comfortable."

"You're very, very kind to me, ma'am," declared Oliver.

"Well, never you mind that, my dear," said the old lady. "That's got nothing to do with your broth; and it's full time you had it. The doctor says Mr. Brownlow may come in to see you this morning; and we must get up our best looks, because the better we look, the more he'll be pleased." Then she applied herself to warming up a basin of broth: strong enough, Oliver thought, to furnish an ample dinner, when reduced to the regulation strength, for three hundred and fifty paupers at least.

"Are you fond of pictures, dear?" inquired Mrs. Bedwin, seeing that Oliver had fixed his eyes most intently on a portrait that hung against the wall, just opposite his chair.

"I don't quite know, ma'am," Oliver replied, without taking his eyes from the canvas. "I have seen so few. What a beautiful, mild face that lady has!"

"Ah!" said the old lady, "painters always make ladies look prettier than they are, or they wouldn't get any custom, child. The man that invented the machine for taking likenesses might have known *that* would never succeed; it's a deal too honest—A deal!" And Mrs. Bedwin laughed very heartily at her own cleverness.

"Is—is that a likeness, ma'am?" inquired Oliver.

"Yes," said his good nurse, looking up for a moment, "*that's* a real portrait."

"Whose, ma'am?" asked Oliver.

"Why, really, my dear, I don't know," answered Mrs. Bedwin, in a good-humored manner. "It's not a likeness of anybody you or I know, I expect. It seems to strike your fancy, dear."

"It is so *very* pretty," replied Oliver.

"Are you sure you're not afraid of it?" queried the old

lady, observing in great surprise the look of wonder with which the boy studied the painting.

"Oh, no, no," returned Oliver, quickly, "but the eyes look so sorrowful. They seem fixed upon me. That look makes my heart beat," added Oliver in a low voice, "as if the lady was alive and wanted to speak to me, but couldn't."

"Lord save us!" exclaimed Mrs. Bedwin, starting. "Don't talk that way, child. You're weak and nervous after your illness. Let me move your chair to the other side, so you won't see the picture—There!" she continued, suiting the action to the word. "You don't see it now, at all events."

But Oliver *did* see it in his mind's eye, as distinctly as if he had not altered his position. However, he thought it better not to worry the kind old lady. So he smiled gently when she looked at him. And Mrs. Bedwin, satisfied that he seemed to be more comfortable, salted and broke bits of toasted bread into the broth, with proper fuss and bustle. Just when Oliver had emptied the bowl, there was a soft rap at the door. "Come in," said Mrs. Bedwin; and Mr. Brownlow entered briskly.

But he had no sooner raised his spectacles to his forehead, and thrust his hands beneath his dressing gown, to take a good long look at Oliver, than his countenance underwent a great variety of odd contortions. Oliver made an attempt to stand up, out of respect to his benefactor, but sank back into the chair again. Then Mr. Brownlow's eyes filled with tears.

"Poor boy, poor boy!" he exclaimed, clearing his throat. "I'm rather hoarse this morning, Mrs. Bedwin. I'm afraid I have caught cold."

"I hope not, sir," said Mrs. Bedwin. "Everything you have had has been well aired, sir."

"I don't know, Bedwin. I don't know," said Mr. Brownlow. "I rather think I had a damp napkin at dinnertime yesterday; but never mind that. How do *you* feel, my lad?"

"Very happy, sir," replied Oliver. "And very grateful indeed, sir, for your goodness to me."

"Good boy!" exclaimed Mr. Brownlow, stoutly. "Have you given him any nourishment, Bedwin?"

"He has just had a basin of strong broth, sir," replied she.

"Ugh!" said Mr. Brownlow, with a slight shudder. "A couple of glasses of port wine would have done him a great deal more good. Wouldn't they, Tom White, eh?"

"My name is Oliver, sir," explained the little patient, with a look of great astonishment.

"Oliver," repeated Mr. Brownlow. "Oliver what? Oliver White, eh?"

"No, sir—Twist: Oliver Twist."

"Queer name!" said the old gentleman. "What made you tell the magistrate your name was White?"

"I never told him so, sir," returned Oliver in surprise.

This sounded so like a falsehood, that the old gentleman looked somewhat sternly at Oliver.

"Some mistake," decided Mr. Brownlow. But, although his motive for looking steadily at Oliver no longer existed, the old idea of the resemblance between his features and some familiar face came upon him so strongly that he could not withdraw his gaze.

"I hope you are not angry with me, sir," said Oliver, raising his eyes pleadingly.

"No, no," replied the old gentleman. "Why! what's this?—Bedwin, look there!"

As he spoke, he pointed hastily to the picture above Oliver's head, and then to the boy's face. There was its living copy. The eyes, the head, the mouth; every feature was the same. The expression was, for the instant, so precisely alike, that the minutest line seemed copied with startling accuracy.

Oliver knew not the cause of this sudden excitement;

for, not being strong enough to bear the start it gave him, he fainted away.

That weakness on his part affords this narrative an opportunity, here, of relieving the reader from suspense in behalf of the other two young pupils of the merry old gentleman; and of bringing their story up to date:

After Bates and the Dodger joined in the hue and cry which was raised at Oliver's heels, they were soon busy thinking of themselves. Therefore, as soon as they were sure that the shouting mob was giving all of its attention to Oliver, they dropped the chase and immediately made for home by the shortest cut.

It was not until the two boys had hurried through many narrow, winding streets and courts, that they ventured to halt beneath a low, dark archway. Having remained silent there just long enough to recover breath to speak, Charley uttered an exclamation of amusement and delight. Then, bursting into an uncontrollable fit of laughter, he flung himself upon a doorstep and rolled thereon in great mirth.

"What's the matter?" inquired the Dodger.

"Ha! ha! ha!" was Charley Bates' reply.

"Hold your noise," warned the Dodger, looking cautiously around. "Do you want to be grabbed, stupid?"

"I—can't help it," said Charley. "I can't *help* it!—To see him splitting away at that pace, and cutting around the corners, and knocking up again' the posts, and starting on again as if he was made of iron as well as them, and me with the wipe in my pocket, singing out after him—oh, my eye!" Whereupon he again rolled upon the doorstep and laughed more loudly than before.

"What'll Fagin say?" inquired the Dodger, taking advantage of the next interval of breathlessness on the part of his friend to ask that important question.

"Why, what *should* he say?" inquired Charley, stopping rather suddenly in his merriment; for the Dodger's manner was impressive.

The Dodger whistled for a couple of minutes; then, taking off his hat, scratched his head and nodded thrice.

"What do you mean?" demanded Charley.

The Dodger made no reply; but, putting his hat on again, and gathering the skirts of his long-tailed coat under one arm, slapped the bridge of his nose some half-dozen times in a familiar but expressive manner. Then, turning on his heel, he slunk down the court, followed by Charley, who had become quiet and very thoughtful.

The noise of footsteps on the creaking stairs, a few minutes later, aroused the crime master, as he sat near the fire. He held a dried pork sausage and a small loaf in his left hand, and a pocketknife in his right. There was a rascally smile on his white face as he turned around; and, glancing sharply out from under his thick red eyebrows, he bent his ear toward the door and listened.

"Why, how's this?" muttered Fagin, looking puzzled. "Only *two* of 'em? Where's the third? They can't have got into trouble—Hark!"

The footsteps approached nearer, then reached the landing. The door was slowly opened; and the Dodger and Charley Bates entered, closing it behind them.

2 Nancy Puts on an Act

"Where's Oliver?" demanded Fagin, rising with a threatening look. "Where's the boy?"

The young thieves eyed their master as if they were alarmed at his manner, and looked uneasily at each other. But they made no reply.

"What's become of the *boy*?" cried the old man, seizing the Dodger by the collar. "Speak out, or I'll strangle you!"

Mr. Fagin looked so very much in earnest, that Charley Bates, who thought it wise in all cases to be on the safe side, dropped upon his knees and raised a loud and continuous roar.

"Will you speak?" thundered Fagin, shaking the Dodger angrily.

"Why, the traps have got him, and that's all about it," said the Dodger, sullenly. "Come, let go o' me, will you!" And, swinging himself by one jerk clean out of the big coat, which he left in Fagin's hands, he snatched up the toasting fork and made a pass at the merry old gentleman's waistcoat. If it had taken effect, it would have let a little more merriment out than could have been easily replaced.

The old one jumped back quickly and, seizing a heavy vessel, prepared to hurl it at the Dodger's head. But Charley Bates, at this moment, attracted Fagin's attention by a terrific howl; and the object was flung toward that young gentleman, instead.

"Why, what the blazes is in the wind now?" growled a deep voice. "Who pitched that 'ere at me? It's well it's the beer, and not the pot, as hit me, or I'd settle somebody. I might have know'd as nobody but an infernal, rich, plundering old fool could afford to throw any drink but water— and not *that*, unless he done the River Company out of its fees. Wot's it all about Fagin? My neck-handerkercher's lined with beer!—Come in, you sneaking warmint. Wot are you stopping outside for, as if you was ashamed of your master? Come in!"

The man who growled those words was a stoutly built fellow of about thirty-five, in a black velveteen coat, soiled drab breeches, lace-up half boots, and gray cotton stockings, which enclosed a bulky pair of legs. He wore a brown hat. The dirty handkerchief around his neck, with its long, frayed ends, served to wipe the beer from his face as he spoke. His broad, heavy face carried a beard of three-days' growth; and one of his scowling eyes showed dark signs of having been damaged recently by a blow.

"Come in, d'ye hear?" roared the rough visitor. A white, shaggy dog, with his face scratched and torn in twenty different places, then skulked into the room.

"Why didn't you come in afore? You're getting too proud to own me in company, are you?—Down!"

This command was enforced with a kick that sent the animal into a corner of the room. He appeared well used to it, however, for he then coiled himself up very quietly and lay still.

"What are you up to? Ill-treating the boys, you stingy, old fence?" asked the ruffian, seating himself deliberately. "I wonder they don't murder you! If I'd been your 'prentice, I'd have done it long ago. And—no, I couldn't have sold you afterward, for you're fit for nothing but keeping as a curiosity of ugliness in a glass bottle. But I suppose they don't blow glass bottles large enough."

"Hush! Hush! Mr. Sikes," warned Fagin, trembling. "Don't speak so loud."

"None of your mistering!" growled Sikes. "You always mean mischief when you play that. You know my name. Out with it! I sha'n't disgrace it when the time comes."

"Well, well, then—Bill Sikes," said the frightened old man. "You seem out of humor, Bill."

"Perhaps I am," replied Sikes. "I should think *you* was rather out of sorts, too, unless you mean as little harm when you throw pots about as you do when you blab and—"

"Are you mad?" hissed Fagin, catching Sikes by the sleeve and pointing toward the boys.

Mr. Sikes contented himself with tying an imaginary knot under his left ear and jerking his head over on his right shoulder. The old man understood perfectly what Sikes meant. Bill then demanded a glass of liquor.

"And mind you don't poison it," he warned, laying his hat upon the table. "I know you *would,* you old devil!"

After swallowing two or three glasses of spirits, Mr. Sikes engaged the young gentlemen in conversation. He thus learned about Oliver's capture in general, with some slight "improvement" upon the truth of the details.

"I'm afraid," Fagin remarked, "that the boy may say something which will get us into trouble."

"That's very likely," returned Sikes with a malicious grin. "You're blowed upon, Fagin!"

"And I'm afraid, you see," added the old man, speaking as if he had not noticed the interruption, and looking at Bill closely as he did so, "I'm afraid that, if the game was up with us, it might be up with a good many more, and that it would come out rather worse for *you* than it would for me, my dear."

There was a long pause. Then:

"Somebody must find out wot's been done at the office," Mr. Sikes announced, in a low tone.

Fagin nodded in agreement.

"If he hasn't peached, and is penned up, there's no fear till he comes out again," said Mr. Sikes. "*Then* he must be taken care on. You must get hold of him somehow!"

Again Fagin nodded.

But how could they get hold of Oliver? No one in that room was anxious to go near a police office on any excuse.

After a long period of silence, the sudden entrance of the two young ladies whom Oliver had seen on a former occasion caused the conversation to flow afresh.

"The very thing!" exclaimed Fagin. "Bet will go, won't you, my dear?"

"Where?"

"Only just up to the office, my dear," replied the old man, coaxingly.

Bet merely expressed an emphatic and earnest desire to be "blessed" if she would.

Quite disappointed, Fagin turned from Bet, who was gaily attired in a red gown, green boots, and yellow curl-papers, to Nancy.

"Nancy, my dear," her chief continued, in a soothing manner, "what do you *say*?"

"That it won't do. So it's no use a-trying it on, Fagin," replied Nancy.

"What do you mean by that?" challenged Mr. Sikes, looking up in a surly manner.

"What I say, Bill," the lady retorted firmly.

"Why, you're the very person for it," argued Bill. "Nobody about here knows anything of you."

"And as I don't want 'em to, neither," Nancy added, in a composed manner. "It's rather more 'no' than 'yes' with me, Bill."

"She'll go, Fagin," Sikes declared.

"No, she won't, Fagin," the girl protested.

"Yes, she *will*, Fagin!" Sikes shouted, commandingly.

And Mr. Sikes was right. By threats, promises, and bribes, Nancy was finally persuaded to undertake the assignment. It just happened that she had moved recently into the neighborhood of Field Lane from the distant but genteel suburb of Ratcliffe. Hence she was not too fearful of being recognized by any of her numerous acquaintances.

Accordingly, with a clean white apron tied over her gown, and her curlpapers tucked up under a straw bonnet, Miss Nancy prepared to go on her errand.

"Stop a minute, my dear," said Fagin, producing a little basket. "Carry that in one hand. It looks more respectable."

"Give her a door key to carry in her t'other one, Fagin," suggested Sikes. "It looks real and genuine like."

"Yes, yes, my dear, so it does," Fagin agreed, hanging a large street-door key on the forefinger of Nancy's right hand. "There. Very good, my dear!"

"Oh, my brother! My poor, dear, sweet, innocent little brother!" exclaimed Nancy, bursting into tears, and swinging the little basket and the street-door key in a show if distress. "What *has* become of him! Where have they taken him to! Oh, do have pity, and tell me what's been done with the dear boy, gentlemen. Do, gentlemen, if you please, gentlemen!"

Having uttered these words in a most heartbroken tone, to the great delight of her hearers, Miss Nancy paused, winked to the company, nodded, and disappeared.

"Ah! she's a clever girl, my dears," said the master, turning toward his young friends, and shaking his head solemnly, as if suggesting that they follow the bright example they had just beheld.

"She's a honor to her sex," announced Mr. Sikes, filling his glass, and striking the table with his heavy fist. "Here's her health and wishing they was all like her!"

Soon Nancy arrived in perfect safety at the police station.

Entering by the back way, she tapped softly with the key at one of the cell doors and listened. There was no sound within. So she coughed and listened again. Still there was no reply. Then she spoke:

"Nolly, dear!" murmured Nancy, in a gentle voice.

There was nobody inside but a miserable, shoeless prisoner who had been taken up for playing the flute. He made no answer, being occupied only in bewailing the loss of the flute, which had been taken from him for the use of the county. So Nancy passed on to the next cell and knocked there.

"Well!" cried a faint and feeble voice.

"Is there a little boy here? inquired Nancy, sobbing.

"No," replied the voice, "God forbid!"

The tenant in that cell was a beggar of sixty-five. In the next cell was a man who had been arrested for selling tin saucepans without a license.

But neither of these prisoners answered to the name of Oliver, or knew anything about him. So Nancy made straight up to the bluff officer in the striped waistcoat. With the most piteous wailings, she demanded possession of her "own dear brother."

"*I* haven't got him, my dear," responded the old man.

"Where *is* he?" screamed Nancy, in a desperate tone.

"Why, the *gentleman's* got him," replied the officer.

"What gentleman? Oh, gracious heavens! *What* gentleman?" exclaimed Nancy.

In reply, the old officer informed the frantic "sister" that Oliver had been taken ill in the office and was discharged after a witness had proved that the robbery had been committed by another boy; and that the prosecutor had taken him away, in an insensible condition, to his own residence—somewhere in Pentonville.

In a dreadful state of doubt, the agonized young woman staggered to the gate. Then, exchanging her faltering walk for a swift run, she returned by a complicated route to Fagin's house.

Mr. Bill Sikes no sooner heard the story of the expedition, than he very hastily called up the white dog; and, putting on his hat, departed without wishing the company good morning.

"We must know where he is, my dears. He *must* be found!" declared their master, greatly excited. "Charley, do nothing but skulk about, till you bring home some news of him! Nancy, my dear, I must have him found. I trust to you, my dear—to you and the Artful for everything! Stay, stay," he added, shakily unlocking a drawer. "There's money! I shall shut up this shop tonight. You'll know where to find me! Don't stop here an instant, my dears!'

Then he pushed them from the room, carefully double-locking and barring the door behind them. After pausing for a moment or two, he drew from its hiding place the box which he had unintentionally disclosed to Oliver and hastily began to hide the watches and jewelry beneath his clothing.

A rap at the door startled him. "Who's there?" he cried in a shrill tone.

"Me!" replied the voice of the Dodger, through the keyhole.

"What now?" cried Fagin, impatiently.

"Is he to be kidnapped to the other den, Nancy says?" inquired the Dodger.

"Yes! Wherever she lays hands on him. Find him, that's all! I shall know what to do next; never fear."

The boy mumbled that he understood and hurried downstairs after his companions.

"He has not peached so far," said Fagin to himself, as he continued his occupation. "If he means to blab us among his new friends, we may stop his mouth yet."

3 Fortune-Telling

When Oliver recovered from his fainting fit, the picture of the beautiful lady was not discussed by Mr. Brownlow and Mrs. Bedwin in the conversations that followed. They spoke only of topics that might amuse without exciting him. He was still too weak to get up for breakfast. But, when he came down into the housekeeper's room next day, he cast an eager glance at the wall, in the hope of looking again on the portrait he loved. He was disappointed, however, for it had been removed.

"Ah!" said the housekeeper, watching the direction of Oliver's eyes. "It is gone, you see."

"I see it is, ma'am," replied Oliver. "Why have they taken it away?"

"Because Mr. Brownlow said that, as it seemed to worry you, perhaps it might prevent your getting well, you know," rejoined the old lady.

"Oh, no, indeed! It didn't worry me, ma'am," said Oliver. "I liked to look at it. I loved it."

"Well, well!" said Mrs. Bedwin, good-humoredly. "You get well fast as ever you can, dear, and it shall be hung up again. There! I promise you that! Now, let us talk about something else."

They were happy days, those of Oliver's recovery.

Everything was quiet, neat, and orderly. Everybody was kind and gentle. In contrast to the noise and ill-treatment in which he had lived before, his new life was heavenly. When he was able to put on his clothes properly, Mr. Brownlow bought him a complete new outfit, telling Oliver he could do what he liked with the old clothes. So the grateful boy gave them to a kind servant, suggesting that she sell them and keep the money for herself. This she did very promptly.

One evening, about a week after the affair of the picture, when the happy boy and Mrs. Bedwin were talking pleasantly, Mr. Brownlow sent word that, if Oliver Twist felt pretty well, he should like to see him in his study and talk to him a little while.

"Bless us, and save us! Wash you hands, and let me part your hair nicely for you, child," said Mrs. Bedwin. "Dear heart alive! If we had known he would have asked for you, we would have put you a clean collar on and made you as smart as sixpence!"

Oliver did as she bade him; and he looked quite presentable when he tapped at the study door. Mr. Brownlow called to him to come in, and he entered a little back room, quite full of books, with a window looking into some pleasant little gardens. There was a table drawn up before the window, at which Mr. Brownlow was seated reading. When he saw Oliver, he told him at once to sit down.

"There are a good many books, are there not, my boy?" said Mr. Brownlow, observing the curiosity with which Oliver gazed at the shelves that extended from floor to ceiling.

"A great number, sir," replied Oliver. "I never saw so many."

"You shall read some of them later, if you behave well," said the old gentleman, kindly. "And you will like that better than looking at their covers—that is, in *some* cases; because there are certain books whose covers are by far the best parts."

Again Oliver stared in wide-eyed wonder at the many different kinds of books that stood like lines of soldiers on the shelves.

"Now," said Mr. Brownlow, speaking very kindly, but in a much more serious manner than Oliver had ever known him to show before, "I want you to pay close attention, my boy, to what I am going to say. I shall speak plainly, for I am sure you are as well able to understand me as many older persons would be."

"Oh, don't tell me you are going to send me away, sir, pray!" exclaimed Oliver, alarmed at the good gentleman's serious tone. "Don't turn me out of doors to wander in the streets again. Let me stay here and be a servant. Don't send me back to the wretched place I came from. Have mercy upon a poor boy, sir!"

"My dear child," said the old gentleman, moved by the warmth of Oliver's sudden appeal, "you need not be afraid of my deserting you, unless you give me cause."

"I never, never will, sir," insisted Oliver.

"I hope not," rejoined Mr. Brownlow. "I do not think you ever will. I have been deceived before in some persons whom I have endeavored to help; but I feel strongly disposed to trust you, nevertheless. And I am more interested in your welfare than I can account for, even to myself. The persons on whom I have bestowed my dearest love now lie in their graves. But, although the happiness and delight of my life buried there, too, I have not made a coffin of my heart and sealed it up, forever, on my best affections. Deep suffering has but strengthened and refined them."

As the old gentleman said this in a soft voice, more to himself than to his companion, and as he remained silent for a short time afterward, Oliver sat quite still.

"Well, well!" said Mr. Brownlow at length, in a more

cheerful tone, "I only say this because you have a young heart; and, knowing that I have suffered great pain and sorrow, you will be more careful, perhaps, not to wound me. You say you are an orphan, without a friend in the world. All inquiries I have been able to make prove the statement. Let me hear your story: where you came from; who brought you up; and how you got into the company in which I found you. Speak the truth, and you shall not be friendless while I live."

Oliver's painful feelings checked his speech for some minutes. When he was on the point of beginning to tell his story, an impatient little double-knock was heard at the street door. Then the servant, running upstairs, announced Mr. Grimwig.

"Is he coming up?" inquired Mr. Brownlow.

"Yes, sir," replied the servant. "He asked if there were any muffins in the house; and, when I told him 'yes,' he said he had come to tea."

Mr. Brownlow smiled and turned to the lad, explaining that Mr. Grimwig was an old friend of his, and saying that Oliver must not mind the visitor's rough manners. "He is a worthy gentleman at heart," added the booklover.

"Shall I go downstairs, sir?" inquired Oliver.

"No; I would rather you remained here."

At that moment, there walked into the room, supporting himself by a thick stick, a stout old gentleman, lame in one leg. He was dressed in a blue coat, striped waistcoat, nankeen breeches and gaiters, and a broad-brimmed white hat, with the sides turned up with green. The variety of shapes into which his face was being twisted defies description. He also had a habit of twisting his head to one side when he spoke; and he looked out of the corners of his eyes at the same time. He greeted his good friend by holding out a small piece of orange peel at arm's length, exclaiming, in a growling voice,

"Look here! Do you see this! Isn't it a most wonderful thing that I can't call at a man's house but I find a piece of this on the staircase? I was lamed with orange peel once, and I know orange peel will be my death at last. It *will,* sir, or I'll be content to eat my own head, sir!"

This was the handsome offer with which Mr. Grimwig supported nearly every statement he made. His head, how-ever, was too large for any man to eat at one sitting—to say nothing of its very thick coating of powder.

"I'll eat my head, sir!" repeated Mr. Grimwig, striking his stick upon the ground—"Hallo! what's that?" looking at Oliver, and retreating a pace or two.

"This is young Oliver Twist, whom we were speaking about," said Mr. Brownlow.

Oliver bowed.

"You don't mean to say that's the boy who had the fever?" said Mr. Grimwig, stepping back a little more. "Wait a minute! Don't speak! Stop—" continued Mr. Grimwig, abruptly. "That's the boy who had the orange! If that's not the boy, sir, who had the orange and threw this bit of peel upon the staircase, I'll eat my head, and his, too."

"No, no, he has not had one," said Mr. Brownlow, laughing. "Come! Put down your hat and speak to my young friend."

"That's the boy, is it?" asked Mr. Grimwig, at length.

"That is the boy," replied Mr. Brownlow.

"How are you, boy?" Mr. Grimwig inquired.

"A great deal better, thank you, sir."

Mr. Brownlow, suspecting that his friend was about to say something disagreeable, asked Oliver to step downstairs and tell Mrs. Bedwin they were ready for tea. As he did not like the visitor's manner, Oliver was very happy to do so.

"He is a nice-looking boy, is he not?" ventured Mr. Brownlow.

"I don't know," answered Mr. Grimwig, pettishly.

"Don't know?"

"No. I don't know. I never see any difference in boys. I only know two sorts of boys: mealy boys, and beef-faced boys."

"And which is Oliver?"

"Mealy. I know a beef-faced boy: a fine boy, they call him, with a round head, red cheeks, and glaring eyes: a horrid boy!"

"Come," said Mr. Brownlow, "Oliver Twist is not like that."

"Well!" exclaimed Mr. Grimwig. "He may be worse."

Here Mr. Brownlow coughed impatiently, which appeared to afford Mr. Grimwig the most exquisite delight.

"He may be worse, I say!" repeated Mr. Grimwig. "Where does he come from? Who is he? What is he? He has had a fever. What of that? Fevers are not peculiar to good people, are they?"

Mr. Brownlow rose and merely replied, "I suppose not. Let's go down to tea now."

In his own heart, Mr. Grimwig was willing to admit that Oliver's appearance and manner were unusually satisfactory. But the stubborn gentleman liked contradiction. So, having determined that no man should dictate to him whether a boy was well looking or not, he had resolved from the first to oppose his friend. Mr. Brownlow had to admit that he knew very little about the boy at the moment, explaining that he had postponed investigation until he thought Oliver was strong enough to bear it. So Mr. Grimwig chuckled threateningly. And he suggested, with a sneer, that the housekeeper might find a tablespoon or two missing some morning.

"And when are you going to hear a full, true, and particular account of the life and adventures of Oliver Twist?" asked Grimwig of Mr. Brownlow, after tea, looking sidewise at Oliver.

"Tomorrow morning," replied Mr. Brownlow. "I would rather he was alone with me at the time. Come to me tomorrow morning at ten o'clock, my boy."

"Yes, sir," Oliver answered, with some hesitation, being somewhat confused by Mr. Grimwig's hard look.

"I'll tell you what," whispered that gentleman to Mr. Brownlow. "He won't come up to you tomorrow morning. I saw him hesitate. He is deceiving you, my good friend."

"I'll swear he is not," insisted Mr. Brownlow.

"If he is not," said Mr. Grimwig, "I'll—" and down went the stick, again indicating that the gentleman would "eat his head."

"I'll answer for that boy's honesty with my life!" exclaimed Mr. Brownlow, knocking the table.

"And I for his falsehood with my head!" rejoined Mr. Grimwig, knocking the table also.

"We shall see!" declared Mr. Brownlow, checking his rising anger.

"We will," agreed his friend, with a provoking smile.

As fate would have it, Mrs. Bedwin brought in, at that moment, a small parcel of books, which Mr. Brownlow had that morning purchased of the bookstall-keeper who has already figured in this history. Having laid them on the table, she prepared to leave the room.

"Stop the boy, Mrs. Bedwin!" ordered Mr. Brownlow. "There is something to go back."

"He has gone, sir," announced Mrs. Bedwin. "I didn't know, sir."

"Dear me, I am very sorry for that!" exclaimed Mr. Brownlow. "I particularly wished some books to be returned tonight. And these are not paid for."

"Send Oliver with them!" challenged Mr. Grimwig. "He will be *sure* to deliver them safely, you know."

"Yes, do let me take them, if you please, sir," begged Oliver. "I'm well enough, sir."

The booklover was just going to say that Oliver should not go out on any account, when a most meaningful cough from Mr. Grimwig convinced him that the lad should go, to prove Grimwig's suspicions unjust.

"You *shall* go, my dear," said the kindly gentleman. "The books are upstairs on a chair by my table. Fetch them down."

Oliver promptly brought down the books under his arm, and waited, cap in hand, for instructions.

"You are to say," said Mr. Brownlow, glancing steadily at Grimwig, "that you have brought those books back; and that you have come to pay the four pound ten I owe the bookseller. This is a five-pound note, so you will have to bring me back ten shillings change."

"I won't be ten minutes, sir," replied Oliver, eagerly. And, having buttoned up the bank note in his jacket pocket, he made a respectful bow and left the room. Mrs. Bedwin followed him to the street door, giving him many directions. Then, after adding various warnings to be sure and not take cold, she permitted him to depart.

"Bless his sweet face!" said Mrs. Bedwin, looking after him. "I can't bear, somehow, to let him go out of my sight." She stood watching him until he turned the corner. Then she closed the door and returned to her own room.

"Let me see. He should be back in twenty minutes, at the longest," said Mr. Brownlow, pulling out his watch and placing it on the table. "It will be dark by that time."

"Oh! you really expect him to come back, do you?" inquired Mr. Grimwig.

"Don't you?" asked Mr. Brownlow, smiling.

"No," replied Grimwig, hammering the table with his fist; "I do not! The boy has a new suit of clothes on his back, a set of valuable books under his arm, and a five-pound note in his pocket. He'll join his old friends, the thieves, and laugh at you. If ever that boy returns to this house, sir, *I'll eat my head*."

With these words, he drew his chair closer to the table. And there the two friends sat waiting, with the watch between them, while the evening shadows slowly gathered round about.

4 *The Tie That Binds*

Mr. William Sikes sat at an old table in a dingy tavern, which was located in the filthiest part of Little Saffron Hill. Drinking from the pewter mug in front of him did not seem to clear away his dark and ugly thoughts. His only companion was his white-coated, red-eyed dog, sitting at his feet. When the dog was not winking at his master with both eyes at once, he licked a large, fresh cut on one side of his mouth.

"Keep quiet, you warmint! Keep quiet!" growled Mr. Sikes, suddenly breaking silence, and giving the dog a heavy kick and a dark curse.

In return, that animal promptly fixed his teeth in one of the half boots. Then, having given it a hearty shake, he retired growling, under a bench, just escaping the pewter measure which Mr. Sikes threw at his head.

"You would, would you?" roared Sikes, seizing the poker in one hand and deliberately opening a large clasp knife with the other. "Come here, you born devil! Come here! D'ye hear?"

The dog no doubt heard; but, evidently objecting to having his throat cut, he remained where he was. He growled more fiercely than before, as he grasped one end of the poker tightly between his teeth.

110

This resistance only angered Mr. Sikes the more. Dropping on his knees, he fought the animal furiously. The dog jumped from side to side, snapping, growling, and barking. Sikes thrust and swore and struck. And the struggle was reaching a critical point when, as the door suddenly opened, the dog darted out, leaving Bill Sikes with the poker and the knife in his hands.

"What the devil do you come in between me and my dog for?" demanded Sikes of his unexpected visitor, with a fierce gesture.

"I didn't know, my dear, I didn't know," replied Fagin, humbly.

"Didn't know, you white-livered thief!" bawled Sikes. "Couldn't you hear the noise?"

"Not a sound of it, as I'm a living man, Bill," was the reply.

"Oh, no! You hear nothing, you don't," retorted Sikes with a sneer. "Sneaking in and out, so as nobody hears how you come or go!—Fagin, I wish *you* had been the dog, half a minute ago."

"Why?" inquired the unwelcome guest, with a forced smile.

"'Cause the government, as cares for the lives of such men as you, lets a man kill a dog how he likes," replied Sikes, shutting up the knife with a very expressive look. "That's why!"

Fagin rubbed his hands and, sitting down at the table, forced a laugh at the "pleasantry" of his friend. He was plainly very ill at ease, however.

"Grin away," said Sikes, replacing the poker and scowling at the old man. "You'll never have a laugh at me, though, unless it's behind a nightcap. I've got the upper hand of you, Fagin, and I'll keep it. If I go, you go, so take care of me!"

"Well, well, my dear. I know all that; we—we—have a mutual interest, Bill—a *mutual* interest."

"Humph," grunted Sikes, as if he thought the interest lay in his favor. "Well, what have you got to say to me?"

"It's all passed safe through the melting pot," replied Fagin, "and this is your share. It's rather more than it ought to be, my dear, but I know you'll do me a good turn another time, and—"

"Cut that talk," shouted the robber, impatiently. "Where is it? Hand over!"

"Yes, yes, Bill. Give me time, give me time," begged the crime master, soothingly. "Here it is! All safe!" As he spoke, he drew forth a small brown-paper packet. Sikes snatched it hastily, opened it, and proceeded to count the gold pieces it contained.

"This is all, is it?" inquired Sikes.

"All." Fagin rubbed his hands together as if pleased.

"You haven't opened the parcel and swallowed one or two coins as you come along, have you?" asked Sikes, suspiciously. "Don't look injured. You've done it many a time. Jerk the bell!"

It was answered by a waiter of vile and repulsive appearance.

Bill Sikes merely pointed to the empty jug. The waiter retired to fill it, exchanging a mysterious look with Fagin, who raised his eyes for an instant, as if expecting it, and shook his head in reply. It was lost upon Sikes, who was tying a bootlace which the dog had torn. If Sikes had observed the brief interchange of signals, he might have thought that it foretold no good to him. Soon the attendant returned with the refilled vessel.

"Is anybody here, Barney?" inquired Fagin (speaking, now that Sikes was looking on, without raising his eyes from the ground).

"Dot a shoul," replied Barney, whose words made their way through his nose with difficulty.

"Nobody?" inquired Fagin, in a tone of surprise, perhaps meaning that Barney was at liberty to tell the truth.

"Dobody but Biss Dadsy," added Barney.

"Nancy!" exclaimed Sikes. "Where? Strike me blind, if I don't honor that 'ere girl for her talents."

"She's bid havid a plate of boiled beef id the bar."

"Send her here," Sikes directed, pouring out a glass of liquor.

Presently Barney returned, ushering in Nancy, with bonnet, apron, basket, and street-door key, complete.

"You are on the scent, are you, Nancy?" inquired Sikes, offering her a drink.

"Yes, I am Bill," replied the young lady, "and tired enough of it I am, too. The young brat's been ill, and—"

"Ah, Nancy, dear!" said Fagin, looking up.

A peculiar contraction of his red eyebrows and a half-closing of his deeply set eyes seemed to warn Nancy that she might say too much. At any rate, with several gracious smiles upon Mr. Sikes, she turned the conversation to other matters. A few minutes later, Mr. Fagin was seized with a fit of coughing, upon which Nancy declared it was time to go. Mr. Sikes left with her. Outside, the dog came from a hiding place and followed Sikes.

Meanwhile, Oliver Twist was on his way to the bookstall. When he entered Clerkenwell, he accidentally turned down a byway which took him somewhat off his course. Halfway down, discovering his mistake, he did not think it worthwhile to turn back. So he marched on, as quickly as he could, with the books under his arm, intending to go in the right direction at the next turning.

He was thinking of his recent good fortune, and how much he would give for only one look at poor little Dick, when he was startled by a young woman screaming, "Oh, my dear brother!" And he had hardly looked up when he was stopped by a pair of arms thrown around his neck.

"Don't!" cried Oliver, struggling. "Let go! Who is it? What are you stopping me for?"

The only reply to this was a great number of loud wails from a young woman who had embraced him, and who carried a little basket and a street-door key.

"Oh, my gracious!" cried the young woman. "I've found him! Oh! Oliver! Oliver! Oh, you naughty boy, to make me suffer sich distress on your account! Come home, dear, come. Thank gracious goodness heavens, I've found him!"

The lady then became dreadfully hysterical.

Two other women and a butcher's boy looked on, wondering what to do.

"What's the matter, ma'am?" inquired one of the women.

"Oh, ma'am," replied Oliver's "sister," "he ran away, near a month ago, from his parents, joined a set of thieves, and almost broke his mother's heart."

"Young wretch!" said one woman.

"Go home, you little brute," ordered the other.

"I am not," replied Oliver, greatly alarmed. "I don't know her. I haven't any sister—father or mother, either. I'm an orphan; I live at Pentonville."

"Only hear him, how he braves it out!" cried the young woman.

"Why, it's Nancy!" exclaimed Oliver. He now saw her face for the first time and started back in astonishment.

"You see, he knows me!" cried Nancy, appealing to the bystanders. "He can't help himself. Make him come home, good people, or he'll kill his dear mother and father, and break my heart!"

"What the devil's this?" said a man, bursting out of a tavern, with a white dog at his heels. "Young Oliver! Come home to your poor mother, you young dog!"

"I don't belong to them. I don't know them. Help! help!" cried Oliver, struggling in the man's powerful grasp.

"Help!" repeated the man. "Yes, I'll help you, you young rascal! What books are these? You've been a stealing 'em, have you? Give 'em here." With these words, the man grabbed the volumes, struck Oliver on the head, and seized him by his jacket collar.

As he dragged poor Oliver away, the ruffian shouted: "Come on, you young villain! Here, Bull's-eye, mind him, boy!"

Weak, terrified, overpowered, and with no help near, Oliver was at the mercy of his captors.

Darkness had fallen, and the lighted gas lamps were few and far between in the many little, narrow courts through which Oliver was forced to go. His pleas fell on deaf ears.

And even the gas lamps near the Brownlow residence were of no help to Mrs. Bedwin, who stood at the door looking anxiously for Oliver. Nor did they help the maid find him, though she ran back and forth along the street many times, while the two old gentlemen still sat waiting in the dark parlor.

5 *Foul Play*

Sikes did not permit his companions to slow up until they entered a large open space that was used as a cattle market. Then he roughly commanded Oliver Twist to take hold of Nancy's hand.

The place was dark and deserted; and Oliver, knowing that resistance would be useless, held out his hand, which Nancy clasped tightly in one of hers. In her other hand she carried the basket into which Sikes had thrown Oliver's parcel of books.

Sikes seized the helpless boy's unoccupied hand, as he called, "Here, Bull's-eye!" to his dog.

The dog looked up and growled.

"See here!" commanded Sikes, putting his free hand to Oliver's throat, "if he speaks ever so soft a word, hold him! D'ye mind!"

The dog growled again and, licking his lips, eyed Oliver as if he were anxious to attach himself to his windpipe without delay.

They were crossing Smithfield. The night was very foggy. All objects were shrouded in gloom; and Oliver felt most dismal and depressed.

After hurrying on a few paces, they heard the deep tones of a church bell strike the hour.

117

"Eight o'clock, Bill," whispered Nancy, as if she were frightened.

"What's the good of telling me that; I can count, can't I?" growled Sikes.

"I wonder whether *they* can hear it," said Nancy.

"Of course they can!"

"Poor fellows!" said Nancy, who was still looking toward the quarter in which the bell had sounded. "Oh, Bill, such fine young chaps as them!"

"Yes; that's all you women think of," countered Sikes. "Fine young chaps! Well, they're as good as dead, so it don't much matter."

With this poor consolation for Nancy, Mr. Sikes tried to control a rising feeling of jealousy; and, clasping Oliver's wrist firmly, pulled him roughly along.

"Wait a minute!" begged the girl. "I wouldn't hurry by if it was you that was coming out to be hung the next time eight o'clock struck, Bill. I'd walk round and round the place till I dropped."

"And what good would that do?" inquired Sikes. "Come on! And don't stand preaching there."

Then they hurried along for about a half hour, finally entering a very filthy, narrow street, lined with many old-clothes shops. The dog ran ahead and stopped before the door of a shop that was closed and apparently vacant. The house was in poor condition. On the door was nailed a "To Let" sign.

Nancy stooped below the shutters. A moment later, Oliver heard a bell ring faintly inside the house. They crossed the street and waited for a little while under a lamp. Then the door softly opened; Mr. Sikes seized the terrified boy by the collar; and all three, with the dog Bull's-eye, quickly entered.

The passage was quite dark, so they waited until the

person who had let them in had chained and barred the door.

"Anybody here?" inquired Sikes.

"No," replied a voice.

"Is the old 'un here?" asked the robber.

"Yes," answered the voice, "and precious down in the mouth he has been. Won't he be glad to see *you*? Oh, no!"

The style of this reply, as well as the sound of the voice which delivered it, seemed familiar to Oliver's ears. But it was impossible to distinguish even the form of the speaker in the darkness.

"Let's have a glim," commanded Sikes, "or we shall break our necks or tread on the dog."

"Stand still a moment, and I'll get you one," continued the voice. And, in another minute, the form of Mr. John Dawkins, the Dodger, appeared. He carried a tallow candle, stuck in the end of a split stick.

That young gentleman did not stop to show any sign of recognizing Oliver, other than a humorous grin; but, turning away, he beckoned the visitors to follow him. They were led down a flight of stairs and into an earthy-smelling room, which seemed to have been built in a small back-yard. There they were received with a shout of laughter.

"Oh, my wig!" cried Master Charley Bates, from whom the laughter had proceeded. "Here he is! Oh, cry, here he is! Oh, Fagin, look at him! I can't bear it! It is such a *jolly* game. Hold me, somebody, while I laugh it out."

And Bates laid himself flat on the floor and kicked convulsively for five minutes, in great joy. Then, jumping to his feet, he snatched the stick from the Dodger and, advancing to Oliver, viewed him round and round; while Fagin, taking off his nightcap, made many low bows to the bewildered boy. The Artful, meantime, rifled Oliver's pockets systematically.

"Look at his togs, Fagin!" said Charley, putting the light dangerously close to Oliver's new jacket. "Superfine cloth, and the heavy, swell cut! Oh, my eye, what a *game*! And his books, too!—Nothing but a gentleman, Fagin!"

"Delighted to see you looking so well, my dear," said the master, bowing. "The Artful shall give you another suit, for fear you should spoil that Sunday one. Why didn't you write, my dear, and say you were coming? We'd have got something warm for supper."

Then there was more laughter, and even the Dodger smiled; but, as he drew forth the five-pound note at that instant, no one knows whether it was the sally or the discovery that awakened his merriment.

"Hallo! what's that?" inquired Sikes, stepping forward as Fagin seized the note. "That's mine, Fagin!"

"No, no, my dear. Mine, Bill, mine! *You* shall have the books."

"If that ain't mine!" said Bill Sikes, putting on his hat with a determined air, "mine and Nancy's, that is, I'll take the boy back again."

Fagin and Oliver were both surprised; and the latter hoped that the dispute might really end in his being taken back.

"Come! Hand over, will you?" demanded Sikes.

"This is hardly fair, Bill; hardly fair, is it, Nancy?" inquired the old man.

"Fair, or not fair," retorted Sikes, "hand over, I tell you! Do you think Nancy and me has got nothing else to do with our precious time but to spend it in scouting after and kidnapping every young boy as gets grabbed through you? Give it here, you grasping old skeleton, give it here!"

Then Mr. Sikes plucked the note from Fagin's fingers; and, looking the old man coolly in the face, folded it up small and tied it in his neckerchief.

"That's for *our* share of the trouble," sneered Sikes,

"and not half enough, neither. You may keep the books, if you're fond of reading. If you ain't, sell 'em."

"They're very pretty," said Charley Bates, pretending to read one of the volumes. Then he shook all over with another laughing fit.

"They—belong to an old gentleman," said Oliver, desperately, "to the good, kind gentleman who took me into his house—and had me nursed when I was near dying of the fever. Oh, pray, send back the books and money! Keep me here all my life long; but pray, pray send them back! He'll think I stole them. The old lady—all who were so kind to me—will think I *stole* them."

Then Oliver fell upon his knees at Fagin's feet and beat his hands together, in great despair.

"The boy's right," remarked Fagin. "You're right, Oliver; they *will* think you have stolen 'em. Ha! ha! It couldn't have happened better if we had chosen our time!"

Oliver had been looking from one to the other as if he were bewildered. But, when Bill wasn't watching, he jumped suddenly to his feet and dashed wildly from the room, uttering shrieks for help that echoed to the roof.

"Keep back the dog, Bill!" cried Nancy, springing toward the door and closing it, after Fagin and his two pupils had darted out in pursuit. "He'll tear the boy to pieces."

"Serve him right!" cried Sikes, struggling to free himself from the girl's grasp. "Stand off, or I'll split your head against the wall."

"I don't care for that, Bill!" screamed Nancy, struggling violently. "The child sha'n't be torn by the dog, unless you kill me first."

"Sha'n't he!" said Sikes, setting his teeth. "I'll soon do that, if you don't keep off."

The housebreaker flung the girl across the room, just as his comrades returned, dragging Oliver with them.

"What's the matter here?" cried Fagin, looking around.

"The girl's gone mad!" replied Sikes, savagely.

"No, she hasn't," said Nancy, pale and breathless from the scuffle. "No, she hasn't, Fagin; don't think it."

"Then keep quiet, will you?" said he, with a threatening look.

"No, I won't do that, neither," cried Nancy, fearlessly. "What do you think of *that*?"

Mr. Fagin now quickly decided to "change the subject" by directing attention again to Oliver.

"So you wanted to get away, my dear, did you?" the old man asked, taking up a jagged club from a corner of the fireplace. "Eh?"

Oliver made no reply. But he watched Fagin closely, and breathed quickly.

"Wanted to get assistance; called for the police—did you?" sneered the master, catching the boy by the arm. "We'll cure you of that!"

He then inflicted a sharp blow on Oliver's shoulders with the club, and was raising it for a second one, when the girl, rushing forward, wrested it from his hand and flung it upon the floor.

"I won't stand by and see it done, Fagin!" cried Nancy. "You've got the boy, and what more would you have?—Let him be—or I shall put that mark on some of you that will bring me to the gallows before my time."

The girl stamped her foot violently on the floor as she made this threat. And, with her lips compressed, and her hands clenched, she defied all of them.

"Why, Nancy!" said Fagin, in a soothing tone, after a pause, "you—you're more clever than ever tonight. Ha! ha! my dear, you are acting beautifully."

"Am I!" she cried. "Take care I don't overdo it. You will be the worse for it, Fagin, if I do, and so I tell you in good time to keep clear of me."

Mr. Fagin was now sure of the reality of Miss Nancy's

rage; and, shrinking back a few paces, cast a glance, half imploring and half cowardly, at Sikes.

Mr. Sikes, thus mutely appealed to, and possibly feeling very important, cursed and threatened Nancy at great length; but in vain. Then he resorted to argument.

"What do you mean by this?" demanded Sikes. "Burn my body! Do you know who you are and what you are?"

"Oh, yes, I know all about it," replied Nancy, laughing wildly and shaking her head from side to side.

"Well, then, keep quiet!" commanded Sikes, with a growl, "or I'll quiet you for a good long time to come."

But the girl laughed again; and, darting a hasty look at Sikes, turned her face aside and bit her lip till the blood came.

"You're a nice one," added Sikes, with a lordly air, "to take up the gen—teel side! A pretty subject for the child, as you call him, to make a friend of!"

"God Almighty help me, I am!" cried the girl, fiercely. "And I wish I had been struck dead in the street, or had changed places with them we passed so near tonight, before I had lent a hand in bringing him here. He's a thief, a liar, a devil, all that's bad, from this night forth. Isn't that enough for the old wretch, without blows?"

"Come, come, Sikes," said Fagin, smoothly, and motioning toward the boys, who were eagerly attentive to all that passed, "we must have civil words, Bill."

"Civil words!" cried Nancy, whose anger was frightful to see. "*Civil words,* you villain! Yes; you deserve 'em from *me.* I thieved for you when I was a child not half as old as this!" pointing to Oliver. "I have been in the same service for twelve years since. Don't you know it? Speak out! Don't you know it?"

"Well, well," replied the master, with an attempt to make peace, "and, if you have, it's your living!"

"Aye, it is!" returned the girl. "It *is* my living; and the cold, wet, dirty streets are my home. And you're the wretch that drove me to them long ago, and that'll keep me there, day and night, day and night, till I die!"

"I shall do you a mischief!" interposed the old one, now thoroughly angered, "a mischief worse than that, if you say much more!" And he raised his club threateningly. Nancy said nothing more; but, tearing her hair and dress in a rage, made such a rush at Fagin as would probably have left marks of her revenge upon him, had not her wrists been seized by Sikes at the right moment. Then she struggled feebly and fainted.

"She's all right now," said Sikes, laying her down in a corner. "She's uncommon strong in the arms, when she's up in this way."

The old man wiped his forehead and smiled, as if it were a relief to have the disturbance over; but no one seemed to consider it in any other light than a common occurrence.

"It's the worst of having to do with women," declared Fagin, lowering his club, "but they're clever, and we can't get on, in our line, without 'em. Charley, show Oliver to bed."

"I suppose he'd better not wear his best clothes to-morrow, Fagin, had he?" inquired Charley Bates, with a grin.

"Certainly not," was the reply, with another grin.

Delighted with his commission, Charley led Oliver into the kitchen, where there were two or three beds on which he had slept before. With many bursts of laughter, and to Oliver's great surprise, Bates produced the identical old suit of clothes which Oliver had so gladly given up at Mr. Brownlow's.

"Pull off the smart ones," said Charley, "and I'll give 'em to Fagin to take care of. What *fun* it is!"

Poor Oliver unwillingly obeyed. Bates rolled up the new

clothes under his arm. Between laughs, he explained how Fagin's discovery of the old clothes in a dealer's window provided the first clue to Oliver's whereabouts.

The noise of Charley's laughter, and the voice of Miss Betsy, who arrived in time to throw water over her friend and help her otherwise, might have kept many people awake. But Oliver, locked in the dark kitchen alone, was sick and weary, and soon fell sound asleep.

6   *A Fee for a Sting*

Mr. Bumble, the beadle, left the workhouse early in the morning and walked with stately steps up the High Street. He was in the full glory and pride of beadlehood. His cocked hat and his coat were dazzling in the morning sun; and he clutched his cane with unusual vigor.

With only a wave of his hand, Mr. Bumble dismissed those who spoke to him as he passed along. And he did not relax until he reached the farm where Mrs. Mann tended the infant paupers with parochial care.

"Drat that beadle!" cried Mrs. Mann, hearing the well-known shaking at the garden gate. "If it isn't *him*, and at this time in the morning!—Lauk, Mr. Bumble, only think of its being *you*! Well, dear me, it *is* a pleasure, this is! Come into the parlor, sir, please. Set right here in this easy chair. And hoping you find yourself well, good sir!"

"Just so-so, Mrs. Mann," replied the beadle. "A parochial life, ma'am, is a life of worrit and trouble; but all public characters must suffer prosecution. Mrs. Mann, I am a-going to *London!*"

"Lauk, Mr. Bumble!" exclaimed Mrs. Mann, starting back.

"I and two paupers, Mrs. Mann! A legal action is

127

a-coming on, about a settlement; and the board has appointed *me* to take charge of the matter."

After Mr. Bumble had laughed a little while in self-
satisfaction, he glanced at the cocked hat on the table and
became very serious.

"We are forgetting business, ma'am," said the beadle.
"Here is your parochial pay for the month." Mrs. Mann
wrote him a receipt and thanked him very much. Mr. Bumble nodded, inquiring how the children were.

"Bless their dear little hearts!" said Mrs. Mann with
mock emotion. "They're as well as can be, the dears! Of
course, except the two that died last week. And little
Dick."

"Isn't that boy no better?" asked Mr. Bumble. "He's a
ill-conditioned, wicious, bad-disposed parochial child, that!
Where is he?"

Having had his face put under the pump and dried
upon Mrs. Mann's gown, Dick was led in to face the greatly
feared official.

The child was pale and thin. His cheeks were sunken;
his eyes were large and bright; and his young limbs had
wasted away like those of an old man. He stood trembling
beneath Mr. Bumble's stern glance.

"What's the matter with you, parochial Dick?" demanded Mr. Bumble.

"Nothing, sir," replied the child, faintly.

"I should think not," said Mrs. Mann. "You want for
nothing, I'm sure."

"I should like," faltered the child, "if somebody would
put a few words down for me on a piece of paper and keep
it for me, after I am laid in the ground. I should like to
leave my dear love to poor Oliver Twist, and to tell him that
I was glad to die when I was very young. Perhaps, then, if
I had lived to be a man, my little sister in heaven might

forget me. And we would be so much happier if we were both children there together."

Mr. Bumble surveyed the little speaker with great astonishment. Then, turning to his companion, he said, "That out-dacious Oliver has ruined them all!—Take Dick away, ma'am!"

Dick was immediately locked up in the coal cellar; and Mr. Bumble left shortly afterward, to prepare for his wonderful journey.

He and the two paupers arrived in London late the next day and stopped at an inn. After disposing of his undesirable companions for the night, the beadle sat down to a big dinner. Then, drawing his chair close to the fire, he settled down to read the newspaper.

The very first item that attracted Mr. Bumble's attention was an advertisement. To the person who could meet the requirements, it offered five guineas. Mr. Bumble thought that sum of money was quite large. The tempting advertisement read as follows:

FIVE GUINEAS REWARD

Whereas a young boy named Oliver Twist ran away, or was kidnapped, on Thursday evening last, from his home at Pentonville, and has not since been heard of, the above reward will be paid to any person who can give information that will lead to the discovery of that boy, or throw some light upon his previous history.

The remainder of the announcement gave a full description of Oliver's dress, person, appearance, and disappearance, and concluded with the name and address of Mr.

Brownlow. In a little more than five minutes, Mr. Bumble was on his way to Pentonville, allowing his imagination free play in counting and re-counting the money he expected to receive, and in picturing the many ways he could spend it. On entering Pentonville, the great beadle found the Brownlow residence very easily.

"Is Mr. Brownlow in?" inquired Mr. Bumble of the girl who opened the door of the booklover's home.

After making some explanations, the hopeful visitor was shown into the little back study, where sat Mr. Brownlow and his friend, Mr. Grimwig.

After courtesies were exchanged, Mr. Bumble was requested to sit down.

"Do you know where the poor boy is now?" Mr. Brownlow asked.

"No more than nobody," replied Mr. Bumble.

"Well, what *do* you know of him?" queried the booklover.

"You don't happen to know any *good* of him, do you?" put in Mr. Grimwig, sourly.

Mr. Bumble shook his head very solemnly.

"You see?" challenged Mr. Grimwig, looking triumphantly at his friend.

Mr. Brownlow then requested Mr. Bumble to tell whatever he knew about Oliver in as few words as possible.

The sum and substance of the beadle's story was: That Oliver was a foundling, born of "low and vicious" parents. That he had, from his birth, displayed no better qualities than treachery, ingratitude, and evil spite. That he had ended his brief career in the place of his birth, by making a bloody and cowardly attack on an innocent lad, and running away in the night from his master's house.

In proof of his being really the person he claimed to be, Mr. Bumble then laid upon the table the official papers he had brought to town.

"I fear it is all too true," Mr. Brownlow remarked, sorrowfully, after looking over the papers. "This is not much money for your story; but gladly would I have given you three times the amount, if it had been *favorable* to the boy."

As it was now too late for Mr. Bumble to change his story, he could only shake his head solemnly. Then, pocketing the five guineas, he withdrew as gracefully as he could, but somewhat deflated.

Mr. Brownlow paced the room for several minutes, evidently so much disturbed by the beadle's tale that even Mr. Grimwig hesitated to vex him further. At length, the disappointed gentleman stopped pacing and pulled the bell cord violently.

"Mrs. Bedwin," said Mr. Brownlow, when the housekeeper appeared, "that boy Oliver is an imposter, a deceiver!"

"It can't be, sir," she ventured, emphatically.

"I tell you he *is*!" retorted the booklover. "What do you mean by 'can't be'? We have just heard a full account of him from the time of his birth. He has been a complete little villain all his life."

"I never will believe it, sir," insisted Mrs. Bedwin. *"Never!* He was a dear, gentle child, sir."

"Silence!" demanded Mr. Brownlow, more angrily than his real feelings dictated. "Never let me hear the boy's name again. I rang to tell you that. Never, on any excuse, *mind!*— You may leave the room, Mrs. Bedwin. Remember! I am serious."

7 Come into My Parlor

"And now, my dear boy," said Mr. Fagin next day, about noon, "at last you and I can have a little heart-to-heart talk in private. The others have gone out to work for their living. Understand?"

"Oh, yes, sir," said Oliver, not knowing what else he could say.

"And you see," Fagin went on, "we took you in and gave you food and shelter, when you were alone and help-less. Remember?"

"I do indeed, Mr. Fagin, sir!"

"You were very, very hungry and footsore and weary when the Artful Dodger found you, early that morning. He provided your breakfast and brought you to our humble home. It was all we had to offer; and we protected you. Did we harm you in any way, Oliver, my dear?" asked the bearded old gentleman, suddenly, watching the boy care-fully.

"No, sir," answered Oliver, "not at all, sir."

"For a long time, we looked after you, demanding noth-ing in return but your loyalty and cooperation. Others would have driven you out into the cold long ago, to shift for yourself in the great wicked city. Then what would you have done? Where would you have gone?"

"I—I don't know, Mr. Fagin," said Oliver, nervously. "Indeed I don't!"

"And I won't even mention how much it cost us to take care of you, these many months. We came between you and starvation. And to be ungrateful is a great sin which often brings severe punishment! I remember how we befriended another young lad, one time, just as we did you. *He was very ungrateful.* He ran away from us as you did and went to the police, thinking he had a good case on us.

"And he *might* have gained his point. You can understand that from personal experience. Although you were innocent, the magistrate fully intended to put you in prison. You were saved in a most unusual manner, my dear! But that other lad I referred to just now was finally *hanged by the neck* until he was *dead!*—Just think of *that*, Oliver, my dear!" Fagin added, staring hard at the poor boy and leaning over close to him.

Oliver's blood ran cold as he said, trembling, "Terrible! Awful! I—will they hang me, too? Oh, please, don't—don't let them hang me, sir!"

Mr. Fagin smiled hideously as he patted the frightened boy on the head and said, "Just stick to us, your best friends, my dear. Be faithful to *us*, and everything will be all right."

Then the old man left the room, locking Oliver's door on the outside.

After being locked in for more than a week with his unhappy, ghostly, and confused thoughts, which often included painful doubts as to what Mr. Brownlow was thinking of him, Oliver was granted the freedom of the house.

It was dirty, run-down, dismal, and dreary. The moldering shutters were all fast closed, admitting only a little light from holes at the top.

One afternoon, after many more days of gloomy loneliness, the Dodger and Bates made Oliver the butt of a conversation which did not seem so amusing to him as it did to them. They "explained," using many words that were unfamiliar to Oliver, how, since most people had to work for a living, Fagin's crew was no exception. There are many, many lines of works to be followed in the world. "But," they argued, "Fagin and his helpers had *fun*!" Not many kinds of work are *just fun*. And the young lawbreakers tried to convince Oliver that if one fellow doesn't steal "pocket-handkerchers" and watches, another will. "The latter is the better off," the Dodger insisted, "and the owner is the loser in any case."

"To be sure, to be sure!" exclaimed Fagin, who had entered unnoticed by Oliver. "All in a nutshell. Take the Dodger's word for it, my dear. Ha! ha! ha!"

The conversation proceeded no further at this time, for Fagin was accompanied by Miss Betsy and a gentleman whom Oliver had never seen before, but who was addressed by the Dodger as Tom Chitling.

Mr. Chitling, at eighteen, was older than the Dodger. He had small, twinkling eyes, and a pockmarked face. He wore a fur cap, a dark corduroy jacket, greasy trousers, and an apron. His wardrobe was, in truth, rather out of repair; but he excused himself to the company by stating that his "time" was out only an hour before. And, he explained, having worn the special "uniform" for six weeks past, he had not been able to give any attention to his own clothes.

"Who's that?" inquired Tom Chitling, casting a sneering glance at Oliver.

"A young friend of mine, my dear," Mr. Fagin replied.

"He's in luck, then," said the young man, with a meaningful look at Fagin.

The boys laughed. After more joking, Bates and the Dodger exchanged a few short whispers with Fagin, and withdrew.

Mr. Chitling and the old man conversed privately for several minutes. Then they, with Miss Betsy and Oliver, sat near the fire. Mr. Fagin led the conversation to the topics most likely to interest his hearers. He spoke of the great advantages of the "trade," the skill of the Dodger, the good-natured Charley Bates, and his own "unselfishness." At length, these subjects were thoroughly discussed. Miss Betsy accordingly withdrew, and left the others to their repose.

From that day, Oliver was seldom left alone, but was almost constantly with the other two boys. They played the old game with Fagin every day. Occasionally, he told them stories of robberies he had committed in his younger days, mixed up with so much that was droll and curious that Oliver could not help laughing heartily, showing that he was amused in spite of all his better feelings.

And so Oliver Twist was held fast in the clever old man's web, which was spun with the many threads of fear, forced gaiety, limited companionship, gloom, and helplessness. Caught thus, the lad was the victim of the daily suggestions by which Fagin hoped to poison and blacken his innocent soul.

8 Oliver Becomes Important

One night, when the foul weather was just right for his kind to be abroad, and for his special purpose, Mr. Fagin bundled up his shriveled body as completely as possible. Then he slunk away from his den, through many winding, narrow ways, until he reached a house in Bethnal Green.

A dog growled as he touched the handle of a room door; and a man's voice demanded to know who was there.

"Only me, Bill; only me, my dear," said Fagin looking in. "Ah! Nancy—

"It *is* cold, Nancy, dear," he added, as he warmed his skinny hands over the fire.

"Well?" inquired Sikes. "What brings *your* old carcass out from the grave on a night like this?"

"About the crib at Chertsey, Bill?" asked the shivering old man in return, pulling his chair forward and speaking in a very low voice. "When is it to be done, Bill, eh? When is it to be done?—Such silver, my dear, such silver!" And Fagin rubbed his hands and elevated his eyebrows in delighted anticipation.

"Not at all," rejoined Sikes. "At least it can't be a put-up job, as we expected. I tell you, that Toby Crackit has been hanging about the place for a fortnight, and he can't get *one* of the servants into line."

"Do you mean to tell me, Bill," asked Fagin, softening as the other grew heated, "that neither of the two men in the house can be got over with us?"

"Yes, I do mean to tell you so," sneered Sikes. "The old lady has had 'em these twenty year; and if you were to give 'em five hundred pound, they wouldn't be in it."

"But do you mean to say, my dear," argued the master, "that the *women* can't be got over, even by flash Toby Crackit?—Think what women are, Bill."

"No, not even by flash Toby Crackit," replied Sikes. "He says he's worn sham whiskers and a canary waistcoat the whole blessed time he's been loitering down there. And it's all of no use."

"He should have tried mustaches and a pair of military trousers," said Fagin, stubbornly.

"So he did," rejoined Sikes, "and they warn't of no more use than the other plant."

Fagin looked blank at this information. And a long silence followed, during which he was in deep thought, with his face wrinkled into a horrible expression.

"Fagin," asked Sikes, abruptly breaking the stillness, "is it worth fifty extra, if it's safely done from the outside?"

"Yes," replied Mr. Fagin, suddenly rousing himself.

"Then," said Sikes, thrusting aside Fagin's hand, "let it come off as soon as you like. Toby and me were over the garden wall the night afore last, sounding the panels of the door and shutters. The crib's barred up at night like a jail; but there's one part we can crack, safe and softly."

"Good!" exclaimed the old man. "Is there no help wanted but yours and Toby's?"

"None," said Sikes. "'Cept the right tool and a boy. The first we've both got; the second you must find us."

"A boy!" cried Fagin. "Oh! then it's a panel, eh?"

"Never mind wot it is!" replied Sikes. "I want a boy, and he mustn't be a big 'un."

"Bill!" exclaimed Mr. Fagin, after a pause.

"What now?" inquired Sikes.

The old master was silent again for a few moments.

"Oh, come now, Fagin," said Nancy with a laugh. "Tell Bill at once about Oliver!"

"Ha! you're a clever one, my dear: the sharpest girl I ever saw!" said Fagin, patting her on the neck. "It *was* about Oliver I was going to speak, sure enough. Ha! ha! ha!"

"What about him?" demanded Sikes.

"He's the boy for you," replied the master, in a hoarse whisper.

"Have him, Bill!" said Nancy. "I would, if I was in your place. He mayn't be so much up, as any of the others; but that's not what you want, if he's only to open a door for you. Depend upon it: He's a safe one, Bill."

"I know he is," rejoined Fagin. "He's been in good training these last few weeks, and it's time he began to work for his bread. Besides, the others are all too big."

"Well, he *is* just the size I want," said Mr. Sikes, thoughtfully.

"And will do everything you want, Bill, my dear," added Mr. Fagin. "He can't help himself, if you frighten him enough."

"Frighten him!" echoed Sikes. "It'll be no sham frightening, mind you. You may not see him alive again, Fagin. Think of that, before you send him. Mark my words!" said the robber, swinging a crowbar, which he had drawn from under the bedstead.

"I've thought of it all," said the old man, with energy. "Once let him feel that he is one of us; once fill his mind with the idea that he has been a thief; and he's ours! Ours for his *life*. Oho! It couldn't have come about better!" Fagin crossed his arms upon his breast and, drawing his shoulders almost up to his ears, literally hugged himself for joy.

"I planned with Toby for the night after tomorrow," Sikes replied in a surly voice, "if he heerd nothing from me to the contrairy."

"Good!" the chief exclaimed. "There's no moon. Is it all arranged about bringing off the swag?"

Sikes nodded.

After some discussion, in which all three took part, it was decided that Nancy should go to Fagin's den next evening and bring Oliver away with her. The master pointed out that the girl could easily persuade the lad to help because she had recently defended him. It was also agreed that Sikes should not be responsible for anything that might happen to Oliver.

Then Mr. Fagin returned through mud and mire to his gloomy abode. There he found the Dodger sitting up, impatiently awaiting his return.

"Is Oliver abed?—I want to speak to him," was the old one's remark as they descended the stairs.

"Hours ago," replied the Dodger, throwing open a door. "Here he is!"

The boy was lying fast asleep on a rude bed. He was pale as death with anxiety and sadness, and the closeness of his prison.

After looking at Oliver for a while, Mr. Fagin whispered, as he turned away quietly, "Not now. Tomorrow. Tomorrow."

⑨ *Deepening Mystery*

As he sat down to breakfast with Mr. Fagin, Oliver said, "Thanks very much, sir, for the nice new shoes that I found by my bed this morning! Shall I now be sent away from here?"

"Yes, my dear," was the reply. "I am sending you to Mr. Sikes' residence tonight."

"To—to—stay there, sir?" asked Oliver, anxiously.

"No, no, my dear," replied the master. "We shouldn't like to lose you. Don't be afraid, Oliver, you shall come back to us again. Ha! ha! ha! We won't be so cruel as to cast you adrift. Oh, no, no!"

The old man, who was toasting a piece of bread, looked around as he bantered Oliver thus. And he chuckled as if to show that he knew the lad would still be very glad to get away if he could. But Mr. Fagin frowned later, when his leading questions did not seem to arouse Oliver's interest as to the reason for his paying Mr. Sikes a visit.

Oliver had no other opportunity to learn the reason, for the old master remained very surly and silent till that night, when he prepared to go out.

"You may burn a candle," he then said to the boy, putting one upon the table. "And here's a book for you to read, till they come to fetch you. Good-night!"

"Thank you, sir. Good-night!" replied Oliver, softly.

On his way to the door, Mr. Fagin looked over his shoulder at the boy. Suddenly stopping, he called Oliver by name. The bewildered lad looked up. Fagin, pointing to the candle, motioned that he should light it. As he did so, he saw that the old man was gazing steadily at him from the other end of the room.

"Take heed, Oliver! Take heed!" directed Mr. Fagin, shaking a finger at him in a warning manner. "He's a rough man, and thinks nothing of blood when his own is up. Whatever happens, say nothing; and do what he bids you. *Mind!*" Placing a strong emphasis on the last word, he favored Oliver Twist with a ghastly grin and, nodding his head, left the room.

Oliver leaned his head upon his hand when the old man disappeared. He was greatly puzzled and not a little afraid. But he could not bewail the prospect of change to any great extent. So he remained lost in thought for some minutes. Then, with a heavy sigh, he took up the book Fagin had left with him and began to read.

The volume was a history of the lives and trials of great criminals; and the pages were soiled. Oliver read of many dreadful crimes that made his blood run cold.

In cold fear, some time later, the boy thrust the book from him. Then, falling upon his knees, he prayed heaven to spare him from such deeds—even by taking his life at once, if need be. After concluding his prayer, Oliver remained on his knees with his face in his hands, when a rustling noise aroused him.

"What's that!" he cried, starting up and seeing a figure standing by the door. "Who's there?"

"Me. Only me," replied a tremulous voice.

It was Nancy. She was very pale. Gently, Oliver inquired if she were ill. The girl threw herself into a chair, with her back toward him.

"God forgive me!" she cried after a while. "I never thought of this."

"Has anything happened?" asked Oliver. "Can I help you?"

She rocked herself to and fro, caught her throat, and, uttering a gurgling sound, gasped for breath.

"Nancy!" cried Oliver. "What is it?"

The girl beat her hands upon her knees for several minutes. Then, suddenly stopping, she drew her shawl close around her and shivered.

Oliver stirred the fire. Drawing her chair close to it, Nancy sat there, for a little time, without speaking; but at length she raised her head, and looked around.

"I don't know what comes over me sometimes," said she, pretending to busy herself in arranging her dress. "It's this damp, dirty room, I think. Now, Nolly, dear, are you ready?"

"Am I to go with you?" asked Oliver.

"Yes, I have come from Bill," replied Nancy.

"What for?" asked Oliver, recoiling.

"What for?" echoed the girl. "Oh! For no harm."

"I don't believe it," said Oliver, who had watched her closely.

"Have it your own way," rejoined Nancy, forcing a laugh. "For no good, then."

Oliver could see that he had some power over the girl's better feelings and, for an instant, thought of appealing to her compassion for his helpless state. But, then, he realized that it was barely eleven o'clock, and that many people were still in the streets, of whom surely some might be found to listen to his tale. Then he stepped forward and said that he was ready.

"Hush," said the girl, pointing to the door as she looked cautiously around. "You can't help yourself. I have tried hard for you, but all to no purpose. You are hedged round and round. If ever you are to get loose from here, this is not the time."

Struck by the energy of her manner, Oliver looked up in her face with great surprise. She seemed to speak the truth. Her countenance was white and agitated.

"I have saved you from being ill-used once, and I will again, and I do now," continued Nancy, "for those who would have fetched you, if I had not, would have been far more rough than me. I have promised for your being quiet. If you are not, you will only harm yourself and me, too, and perhaps be my death. See here! I have borne all this for you already, as true as God sees me show it."

She pointed hastily to some red marks on her neck and arms, and continued, with great rapidity:

"Remember this! And don't let me suffer more for you, just now. If I could help you, I would. They don't mean to harm you. Whatever they make you do is no fault of yours. Hush! Every word from you is a blow for me. Make haste! Your hand!"

Outside, a cab was waiting. Nancy pulled Oliver in with her and drew the curtains close. The driver wanted no directions, but lashed his horse into full speed at once.

The girl still held Oliver fast by the hand. All was so quick and hurried that he scarcely knew where he was, when the carriage stopped at the house which was visited by Fagin on the previous evening.

For one brief moment, Oliver cast a hurried glance along the empty street, and a cry for help hung upon his lips. But Nancy begged him in such tones of agony to remember her, that he had not the heart to cry out. Soon he was in the house, and the door was shut.

"This way," said the girl, releasing her hold for the first time. "Bill!" she called out.

"Hallo!" replied Sikes, appearing at the head of

the stairs with a candle. "Oh! That's the time of day. Come on!"

This was an unusually hearty welcome from Mr. Sikes. Nancy, appearing much gratified, greeted him cordially.

"Bull's-eye's gone home with Tom," observed Sikes.

"That's right," rejoined Nancy.

"So you've got the kid," said Sikes, closing the door.

"Yes," replied Nancy.

"Did he come quiet?" inquired Sikes.

"Like a lamb."

"I'm glad to hear it," said Sikes, looking grimly at Oliver. "Come here, young'un; and let me read you a lectur', which is as well got over at once." Mr. Sikes then threw Oliver's cap into a corner and stood the boy in front of him.

"Now, first: Do you know wot this is?" inquired Sikes, taking up a pistol from the table. Oliver replied in the affirmative.

"Well, then, look here," continued Sikes. "This is powder; that 'ere's a bullet; and this is a little bit of a old hat for waddin',"

Then Mr. Sikes proceeded to load the pistol, with great care.

"Now it's loaded," said Mr. Sikes, when he had finished.

"Yes, I see it is, sir," replied Oliver.

"Well," said the robber, grasping Oliver's wrist and putting the gun against his temple. "If you speak a word when you're out o' doors with me, except when I speak to you, that loading will be in your head without notice. So, if you *do* make up your mind to speak without leave, say your prayers first."

Scowling at Oliver, Mr. Sikes continued:

"As near as I know, there isn't anybody as would be asking very partickler after you, if you *was* disposed of. So I needn't take this devil-and-all of trouble to explain matters to you, if it warn't for your own good. And now, Nancy, let's have some supper and then get a snooze before starting."

After supper—it may be easily understood that Oliver had no great appetite for it—Mr. Sikes disposed of a couple of glasses of spirits and water, and threw himself on the bed. Then, with many threats, he ordered Nancy to call him at five precisely.

Oliver stretched himself in his clothes, by command of the same authority, upon a mattress on the floor. The girl sat before the fire to await the appointed time.

For a long time, Oliver lay awake, wondering what was going to happen. Finally he fell asleep from exhaustion.

When he awoke, Mr. Sikes was thrusting the pistol and various other articles into the pockets of his greatcoat. Nancy was preparing breakfast. The candle was still burning. A sharp rain was beating against the windowpanes; and the sky looked black and cloudy.

"Now, then!" growled Sikes, as Oliver started up, "half-past five! Look sharp, or you'll get no breakfast."

A little while later, having eaten some breakfast, Oliver

replied to a surly inquiry from Sikes that he was quite ready to go.

Nancy, scarcely looking at the boy, threw him a handkerchief to tie around his throat. Sikes gave him a large, rough cape to button over his shoulders. Then, after a grumbled farewell to Nancy, the robber took Oliver by the hand and led him away.

10 *The Winding Trail*

It was a cheerless morning for any kind of journey. Large pools of water had collected in the road. The windows of the houses were all closely shut; and the streets through which Mr. Sikes and Oliver trudged were then noiseless and empty.

By the time they had turned into the Bethnal Green Road, the day had fairly begun to break. Many of the street lamps were already extinguished; and a few country wagons were slowly toiling toward London. Now and then, a stagecoach, covered with mud, rattled briskly by. The taverns, with gaslights burning inside, were already open. By degrees, other shops showed signs of life, and a few scattered people appeared.

As Sikes and Oliver approached the center of London, the noise and traffic gradually increased. When they traveled the streets between Shoreditch and Smithfield, there was a great roar of sound and bustle. The day was as light now as it was likely to be at any other hour; and half the London population had begun their many activities.

A roar of discordant sounds that filled Oliver Twist with amazement arose in Smithfield, for it was market morning. The ground was covered, nearly ankle-deep, with filth and mire. A thick stream, constantly rising from the reeking bodies of the cattle, and mingling with the fog, which seemed to rest upon the chimney tops, hung heavily above. The noise, confusion, and filthy odors were sickening to poor Oliver.

Mr. Sikes, dragging Oliver after him, elbowed his way through the thickest of the crowd, until they were clear of the turmoil and had made their way through Hosier Lane into Holborn.

"Now, young 'un!" said Sikes, looking up at the clock of St. Andrew's Church. "Hard upon seven! You must step out!"

Bill Sikes accompanied this speech with a jerk at his companion's wrist. Oliver kept up with the rapid strides of the housebreaker as well as he could, until they had passed Hyde Park Corner and were on their way to Kensington. Then Sikes relaxed his pace, until an empty cart drew up. Seeing "Hounslow" lettered on it, he asked the driver if he would give them a lift as far as Isleworth.

"Jump up," said the man. "Is that your boy?"

"Yes; he's my boy," replied Sikes, looking hard at Oliver, and putting his hand into the pocket where the pistol was.

"Here, Ned. In with you!"

Thus addressing Oliver, Bill helped him into the cart. The driver, pointing to a heap of sacks, told the weary lad to lie down there and rest himself.

As they passed the different milestones, Oliver wondered where his companion meant to take him. Kensington, Hammersmith, Chiswick, Kew Bridge, Brentford were all passed. At length, they came to a public house called the "Coach and Horses." A little way beyond, another road appeared to turn off; and here the cart stopped.

Sikes dismounted quickly and then lifted Oliver down.

"Good-bye, boy," said the driver.

"He's sulky," replied Sikes, giving Oliver a shake. "Don't mind him."

"Not I!" rejoined the other. And he drove away.

Mr. Sikes led his companion on for a long time, until they were close to Hampton. They lingered in the fields for some hours. Then they entered the town and, turning into an old public house with a defaced signboard, ordered some dinner by the kitchen fire, where they could be by themselves.

They had some cold meat for dinner, and sat so long after eating it, while Mr. Sikes indulged himself with three or four pipefuls, that Oliver began to feel quite certain they were not going any farther. At any rate, he was very tired and soon fell asleep.

It was quite dark when Sikes wakened him. He sat up straight, and heard Bill and another man conversing in low tones over a pint of ale. After listening awhile, Oliver learned that Sikes' acquaintance would take the two travelers in his empty cart as far as Halliford.

The horse, whose health had been drunk in his absence, was standing outside, harnessed to the cart. Oliver and Sikes got in without ceremony; and the driver mounted his seat. Soon they were off at great speed and rattled their way out of the town right gallantly.

The night was very dark. A damp mist arose from the river and the marshy ground, and spread itself over the dreary fields. The wind was piercing cold. Few words were exchanged, for the driver had grown drowsy, and Sikes was in no mood for conversation. Oliver sat huddled in a corner of the cart, confused, alarmed, and weary, imagining that he saw strange objects in the gaunt trees, whose branches waved grimly to and fro.

Two or three miles beyond Sunbury, the cart stopped.

Sikes alighted, took Oliver by the hand, and they once again walked on.

Through Shepperton and on they trudged in mud and darkness, until they came within sight of the lights of another town. On looking intently forward, Oliver saw water just below them and noticed that they were coming to the foot of a bridge.

Sikes kept straight on until they were close to Chertsey Bridge. Then he turned suddenly down a bank upon the left.

"The water!" thought Oliver, turning sick with fear. "He has brought me to this lonely place to murder me!"

He was about to throw himself on the ground and make one desperate struggle for his young life, when he saw that they stood before a solitary house: all ruinous and decayed. It was dark and, to all appearance, uninhabited.

Sikes, with Oliver's hand still in his, softly approached the low porch and raised the latch. The door yielded, and they passed in together.

11 *How the Boy Bleeds!*

"Hallo!" cried a loud, hoarse voice, as soon as Bill Sikes and Oliver set foot in the passage.

"Don't make such a row," Sikes growled, bolting the door. "Show a glim, Toby."

"Aha! my pal!" cried Toby. "A glim, Barney, a glim! Show the gentleman in, Barney. Wake up first, if convenient."

The speaker threw a bootjack at Barney to arouse him from his slumbers. The response was an indistinct muttering. A little later, there came from a door a feeble candlelight. It was followed by the man who has been already described as having an obstruction in his nose, and as being a waiter at the tavern on Saffron Hill.

"Bister Sikes!" exclaimed Barney, "cub id, sir; cub id."

Sikes pushed Oliver forward into a low, dark room, where the lad saw a smoky fire, two or three broken chairs, a table, and a very old couch. On it lay a man somewhat above middle size. He wore a snuff-colored coat, with large brass buttons; an orange neckerchief; a coarse, shawl-pattern waistcoat; and drab breeches. Mr. Toby Crackit (for he it was) had a little reddish hair that was twisted into long corkscrew curls, through which he occasionally thrust his dirty fingers, ornamented with large, cheap rings.

152

"Bill, my boy!" said Mr. Crackit, "I'm glad to see you. I was almost afraid you'd given it up, in which case I should have made a personal wentur'—Hallo!" This exclamation showed his surprise at seeing Oliver; and Toby sat up, demanding to know who that was.

"Only the boy!" replied Sikes, drawing a chair toward the fire.

"Wud of Bister Fagin's lads," added Barney, with a grin.

"Fagin's, eh!" exclaimed Toby, looking closely at Oliver. "Wot an inwal'able boy he'll make for the old ladies' pockets in chapels! His mug is a fortun' to him."

"Now," said Sikes to Barney, after whispering something about Oliver that made Toby laugh, "if you'll give us something to eat and drink while we're waiting, you'll put some heart in us, or in me, at all events. Sit down by the fire, younker, and rest yourself; for you'll have to go out with us again tonight."

Oliver looked at Sikes in helpless wonder, and sat on a stool by the fire with his aching head upon his hands.

"Here," Toby said, as Barney placed some fragments of food and a bottle of liquor upon the table. "Success to the crack!" And Crackit and Sikes drank to their expected good fortune.

Oliver was so frightened that he could cat nothing but a small crust of bread. But Bill Sikes ate ravenously until he was satisfied. Then the two men lay on chairs for a short nap. Oliver remained on his stool by the fire. Barney, wrapped in a blanket, stretched himself on the floor.

Then the men slept, or appeared to sleep, for some time. Oliver fell into a restless doze from which he was aroused by Toby Crackit, who jumped up and declared it was half-past one.

In an instant all were actively engaged in preparation. Sikes and his companion wrapped their necks in large, dark shawls and drew on their greatcoats. Barney opened a cupboard and brought forth pistols and burglars' tools, which he hastily crammed into the pockets. Soon the two robbers, carrying dark lanterns and heavy clubs, were satisfied with their preparations.

After fastening on Oliver's cape for the poor lad, Sikes said, "Now, then!" and grasped one of the boy's hands, directing Toby to hold the other.

Barney quietly opened the door to peep outside and announced that all was quiet. Then the two robbers went out with Oliver between them. Barney fastened the door behind them, rolled himself up as before, and was soon asleep again.

The fog was much heavier than it had been earlier, and, although no rain was falling, Oliver shivered with dampness and cold. The three dark figures hurriedly crossed the bridge and soon arrived at Chertsey.

"Slap through the town," whispered Sikes. "There'll be nobody in the way at this hour to see us."

He was right. Dogs barked here and there. Oliver saw lights in several houses, but no stragglers were abroad. And Sikes and Crackit had dragged the trembling lad through the town just before the church bell struck two.

Then, quickening their pace, they turned off the main road for a short distance and stopped before a house surrounded by a wall. In a twinkling, Toby Crackit climbed to the top of the wall.

"The boy next," said he. "Hoist him up; I'll catch hold of him."

Before Oliver realized what was happening, he and Toby were lying on the grass on the other side. Sikes followed directly. And the three crept cautiously toward the house.

Then Oliver Twist, well-nigh mad with grief and terror, was sure that housebreaking and robbery, if not murder, were the objects of the expedition. A mist came before his

eyes; the cold sweat stood upon his ashy face; and he fell upon his knees.

"Get up!" murmured Sikes, trembling with rage and drawing the pistol from his pocket. "Get up, or I'll strew your brains upon the grass!"

"Oh! for God's sake, let me go!" begged Oliver. "Let me run away and die in the fields." With an oath, Bill Sikes aimed his pistol at Oliver's head. But Toby struck it from his grasp. Then, placing his hand upon the boy's mouth, Mr. Crackit dragged him to the house, warning Sikes about the noise of shooting. "I can put the boy out with a crack on the head, if I must," he added. "Here, Bill, wrench the shutter open."

Sikes, cursing Fagin for sending Oliver on such an errand, plied the crowbar vigorously, but quietly. Toby assisted; and soon the shutter swung open.

Inside was a little lattice window, about five and a half feet above the ground, at the back of the house. It belonged to a scullery, or a small brewing place, at the end of the passage. The opening was just large enough to admit a boy of Oliver's size. Sikes opened the window easily.

"Now, listen, you young limb!" whispered Bill, taking a dark lantern from his pocket. "Take this light. I'm a-going to put you through there. Then go softly up the steps straight afore you, and along the little hall to the street door. Unfasten it, and let us in. Barney 'ticed the dog away tonight, so neat!"

Oliver was in great terror as he waited and heard Sikes command Mr. Crackit to get to work. Toby first produced his lantern and placed it on the ground. Then he planted himself firmly beneath the window, with his head against the wall and his hands upon his knees, forming a step with his back. Sikes mounted him and lifted Oliver gently through the window, feet first, to the floor inside.

"Now! Your lantern," directed Bill, looking into the room. "See the stairs afore you?"

Oliver, seemingly more dead than alive, gasped, "Yes." Sikes, pointing to the street door with his pistol barrel, informed the trembling boy that he was within range all the way and warned him that, if he faltered, he would fall dead that instant.

By this time, Oliver had decided on one thing at least: Whether he died in the attempt or not, he would make an effort to dart upstairs from the hall and alarm the family. With that in mind, he advanced at once, but stealthily.

A moment or two later, he was interrupted: "Come back!" called Sikes. "Back! back!"

Then came a loud outcry. Oliver dropped his lantern. The crash added to his fright, and he knew not which way to turn.

The cry was repeated—a light appeared. Oliver saw two terrified, half-dressed men at the top of the stairs. There was a flash—a loud noise—smoke—and he staggered back.

Sikes had disappeared for an instant, but now had the lad by the collar. After firing his own pistol at the men, who were already retreating, the robber lifted the boy up to the windowsill.

"Clasp your arm tighter," Sikes directed, as he drew the wounded boy through the opening. "Give me a shawl here, someone. They've hit him! Quick. How the boy bleeds!"

Then came the loud ringing of a bell, the noise of firearms, and the shouts of men; and Oliver had the sensation of being carried over uneven ground at a rapid pace. Soon a cold, deadly feeling crept over the boy's heart; and he neither saw nor heard anything more.

Part 3
The Fateful Bullet

1 *Mr. Bumble Searches for Honey*

On the third night after the attempted robbery, the ground was covered with snow. Bleak, dark, and piercing cold, it was a night for the well-housed and well-fed to gather round the hearth fire and thank God they were at home; and for the homeless, starving wretch to lay him down and die.

Mrs. Corney, the matron of the workhouse where Oliver Twist was born, sat down before a cheerful fire in her own little room. She glanced with satisfaction at a small round table, on which was a large tray. Mrs. Corney was about to enjoy a cup of tea. She looked toward the little kettle in the fireplace and smiled as she listened to its little piping song.

"Well!" said she, "I'm sure all of us have a great deal to be thankful for, if we did but know it."

A little later, however, the small teapot and the single cup awakened in her mind sad memories of Mr. Corney, who had died about twenty-five years previously.

"I shall never get another!" she complained. "I shall never get another—like *him*."

She had just tasted her first cup of tea when she heard a soft tap at the door.

"Oh, come in with you!" Mrs. Corney called out,

sharply. "Some of the old women dying, I suppose. They always die when I'm at meals. Don't stand there, letting the cold air in! What's amiss now, eh?"

"Nothing, ma'am, nothing," replied a man's voice, ever so softly.

"Dear me!" exclaimed the matron, sweetly. "Is that Mr. *Bumble*?"

"At your service, ma'am," Mr. Bumble announced. And he entered the room, closing the door after him without waiting for permission.

The beadle and the matron then discussed the weather and all the problems connected with providing "comforts" and food for the poor. And both agreed that the paupers are treated much better than they deserve; that they are never contented; that there are always too many of them; and that they die because they are obstinate—but not soon enough.

"But, however," said Mr. Bumble, after a while, as he began to unwrap a bundle he had under his arm, "these secrets, ma'am, are not to be spoken of, except, as I may say, among the parochial officers, such as ourselves. And here is the port wine, ma'am, two bottles, that the board ordered for the sick."

Having held the first bottle up to the light and shaken it well, Mr. Bumble placed them both on the top of a chest of drawers. He then reached for his hat, as if to go.

"You'll have a very cold walk, Mr. Bumble," Mrs. Corney suggested.

"It blows, ma'am," he replied, turning up his coat-collar, "enough to cut one's ears off."

The matron looked from the little kettle to the beadle, who was moving toward the door. As he coughed, preparatory to bidding her good-night, Mrs. Corney bashfully inquired whether—whether he wouldn't take a cup of tea?

The official immediately turned back his collar; laid

his hat and stick upon a chair; and drew another chair up to the table. As he slowly seated himself, he looked at the lady. She fixed her eyes upon the little teapot. Mr. Bumble coughed again and smiled slightly.

Mrs. Corney arose to get another cup and saucer from the closet. As she sat down, her glance once again met that of the gallant beadle. She blushed and applied herself to the task of preparing his tea. Mr. Bumble coughed more loudly than before.

"Sweet? Mr. *Bumble*?" inquired the matron, taking up the sugar bowl.

"Very sweet, *indeed*, ma'am," replied he, very tenderly.

The tea was made and handed to him in silence.

"You have a cat, ma'am, I see," observed Mr. Bumble. "And kittens, too, I declare!"

"I am so fond of them, Mr. Bumble, you can't think," the matron assured him. "They're *so* happy, *so* frolicsome, and *so* cheerful, that they are real companions for me."

"Very nice animals, ma'am," Mr. Bumble decided, "so very domestic."

"Oh, yes!" added the matron with enthusiasm. "So fond of their home, too."

"Mrs. Corney, ma'am," said Mr. Bumble, slowly, "I mean to say this, ma'am: that any cat or kitten that could live with *you*, ma'am and *not* be fond of its home, must be a ass, ma'am."

"Oh, Mr. Bumble!" exclaimed Mrs. Corney, modestly.

"It's of no use disguising facts, ma'am," the beadle insisted, waving his teaspoon. "I would drown it myself, with pleasure."

"Then you're a cruel man," the matron declared, in a kittenish manner, as she held out her hand for the beadle's cup, "and a very hard-hearted man besides."

"Hard-hearted, ma'am?" queried Mr. Bumble. "Hard?" He yielded his cup without another word and squeezed

Mrs. Corney's little finger as she took it. Then, after inflicting two open-handed slaps upon his laced waistcoat, he sighed deeply and moved his chair just a little farther from the fire. Every moment or two, the chair was budged again; and, as the table was round, the distance between the two chairs became gradually shorter.

If Mrs. Corney had moved her chair to the right, she would have been scorched by the fire; and if left, she must have fallen into Mr. Bumble's arms. So, being a genteel matron, she remained where she was and handed the gentleman another cup of tea. At that moment, the two chairs touched each other.

"Hard-hearted, Mrs. Corney?" asked Mr. Bumble again, stirring his tea and looking up into the matron's face. "Are *you* hard-hearted, Mrs. Corney?"

"Dear me!" exclaimed the matron, fluttering, "what a very curious question from a single man. What can you want to know for, Mr. Bumble?"

The beadle drank his tea to the last drop; finished eating a piece of toast; whisked the crumbs off his knees; wiped his lips; and deliberately kissed the matron.

"Mr. *Bumble!*" whispered that discreet lady, excitedly. "Mr Bumble, I shall *scream!*" But the determined Bumble made no reply. Instead, he put his arm around the matron's waist in a slow and dignified manner.

It was not necessary for her to scream. A hasty knocking at the door caused her lover to dart quickly from his chair to the wine bottles. And he began dusting them with great care, while the matron sharply demanded who was there.

"If you please, mistress," begged a withered old female pauper, putting her head in at the door, "Old Sally is a-going fast."

"Well, what's that to me?" angrily demanded the matron. "I can't keep her alive, can I?"

"No, no, mistress," replied the old woman, "nobody can. She's far beyond the reach of help. But she's troubled in her mind. She says she has something to tell, which you must hear. She'll never die *quiet* till you come, mistress."

Mrs. Corney scowled and muttered a variety of terms that were not exactly complimentary to old women who couldn't die without purposely annoying their betters. Then, muffling herself in a thick shawl, she kindly requested Mr. Bumble to stay till she came back, lest "anything particular" should occur. Bidding the messenger hurry ahead, she flounced from the room, scolding all the way.

The beadle's conduct, on being left alone, was rather unusual. He opened the closet, counted the teaspoons, lifted the sugar tongs, and closely inspected a silver milk pot. Then, having satisfied his curiosity, he put on his cocked hat cornerwise and pranced with much dignity four times around the table. After this strange performance, he removed his hat again; and, spreading himself with his back toward the fire, seemed to be mentally engaging in placing a value upon the furniture.

2 *Deathbed Gold!*

The skinny, twisted old hag tottered along the passages and up the stairs, muttering indistinct answers to the grumblings of Mrs. Corney. At length, compelled to pause for breath, the trembling figure gave the light to the matron and remained behind to follow as best she might. Her more nimble superior hurried to the room where the dying woman lay.

It was a bare garret room, with a dim light burning at the farther end. There was another old woman watching by the bed. The parish doctor's apprentice was standing by the fire, making a toothpick out of a quill.

"Cold night, Mrs. Corney," said that young gentleman, as the matron entered.

"Very cold, indeed, sir," agreed Mrs. Corney, in her most civil tones, and bowing slightly as she spoke.

The conversation was here interrupted by a moan from the sick woman.

"Oh!" exclaimed the young man, turning toward the bed, as if he had quite forgotten the patient, "it's all *up* with her, Mrs. Corney."

"It is, is it, sir?" asked the matron.

"If she lasts a couple of hours, I shall be surprised,"

announced the medical student, examining the toothpick. "Complete breakdown—Is she dozing, old one?"

The attendant stooped over the bed and then nodded.

"Perhaps she'll go off in that way, then, if you don't make a row," suggested the young man. "Put the light on the floor. She won't see it there."

The attendant did as she was told, shaking her head to indicate that the patient would not die so easily. Then she resumed her seat by the side of the other nurse, who had returned. The mistress wrapped herself impatiently in her shawl and sat at the foot of the bed.

The doctor's assistant, satisfied with the shape of his toothpick, grew weary of the scene a few minutes later, wished Mrs. Corney joy of her job, and left on tiptoe.

Soon the two old women crouched together over the fire and whispered to each other: "Did she say any more, Annie dear, while I was gone?" inquired the messenger.

"Not a word," was the reply.

"Did she drink the hot wine the doctor said she was to have?"

"She couldn't," answered the other. "Her teeth were set. So *I* drank it; and it did me good!" Then both old hags indulged in a quiet, cackling laugh.

A little while later, the matron, who had been impatiently waiting for the patient to awaken from her stupor, joined them by the fire, and sharply asked how long she was expected to wait?

"Not long, mistress," replied the second woman, looking up into her face. "None of us must wait long for death."

"Hold your tongue, you doting idiot!" ordered the matron, sternly. "You, Martha, tell me: Has she been this way before?"

"Often."

"But will never again," added Annie; "that is, she'll

never wake again but once—and mind, mistress, that won't be for long!"

"Long or short," said the matron, snappily, "she won't find me here when she does wake. Take care, both of you, how you worry me again for nothing. Mind that, you impudent old witches. If you make a fool of me again, I'll soon cure you!"

She was about to leave when the patient raised herself upright, stretching her arms toward her attendants.

"Who's that?" she asked, in a hollow voice.

"Hush, hush!" commanded one of the women, stooping over her. "Lie down, lie down!"

"I'll never lie down again—alive!" the woman insisted, struggling. "I *will* tell her! Come here!—Nearer! Let me whisper—in your ear."

She clutched the matron by the arm and, pulling her toward a chair by the bedside, was about to speak. But, looking around, she caught sight of the two old women bending forward in the attitude of eager listeners.

"Turn them—away," urged the dying one, drowsily. "Make haste!—Make haste!"

The two old crones, chiming in together, protested. But their superior pushed them from the room, closed the door, and returned to the bedside. Then the old ladies changed their tone and cried through the keyhole that Old Sally was drunk.

"Now—listen," begged the dying woman aloud, as if making a great effort to revive one remaining spark of energy. "In this very room—in this very bed—I once nursed—a pretty young creatur' that was—brought into the house with her—her feet cut and bruised from walking. She—gave birth to a boy—and died."

"What about her?" queried her listener, impatiently.

"Ay," murmured the sick woman, "what about her?—

What about—I know!" She whispered. "I robbed her—so I did! She wasn't cold—when I stole it!"

"Stole what, for God's sake?" demanded the matron.

"*It!*" replied the other. "The only thing she had. She had—kept it safe—in her bosom. It was gold, I tell you! Rich gold—that might have—saved her life!"

"Gold!" echoed the matron, bending eagerly over the suffering woman. "Go on, go on—yes—what of it? Who was she? When was it?"

"She charged me to—to keep it safe," came the reply, with a groan, "and trusted me as—the only woman about her. And the child's death—perhaps— is on *me,* besides! They—would have treated him better if—they had known it all!"

"Known what?" asked Mrs. Corney. "Speak!"

"The boy grew—so like his mother, that I could—never forget it—when I saw his face. Poor girl!—Wait: There's more to tell."

The matron inclined her head to catch the words as they came more faintly from the dying woman. "Be quick, or it may be too late!"

"She—when the pains of death first came upon her—whispered—in my ear that—if her baby was born alive—and thrived—the day might come when it would not—feel so much disgraced to hear its poor young mother named. 'And oh, kind heaven!' she said—folding her thin hands together, 'whether boy or girl, raise up—some friends for it. Take pity on a poor child!' "

"The boy's name?" demanded the matron.

"They *called* him—Oliver," replied the woman, feebly. "The gold I stole was—"

"Yes, yes—what?" cried the other, desperately.

Mrs. Corney stooped down more closely to hear, but drew back as the poor woman once again raised herself and tried to speak. But, clutching the cover with her hands, Old Sally muttered indistinctly and fell lifeless on the bed.

"Stone dead!" piped one of the old women, hurrying in as soon as the door was opened.

"And nothing to tell, after all!" rejoined the matron, bouncing carelessly away.

The two hags, seemingly too much occupied with deathbed duties to make any reply, were then left alone, hovering about the body.

3 *Alive or Dead?*

Meantime, that same cold evening, Mr. Fagin sat in the old den from which Oliver had been recovered by the girl. The old man was in deep thought.

At a table behind him sat the Artful Dodger, Master Charles Bates, and Mr. Chitling, playing cards. The Dodger wore his hat, as was often his custom within doors. Betsy was looking on with interest. There was much poking of fun, especially when the conversation turned toward Tom Chitling, who was accused of being "sweet" on Betsy.

Some of the joking centered also around Mr. Chitling's six-weeks' recent "rest" in the reformatory; but the "vacationer" was rubbed the wrong way. The "fur" flew for a few minutes, during which time Tom made Fagin feel quite uncomfortable. And finally there wasn't much to laugh at, for, when Tom aimed a blow at Charley for laughing, the latter ducked and the blow fell on Mr. Fagin's chest.

"Hark!" cried the Dodger, somewhat later, "I heard the tinkler." Catching up the light, he crept softly upstairs.

The bell was rung again, with some impatience, while the group was in darkness. After a short pause, the Dodger reappeared and whispered to Fagin mysteriously.

"What!" cried he. "Alone?"

The Dodger nodded and, shading the flame of the

candle with his hand, gave Charley Bates a private suggestion, in dumb show, that he had better not be funny
just *then*. So the Artful fixed his eyes on the old man's face
and awaited instructions.

Fagin bit his yellow fingers thoughtfully for some seconds. His face showed that he dreaded something and
feared to know the worst. At length he raised his head.

"Where is he?" he asked.

The Dodger pointed to the floor above and made a sign
as if he would leave the room.

"Yes," said Fagin, "bring him down. Hush! Quiet,
Charley! Go gently, Tom. Quiet, quiet!"

These brief directions to Charley Bates and Tom were
immediately obeyed. There was no sound of their whereabouts when the Dodger descended the stairs, bearing the
light, and followed by a man in a coarse old robe. The latter,
after casting a hurried glance around the room, pulled off
his hat and a large cloth that had concealed the lower portion of his face, showing the pale unwashed and unshaved
features of flash Toby Crackit.

"How are you, Faguey?" the visitor inquired, nodding
to his master. "Pop that shawl away in my hat, Dodger, so
that I may know where to find it when I cut. That's the
time of day! You'll be a fine young burglar some day."

With these words, he pulled up the robe; and, winding
it around his middle, drew a chair to the fire and placed
his feet upon the hob.

"See there, Faguey," he said, pointing unhappily to his
top boots. "Not a drop of blacking since you know when,
by Jove! But don't talk about business till I've eat and drank.
So produce the sustenance, and let's have a quiet fill-out
for the first time these three days."

Fagin motioned to the Dodger to place some leftover
food upon the table. Then, seating himself opposite the
housebreaker, he waited for his story.

To judge from appearances, Toby was by no means in a hurry to talk. At first, his chief contented himself with patiently watching Toby's face, as if to gain from its expression some clue of information, but in vain. Toby looked tired and worn, but his normal expression of ease appeared upon his features. And, through dirt and beard, his self-satisfied grin was still present.

Then, in an agony of impatience, Fagin watched every morsel the young criminal put into his mouth, pacing up and down the room, meanwhile, in unbearable excitement. It was all of no use. Toby continued to eat in a quiet, care-free manner, until he could eat no more. Finally, ordering the Dodger to leave, he closed the door, mixed a glass of spirits and water, and settled himself for talking.

"First and foremost, Faguey," Toby began.

"Yes, yes!" cut in the old man, drawing up his chair.

Mr. Crackit stopped to take a drink and to declare that it was excellent. Then, placing his feet against the low mantelpiece, so as to bring his boots up to about the level of his eyes, he quietly resumed:

"First and foremost, Faguey," said the housebreaker, "how's Bill?"

"What!" screamed Fagin, starting from his seat.

"Why, you don't mean to say—" Toby went on, turning pale.

"Mean!" cried the master, stamping furiously on the ground. "Where are they? Sikes and the boy! Where have they been? Where are they hiding? Why have they not been here?"

"The crack failed," announced Toby, faintly.

"I know it," replied Fagin, snatching a newspaper from his pocket and pointing to it. "What more?"

"They fired and hit the boy. We cut over the fields at the back, with him between us—straight as the crow flies—through hedge and ditch. They gave chase. Damme! the whole country was awake, and the dogs upon us."

"The boy!" Fagin insisted.

"Bill had him on his back and scudded like the wind. We stopped to take him between us. His head hung down, and he was cold. Pursuers were close upon our heels; every man for himself; and each from the gallows!—We parted company and left the youngster lying in a ditch. Alive or dead, that's all I know about him!"

The frightened old man waited to hear no more. Uttering a loud yell, and twining his hands in his hair, he rushed from the room and from the house.

4 *Enter Mr. Monks*

Old Fagin avoided all the main streets wherever he could, hurrying through the byways and alleys. Some distance beyond Snow Hill, where he felt more at home, he slowed up to his usual shuffling pace and seemed to breathe more freely.

Near the spot where Snow Hill and Holborn Hill meet, there opens a narrow, dismal alley, called Field Lane, which leads to Saffron Hill. In the filthy Field Lane shops are shown huge bunches of second-hand silk handkerchiefs of all sizes and patterns; for here reside the traders who purchase them from pickpockets. And here, also, the clothesman, the cobbler, the rag merchant, and many others display their goods, as signboards to the petty thief.

As the worried old man passed along in Field Lane, he nodded here and there in recognition of a few of his cronies who were on the lookout to buy or sell. But he was headed directly for the Three Cripples, the tavern where Sikes and his dog, earlier in this story, put on their little show. Fagin stopped only once, near the farther end of the lane, where he inquired after Sikes but obtained no helpful information.

Arriving at the public house, and merely making a sign to the bartender, the old man walked upstairs. There he opened the door of a room and softly stepped inside, looking anxiously about, and shading his eyes with his hand, as if in search of someone.

In the dingy, smoke-filled room were many rough characters of both sexes, drinking and engaging in all kinds of boisterous conduct. There was much noise and confusion, aided no little by a gentleman who was playing a cheap and jangling piano. At intervals there were attempts at singing songs that were not too refined.

The landlord was seated at the head of the long table around which the crowd was gathered. He seemed to be acting the part of chairman for a meeting. When Fagin saw him, he beckoned to him to step outside.

"What can I do for you, Mr. Fagin?" inquired the landlord, when they were both out on the landing. "Won't you join us? They'll be delighted, everyone of 'em."

Fagin simply shook his head impatiently and whispered, "Is *he* here?"

"No," was the quiet reply.

"And no news of Barney?"

"None," answered the landlord. "He won't stir till it's all safe. Depend on it! They're on the scent, down there. Barney's all right enough, else I should have heard of him."

"Will *he* be here tonight?" asked Fagin.

"Monks, do you mean?"

"Hush!" said the old man. "Yes."

"Certain," declared his friend, looking at his gold watch. "I expected him here before now. If you'll wait ten minutes—"

"No, no!" exclaimed Fagin, hastily. "Tell him I was looking for him, and that he must come to me tomorrow."

"Good!" said the landlord. "Nothing more?"

"Not now," the old man replied, descending the stairs. "Good night," and Fagin left the tavern hastily.

Some time later, he stood before the door of Mr. Sikes' residence and tapped on it softly. "Now," he muttered to himself, "if there is any deep play here, I shall have it out of you, my girl, cunning as you are!"

He found Nancy alone, lying with her head upon the table, and her hair straggling over it. "She has been drinking," mumbled her master, "or perhaps she is only miserable."

She eyed his crafty face narrowly after she inquired whether there was any news, and listened closely to the old man's report on Toby Crackit's story. Then she sank into her former attitude, but said nothing.

During the silence, Mr. Fagin looked slyly about the room for signs of Sikes' possible secret return. He seemed to be satisfied with his inspection. Then he rubbed his hands together and asked, in his most friendly tone,

"And where should you think Bill was now, my dear?"

The girl moaned and was apparently crying, but managed to mutter that she did not know.

"And the *boy*, too," said Fagin, straining his eyes to catch a glimpse of Nancy's face. "Poor leetle child! Left in a ditch, Nance; only *think!*"

"The child," said the girl, suddenly looking up, "is better where he is than among us. And, if no harm comes to Bill from it, I hope he lies *dead* in the ditch, and that his young bones may rot there."

"What!" cried her chief, in amazement.

"Ay, I do," insisted the girl. "I shall be glad to have him away from my eyes, and to know that the worst is over. The sight of him turns me against myself and all of you."

"Pooh!" Fagin said, scornfully. "You're drunk, but you can hear me. Now, listen! I could have Sikes strangled with six words. But you may think it better to murder him yourself before this is all over. And don't wait till it is too late!"

"What is all this?" mumbled the girl.

"What is it?" Fagin went on, mad with rage. "When the boy's worth hundreds of pounds to me, am I to lose what chance threw me in the way of getting safely?—And me bound, too, to a born devil that only wants the will, and has the power to, to—"

Panting for breath, the old man then checked his wrath and changed his whole manner, observing that Nancy had seemed to lose interest again.

"Nancy, dear!" he pleaded, in his usual tone. "Did you hear me, dear?"

"Don't—worry me now, Fagin!" replied the girl, raising her head slightly. "If Bill has not done it this time, he will another. He has done many a good job for you. The boy must take his chance with the rest. I—I hope he is out of harm's way, and out of yours—that is—if *Bill* comes to no harm."

Fagin put several other questions, but could get little more out of her that was worthwhile to him. Most of her short replies or exclamations simply convinced him that she was thoroughly muddled with liquor. Her moods changed every now and then. And Fagin was really pleased to observe her condition. Finally, when she was apparently asleep, he left her.

It was then within an hour of midnight; and Mr. Fagin started for his home. The piercing cold made him move faster than usual. Few other persons were abroad. He had reached the corner of his own street and was fumbling in his pocket for the door key, when a dark figure moved quietly toward him from a doorway that lay in deep shadow.

"Fagin!" whispered a voice close to his ear.

"Ah!" said the old criminal, turning quickly around, "is that—*Monks*?"

"Yes!" Monks answered, softly. "I have been freezing here these two hours. Where the devil have you been?"

"On *your* business, my dear," whispered Fagin, glancing uneasily at his companion, and slackening his pace.

"Oh, of course!" said Monks, with an ugly grin. "Well, and what's come of it?"

"Nothing good."

"Nothing bad, I hope?" Monks inquired, looking rather startled.

Not too willing to entertain his unexpected midnight guest, Fagin nevertheless unlocked the door of his house, before which the two soon found themselves. Whispering to Monks, "Close the door softly," he admitted him and went to get a light.

"It's dark as the grave," grumbled Monks, groping forward. "Make haste!"

"Toby's asleep in the back room below," Fagin assured his visitor, upon returning quietly with a lighted candle. "The boys are in the front room. Come upstairs."

In a room above, the two men whispered together for a time. Then Monks raised his voice somewhat.

"I tell you again, it was badly planned. Why didn't you keep him here among the rest and make a sneaking, sniveling pickpocket of him, like the others? With patience, you could have got him convicted and sent away, perhaps for life."

"Whose turn would that have served, my dear?" inquired Fagin, humbly.

"Mine," replied Monks.

"But not *mine!*" the old man exclaimed. "With him, I found it was not easy. It was different. I seemed not to have the right hold on him. And once sending him forth with Charley and the Dodger was no good."

"*That* was not my doing," Monks pointed out.

"No, no, my dear!" agreed Fagin. "If it had never happened, you might never have clapped eyes upon the boy to discover that it was him you were looking for. Well! I got him back for you by means of the girl; and then *she* begins to favor him."

"Throttle the girl!" growled Monks, impatiently.

"Not just now, my dear," observed the old one, with a

twisted smile. "If the boy becomes hard, she'll care nothing for him. You want him made a thief. Well, if he is alive, I can make him one from this time; and if—if—it's not likely, mind—but if the worst comes to the worst, and he is dead—"

"It's no fault of mine if he is!" interrupted Monks, with a look of terror. "Mind that, Fagin! Anything but his death, I told you from the first. If they shot him dead—what's that?"

"What!" cried Fagin, jumping up. "Where?"

"Yonder!" exclaimed Monks, glaring at the opposite wall. "I saw the shadow of a woman wearing a cloak and bonnet pass along there like a breath!—Your candle is in the hallway, you know."

They rushed from the room. The candle was burning low. It showed them only the empty staircase, and their own white faces. They listened intently.

"It's your fancy," Fagin declared, taking up the light.

"I'll swear I saw it!" replied Monks, trembling. "It was bending forward when I saw it first. When I spoke, it darted away."

Fagin sneered at Monks' pale face and led the way up a flight of stairs. They looked into all the rooms, only to find them cold, bare, and empty. They descended into the passage and into the cellars below. But all was still as death.

"What do you think now?" the old man asked, when they were in the front passage again. "Besides ourselves, there's not a creature in the house except Toby and the boys; and they're safe enough. They are all locked in."

Then Mr. Monks had to laugh in spite of himself, saying, "Imagination, I suppose." But he did not want any more conversation that night. And it was past one o'clock when he again braved the wintry blasts.

5 *Mr. Bumble Gathers Honey*

No one who was acquainted with Mr. Bumble would have been surprised at any time to discover him improving each shining hour for himself—whether in company or alone. Did he sit in idleness and stare vacantly into vacant space, after sweet Mrs. Corney was so rudely called from his presence? Not he! As the time of her absence lengthened, was he satisfied after only *one* thorough inspection of the dear lady's furniture, silverware, and contents of her chest of drawers? Not Mr. Bumble! Did he feel that he wasted his precious time when his thorough searching led his hand where he could grasp and shake a padlocked box, whose contents gave forth the pleasant sound of jingling coin? Not he! And then, after listening at the keyhole of the room once more, to make sure that he had not been spied upon, and looking around carefully to see that all was in proper order, did he declare, "I'll do it!" in a very decided manner? He certainly did!

He was indulging in very pleasant thoughts when Mrs. Corney, hurrying back to her room, threw herself upon a chair by the fireside. Then she covered her eyes with one hand, placed the other over her heart, and gasped for breath.

"Mrs. Corney," demanded Mr. Bumble, gently stooping

over her, "what is this, ma'am? Has anything happened, ma'am? Pray answer me! I'm on—on—" Mr. Bumble, in his alarm, could not immediately think of the term "pins and needles," so he said, "—broken bottles."

"Oh, Mr. Bumble!" cried the lady, "I have been so *dreadfully* put out! It is too *terrible* to think of!"

"Then *don't* think of it, ma'am," Mr. Bumble advised. "Just tell me what upset you, and let *me* think."

"Nothing, really," replied Mrs. Corney. "I'm just a foolish, excitable, weak creatur'."

"Not weak, ma'am," objected Mr. Bumble, drawing his chair a little closer. "Are you a *weak* creatur', Mrs. Corney?"

"We are all weak creatur's," announced Mrs. Corney, on general principles.

"Yes; so we are," agreed the beadle, thoughtfully.

Nothing more was said for a minute or two. Then Mr. Bumble moved his left arm from the back of Mrs. Corney's chair to her apron string. And his arm was soon bound tightly by a number of twists and turns of that long strip of cloth.

Mrs. Corney sighed.

"Don't sigh, Mrs. Corney," Mr. Bumble rumbled.

"I can't help it," said Mrs. Corney. And she sighed again, as if she were utterly helpless.

"This is a very comfortable room, ma'am," the beadle made clear, looking around. "Another room, and *this*, ma'am, would be a complete thing.

"It would be too much for one," murmured the lady.

"But not for *two*, ma'am," Mr. Bumble observed officially, in soft, cooing accents. "Eh, Mrs. Corney?"

The matron lowered her head, ever so modestly. The beadle lowered his to look into her face. Mrs. Corney very properly turned her face aside and, reaching for her handkerchief, unintentionally placed her hand in Mr. Bumble's free one. He quickly held it prisoner.

"The board allow you coals, don't they, Mrs. Corney?" inquired the beadle, squeezing her hand gently.

"And candles," she added, returning the pressure of his hand just the least bit.

"Coals, candles—and house-rent free," Mr. Bumble summarized. "Oh, Mrs. Corney, what a *angel* you are!"

The lady was not fortified against all this. She just sank right into the beadle's arms! And that gentleman, of *all* persons, lost his dignified control and planted a kiss very definitely upon her respectable nose.

"Such parochial perfection!" her lover exclaimed, delightedly. "Do you know that Mr. Slout is worse tonight, my fascinator?"

"Yes," replied the matron, bashfully.

"He can't live a week, the doctor says. He is the master of this establishment. His death will cause a wacancy, which must be filled. Oh, Mrs. Corney, what a possibility! What a opportunity for a-j'ining of hearts and housekeepings!"

Mrs. Corney simply sobbed quietly.

"The little word?" Mr. Bumble gently asked, and bent over the bashful beauty. "The one little, little, little word, my blessed Corney?"

"Ye—ye—yes!" sighed the matron, almost gasping.

"One more," pursued the beadle. "Compose your darling feelings for only one more: When is it to come off?"

The sweet lady twice tried to speak, and twice failed. But, soon gathering courage, she threw her arms around the humble Mr. Bumble's neck, saying that it might be as soon as ever he pleased. And she added, ever so kittenishly, as he held her tightly, "You—irre—sistible duck!"

Having thus satisfactorily arranged their affairs, the contract was solemnly made secure by two teacupfuls of a certain peppermint mixture. Such fortification was the more necessary because the bride-to-be was all a-flutter.

As she felt her strength returning, she told her Bumble of the old woman's death.

"Very good," decided that gentleman, sipping his peppermint. "I'll call at Sowerberry's as I go home and tell him to send over tomorrow morning. Was it that as frightened you, love?"

"It wasn't anything particular, dear," the lady said, trying to avoid the subject.

"It must have been *something,* love," urged Mr. Bumble. "Won't you tell your own *B.?*

"Not now. One of these days. After we're married, dear."

"*After* we're married!" exclaimed the lady's dear B. "It wasn't any impudence from any of them male paupers as—"

"No, no, love!" insisted B.'s sweet one, hastily.

"If I thought it was," continued the "irresistible duck." "If I thought as any one of 'em had dared to lift his wulgar eyes to that lovely face—"

"They wouldn't have dared to do it, love," the lady assured him.

"They had better not!" said her gallant B., clenching his fist. "Let me see any man, parochial or extra-parochial, as would even try! He—wouldn't do it a second time!"

This show of protection might have seemed no very high compliment to the sweet lady's charms; but the weighty Mr. Bumble accompanied the threat with many warlike gestures. Hence she was much touched with this proof of his devotion. In fact, she insisted, with great admiration, that he was indeed a dove.

The "dove" promptly turned up his coat collar and put on his cocked hat. Then, having indulged in an affectionate embrace with his future partner, he ducked forth bravely into the cold winds of the night. He paused for a few minutes in the male paupers' ward to abuse them a little and thus satisfy himself that he could fill the office of workhouse master with necessary sharpness.

Pleased with his qualifications, the dovelike B. left there with a light heart and bright visions of a happy marriage and his promotion. Then, head high, and swinging his cane officially, he set out upon his pleasant errand to the undertaker's shop on his way home.

6 *I Shot Him, Miss!*

"Wolves tear your throats!" growled Sikes, grinding his teeth together. "I wish I was among you. You'd howl the hoarser for it."

Sikes issued this desperate threat into the early morning air after the attempted burglary failed and Oliver Twist was wounded. Bill had stopped to rest in his wild effort to escape. He laid poor Oliver on his knee and looked back.

There was little that Sikes could see in the mist and darkness; but he heard loud shouts of men, and the barking of dogs aroused by the sound of the alarm bell.

"Stop, you white-livered hound!" the robber shouted at Toby Crackit, who, making the best use of his long legs, was already ahead. "Stop!"

Toby stopped.

"Bear a hand with the boy," demanded Sikes. "Come back!"

Bill then laid the boy in a ditch at his feet and drew his pistol, as the noise of the pursuers grew louder.

"It's all up, Bill!" called Toby. "Forget the kid and run."

Mr. Crackit then took the chance of being shot by his friend and darted off at full speed. Sikes clenched his teeth; took one look around; threw a cape over Oliver's motionless body in the ditch; and, holding his pistol above his head, leaped over a hedge and was gone.

"Ho, ho, there!" cried a shaky voice in the rear. "Pincher! Neptune! Come here, come here!"

The dogs obeyed; and three pursuers in the field stopped to talk over the situation. Two of them, Giles and Brittles, were in the service of the old lady of the mansion that Sikes had tried to "crack." The third was a traveling tinker who had been permitted to spend the night in an old shed.

They had already overexerted themselves in the chase, beyond their interest and physical powers, without much success. And their conversation caused a welcome delay. They were frightened. So it was easy for them to agree that they could never catch up with the robbers. Then they turned toward the mansion at trot speed, often looking back fearfully. As they approached the house and safety, they felt more cheerful.

The air grew colder as day slowly dawned; and the mist rolled along the ground like a dense cloud of smoke. The grass was wet; the pathways and low places were all mire and water.

Oliver Twist lay motionless on the spot where Sikes had left him.

Later in the morning, the rain came down thick and fast. But Oliver did not feel it as it beat upon him.

At length, on his bed of wet clay, the boy awoke with a low cry of pain. His left arm, rudely wrapped in a bloody shawl, hung heavy and useless at his side. Forcing himself to sit up, Oliver looked feebly around for help, groaning in agony. Trembling in every joint from cold and exhaustion, he made an effort to stand upright, but fell back into the mud and water of the ditch.

He became unconscious again for a while and awoke

again much later. Then he seemed to realize only one thing clearly: He must get upon his feet and leave that place, or the ditch would surely be his grave. But he was very weak, sick, and dizzy. He tried several times to stand, before he managed finally to crawl out of the ditch and stagger away. More than once he stumbled to his knees and cried out in pain, when he struck his wounded arm against the ground.

Creeping between the bars of gates, or through hedge-gaps, as they came in his way, he staggered on until he reached a road. There, stopping to rest, he looked around. Through the driving rain, the wounded boy saw a house that he thought was not too far away for his legs to carry him. He summoned all his strength and forced his uncertain steps toward it.

As he drew nearer to the house, he slowly became sure that he had seen it before. And that garden wall! On the grass inside, he had fallen on his knees last night and begged for mercy. The mansion was the one that was to be robbed!

Oliver now became almost paralyzed with fear and for a moment forgot the agony of his wound. He thought only of running, but could scarcely stand. And, even if he had all his strength, where could he have run? He pushed against the garden gate. It swung open. He tottered across the lawn, climbed the steps, and knocked faintly at the door. Then he collapsed and fell heavily against one of the pillars of the porch.

Giles, Brittles, and the tinker were refreshing themselves with tea and toast in the kitchen, after the labors and terrors of the night. Their expanded tales of great heroism, well dramatized, were being absorbed by the cook and a maid in open-mouthed wonder and admiration. Just when those ladies felt that they could not endure any more of such thrills of horror, Mr. Giles was interrupted by hearing a violent thump. The sound seemed to come from the front door.

That was the "last straw" for the ladies. At once and together, they let out piercing screams.

"It was a knock," declared Mr. Giles, acting as if he were perfectly at ease. "Open the door, somebody."

Nobody moved.

"It seems a strange sort of a thing—a knock coming at such a time in the morning," added Mr. Giles, watching the pale faces that surrounded him, and looking very blank himself, "but the door must be opened. Do you hear, *somebody?*"

He again looked from one to the other, but neither of the other men seemed eager for the job. It was finally agreed, however, that the men should go together. With the dogs leading, they then started upstairs. The two women followed because they were afraid to remain alone in the kitchen.

Advised by Giles, all made as much noise as possible. And, in the hall, they pinched the dogs' tails to make them bark savagely. Then, inside the door, Mr. Giles held the tinker's arm so that he could not run away and commanded Brittles to open the door. He did so; and the little "army," peeping timidly outside, saw only Oliver Twist, speechless and exhausted. He opened his eyes slowly and with them prayed for pity and help.

"A boy!" exclaimed Giles, suddenly becoming masterful and brave. "What's the matter with the—eh?—Why, Brittles, look here—don't you know?"

Brittles came forward, saw Oliver, and uttered a loud cry. Mr. Giles, seizing the boy, lugged him into the hall, and placed him full length upon the floor.

"Here he is!" bawled Giles, calling in great excitement up the staircase. "Here's one of the thieves, ma'am! Here's

a thief, miss! Wounded, miss! I shot him, miss; and Brittles held the light." The two women-servants ran upstairs.

A few minutes later, in the midst of all this noise and commotion, there was heard a sweet female voice, and all the shouting ceased.

"Giles!" the voice spoke from the stairs, in a half-whisper.

"I'm here, miss," replied Mr. Giles. "Don't be frightened, miss. I ain't much injured. He didn't make a very desperate resistance, miss!"

"Hush!" replied the young lady, "you frighten my aunt as much as the thieves did. Is the poor creature hurt badly?"

"Wounded desperate, miss," Giles answered.

"Wait quietly only one instant, while I speak to my aunt," ordered the lady.

She soon returned, directing them to carry the wounded one carefully up to Giles' room. She also ordered Brittles to saddle the pony and ride to Chertsey with all speed for a doctor.

"Oh! treat him kindly, Giles, for my sake!" the kind lady begged, as she left them again.

7 *Doubtful Glory*

"And Brittles has been gone upwards of an hour, has he?" asked Mrs. Maylie, the elderly mistress.

"An hour and twelve minutes, ma'am," Mr. Giles replied, on the authority of his silver watch.

"He is always slow," remarked the old lady.

"Yes, Brittles always *was* a slow boy, ma'am," the attendant informed her, more for his own good than for any other reason.

This dialogue took place in a well-furnished dining room that had the appearance of old-fashioned comfort. Mrs. Maylie and young Miss Rose Maylie sat at a well-spread breakfast table. Mr. Giles was dressed with great care in a black suit. His whole dignified manner showed that he had a high regard for his own merits and the importance of his position as butler and steward.

Mrs. Maylie, sitting very straight in her high-backed oak chair, was dressed with utmost nicety. Her eyes, only slightly dimmed with age, were attentively fixed upon the young lady.

Miss Rose, scarcely seventeen, was in the lovely bloom and springtime of womanhood. She was slight in build, and as beautiful in character as she was to look upon. Intelligence shone in her deep blue eyes and was indicated by her noble head. She seemed not at all a part of the rough world; for her sweetness, good humor, and cheerful, happy smile were made for home and fireside peace and happiness.

After a pause of several minutes in the conversation, a gig drove up to the garden gate. Out jumped a fat gentleman who ran straight up to the door. He entered the house without waiting to be announced and burst into the room, nearly overturning Mr. Giles and the breakfast table together.

"I never hear of such a thing!" exclaimed the fat gentleman. "My *dear* Mrs. Maylie—bless my soul—in the silence of night, too—I *never* heard of such a thing!"

With these expressions of sympathy, the fat gentleman shook hands with both ladies and, drawing up a chair, inquired how they found themselves.

"You ought to be dead—positively dead with the fright," declared he. "Why didn't you send? Bless me, my man should have come in a minute; and so would I; and my assistant would have been delighted; or *anybody*, I'm sure, under such circumstances. Dear, dear! So unexpected! In the dead of night, too!

"And you, Miss Rose," the excited gentleman continued, turning to her. "I—"

"Oh! very much so, indeed, Dr. Losberne," said Rose, interrupting him, "but there is a poor creature upstairs whom my aunt wishes you to see."

"Ah! to be sure," returned the doctor, "so there is!— That was your handiwork, Giles, I understand."

Mr. Giles, who had been hurriedly assembling the teacups, blushed very plainly, admitting that he had had the honor.

"Honor, eh?" queried the doctor. "Well, I don't know. Perhaps it's as honorable to hit a thief in a back kitchen, as to hit your man at twelve paces."

Talking all the way, he followed Mr. Giles upstairs. His attentions to the patient took the surgeon much longer than anyone expected. A large flat box was fetched from the gig.

The bedroom bell was rung very often for the servants, who ran up and down stairs frequently. All of this activity was proof enough that important work was being done. At length Dr. Losberne returned; and, in reply to an anxious inquiry after his patient, looked very mysterious.

"This is a very extraordinary thing, Mrs. Maylie," he declared, standing with his back to the door of the room wherein he found Mrs. Maylie and the girl.

"He is not in danger, I hope?" the elderly lady inquired.

"Why, *that* would not be an extraordinary thing, under the circumstances," replied the surgeon, "though I don't think he is. Have you seen this thief?"

"No."

"Nor heard anything about him?"

"No," repeated Mrs. Maylie, her curiosity aroused.

"I beg your pardon, ma'am," Mr. Giles chimes in, "but I was going to tell you about him when Dr. Losberne arrived."

The fact was that Mr. Giles had not, at first, desired to make it generally known that he had shot a mere boy. He was fully enjoying his "glory" as a hero and wanted it to last as long as possible.

"Rose wished to see the man," said Mrs. Maylie, "but I would not hear of it."

"Humph!" exclaimed the doctor. "There is certainly nothing very alarming in his appearance. Have you any objection to seeing him in my presence?"

"If it be necessary," consented the old lady. "Certainly not."

"I think it *is* necessary," the doctor made plain. "At all events, I am quite sure that you would deeply regret not seeing him, if you delayed. He is perfectly quiet and comfortable now. Allow me—Miss Rose. Will you permit me?—Not the slightest danger, I assure you on my honor!" And Dr. Losberne, saying the same things again and again, fussily assisted the ladies up the stairs.

8 Unofficial Investigation

"Now, ladies," said the doctor, in a whisper, as he softly turned the handle of a bedroom door, "tell me what you think of him. He has not been shaved very recently, but he doesn't look at all ferocious. Stop, though! Let me first see that all is in order for visitors."

Stepping before them, he looked into the room. Then, motioning that they should enter, he closed the door after them and gently drew back the bed curtains. Instead of the ruffian they had expected to see on the bed, there lay a mere youth, worn with pain and exhaustion, sleeping soundly. His wounded arm, now bound in splints, was lying over his breast.

The surgeon held back the curtain for several minutes in silence. And the younger lady, seating herself by the bedside, lifted Oliver's long, fair hair from where it streamed over his face. As she stooped over him, her tears fell upon his forehead.

"What can this mean?" inquired Mrs. Maylie, as she, too, looked at Oliver. "This poor boy is certainly not a robber!"

"Vice," sighed Dr. Losberne, replacing the curtain a moment later, "is too often hidden by a fair outside."

"But at so early an age!" Rose objected.

"My dear young lady," replied the surgeon, mournfully, "crime, like death, is not confined to old persons."

"But, can you really believe that this delicate boy has willingly joined a band of robbers?" asked Rose.

The doctor shook his head as if to say he had his doubts. Then, warning the ladies that they might disturb the patient, he led them into another room.

"But even if he has been wicked," argued Rose, "think how young he is! He may never have known a mother's love, or the comfort of a home. And ill-usage, blows, or hunger may have driven him into crime. Aunt, dear aunt! for mercy's sake, think of this before you let them drag this sick lad to a prison. Oh! as you love me, I beg you have pity upon him before it is too late!"

"My dear love," said the elder lady, embracing the distressed girl, "do you think I would permit more harm to come to him?"

"Oh, no!" Rose exclaimed, smiling in spite of her tears.

"My days are drawing to their close," continued Mrs. Maylie. "Doctor, what can I do to save him, sir?"

"Let me think, ma'am," said he. "Let me think." Then the doctor thrust his hands into his pockets and paced back and forth across the room for several minutes in silence.

"Well," said Dr. Losberne, at last, halting before the two ladies, "Mrs. Maylie, I have a plan to suggest—the only one I can think of. The boy will wake in an hour or so, I dare say. And I have told that thick-headed constable-fellow downstairs that the patient mustn't be moved or spoken to at present. But he may be strong enough for conversation after his rest. If you agree, I shall question him in your presence. Then, if you are convinced that he is a real and thorough bad one (which is more than possible), he shall be left to his fate, without any further interference on my part, at all events."

"Oh, no, aunt!" Miss Maylie begged.

"Oh, yes, aunt!" insisted the doctor. "Is it a bargain?"

"He cannot be hardened in vice," said Rose. "It is impossible."

"Very good," retorted Dr. Losberne. "Then so much the more reason for agreeing to my proposition."

Finally, the plan was entered into.

Oliver Twist slept heavily until evening. When he awoke, the doctor made sure that his patient was rested enough for him to endure the questioning that was in store for him. Besides, although the lad was ill and weak from loss of blood, he seemed to be very eager to tell something. Therefore, Dr. Losberne informed the ladies that the plan agreed upon would be tried at that time.

The conference was a long one. Oliver told them his story, often being interrupted by pain and weakness. All were impressed by hearing, in the darkened room, the feeble voice of the sick youth reviewing his sad record of evils and troubles that hard men had brought upon him.

Oliver's pillow was smoothed by gentle hands that night; and loveliness and virtue watched him as he slept. He felt calm and peaceful, and could have died happily right there.

Even the doctor, who had been hardened to many of life's circumstances, touched his eyes with his handkerchief, after Oliver concluded his story. Then he hastened down the stairs to find the servants. They were in the kitchen with the tinker and the constable.

The adventures of the previous night were being discussed again in full detail. Mr. Giles was praising himself highly for his presence of mind and bravery when the doctor entered. Mr. Brittles, with a mug of ale in his hand, agreed with everything Mr. Giles said. The latter offered his chair to Dr. Losberne.

"Sit still," said the doctor, waving his hand.

"Thank you, sir," Mr. Giles remarked, with some relief.

"The mistress said some ale should be given out. How is the patient tonight, sir?"

"So-so," replied the doctor. "I am afraid you have got yourself into a scrape there, Mr. Giles."

"I hope you don't mean to say, sir," said Mr. Giles, trembling, "that he's going to die. If I thought it, I could never be happy again. I wouldn't knowingly cut a boy off. No; not even Brittles here—not for all the plate in the country, sir."

"That's not the point," continued the doctor, mysteriously. "Mr. Giles, are you a religious man?"

"Yes—sir; I—hope so," faltered Mr. Giles, who had turned very pale.

"And what are *you*, boy?" demanded the doctor, turning sharply upon Brittles.

"Lord bless me, sir!" Brittles exclaimed, showing great surprise; "I'm—the same as Mr. Giles, sir."

"Then tell me this," ordered the doctor. "Both of you! Can you truthfully swear that the boy upstairs is the robber that was put through the little window last night? Out with it! We are prepared for you!"

The surgeon made this demand in such a dreadful tone of anger that Giles and Brittles, who were considerably muddled by ale and excitement, just stared helplessly at each other.

"Pay attention to the reply, constable, will you?" said Dr. Losberne, shaking his forefinger at the group very solemnly. "Something may come of this before long."

The constable nodded and looked as wise as he could.

"Here's a house broken into," added the doctor, "and a couple of men catch one moment's glimpse of a boy, in the midst of gunpowder smoke, confusion, and darkness. Then a boy comes to this house, next morning. Because he happens to have his arm tied up, these men lay violent hands upon him—thus placing his life in great danger—

and say he is the thief. Now, the question is, whether these men are justified by the fact. If not, in what situation do they place themselves?"

The constable nodded in full agreement and said, "If that ain't law, I'd be glad to know what is."

"I ask you again," thundered the surgeon. "Can you, on your solemn oaths, identify—do you *recognize* that boy?"

Brittles looked doubtfully at Mr. Giles. Mr. Giles looked doubtfully at Brittles. The constable put his hand behind his ear, to catch the reply. The two women and the tinker leaned forward to listen. The doctor glanced keenly around. Just then a ring was heard at the gate, and the rattling sound of wheels.

Brittles and Giles looked very much relieved; and the former, mumbling, "Expected them sooner," dashed out of the kitchen.

9 Is This the Robber?

"Who's that?" inquired Brittles, opening the door an inch or two, and peeping out, shading the candle with his hand.

"Open the door!" commanded a man outside. "It's the officers from Bow Street Police Station, as was sent to, today."

Much comforted by this assurance, Brittles opened the door to its full width and confronted a heavy man in a greatcoat. He walked in, without saying anything more, wiping his shoes on the mat as coolly as if he lived there.

"Just send somebody out to relieve my mate, will you, young man? requested the officer. "He's in the gig. Can you put it up for five or ten minutes?"

Brittles replied in the affirmative, pointing out the coach house. Then he got his lantern and proudly went with them to put up the gig. This done, they returned to the house, where Brittles showed them into a parlor.

"Tell your governor that Blathers and Duff is here, will you?" ordered the stout constable, smoothing down his hair and laying a pair of handcuffs on the table. "Oh! Good evening, master. Can I have a word or two with you in private, if you please?"

This was addressed to Dr. Losberne, who had just

entered. He motioned Brittles to retire, brought in the two ladies, and shut the door.

"Here is the lady of the house," said the doctor, presenting Mrs. Maylie. "And this is Miss Maylie. I am Dr. Losberne."

Blathers made a bow. After being invited to sit down, he put his hat on the floor, seated himself, and motioned Duff to do the same. The latter did so, but was plainly very uneasy.

"Now, with regard to this here robbery," Blathers began, "what are the circumstances?"

Mrs. Maylie lifted her hand toward Dr. Losberne, who told the story fully, but in a very roundabout manner. The police officers looked very knowing, meanwhile, and occasionally exchanged nods of understanding and agreement. When the tale was concluded, they agreed, unofficially, that the "work" must have been done by professional burglars.

"Now, what about this here boy that the servants are a-talking on?" asked Blathers.

"Nothing at all," replied the doctor. "One of the frightened servants thought that the child had something to do with the attempted robbery; but it's only nonsense!"

"Wery easy diposed of, if it is," remarked Duff.

"What he says is quite correct," observed Blathers, playing carelessly with the handcuffs. "But who is the boy? Where did he come from? He didn't drop out of the clouds, did he, sir?"

"Of course not," answered the surgeon, with a nervous glance at the two ladies. "I know his whole history; but we can talk about that presently. I suppose you would like, first, to see the place where the thieves made their attempt."

"Certainly," agreed Mr. Blathers.

Lights were then brought, and a complete inspection was made of the scene of the housebreaking. There was a full attendance of witnesses. All the known details were repeated and confirmed. Imaginary points of many kinds were suggested amid the excitement. Giles and Brittles were six times required to re-dramatize the heroic parts they played in the famous affair, contradicting each other again and again. Then Blathers and Duff cleared the room of witnesses, and held a long, secret, and solemn council together.

Meanwhile, the doctor walked restlessly around the next room; and Mrs. Maylie and Rose watched him and waited anxiously. They discussed the whole case at great length, realizing that Oliver's life-story, to date, contained many points that might be turned against him in the opinion of the police.

"The more I think of it," declared the doctor, "the more I see trouble ahead, if these officers hear the boy's whole story. For their own purpose, they will believe one thing and disbelieve another. Time will drag on. Publicity will be cruel. And your merciful plans for rescuing the lad from his misery might be defeated."

"Oh! what is to be done?" cried Rose. "Dear, dear! why did Brittles send for these people without consulting my aunt?"

"Why, indeed!" exclaimed Mrs. Maylie. "I would not have had them here for the world."

"All I know is," said Dr. Losberne, with a kind of desperate calmness, "that we must try to carry it off with a bold face. Our object is a good one. And the boy has strong symptoms of fever upon him. He is in no condition to be talked to any more at present. We must make the best of it; and if bad be the best, then it is no fault of ours—Come in!"

"Well," said Blathers, entering the room, followed by his associate, and closing the door carefully behind him, "this warn't a put-up thing."

"And what the devil's a 'put-up' thing?" demanded the doctor, impatiently.

"We call it a put-up robbery," replied Blathers, "when the servants is in it."

"Nobody suspected them, in this case," insisted Mrs. Maylie.

"Wery likely not, ma'am," Blathers put in, "but they might have been in it, for all that."

"More likely on that wery account," Duff added.

"We find it was a town hand," Blathers continued, "for the style of work is first-rate."

"Wery pretty, indeed, it is," echoed Duff, in an under-tone.

"There was two of 'em in it," continued Blathers, "and they had a boy with 'em. That's plain, from the size of the window. That's all to be said at present. We'll see this lad you've got upstairs at once, if you please."

"Perhaps they will have a little wine first, Mrs. Maylie," the doctor suggested, brightly.

"Oh! to be sure!" exclaimed Rose, eagerly. "You shall have some immediately, if you wish, gentlemen."

"Why, thank you, miss!" Blathers agreed, drawing his coat sleeve across his mouth. "It's dry work, this sort of duty. Anything that's handy, miss. Don't put yourself out of the way for us. It's a cold ride from London, miss."

Miss Rose went over to the sideboard to get the wine, while Mrs. Maylie engaged the policemen in further conversation. The doctor left the room quietly.

Soon the Bow Street officers became quite friendly and seemed to be enjoying a kind of social visit. Blathers related a long story of a case that he and Duff thought was similar to the present case in many ways. Dr. Losberne returned before the story had gone very far into fine points; and the little plan for delaying action seemed to be working out satisfactorily for Oliver's new friends. They encouraged the investigators to continue talking for a long time.

Finally, Blathers rattled his handcuffs and stood up straight, as if to remind everybody present that, after all, he was there on official business. The doctor "took the hint," and, sending for Mr. Giles and a light, he directed that famous hero to lead the group to the patient's room.

Oliver had been dozing, but looked worse and was more feverish than he had as yet appeared. Assisted by the surgeon, he managed to sit up in bed. He looked at the strangers without understanding what was going on. In fact, he did not seem to remember where he was.

"This," said Dr. Losberne, speaking softly, but with great feeling, and supporting Oliver with one arm, "is the lad, who was accidentally wounded by a spring gun in some boyish trespass on Mr. What-d'ye-call-him's grounds, at the rear of this house. He comes here, half-dead, for assistance this morning, and is immediately laid hold of and ill-treated by that brave gentleman there, holding the candle. His rough handling of the boy has placed his life in considerable danger. I can swear to that fact professionally!" The doctor kept his voice low, but anger flashed in his eyes.

Blathers and Duff looked pointedly at Mr. Giles. The bewildered butler gazed from them toward Oliver, and from Oliver toward Dr. Losberne, with a really comical mixture of fear and confusion.

"You don't mean to deny *that*, I suppose?" inquired the doctor, laying Oliver gently down again.

"It was all done for the—for the best, sir," answered Giles. "I am sure I thought it was the boy, or I wouldn't have meddled with him. I am not inhuman, sir."

"Thought it was *what* boy?" asked the senior officer.

"The housebreakers' boy, sir!" replied Giles. "They—they certainly had a boy."

"Well? Do you think so now?" inquired Blathers.

"Think what, now?" returned Giles, looking vacantly at his questioner.

"Think it's the *same* boy, stupid-head?" persisted Blathers, impatiently.

"I don't know, sir. I really don't know," said Giles, with a painful look. "I wouldn't swear to him."

"What do you *think*?" asked Mr. Blathers.

"I don't know what to think," replied poor Giles. "I don't think it *is* the boy. Indeed, I'm almost certain that it ain't."

"Has this man been a-drinking, sir?" inquired Blathers, turning to Dr. Losberne.

Dr. Losberne had been feeling the patient's pulse at times during this dialogue. He now rose from his chair and remarked that if the officers had any doubts concerning the sick lad, they should perhaps like to step into another room and question Brittles.

They thought they had better make sure; and the group adjourned to the next room. Mr. Brittles was called before them there. He involved himself and his heroic superior in a wonderful puzzle of fresh contradictions and impossibilities. His statements threw no certain light on anything but his own confusion, except as follows: He declared that he wouldn't know the real boy if he were put before him that instant; that he had thought the wounded boy was a robber, only because Mr. Giles had said so; and that Mr. Giles had admitted a short while ago in the kitchen that he was afraid he had been too hasty.

The question was then raised as to whether Mr. Giles had really wounded *anybody*. Besides, examination of the undischarged barrel of his pistol showed that it was loaded with nothing more destructive than gunpowder and brown paper. That discovery made a considerable impression on everybody but the doctor, who had removed the ball about ten minutes before. But Mr. Giles was more deeply impressed thereby than anyone else. After laboring for some hours under the fear of having mortally wounded a fellow creature, he caught at the new discovery eagerly. It relieved his fears. Finally, the Bow Street officers, without troubling themselves very much about Oliver, left the Chertsey constable on guard in the house and went into the town that night to rest, promising to return next day.

In the morning, further checking by those officials brought no new facts to light. Therefore, a neighborhood magistrate was readily persuaded to take the joint bail of Mrs. Maylie and Dr. Losberne for Oliver's appearance, if he should ever be called upon. And Blathers and Duff, after cheerfully accepting a couple of guineas for their trouble, returned again to London with divided opinions on the whole case.

10 *From Darkness to Daylight*

"Poor fellow!" exclaimed Rose one day, after Oliver had told her that, when he became really strong enough, he would do everything possible to show his gratitude for all that his kind friends had done for him. "We are going into the country, and my aunt intends that you shall accompany us. All the pleasures and beauties of spring will restore you in a few days. We will let you help in a hundred ways. And if you try to please us, you will make me very happy, indeed."

"Happy, Miss Rose!" cried Oliver. "How kind of you to say so!"

"You will make me happier than I can tell you," replied the young lady. "To think that my dear aunt has rescued one from such misery as you have seen would be a great pleasure to me. And then to find that the object of her goodness and mercy is sincerely grateful would delight me more than you can imagine. Do you understand me?" she inquired, watching Oliver's thoughtful face.

"Oh, yes, Miss Rose, yes!" declared Oliver, eagerly, "but I believe I am ungrateful now to certain persons."

"To whom?" the young lady asked.

"To the kind gentleman and the dear old nurse who

took such good care of me before," explained Oliver. "If they knew how happy I am, they would be pleased."

"I am sure they would," the kind young lady agreed, "and Dr. Losberne has already promised that he will take you to see them, as soon as you can bear the journey."

"How good of him!" cried Oliver, his face brightening. "I don't know what I shall do for joy when I see their kind faces again!"

Soon thereafter Oliver was sufficiently recovered to undertake that expedition. And one morning he and the doctor set out in a little carriage that belonged to Mrs. Maylie. When they came to Chertsey Bridge, Oliver looked frightened and uttered a loud exclamation.

"What's the matter?" queried Dr. Losberne, excitedly. "Do you see anything—hear anything—feel sick—eh?"

"*That*, sir!" cried Oliver, pointing out of the carriage window. "That house!"

"Yes; well, what of it?—Stop coachman! Pull up here," ordered the doctor. "*What* of the house, my man, eh?"

"The thieves—the house they took me to!" whispered Oliver.

"The devil it is!—Halloa, there! let me out!"

But before the coachman could dismount from his box, Dr. Losberne had jumped out of the coach. He ran down to the ramshackle place and began kicking at the door like a madman.

"Halloa!" called out a little, ugly humpbacked man, opening the door. "What's the matter here?"

"Matter!" the doctor exclaimed, collaring the stooped man without a moment's hesitation. "A good deal. Robbery is the matter!"

"There'll be murder the matter, too," threatened the humpbacked man, coolly, "if you don't take your hands off me! Do you hear?"

"I hear you," said Dr. Losberne, shaking his captive

roughly. "Where's—confound the fellow—what's his rascally name? *Sikes;* that's it! Where's Sikes, you thief?"

The humpbacked man stared in great surprise and anger. Then, twisting himself cleverly from the doctor's grasp, he growled forth a volley of horrid curses and turned back into the house. Before he could shut the door, however, the doctor had entered the front room. He looked anxiously around, but nothing that he saw there seemed to correspond with the description Oliver had previously given him of the place!

"Now!" shouted the humpbacked man, who had watched the doctor keenly, "what do you mean by coming into my house, in this violent way? Do you want to rob or murder me? Which is it?"

"Did you ever know a man come out to do either, in a chariot and pair, you ridiculous old leech?" asked the angry doctor.

"What do you want, then?" demanded the hunchback. "Will you take yourself off, before I do you a mischief? Curse you!"

"As soon as I think proper," replied Dr. Losberne, looking into another room, which, like the first, bore no resemblance whatever to Oliver's account of it. "I shall find you out someday, my friend!"

"Will you?" sneered the angry man. "If you ever want me, I'm here. I haven't lived here mad, and all alone, for twenty-five years, to be scared by you. You shall pay for this!" And so saying, he set up a yell and danced about as if wild with rage.

"Stupid enough, this," muttered the doctor to himself. "The boy must have made a mistake. Here! Put that in your pocket and shut yourself up again." With these words, the visitor flung the hunchback a piece of money and returned to the carriage.

But the man followed to the carriage door, uttering the

wildest threats and curses all the way. As Dr. Losberne turned to speak to the driver, the furious man looked into the carriage at Oliver with a glance so sharp and fierce that, waking or sleeping, the youth could not forget it for months afterward. Even after the driver had resumed his seat, and they were once more on their way, they could see the hunchback beating his feet upon the ground and tearing his hair in a great rage.

"I am a fool!" the doctor announced, after a long silence. "Did you know that before, Oliver?"

"No, indeed not, sir."

"Then don't forget it another time," continued the doctor. "An ass! Even if it had been the right place, and the right fellows had been there, what could I have done, single-handed? And if I had had assistance, I see no good that I should have done. I should have been compelled to make a statement of the manner in which I have hushed up this business. That would have served me right, though. I am always involving myself in some scrape or other by acting on impulse. It might have done me good—if I had lived through it."

Now the fact was that the excellent doctor enjoyed the warmest respect and esteem of all who knew him. But the affair with the hunchback left him out of temper for a while. He was disappointed in failing to find some proof of Oliver's story on the very first opportunity that presented itself. However, on questioning the lad further, and observing that his replies were now as straightforward as before, he felt better and decided that he would believe the young man fully.

As Oliver knew the name of the street in which Mr. Brownlow resided, they found it directly. On recognizing it, the lad's heart beat so violently that he could scarcely breathe.

The coach rolled on. When it stopped before the house

indicated by Oliver, however, his happy expectation received a cruel blow. There was a "To Let" card in the window, and the house was vacant! Worse yet, they learned from neighbors that Mr. Brownlow had sold his goods and gone to the West Indies, six weeks before. He was accompanied by a gentleman friend and Mrs. Bedwin. Oliver could scarcely endure the shock of that news. Nor did the doctor's refusal to try to find the bookseller make him feel any better!

"My poor boy, we have had disappointment enough for one day," insisted the doctor. "Quite enough for both of us. If we look for the bookseller, we shall certainly find that he is dead, or has set his house on fire, or run away. No; home again, straight!" And in obedience to the doctor's wishes, home they went.

That fruitless journey caused Oliver much sorrow, even amid his happy surroundings. He had pleased himself, many times during his illness, thinking of all that Mr. Brownlow and Mrs. Bedwin would say to him, and of all he would tell them about his recent adventures and his cruel separation from them. His heart was bursting with the desire to explain to them why he did not return from his errand with the books. Surely they had decided that he was a cheat and a robber.

But he still received an overflowing measure of kindness from his new friends. And, two weeks later, when the signs of spring were everywhere, Oliver Twist left the Chertsey home with the good ladies for a long stay in the country. The silver plate was placed in the hands of their banker; and Giles and another servant were made responsible for the town residence.

The country place was a lovely spot. Oliver seemed to enter upon a new life there. All of the beauties of the scene attracted him. The days were peaceful and serene. The nights brought him neither fear nor care. Every morning he went to a white-haired gentleman, who lived near the little church and who taught him to read better and to write. In his teaching, the learned gentleman was patient, kind, and painstaking; and Oliver could never try hard enough to please him.

After each period of instruction, the happy boy would walk with Mrs. Maylie and Rose, and hear them talk of books. Or he would simply sit near them, in some shady place, and listen while the young lady read aloud. In the late afternoons, he prepared his lessons. Between times, he ran errands and did everything he could think of to please the good ladies. In the evenings, Miss Rose played the piano and sang sweetly, to Oliver's great delight. And he looked

forward to each Sunday; for churchgoing, as well as Bible reading at home, were peaceful new experiences that seemed to help him, though he knew not why.

So passed three months of happiness for Oliver, before he realized how fast the days slipped by. But the youth who had known so much trouble and grief had grown stronger in spirit, mind, and body. And a deep and lasting affection had sprung up between him and his good friends, whom a kind fate had appointed as his guardians when he needed them most.

Part 4
Nancy's Decision

1 *Death Casts a Shadow*

Then came summer, in all its glory, to the countryside. The earth had put on her mantle of brightest green and shed her richest perfumes abroad. All things were glad and flourishing. And the same quiet and cheerful life went on at the little cottage.

One beautiful night, Mrs. Maylie, Miss Rose, and Oliver had taken a longer walk than usual. There was a brilliant moon, and a light wind had sprung up to refresh them after a very warm day. Rose had been in high spirits. But, after returning home and playing the piano for a few minutes, she showed signs of trying to control an outburst of weeping.

"My child!" exclaimed the elderly lady, going quickly to Rose and embracing her. "I never saw you this way before. Are you ill?"

"I would not alarm you if I could avoid it," Rose answered, "but indeed I have tried very hard, and cannot help this. I fear—I *am* ill, aunt!" Then she wept freely, as Oliver and Mrs. Maylie helped her to the sofa.

When candles were brought, it was plain to see that the girl was ill. Her face became very pale. And she had violent chills and a burning fever.

Oliver, who watched Mrs. Maylie anxiously, observed that she was alarmed by these signs; and so, in truth, was he. But, seeing that she tried to make light of them, he subdued his fears. Everything possible was done to relieve Miss Rose; and, later in the evening, when she seemed to feel better, she was removed to her own bed with aid of the servants.

"I hope," said Oliver, when Mrs. Maylie returned, "that nothing serious is the matter? She doesn't look well tonight, but—"

The good lady motioned to him not to speak and, sitting down in a dark corner of the room, remained silent for some time. At length, she said, in a trembling voice,

"She is very ill now and will be worse, I am sure. My dear, dear Rose! Oh, what should I do without her!"

Mrs. Maylie then gave way to such grief that Oliver, suppressing his own emotion, ventured to reason with her. He begged earnestly that, for the sake of the dear young lady herself, Mrs. Maylie should be more calm.

"And consider, ma'am," said Oliver, as the tears forced themselves into his eyes, despite his efforts to the contrary. "Oh! consider how young and good she is, and what pleasure and comfort she gives to all about her. I am sure that, for your sake, who are so good yourself, and for her own, and for the sake of all she makes so happy, she will not die. Heaven will never let her die so young."

"*Hush!*" requested Mrs. Maylie, laying her hand on Oliver's head. "You think like a child, poor boy. But you teach me my duty just the same! I had forgotten it for a moment, Oliver, but I hope I may be pardoned. I am old and have seen enough of illness and death to know the agony of separation from those we love. I have learned, too, that it is not always the youngest and best who are spared to us. But heaven is just. There is a brighter world than this, and the passage to it is speedy. God's will be done! I love her; and He knows how well!"

After that first anxious night, the morning revealed that Mrs. Maylie's predictions were too-well fulfilled. Rose was in the first stage of a dangerous fever.

"We must be active, Oliver, and not give way to useless grief," said Mrs. Maylie, laying her finger on her lip, as she looked steadily into his face. "This letter must be sent with all speed to Dr. Losberne. It must be carried to the market town, four miles away, by the footpath across the fields, and thence dispatched, by messenger on horseback, straight to Chertsey. The people at the inn will undertake to do this. I know I can trust you to see it done."

Oliver immediately showed his eagerness to do her bidding.

"Here is another letter," said Mrs. Maylie, pausing to think, "but whether to send it now, or wait until I see how Rose goes on, I scarcely know. I would not forward it, unless I feared the worst."

"Is it for Chertsey, too, ma'am?" inquired Oliver, impatiently holding out his hand for the letter.

"No," replied the old lady, giving it to him mechanically. Oliver glanced at it and saw that it was directed to Harry Maylie, Esquire, at some great lord's house in the country.

"Shall it go, ma'am?" asked Oliver, looking up anxiously.

"I think not now," replied Mrs. Maylie, taking it back. "I will wait until tomorrow."

With these words, she gave Oliver her purse, and he started off, without more delay, at the greatest speed he could muster.

Swiftly he ran across the fields and down the little lanes which divided them. Nor did he stop, except now and then for a few seconds, to recover breath, until, very hot and covered with dust, he entered the little marketplace of the town.

Finally locating the inn called "The George," he explained his errand to the landlord.

That gentleman walked slowly into the bar and still more slowly made out the bill for the service required. After Oliver paid him, a horse had to be saddled, and a man had to be dressed. Ten more minutes passed. Meanwhile, Oliver was in a desperate state of impatience and anxiety. At last, all was ready. The rider received the little parcel and full instructions from Oliver, set spurs to his horse, and galloped away.

Relieved by the knowledge that assistance had been sent for, Oliver hurried up the inn yard and out of the gateway. In his haste, he accidentally stumbled against a tall man wrapped in a cloak.

"Hah!" cried the man, glaring at Oliver and suddenly recoiling. "What the devil's this?"

"I beg your pardon, sir," said Oliver. "I was in a great hurry to get home—and didn't see you coming."

"Death!" muttered the man to himself, anger flashing from his large, dark eyes. "Who would have thought it! Grind him to ashes! He'd start up from a stone coffin to come in my way!"

"I—am sorry, sir," stammered Oliver, confused by the man's wild look and strange sayings. "I hope I have not hurt you!"

"Rot you!" grumbled the man, in a horrible rage. "If I had only had the courage to say the word, I might have been free of you in a night. Curses on your head, and black death on your heart, you imp! What are you doing here?"

Then the man shook his fist, advancing toward Oliver as if intending to strike him. The blow did not fall, but the man did; and Oliver was amazed to see him at his feet, writhing and foaming in a fit.

The frightened youth darted into the house for help. Several men hurried forth and carried the stricken man into the hotel. Then Oliver hurried homeward as fast as he could, to make up for lost time. He was filled with astonishment and fear as he thought of the horrible behavior of the stranger.

But, when he reached the cottage, there were other matters to occupy his attention. And all thoughts of himself were driven from his mind.

Rose Maylie had rapidly grown worse. Before midnight, she was delirious. A neighborhood doctor was attending her. After first seeing the patient, he had taken Mrs. Maylie aside and pronounced the girl's disorder to be one of a most alarming nature. "In fact," he said, "it would be little short of a miracle if she should recover."

The worried lad did not rest that night. He trembled every time he heard a sudden trampling of feet in or near the young lady's bedroom. And many were the prayers he offered to heaven for her recovery. To make his agony worse, he knew he could not help her directly.

Morning came at last; and the little cottage was lonely and still. People spoke in whispers; anxious faces appeared at the gate, from time to time; women and children went away in tears. Whenever there were no little services for him to perform that day, Oliver paced up and down the garden, often glancing anxiously at the bedroom window.

It was late at night when Dr. Losberne arrived. "It is too bad," said he at last, turning away from Rose as he spoke. "So young; so much beloved; but there is very little hope."

Another fearful night gave way to another morning. The sun shone bright; and, except for a few errands, Mrs. Maylie told Oliver he should feel free to roam about the fields. "None of us can do much more for dear Rose at present. Run in the sun and fresh air," she added, when she noticed that Oliver hesitated to be out of reach of her call.

The peace, beauty, and brightness everywhere improved Oliver's thoughts and made him more hopeful for Miss Rose, in spite of his cloud of anxiety. "Surely," he said to himself, "this shadow of death must be driven away from us. This is not a time for death. Rose must live!"

The afternoon wore on; and Oliver turned homeward. As if he were speaking to the songbirds overhead, he said, "She loves you and the flowers and all things beautiful. She had done so much to make our lives brighter. Oh, if only I could repay her now, for her kindness to me, by bringing back her health!"

At the cottage, Oliver found Mrs. Maylie sitting in the little parlor. Oliver's heart sank at the sight of her; for she seldom left the bedside of Miss Rose. What change could have taken place in his absence? Mrs. Maylie read his question in his face and simply said, "Rose is now in a deep sleep. She will waken either to recovery or to bid us farewell."

They sat listening and afraid to speak for hours. The evening meal, almost untasted, was removed. With looks which showed that their thoughts were elsewhere, they saw the sun sink lower and lower. After the sunset colors began to fade, their quick ears caught the sound of approaching footsteps. Dr. Losberne entered.

"What of Rose?" asked the elderly lady. "Tell me at once! I can bear it; anything but suspense! Oh, tell me! in the name of heaven!"

"You must compose yourself," said the doctor, supporting her. "Be calm, my dear ma'am, please."

"Let me go to her, in God's name!—My dear child!— She is dead!—She is dying!"

"No!" the doctor replied, emphatically. "As God is good and merciful, she will live to bless us all, for years to come."

The lady fell upon her knees and tried to fold her hands together in thanksgiving. But the shock of joy was too great for the weary lady; and Dr. Losberne caught her before her head could strike the floor.

2 *Hopes and Fears*

The good news meant almost too much happiness for Oliver to bear. He could not speak and could not sit still. He simply ran out of the house—ran across the fields until he had to stop to rest. Then the thrilled lad rambled around aimlessly in the quiet evening air.

Night was fast closing in when he turned homeward with flowers for the sick chamber. Oliver walked briskly along the road and soon came to the turning from which he could see the entrance to the Maylie cottage grounds. Just then he heard behind him the noise of some vehicle approaching at a furious pace. Looking around, he saw that it was a light carriage drawn by two fine horses. He stood against a gate, to be safe. As the post chaise dashed by him, the boy caught a glimpse of a man inside whose face seemed familiar to him. To his surprise, Oliver saw that the horses were now being slowed to a stop. Then he recognized Mr. Giles leaning out of the carriage and calling to him excitedly:

"Oliver, what's the news?—Miss Rose?"

Giles was suddenly pulled back by a young gentleman who occupied the other corner of the chaise, and who eagerly asked the same question, as Oliver came running up to them.

"Better—*much* better!" cried Oliver, trying to catch his breath.

"Thank heaven!" exclaimed the gentleman. "You are sure?"

"Quite, sir," replied Oliver. "The change took place only a few hours ago; and Dr. Losberne says that all danger is past."

The gentleman leaped out and took Oliver hurriedly by the arm, saying, as he led the boy aside,

"You are quite *certain*?—There is no possibility of any mistake on your part, my boy, is there? Do not awaken hopes in me that are not to be fulfilled." The stranger seemed to be very nervous.

"I would not for the world, sir," declared Oliver. "Indeed, you may believe me! Dr. Losberne declared that she would live to bless us all for many years to come. I heard him say so."

As the gentleman turned his face away and remained silent for a while, Oliver could see that he was greatly affected. So the lad remained respectfully silent. Giles, who had heard what was said, was also speechless with joy for the moment. Then the young gentleman turned around and addressed him:

"I think you had better go ahead in the chaise to mother, Giles. I would rather walk slowly on, so as to gain a little time before I see her. You can say I am coming."

"I beg your pardon, Mr. Harry," replied Giles, "but if you would leave the postboy to say that, I should be very much obliged to you. I don't want the maids to see me in this state, sir."

"Well," rejoined Mr. Harry Maylie, smiling, "you can do as you like. Let him go on with the luggage. You follow with us. But first exchange that nightcap for some more appropriate covering, or we shall be taken for madmen."

As the two men and he walked along, Oliver glanced

from time to time with much interest and curiosity at Mr. Maylie. He seemed to be about twenty-five years of age and was of average height. His countenance was frank and handsome, and his manner easy and friendly. Oliver observed that he bore a strong likeness to Mrs. Maylie.

She was anxiously waiting to receive her son when he reached the cottage. They did not try to hide their feelings when they met. After embracing his mother, Harry said, quietly, pleadingly,

"Mother! why did you not write me before?"

"I did," replied Mrs. Maylie, "but then decided to hold the letter until I had heard Dr. Losberne's opinion."

"But," insisted the young man, "why run the chance of that occurring which so nearly happened? If Rose had— I cannot utter that word now. If this illness had ended differently, how could you ever have forgiven yourself! How could *I* ever have known happiness again!"

"If that *had* been the case, Harry," said Mrs. Maylie, "I fear your happiness would have been surely blighted. Then your arrival here, a day sooner or a day later, would have been of little importance."

"And who can wonder if it be so, mother?" argued the young man. "Oh, why should I say *if?*—It *is*—you know it, mother—you must know it!"

"I know that she deserves the best and purest love the heart of man can offer," said Mrs. Maylie. "I know that her devotion requires no ordinary return, but one that shall be deep and lasting. If I did not feel this and know, besides, that a changed behavior in one she loved would break her heart, I should not feel my task so difficult when I take what seems to be the strict line of duty."

"This is unkind, mother," Harry continued. "Do you still suppose that I am a mere boy, ignorant of my own mind and mistaking the impulses of my own soul?"

"I think, my dear son," returned Mrs. Maylie, laying

her hand upon his shoulder, "that youth has many generous impulses, some of which do not last. Above all, I think that, if an enthusiastic and ambitious man marry a girl on whose name there is a stain, though it was not caused by her, it may bring cruel gossip upon her and upon his children also. And *he* may, no matter how generous his nature, one day repent of that marriage. Besides, his wife may suffer by knowing his regrets."

"Mother," declared the young man, impatiently, "he would be a selfish, unworthy brute who acted thus. My heart and soul—all my thoughts and plans—are wrapped up in my deep love for sweet, gentle Rose!"

"Dear Harry," said Mrs. Maylie, "it is because I think so much of warm and sensitive hearts that I would spare them from being wounded. But we have said enough—and more than enough—on this matter, just now."

"Let it rest with Rose, then," begged Harry. "You will not press these opinions of yours so far as to throw any obstacle in my way?"

"I will not," Mrs. Maylie assured him, "but I would have you consider—"

"I *have* considered!" was the impatient reply. "Mother, I have considered everything, for years. My feelings remain unchanged, as they ever will. Before I leave this place, Rose shall hear me."

"She shall," agreed Mrs. Maylie. "But, before you stake your all on this chance, just reflect for a few moments, my dear child, on Rose's history. Consider what effect the problem of her mysterious background may have on her decision, devoted as she is to both of us!"

"What do you mean?"

"That I leave for *you* to discover," replied Mrs. Maylie. "I must go back to her—God bless you!"

"I shall see you again tonight?" asked the young man, eagerly.

"By and by," replied the lady, "when I leave Rose."

"You will tell her I am here?"

"Of course," promised Harry's mother. "I will tell her all." Then, pressing her son's hand, affectionately, Mrs. Maylie hastened from the room.

Dr. Losberne and Oliver had remained at another end of the room while this hurried conversation was proceeding. The former now held out his hand to Harry; and the two exchanged hearty greetings. The doctor then told the young gentleman the whole story of Miss Rose's illness, assuring him she would recover. Harry showed great joy in his whole manner. Giles, who seemed to be busy about the luggage, listened meanwhile with greedy ears.

"Have you *shot* anything particular, lately, Giles?" inquired the doctor, when he had concluded his report to Harry.

"Nothing particular, sir," replied Mr. Giles, coloring up to the eyes.

"Nor catching any thieves, nor identifying any housebreakers?"

"None at all, sir," replied Mr. Giles, solemnly.

"Well," said the doctor, "I am sorry to hear it, because you do that sort of thing admirably. And, by the way, Giles, seeing you here reminds me: On the day before that on which I was called away so hurriedly, I completed, at the request of your good mistress, a small commission in your favor. Just step into this corner a moment, will you, Giles?"

Dr. Losberne then informed him in whispers that the favor, because of his watchfulness and gallantry during the attempted robbery, made the faithful servant twenty-five pounds richer than before: "It is in the bank, Giles! You may use it as you see fit."

With many bows and stammered thanks, Mr. Giles received the good news. Then he straightened up majestically and suddenly "remembered" something he had to do in the kitchen at once.

In the parlor, the remainder of the evening passed cheerfully, mainly because of the doctor's high spirits. He told many humorous stories, unmatched by the others. But everyone felt better, when, at a late hour, all retired for a much-needed rest. Oliver had no funny stories to tell, but was permitted to remain as a member of the party.

He arose next morning in better heart and went about his usual occupations with more hope and pleasure than he had known for many days. The dew seemed to sparkle more brightly on the green leaves; the air to rustle among them with a sweeter music; and the sky itself to look more blue and bright.

But Oliver's morning expeditions were no longer made alone. Harry Maylie accompanied him, helping to select fresh flowers to delight the heart of the young lady who was rapidly recovering. Otherwise, Oliver spent his time gladly performing his small duties and making rapid progress in his studies.

The little room in which he was accustomed to study was on the ground floor, at the back of the house. From the lattice window he could look into a garden, whence a wicket gate opened into a small paddock. Beyond was fine meadowland and wood.

One beautiful evening, at the end of a very sultry day, Oliver sat at the little window, intent upon his books. But, because of the heat and a strenuous day, he soon grew weary. He tried his best to keep fully awake, but a kind of half-conscious sleep overtook him.

The lad seemed to know perfectly well that he was in his own little room; that his books were lying on the table before him; and that the sweet air was stirring among the plants outside. Suddenly, the scene changed; the air became stifling; and he thought, with a feeling of terror, that

he was in Fagin's house again. There sat the hideous old man in his corner, pointing at Oliver and whispering to another man who sat beside him.

"Hush, my dear!" Oliver thought he heard the old man say. "*It is he,* sure enough. Come away!"

"*He!*" the other man seemed to answer. "Could I mistake him, think you? If a crowd of ghosts were to put themselves into his exact shape, and he stood among them, there is something that would tell me how to point *him* out. If you buried him fifty feet deep and took me across his grave, I fancy I should know, if there wasn't a mark above it, that he lay buried there."

Oliver felt that the man spoke with dreadful hatred. And it was then that the lad awoke with fear and jumped up.

Good heaven! What was that which sent the blood tingling to his heart, but which deprived him of his voice and strength? There—there—at the window—close before him—so close that Oliver could have almost touched him before he started back: With his eyes peering into the room, *there stood Fagin!* And beside him, white with rage or fear, or both, were the scowling features of the very man who had confronted the boy previously in the inn yard.

It was but an instant: a glance, a flash, before Oliver's eyes; and the figures were gone. But they had recognized him, and he them! And their gaze was as firmly impressed upon his memory as if it had been deeply carved in stone and set before him from the time of his birth. He stood immovable for a moment. Then, leaping from the window into the garden, the frightened youth called loudly for help.

3 *Love's Problems*

"Fagin! Fagin!"

Oliver practically screamed the name, as soon as he was in full possession of his wits.

"Fagin! Fagin!"

The frightened boy was standing, pale and highly excited, pointing in the direction of the meadows, when Giles and Harry Maylie came running to his aid.

"What direction did he take?" asked Mr. Maylie, catching up a heavy stick which was standing in a corner.

"That way," replied Oliver, staring across the meadows.

"Then they are in the ditch!" exclaimed Harry. "Follow!—You, Giles, keep as near me as you can." Springing lightly over the hedge, Mr. Maylie then darted off at great speed. He was eager for this chase, for his mother had told him Oliver's story.

Giles followed as fast as he could; and Oliver ran along, too. A minute or two later, Dr. Losberne, who had returned from a walk, tumbled over the hedge and dashed after them, shouting all the while, demanding to know what was the matter.

The search was continued for a long time, but all in vain. No traces of strange footsteps could be seen.

"It must have been a dream, Oliver," said Harry Maylie, during a pause.

"Oh, no, indeed, sir!" replied Oliver, shuddering at the very thought of the old wretch's face. "I saw Fagin too plainly for that. I saw them both, as surely as I see you now."

"Who was the other?" inquired both Harry and Dr. Losberne.

"The one I told you of, who came so suddenly upon me at the inn," said Oliver. "We had our eyes fixed full upon each other; and I could swear as to him. The tall man leaped over that hedge, just there; and Fagin, running a few paces to the right, crept through that gap, yonder there!"

The two gentlemen watched Oliver's earnest face, as he spoke; and, looking from him to each other, seemed to feel satisfied of the accuracy of what he said. Still, in no direction—not even in the damp ditches—were there any telltale signs of men in hurried flight.

"This is strange!" said Harry.

"Strange?" echoed the doctor. "Blathers and Duff, themselves, could make nothing of it."

Nevertheless, darkness having stopped the search in the fields, Giles was sent forth to the different alehouses in the village, furnished with the best description Oliver could give of the intruders. But the butler returned without any information that might have helped solve the mystery. Further efforts to trace Fagin and his companion, during the next several days, were also fruitless.

Meanwhile, Rose was rapidly recovering. She was now able to leave her room and go outdoors for short walks. Her presence brought joy to the hearts of all.

There were times, however, when Oliver felt as if happiness within the circle was dampened for some strange reason. Mrs. Maylie and her son were often closeted together for a long time; and more than once Rose showed traces of weeping. After Dr. Losberne had set the day for his return to Chertsey, these signs of trouble appeared oftener.

And then, one morning, when Rose was alone at breakfast, Harry Maylie entered. With some hesitation, he begged permission to speak with her for a few moments.

"A short time will suffice, Rose," said the young man, drawing a chair toward her. "What I have to say has already presented itself to your mind. My most cherished hopes are known to you, though you have not yet heard them from my own lips."

Rose had been very pale from the moment of his entrance. She merely nodded and, bending over some plants that stood near, waited in silence for him to speak.

"I—I—ought to have left here, before," Harry began.

"You should, indeed," replied Rose. "Forgive me for saying so; but—I wish you had."

"I was brought here by the most dreadful of all fears," continued Harry, "the fear of losing the dear one on whom my every wish and hope are fixed. You were at death's door. We all know, heaven help us, that the best and fairest of our kind too often fade in blooming!"

Tears came to the eyes of the gentle girl. One fell upon the flower over which she bent and glistened brightly in its cup.

"A fair and innocent creature," Harry resumed with great emotion, "fluttered between life and death. Rose, dear! Thoughts of what might happen filled me with great despair. Day and night I suffered an agony of fears and selfish regrets. I could not bear thinking that you might die without knowing my great love for you!—You recovered, little by little. I have watched you change, almost from death to life; and I became more certain each day of my deep affection for you. Do not tell me that you wish I had

lost all this, for it has softened my heart to all mankind."

"I do not mean that," said Rose, sobbing. "I only wish you had left here, that you might have turned to high and noble interests again: to pursuits well worthy of you."

"There is no pursuit more worthy of me, more worthy of the highest nature that exists, than the struggle to win a heart like yours," pleaded the young man, taking her hand. "Rose, my own dear Rose! For years I have loved you, hoping to win my way to fame and then come proudly home to tell you it was all for you to share. I dreamed of how I would remind you, in that happy moment, of the many silent tokens I had given you of a boy's attachment. I dreamed of how I would then claim your hand, as if to fulfill some silent contract that had been sealed between us! That time has not arrived. But here, with no fame won, and no young dream realized, I offer you the heart that has been so long your own, and stake everything upon the words with which you greet the offer."

"Your behavior has ever been kind and noble," said

Rose, controlling her deepest feelings. "As you believe that I understand and am not ungrateful, so hear my answer: You must try to forget me as the object of your love. Look into the world, where there are many hearts you would be proud to gain. Center some other feeling in me, if you will. I will be your truest friend."

There was a pause, during which Rose, who had covered her face with one hand, freely gave way to tears. Harry still held her other hand.

"And why, Rose," he said at length, in a low voice, "why this decision?"

"You have a right to know," responded Rose. "You can say nothing to alter my resolution. It is a duty that I must perform. I owe it to others and to myself."

"To yourself?"

"Yes, Harry. I owe it to myself, that I, a poor and friendless girl, with a blight upon my name, should not give your friends cause to suspect that I had schemed to fasten myself as a weight upon your future. I owe it to you and yours to prevent you from opposing such great obstacle to your progress."

"If your inclinations chime with your sense of duty—" Harry began.

"They do not," replied Rose, coloring deeply.

"Then you return my love?" asked Harry. "Say but that, dear Rose! Say but that; and thus soften the bitterness of this cruel disappointment."

"If I could have done so, without doing great wrong to him I loved," Rose answered, "I could have –"

"Could have received my declaration very differently?" continued Harry. "Do not conceal that from me, at least, Rose!"

"I could," Rose admitted. "Stay!" she added, taking her hand from his. "Why should we prolong this interview? It is most painful to me, and yet productive of lasting happiness, nevertheless. It *will* mean happiness for me to know that I once held the high place in your regard that I now occupy. And every triumph you gain in life will give me new strength. Farewell, Harry! As we have met today, we meet no more. But in relations other than those in which this conversation might have placed us, we can be long and happily associated. And may my earnest prayers bring forth many blessings to cheer and prosper you!"

"Another word, Rose," Harry begged. "Your *real* reason, from your own lips; let me hear it!"

"The prospect before you," answered Rose, "is a brilliant one. All the honors to which great talents and powerful connections can help men in public life are in store for you. But your connections are proud; and I will not mingle with those who may scorn the mother who gave my life. Nor will I allow myself to bring disgrace or failure to the son of her who has so well taken my own mother's place. In a word, there is upon my name a stain which the world visits on innocent heads. I will carry it into no blood but my own. I will bear it alone."

"One word more, dearest Rose!" cried Harry. "If I had been less—less 'fortunate,' the world would call it—if some hidden and peaceful life had been my destiny—if I had been poor, sick, helpless—would you have turned from me, then? Or has my probable advancement to riches and honor given you this idea?"

"Do not press me to reply," answered Rose. "The question does not arise, and never will. It is unfair—almost unkind—to urge it."

"If your answer be what I almost dare hope it is," retorted Harry, "it will shed a gleam of happiness upon my lonely way and light the path before me. Oh, Rose! in the name of my deep and enduring love; in the name of all I have suffered for you, and all that you doom me to undergo, answer me this one question!"

"Well, then, let's suppose your lot had been differently cast," rejoined Rose. "If you had been just a *little* above me, so that I could have been a help to you in some humble scene, instead of a drawback in high places, I should have been spared this trial. I have every reason to be happy now; but then, Harry, I admit I should have been happier—And now, I must indeed leave you," she concluded, extending her hand.

"I ask one promise," insisted Harry. "Once, and only once more—say, within a year, if not sooner—may I speak to you again on this subject, for the last time?"

"Not to press me to change my decision!" replied Rose, trying to smile. "It will be useless."

"No," said Harry, "to hear you repeat it, if you must— *finally* repeat it! I will lay at your feet whatever position I may hold. Then, if you still cling to your present resolution, I will not try to make you change it."

"Then let it be so," agreed Rose. "It means still more pain; but by that time I may be able to bear it better."

Then her lover embraced her impulsively, kissed her, and hurried from the room.

4 *A Departure and a Secret*

"And so you are resolved to be my traveling companion this morning, eh?" said Dr. Losberne, as Harry Maylie joined him and Oliver at breakfast. "Why, you are not of the same mind or intention two half hours together!"

"You will speak differently, one of these days," Harry predicted, coloring.

"I hope I may have good cause to do so," commented the doctor, "though I confess I don't think I shall. Yesterday morning, you had made up your mind suddenly to stay here a little longer and to accompany your mother like a dutiful son to the seaside. Before noon, you announce that you are going to do me the honor of accompanying me as far as I go, on your way to London. And at night, you urge me, with great mystery, to start before the ladies are stirring. The result is that young Oliver here is pinned down to his breakfast when he ought to be ranging the meadows. Too bad, isn't it, Oliver?"

"I should not want to be away from home when you and Mr. Maylie leave, sir," Oliver replied.

"That's a fine fellow!" exclaimed the doctor. "You shall come and see me when you return from the seashore. But, to speak seriously, Harry: Has any communication from the great nobs produced this sudden anxiety on your part to be gone?"

"The great 'nobs,'" replied Harry, "by which term I suppose you refer to my most stately uncle, has not communicated with me at all since I have been here. Besides, at this time of the year, it is not likely that there would be any reason for us to join in correspondence."

"Well," said the doctor, "you *are* a puzzling fellow. But of course they will elect you for Parliament before Christmas. And these sudden shiftings and changes are good preparation for political life."

Harry Maylie looked as if he could have followed up this dialogue by one or two remarks that would have staggered the doctor. But he contented himself with saying, "We shall see," and pursued the subject no further. The post chaise drove up to the door shortly afterward; and Giles came in for the luggage. Then Dr. Losberne bustled out to see it securely placed.

"Oliver," said Mr. Maylie, in a low voice, "let me have a word with you."

Oliver walked into the window recess to which Harry beckoned him. The boy was much surprised at the mixture of sadness and boisterous spirits displayed by young Maylie.

"You can write well now?" asked Harry, laying his hand upon Oliver's arm.

"I hope so, sir."

"I shall not be at home again, perhaps for some time. I wish you would write me—say, every other Monday, to the General Post Office in London. Will you?"

"Oh! certainly, sir; I shall be proud to do so," exclaimed the lad, with delight.

"I should like to know how—how my mother and Miss Rose are," said the young man. "And you can fill up a sheet by telling me about your walks, your conversations, and whether she—they, I mean—seem happy and quite well. You understand me?"

"Oh! quite, sir, quite."

"I would rather you did not mention this plan to them," Harry continued, hurrying over his words, "because it might make my mother anxious to write to me oftener. That would be a trouble and worry to her. Let this be a secret between us. And tell me *everything!* I'll depend upon you."

Oliver, pleased and honored by a new sense of his importance, faithfully promised secrecy and that his reports would be complete. Then Mr. Maylie took leave of him, with many assurances of his regard and protection.

The doctor was now in the chaise. Giles (who, it had been arranged, should be left behind) held the door open; and the women-servants were in the garden, looking on. Harry cast one quick glance up toward the latticed window and jumped into the carriage.

"Drive on!" he cried. "Hard, fast, full gallop! Nothing short of flying will keep pace with me today."

"Halloa!" cried the doctor, letting down the front glass in a great hurry and shouting to the driver. "Something *very* short of flying will keep pace with *me*. Do you hear?"

Jingling and clattering, the vehicle wound its way along the road, almost hidden in a cloud of dust. And one witness to the departure remained with eyes fixed a long time upon the spot where the carriage finally disappeared. Behind the white curtain, which had shrouded her from view when Harry raised his eyes toward the window, sat Rose herself.

"He seems in high spirits and happy," she said softly, as if someone were near her. "I feared for a time he might be otherwise. I am very, very glad."

But joy and gladness did not show themselves in her face, as she continued staring vacantly into the distance.

5   *Mr. Bumble's Fickle Fortune*

"I sigh," sighed Mr. Bumble. "I sigh ever so deeply! I sigh for things as once was. I am now master of the workus—but promoted out of my gold-braided coat and cocked hat and gilt-knobbed staff. A new beadle now wears my special dignity. Oh, dear; oh, dear!—And tomorrow, two months, it was done. It seems a age. I sold myself in marriage for six teaspoons, a pair of sugar tongs, a milk pot, some second-hand furniture, and twenty pound money. I went cheap—dirt cheap!"

Thus did Mr. Bumble bemoan the new state of affairs in which he found himself, early in the summer, as he sat drooping in the workhouse parlor.

"Cheap!" cried a shrill voice in his ear. "You would have been dear at any price; and dear enough I paid for you, as Lord above knows!"

Mr. Bumble turned to face the angry Mrs. B., who had heard at least the last few words of his complaint.

"Mrs. Bumble, ma'am!" exclaimed Mr. Bumble, with sentimental sternness.

"Well!" cried the lady, showing no signs of fear.

"Have the goodness to look at me," continued Mr. Bumble. Then he mumbled to himself: "If she stands such a eye as that, she can stand anything. It is a eye I never knew to fail with paupers. If it fails with her, my power is gone."

But the fierce glare that made paupers tremble did not overpower Mrs. B. Instead, she treated it with great scorn and even laughed in the great official's face.

Her own "B." could not believe his eyes or ears. He was completely amazed and did the only thing he could do safely—slumped down into his chair as if he were thoroughly beaten, with his once-powerful eyes tightly closed.

Then he breathed deeply, pretending to sleep, and awaited developments. But he did not have to wait long.

"Are you going to sit snoring there, all day?" demanded Mrs. Bumble, in a high-pitched voice. Hoping to regain a little of his dignity, Mr. Bumble let the clock tick along a few times before replying:

"I am going to sit here as long as I think proper, ma'am. And although I was *not* snoring, I shall snore, gape, sneeze, laugh, or cry, as the humor strikes me; such being my prerogative."

"*Your* prerogative!" sneered Mrs. Bumble, with supreme contempt.

"I said the word, ma'am! The *right* of a man is to *command*."

"And what's the privilege of a *woman,* in the name of goodness?" cried the relic left by poor Mr. Corney.

"To *obey,* ma'am!" thundered Mr. Bumble. "Your late unfortunate husband should have taught you that; and then, perhaps, he might have been alive—I wish he was, poor man!"

Mrs. Bumble was certain that the great moment had now arrived. She felt sure that a blow struck for control on one side or the other must now be necessarily final. Therefore, having heard that reference to the departed dear one, she dropped into a chair. Then, with a loud scream to the effect that Mr. Bumble was a hard-hearted brute, she gave way to a crying fit that should have temporarily softened the hardest of stony hearts.

"Crying opens the lungs, washes the countenance, exercises the eyes, and softens down the temper," lectured Mr. Bumble. "So cry away!"

As he delivered himself of this scientific knowledge, Mr. Bumble took his hat from a peg. He put it on rather rakishly, with a superior air. Then he thrust his hands into his pockets and sauntered toward the door.

Now the former Mrs. Corney had tried tears because they were less troublesome than physical combat. But she was quite prepared to try the latter mode of offense, if necessary, as Mr. Bumble was not long in discovering.

The first proof he experienced of that fact was a hollow sound, immediately succeeded by the sudden flying off of his hat to the opposite end of the room. As this preliminary laid bare his head, the expert lady, clasping him tightly around the throat with one hand, inflicted a shower of heavy, well-aimed blows upon that head with the other. This done, she created a little variety by scratching his face and tearing his hair. Then, pleased with Mr. Bumble's exterior decorations, she pushed him over a chair, which was luckily well placed for the purpose, and defied him to talk about his prerogative again.

"Get up!" cried Mrs. Bumble, in a voice of command. "And take yourself away from here, unless you want me to do something desperate."

Mr. Bumble rose slowly and painfully, looking quite abused, indeed, and wondering just what "something desperate" might be. Then, picking up his hat, he squinted uncertainly toward the door.

"Are you going?" demanded lovely Mrs. Bumble.

"Of course, my dear," rejoined Mr. Bumble, making a quick motion toward the door. "I didn't intend to—I'm going, my dear! You are so very violent, that really I—"

At that instant, Mrs. Bumble stepped hastily forward to replace the carpet which had been kicked up in the scuffle. Mr. Bumble immediately darted out of the room, leaving the former Mrs. Corney in full possession of the field.

But the measure of his disgrace was not yet full. After making a tour of the house, Mr. Bumble came to a room in which female paupers were washing the parish linen. Stopping outside the door, he heard the sound of loud voices.

"Hem!" said Mr. Bumble, summoning up all his natural dignity. "These women at least shall continue to respect the prerogative—Hallo! hallo, there! What do you mean by this noise, you hussies?"

Mr. Bumble opened the door and walked in with a very fierce and angry manner. But it was at once replaced by a frightened expression and bearing, for he unexpectedly beheld his gentle wife standing near the door.

"My dear," mumbled Mr. Bumble, "I—didn't know you were here."

"Didn't know I was here!" repeated Mrs. Bumble. "What do *you* do here?"

"I thought they were—talking rather too much to be—doing their work properly, my dear," ventured Mr. Bumble, glancing undecidedly at a couple of old women at the washtub. They had dropped their work and were looking him over, gleefully sneering at his appearance and defeat.

"*You* thought they were talking too much? What business is it of yours?"

"Why, my dear—" urged Mr. Bumble, pleadingly.

"What business is it of *yours*?" demanded Mrs. Bumble again.

"It's very true: You're matron here, my love," submitted Mr. Bumble. "But I thought you mightn't be on hand just then."

"I'll tell you *what,* Mr. Bumble," cried the sweet lady. "We don't want any of your interference. You're a great deal too fond of poking your nose into things that don't concern you, making everybody in the house laugh, the moment your back is turned, and making yourself look like a fool every hour in the day. Be off; come!"

Her own B., painfully observing the delight of the two old paupers, hesitated for an instant. Mrs. Bumble, impatient and determined, caught up a bowl of soapsuds and started toward him with it in her hands, ordering him instantly to depart.

What could the loser do? He looked helplessly around and slunk away. As he reached the door, the titterings of the paupers broke into shrill chuckles of delight. He was now degraded in their eyes.

"All in two months!" exclaimed the humble Mr. Bumble, as he left the house.

It was too much!—The brave gentleman boxed the ears of the boy who opened the gate for him and walked into the street.

He walked until exercise had subdued his fierce anger. Then he became thirsty. He passed a great many public houses, but at length paused before one in a byway. He peeped over the blinds. Only one customer was within. Then a heavy rain began to fall, and the retreating Bumble made his decision. Inside the tavern, he ordered something to drink as he passed the bar and continued through to the room wherein he had seen the lone patron.

Tall and dark, and wearing a large cloak, Mr. Bumble sized him up as a stranger. Judging from his haggard face and dusty clothes, the defeated one concluded that the man at the table had traveled some distance. Only cold, questioning eyes met Mr. Bumble's nod.

But the former beadle could show dignity enough for two; so he sat down and drank in silence, while reading a

paper as if nothing else were of interest to him. Every now
and then, however, he stole a glance at the stranger, only
to discover, each time, that the latter was also looking at
him, with distrust and suspicion. And Mr. Bumble would
then quickly turn his attention again to his paper, for he
did not like his fellow patron's scowl and sharp eyes.

"Were you looking for me when you peered in at the
window?" inquired the stranger, in a harsh, deep voice, at
least breaking the silence.

"Not that I am aware of, unless you're Mr.—" Here
Bumble stopped short, hoping the blank might be filled in.

"I see you were not," said the other customer, with a
slight, sarcastic smile," or you would have known my name.
I would recommend you not to ask for it."

"I meant no harm, young man," observed Mr. Bumble,
majestically.

"And have done none," said the stranger.

After another silence, the latter spoke again.

"I have seen you before, I think?" suggested he. "You
were differently dressed at that time. I only passed you in
the street, but I remember you. You were beadle here, once,
were you not?"

"I was," admitted Mr. Bumble, in some surprise. "Parochial beadle."

"Just so," added the other, nodding his head. "It was
in that character I saw you. What are you now?"

"Master of the workhouse," announced Mr. Bumble,
slowly and impressively, to check any possible undue fa-
miliarity. "Master of the workhouse, young man!"

"You have the same eye to your own interest that you
always had, I doubt not?" resumed the man of mystery,
looking keenly into Mr. Bumble's eyes, as they were raised
in astonishment. "Don't hesitate to answer freely, man. I
know you pretty well, you see."

"I suppose a married man," ventured Mr. Bumble, puzzled, surveying his companion from head to foot, "has no

more objections to turning an honest penny, when you can, than a single one. Parochial officers are not paid too well, you know."

The man across the table smiled and nodded his head again, as if to say he had not mistaken Bumble. Then he rang the bell and ordered the landlord to refill Bumble's empty glass.

"Now listen to me," said the stranger, a little later, after closing the door and window. "I came down to this place today to find you out. And, by one of those chances which the devil throws in the way of his friends, sometimes, you walked into the very room I was sitting in, while you were uppermost in my mind. I want some information from you. I don't ask you to give it for nothing, slight as it is. Put up *that,* to begin with."

As he spoke, he pushed a couple of one-pound gold coins very quietly toward his companion. With wide-open eyes, the humble Bumble carefully examined the coins, then slipped them into his waistcoat pocket. The stranger continued:

"Carry your memory back—let me see—twelve years, last winter."

"It's a long time," said Mr. Bumble. "Very good. I've done it."

"The scene: the workhouse?"

"Good!"

"And the time: night?"

"Yes."

"And the place: the crazy hole, wherever it was, in which miserable drabs gave birth to weak children for the parish to rear; and then hid their own shame, rot 'em, in the grave!"

"The lying-in room, I suppose?" suggested Mr. Bumble, not quite following the stranger's excited description.

"Yes," said the later. "A boy was born there."

"A-many boys," observed Mr. Bumble, shaking his head sadly.

"A plague on the young devils!" cried his fellow patron. "I speak of one: a meek-looking, pale-faced boy, who was apprenticed down here to a coffin maker. I wish he had made the boy's coffin and put him away in it. I mean the boy who afterward ran away to London, as it was supposed."

"Why, you must mean *Oliver!*—young Twist!" exclaimed Mr. Bumble. "I remember *him,* of course. There wasn't a obstinater young rascal—"

"It's not of him I want to hear. I've heard enough of him," declared the stranger, stopping Mr. Bumble at the outset of a long tale about poor Oliver's "vices." "It's of a woman: the hag that nursed his mother. Where is she?"

"Where is she?" asked Mr. Bumble, in his turn. "It would be hard to tell. There's no midwifery *there,* whichever place she's gone to. So I suppose she's out of employment, anyway."

"What do you mean?" came the stern demand.

"That she died last winter," Mr. Bumble explained.

The questioner looked fixedly at Bumble for some time afterward and seemed lost in thought. Finally, he breathed more freely, observing that it was no great matter. Then he arose, as if to depart.

But foxy Mr. Bumble at once got the scent of an opportunity for selling some secret possessed by his better half. He well remembered the night of Old Sally's death, for it was then that he had proposed to Mrs. Corney. True, that honey-sweet lady had never told him the whole story; but he had heard enough to know that Sally's last words had *some* connection with Oliver Twist's mother. So, thinking quickly, he informed his companion, with an air of mystery, that he knew *one* woman who had been close to the old hag at her death. And he hinted that the woman he referred to could probably throw some light on the stranger's inquiry.

"How can I find her?" asked the searcher, off his guard, but plainly showing that he was afraid of something.

"Only through *me*," suggested Mr. Bumble.

"When?"

"Tomorrow."

"At nine in the evening," the dark gentleman decided, writing upon a scrap of paper the address of a place by the waterside. "Bring her to me there. I needn't tell you to be secret. It's to your interest."

With these words, the mysterious one led the way to the door, after paying the bill. Then, repeating the hour of the appointment for the following night, he drew his black cloak tightly about him and stepped out into the driving rain.

On glancing at the address, the workhouse master observed that it contained no name. And, as the stranger had not gone far, he hurried after him.

"What do you want?" growled the man in the cloak, as Bumble touched him on the arm. "Are you following me?"

"Only to ask one little question," said Mr. Bumble, meekly, pointing to the scrap of paper. "What name?"

"Monks!" was the answer, as that gentleman strode hastily away.

6 *Can the Dead Tell Tales?*

"The place should be somewhere near here," mumbled Mr. Bumble, trying to read the scribbling on a scrap of paper that he held in his hand, as he and sweet Mrs. Bumble stood before an old ramshackle building in the rain.

The rumblings they had heard when they started off seemed to be coming closer now, giving promise of a heavy thunderstorm that was gathering force. Their shabby outer garments served the double purpose of protecting the couple from the rain and hiding them from observation. At that moment, however, no other human beings were abroad along the riverfront. The old factory and other scattered, broken-down buildings looked as if they might not remain standing much longer on the swampy ground.

"Halloa, there!" cried someone from overhead. Mr. and Mrs. Bumble felt uncomfortable for a number of reasons. One was that they believed gangsters made that district their headquarters.

Mr. Bumble glanced up and saw a man looking out from the second story.

"Stand still a minute!" came the command. "I'll be with you directly." And the head disappeared.

"Is that the man?" asked Mr. Bumble's worthy helpmate.

She could see Mr. Bumble nod in the affirmative.

"Then, mind what I told you," ordered the matron, "and be careful to say as little as you can, or you'll betray us at once."

If the truth must be told, the brave Bumble would have hurried homeward gladly at that moment. But Monks appeared at a small door near which they stood and beckoned them to enter.

"Hurry!" he cried impatiently, stamping his foot upon the ground. "Don't keep me here!"

Mrs. Bumble hesitated only slightly before entering. Mr. Bumble, who was ashamed or afraid to lag behind, followed, but was very ill at ease. And he seemed to lose some of his remarkable dignity.

Inside the damp and dingy old place, Monks first turned to the matron and then asked Mr. Bumble, "This is the woman, is it?"

"Hem!—*That* is the woman," replied Mr. Bumble, mindful of his wife's warning to be brief.

"You think women never can keep secrets, I suppose?" said Mrs. Bumble, returning Monks' searching look.

"I know they will always keep *one* till it's found out," said he.

"And what may *that* be?"

"The loss of their own good name," replied Monks. "So, by the same rule, if a woman is a party to a secret that might hang her, I'm not afraid she will tell it to anybody; not I!"

With half a smile and half a frown, Monks again beckoned them to follow him. He was preparing to ascend a steep ladder leading to another floor of storerooms, when a bright flash of lightning streamed down the opening. A peal of thunder followed, which made the crazy building and the two worthy visitors tremble.

"Hear it!" Monks cried, shrinking back and covering

his face with his hands. "Hear it! Rolling and crashing as if it echoed through a thousand caverns where the devils were hiding from it. I *hate* the sound!"

He remained silent for a few moments. Then, removing his hands suddenly from his face, showed, to the great discomfort of Mr. Bumble, that it was much distorted and discolored.

"These fits come over me now and then," said Monks, "and thunder sometimes brings them on. Don't mind me now. It's all over for this time. Follow me up the ladder."

On the floor above, they entered a very dirty room.

Hastily closing the window shutter, Monks lowered a lantern which hung at the end of a rope and pulley, and which cast a dim light upon an old table and three old chairs.

"Now," said Monks, when they had seated themselves, "the sooner we come to our business, the better for all. The woman knows what it is, does she?"

The question was addressed to Bumble; but his wife spoke quickly, making clear that she knew.

"Is he right in saying that you were with that old hag the night she died, and that she told you something—"

"About the mother of the boy you named," replied the matron, interrupting him. "Yes."

"What was the nature of her communication?" demanded Monks.

"Your question should be," observed the woman, coolly, " 'What may the communication be worth?' "

"Who can tell that, without knowing of what kind it is?" Monks asked, as a reply.

"Nobody better than you, I am sure," answered Mrs. Bumble, holding her ground.

"Humph!" cried Monks, meaningly, and with a look of eager inquiry. "There may be money's worth to get, eh?"

"Perhaps there may," was the cool reply.

"Something that was taken from her," suggested Monks. "Something that she wore. Something that—"

"You had better bid," interrupted Mrs. Bumble. "I have heard enough already to assure me that you are the man I ought to talk to."

Mr. Bumble, who had not yet been told much about the secret, listened with surprise.

"What's it worth to you?" demanded his beloved, eyeing Monks calmly.

"It may be nothing; it may be twenty pounds," Monks hinted. "Speak out, and I will know which."

"Add five pounds. Give me twenty-five pounds in gold," said Mrs. B., "and I'll tell you all I know; not before."

"Twenty-five pounds!" exclaimed Monks, drawing back.

"I spoke as plainly as I could," was the reply. "It's not a large sum, either."

"Not a *large* sum, for a little secret that may mean nothing when it's told!" cried Monks impatiently, "and which has been lying dead for twelve years past or more!"

"Such matters keep well and, like good wine, often double their value in time," continued the matron, still maintaining her outward indifference.

"What if I pay for nothing?" asked Monks, hesitating.

"You can easily take it away again," replied the matron. "I am but a woman, alone here and unprotected.

"Not alone, my dear, nor unprotected neither," suggested Mr. Bumble, in a voice trembling with fear. "*I* am here, my dear. And besides, Mr. Monks is too much of a gentleman to attempt any violence on parochial persons. He knows that I am not a young man; but he has heerd, my dear, that I am a wery determined officer, with uncommon strength, if I'm once roused. I only want a little rousing; that's all."

As Mr. Bumble spoke, he made a sad effort to grasp his lantern with fierce determination. And his alarmed expression showed plainly that he *did* require a little rousing before making any warlike move against Monks.

"You are a fool," declared Mrs. Bumble, in reply, "and had better hold your tongue!"

"He should have cut it out before he came!" exclaimed Monks, grimly. "So! He's your husband, eh?"

Mr. B.'s beloved merely tittered in reply.

"So much the better," rejoined Monks. "I have less hesitation in dealing with two people when I find that there's only one *will* between them. I'm in earnest. See here!"

He thrust his hand into a side pocket and, producing a canvas bag, counted out twenty-five sovereigns on the table and pushed them over to the woman.

"Now," he said, "gather them up!—And, when this cursed peal of thunder, which I feel is coming to break over the housetop, is gone, let's hear your story."

The thunder indeed seemed to break almost over their heads. Then Monks raised his head from the table and bent forward to listen to what the matron should say. The sickly rays of the suspended lantern made the three faces look extremely ghastly.

"When Old Sally died," whispered Mrs. Bumble, "she and I were alone."

"Was there no one else by?" asked Monks, in a hollow whisper. "And no wretch or idiot in some other bed? No one who could hear and understand?"

"Not a soul," replied the matron. "We were alone. *I* stood alone beside the body when death came."

"Good," said Monks, regarding her attentively. "Go on."

"She spoke of a young creature who had brought a child into the world some years before, not merely in the same room, but in the same bed in which she then lay dying."

"Ay?" said Monks, with quivering lip, and glancing over his shoulder. "Blood! How things come about!"

"The child was the one you named to *him* last night," continued Mrs. Bumble, nodding carelessly toward her husband. "It was the child's mother that old Sally had robbed."

"In life?" asked Monks.

"In death," replied Mrs. Bumble, with something like a shudder. "She stole from the corpse—when it had hardly become one—something which the dead mother, with her last breath, had begged that she should keep for the infant's sake."

"She sold it?" cried Monks, with desperate eagerness. "Did she *sell* it? Where? When? To whom? How long before?"

"As she told me, with great difficulty, that she *had* done this, she fell back and died."

"Without saying more?" queried Monks, in a voice which, from its very suppression, seemed only the more furious. "It's a lie! I'll not be played with. She said *more*. I'll tear the life out of you both; but I'll know what it was."

"She didn't utter another word," Mrs. Bumble insisted, to all appearance unmoved (as Mr. Bumble was very far from being) by the strange man's threat. "But she clutched my gown with one hand. And, when I saw that she was dead, and removed the hand by force, it held a scrap of dirty paper—a pawnbroker's duplicate."

"For what?" demanded Monks.

"In good time I'll tell you," the matron answered. "I think she had kept the trinket for some time, hoping to turn it to better account, and then had pawned it. But she must have scraped together enough money to pay the pawnbroker's interest, year by year, so that, if anything came of the trinket, it could still be redeemed. Nothing *had* come of it; and, as I say, she died with the worn paper in her hand. The time was to be out in two days. I thought, too, that something might one day come of it and so redeemed the pledge myself."

"Where is the trinket now?" asked Monks, quickly.

"There!" And, as if glad to be rid of it, Mrs. Bumble threw upon the table a small bag. Monks grabbed it and opened it with trembling hands. The trinket was a little gold locket, containing two locks of hair and a plain gold wedding ring.

"It has the name 'Agnes' engraved on the inside," the matron pointed out. "There is a blank left for the surname; and then follows the date, which is within a year before the child was born. I found out about that!"

"And this is all?" asked Monks, after closely and excitedly examining the locket.

"All."

Mr. Bumble drew a long breath, as if he were glad that the story was over, and that no mention was made of taking the twenty-five pounds back again. Then he wiped the perspiration off his face.

"I know nothing of the history. I can only guess," said his wife to Monks, after a short silence, "and I want to know nothing, for it's safer not. But may I ask you two questions?"

"You may ask," Monks replied with some show of surprise, "but whether I answer or not is another matter."

"Is that what you expected to get from me?"

"It is," admitted Monks. "The other question?"

"What do *you* propose to do with it? Can it be used against me?"

"Never!" declared Monks, "nor against me, either. See here!—But don't move a step forward, or your life will be the forfeit."

Then Mr. Monks suddenly pushed the table aside, and, grasping an iron ring in the floor, he threw back a large trapdoor. It opened near Mr. Bumble's feet, causing that brave gentleman quickly to move several paces backward.

"Look down," said Monks, lowering the lantern into the opening. "Don't fear me. I could have let you both down there quietly enough, if that had been my game."

Thus encouraged, the couple looked over the brink. The dark, muddy river water was rushing rapidly below. All other sounds were lost in the noise of its splashing against the green, slimy piles.

"If you flung a man's body down there, where would it be tomorrow morning?" asked Monks, swinging the lantern to and fro in the dark well.

"Twelve miles down the river—and cut to pieces besides," replied Bumble, shuddering at the thought.

Monks drew the telltale trinket from his breast pocket and, after tying it to a leaden weight that had been lying on the floor, dropped it into the stream.

The three, looking at one another, now seemed to breathe more freely.

"There!" exclaimed Monks, closing the heavy trapdoor. "If the sea ever gives up its dead, as books say it will, it will keep its gold and silver to itself, and *that* trash among it! We have nothing more to say and may now break up our pleasant party."

"By all means," observed Mr. Bumble, with great delight.

"*You'll* keep a quite tongue in your head, will you?" inquired Monks of him, with a threatening look. "I know your wife will."

"You may depend upon me, young man," promised Mr. Bumble, bowing himself gradually toward the ladder, with extreme politeness.

"I am glad, for your sake, to hear that," remarked Monks. "Light your lantern and get away from here as fast as you can!"

It was fortunate that the conversation ended then. Otherwise, Mr. Bumble, who had bowed himself back to within six inches of the ladder, would have fallen to the room below. He lighted his lantern and descended the ladder in silence, followed by his wife. Before Monks came down, he paused a moment to make sure that there were no sounds to be heard other than the beating of the rain without and the rushing of the water below.

In the lower room, he seemed frightened at every shadow. And Bumble, holding his lantern close to the ground, walked carefully and lightly, looking nervously around for hidden trapdoors. Monks opened the gate quitely. Then the two lovebirds, merely exchanging a nod with their mysterious host, were soon lost to view in the heavy rain and the blackness of the night.

Mr. Monks closed the gate after them as softly as he had opened it. Evidently he did not like to be left alone, for he then called to a boy who had been hidden in an old storeroom.

"Take the lantern and light my way up the ladder," Monks commanded him, and climbed after the boy to the room in which only the shadows and Monks himself held Mrs. Bumble's secret.

7 *Fair Wind or Foul?*

"Wot—wot's the time?"

Mr. William Sikes was awakening from a nap on the following evening when he growled forth that inquiry.

His cheap, poorly furnished room, was located not far from his former lodgings. It was very small, lighted only by one narrow window in the shelving roof, and overlooking a dirty lane. Clearly, Mr. Sikes had gone down in the world lately, as shown not only by the kind of room he was occupying, and its location, but also by the poor quality of its few pieces of furniture.

And Bill's appearance likewise was proof of his reduced circumstances. He was lying on an old bed, in his soiled and worn dressing gown. On his head was a dirty nightcap. In spite of a week's growth of black beard, his face showed that he now was and had been very ill.

Bull's-eye sat at the low bedside, eyeing his master closely, pricking his ears and growling whenever he heard the slightest noise.

A girl was sitting by the window, patching an old waistcoat of Bill's. She was thin and pale, for want of proper food, and because of taking care of Mr. Sikes. But for her voice, when she replied to Bill's inquiry, it would have been difficult to recognize her as Nancy.

261

"Not long after seven. How do you feel tonight?"

"As weak as water," replied Mr. Sikes, cursing his eyes and limbs. "Here: Lend a hand, and let me get off this imitation bed."

Illness had not improved Bill's temper. As the girl helped him to a chair, he muttered various curses on her awkwardness and struck her. Nancy turned away in tears.

"Whining, are you?" jeered Sikes. "Come! Don't stand crying there. If you can't do anything better than that, cut off altogether. D'ye hear me?"

"I hear you," replied Nancy, forcing a laugh. "What fancy have you got in your head now?"

"Oh! you've thought better of it, have you?" growled Sikes. "All the better for you, if you have!"

"Why, you don't mean to say you'd be hard upon me tonight, Bill," pleaded the girl, laying her hand upon his shoulder.

Mr. Sikes shouted, "Why not?"

"Many nights," answered the girl, with a touch of woman's tenderness in her voice, "I've been patient with you, nursing and caring for you, as if you had been a child. And this is the first time that I've seen you like yourself. You wouldn't have served me as you did just now, if you'd thought of that, would you? Come, come. Say you wouldn't."

"Well, then," admitted Mr. Sikes, "I wouldn't. Why, look, now, you're whining again!"

"It's nothing," said the girl, dropping into a chair. "Don't mind me. It'll soon be over."

"What'll be over?" demanded Bill in a savage voice. "What foolery are you up to now, again? Get up and bustle about, and don't try me with your woman's nonsense!"

But Nancy, being very weak, leaned back in the chair and fainted, before Mr. Sikes could swear at her in his usual

fashion. Not knowing just what to do alone, under the circumstances, Bill called for assistance.

"What's the matter here, my dear?" asked Fagin, looking in.

"Help her, can't you?" growled Sikes, impatiently. "Don't stand chattering and grinning at me!"

With an exclamation of surprise, Fagin hastened to the girl's assistance, while Mr. John Dawkins (the Artful Dodger), who had followed his dear friend into the room, hastily deposited on the floor a large bundle he was carrying. Then he snatched a bottle from the grasp of Master Charles Bates, who stood nearby, and, after tasting its contents, poured a portion down the patient's throat.

"Give her a whiff of fresh air with the bellows, Charley," ordered Mr. Dawkins, "and you slap her hands, Fagin."

Thanks to either these proceedings or nature's secret powers, Nancy gradually recovered. Then Sikes turned at once upon his unexpected visitors.

"Why, what evil wind has blowed you here?" he demanded of Fagin.

"No evil wind at all, my dear, for evil winds blow nobody any good. I've brought something good with me that you'll be glad to see. Dodger, my dear, open the bundle and give Bill the little trifles that we spent all our money on this morning."

Obeying, the Artful untied his bundle and handed the articles it contained, one by one, to Charley Bates. That cheerful gentleman placed them on the table, with various complimentary remarks about their rare and excellent qualities.

"Ah!" said Fagin, rubbing his hands with great satisfaction at the display. "You'll do, Bill; you'll do now. Fine expensive food and drink for you."

"Do!" exclaimed Mr. Sikes. "I might have been *done*

for, twenty times over, afore you'd have come to help me. What do you mean by leaving me in this state, three weeks and more, you false-hearted wagabond?"

"Only hear him, boys!" cried Fagin, shrugging his shoulders. "And us come to bring him all these beautiful things."

"The things is well enough, in their way," observed Mr. Sikes, a little soothed as he glanced over the table. "But what have you got to say for *yourself,* why you should leave me here, down in the mouth and everything else, and take no more notice of me, all this time, than if I was that 'ere dog?—Well, what have you got to say?"

"Easy, my dear, easy!—I was away from London, a week and more, on a plant," replied the old man.

"And what about the other two weeks?" demanded Sikes—"that *other* fortnight, when you left me here like a sick rat in his hole?"

"I couldn't help it, Bill. I can't explain before company. But I couldn't help it, upon my honor."

"Upon your *what?*" jeered Sikes. "Here! Cut me off a piece of that meat pie, one of you boys, to take the taste of that cheap wine out of my mouth, or it'll choke me to death."

"Don't be out of temper, my dear," urged Fagin, softly. "I have *never* forgot you, Bill; never once."

"No! I'll bet a pound that you hadn't," replied Sikes, with a bitter grin. "You've been scheming every hour that I have laid shivering and burning here. You were planning how Bill could do *this;* how Bill could do *that;* and how Bill could do it *all,* dirt cheap, as soon as he got well and was quite *poor* enough. If it hadn't been for the girl, I might have died."

"There now, Bill—If it hadn't been for the girl!—Who but poor old Fagin was the means of your having such a handy girl about you?"

"He says true enough there!" cried Nancy, coming hastily forward. "Let him be; let him be!"

Nancy's presence gave a new turn to the conversation, for the boys, receiving a sly wink from their clever old master, began to offer her wine. She took very little, however. And Fagin, playing his part, gradually brought Mr. Sikes around to a better temper by pretending that his threats were just in fun. Furthermore, the old man laughed at the rough jokes that Sikes told after taking several strong drinks. But the robber kept his wits, for, suddenly turning on Fagin after a while, he said,

"It's all very well; but I must have some money from you tonight!"

"I haven't a coin about me," whined the master.

"Then you've got lots at home!" Sikes flared back. "Get me some from there."

"Lots!" cried Fagin holding up his hands. "I haven't so much as would—"

"I don't know how much you've got! And I dare say you hardly know yourself, as it would take a pretty long time to count it," bawled Sikes. "But I must have some *now;* and that's flat!"

"Well, well," said Fagin, with a sigh, "I'll send the Artful around presently."

"You won't do nothing of the kind!" shouted Mr. Sikes. "The Artful's a deal too artful, and would forget to come back, or lose his way—or anything for an excuse, if you put him up to it. *Nancy* shall go to the den and fetch it, to make all sure, while I lie down and have a snooze."

After a great deal of squabbling, Fagin beat down the amount of the required advance from five pounds to three pounds and a little over four shillings, protesting with many curses that that would leave him only a few pennies for housekeeping. Then the chief told Nancy to accompany him home and directed the boys to put the eatables in the cupboard and go along. With a loving "good-bye" to Bill, Fagin next gave the signal for his three followers to leave the room quietly. Sikes sprawled upon the bed and was soon sleeping heavily.

When they arrived at Fagin's hideout, they found Toby Crackit and Mr. Chitling playing cards. The latter fine gentleman had lost, and Toby was poking fun at him. Sweetly but firmly, their master ordered them to leave, after he learned that no visitors had stopped in.

Then, turning to the boys who had entered with him, he spoke sharply: "Dodger! Charley! It's time you were on the lay. Come! It's near ten, and nothing done yet."

Obediently, the boys, nodding to Nancy, took up their hats and left the room.

"Now," said Fagin to Nancy, "I'll get you that cash. Here is my key to the little cupboard where I keep a few odd things for the boys, my dear. I never lock up my money, for I've got none to lock up, my dear—ha! ha! ha!—none to lock up. It's a poor trade, Nancy, and no thanks! But I'm fond of seeing the young people about me. And I bear it all; I bear it all—Hush!" he said, hastily thrusting the key into a pocket. "Who's that? Listen!"

The girl, who was sitting at the table with her arms folded, appeared in no way interested until she heard the sound of a man's voice outside. Then she instantly removed her bonnet and shawl, thrusting them under the table, while Fagin stood listening at the door. When he turned toward her, she acted as unconcerned as before and, in a careless tone, complained of the hot room.

"Bah!" whispered Fagin, as if annoyed by the interruption. "It's the man I expected before; he's coming here. Not a word about the money while he's here, Nance! He won't stop long. Not ten minutes, my dear."

Laying a skinny finger upon his lips, the master reached for a lighted candle, as a man's step was heard upon the stairs. After being admitted, the visitor was close to the girl before he noticed her.

Their guest was Monks!

"Only one of my young people," said Fagin, observing that Monks drew back on beholding a stranger. "Don't leave, Nancy."

The girl moved closer to the table and, glancing quickly at Monks with a carefree smile, as quickly turned away. But, when he turned toward Fagin, she stole another look: keen, searching, and full of purpose.

"Any news?" inquired Fagin.

"Great. Well, not bad, at any rate," Monks replied with a smile. "I have been prompt enough this time. Let me have a word with you."

Fagin pointed upward; and he and Monks then left the room.

"Not that infernal hole we were in before!" she heard the visitor say, as they went upstairs. Fagin laughed and, making some reply which Nancy could not hear, seemed, by the creaking of the boards, to lead his companion to the second story.

Before the sound of their footsteps had ceased to echo through the house, the girl had removed her shoes. Then, drawing her shawl loosely over her head, and covering her arms with it, she stood at the door, listening with great interest. The moment the noise above ceased, she glided from the room, went up the stairs very softly, and stood quietly on the landing in the darkness.

A quarter of an hour later, Nancy crept back with the same silent tread. Almost immediately afterward, she heard the two men descending. Monks went at once into the street; and Fagin shuffled upstairs again. When he returned, the girl was putting on her shawl and bonnet, as if preparing to leave.

"Why, Nance," exclaimed Fagin, starting back as he put down the candle, "how pale you are!"

"Pale!" echoed the girl, shading her eyes with her hands and looking steadily at him.

"Quite horrible! What have you been doing?"

"Nothing that I know of, except sitting in this close place for I don't know how long, and all," replied the girl, carelessly. "Come! Let me get back; that's a dear."

With a sigh for every piece of money, Fagin counted out the required amount into her hand. Then they parted, exchanging with each other only a "good night."

In the open street, Nancy sat down upon a doorstep and seemed, for a few moments, quite confused. Suddenly she arose and hurried away, but not in the direction that would have led her toward Sikes. For a while she actually ran, but became completely exhausted and had to stop to rest.

As if suddenly remembering her real errand, and regretting that she could not do what she had planned, she began to cry. A short time later, she managed to control her outburst and, probably realizing that there was no other way, turned back. Forcing herself to hurry as much as possible, she soon reached the dwelling in which she had left the robber, but paused long enough outside to catch her breath before entering.

If Nancy betrayed any nervousness when she presented herself to Mr. Sikes, he did not observe it. He sat up in bed only long enough to make sure that she had brought the money. Then, with a growl of satisfaction, he dropped back and fell asleep again.

Next day, the possession of money gave Bill plenty of employment in the way of eating and drinking. His temper smoothed down so much that he paid little attention to Nancy. That was lucky for her, because otherwise, he would have noticed her restless manner, which showed signs of some bold scheme in the making.

But the girl's excitement increased during that day. As night came on, she sat watching until Sikes should drink himself to sleep. There was an unusual paleness in her cheeks and a fire in her eyes. Suddenly, as he pushed his glass toward her to be filled, he happened to look directly into her face.

"Why, burn my body!" cried Bill, raising himself from the bed. "You look like a corpse come to life again. What's the matter?"

"Matter!" replied the girl. "Nothing! Why do you look at me that way?"

"What foolery is this?" demanded Sikes, grasping her by the arm and shaking her roughly. "What is it? What do you mean? What are you thinking of?"

"Of many things, Bill," answered Nancy, shivering and pressing her hands upon her eyes. "But, Lord! What odds in that?" She laughed, pretending to be gay.

"I tell you wot it is," said Sikes. "If you haven't caught the fever and got it comin' on, now, there's something unusual in the wind, and something dangerous, too! You're not a-going to—No! you wouldn't do *that*!"

"Do what?" asked the girl.

Sikes stared at her steadily, saying, as if to himself, "There ain't a stauncher-hearted gal going, or I'd have cut her throat three months ago. She's got the fever coming on; that's it."

Then, with many grumbling oaths, the robber called for his medicine. The girl jumped up quickly, poured it with her back toward him, and held the vessel to his lips. He drank the mixture and scowled.

"Now," said Sikes, "come, sit beside me, and put on your *own* face, or I'll alter it so that you won't know it again when you *do* want it."

The girl obeyed. Sikes, locking her hand in his, fell back upon the pillow. His eyes closed, opened again, and closed once more. He tried to raise himself, fighting the heavy sleep that was coming upon him, but finally gave up the struggle.

"The *laudanum* has put him to sleep at last!" murmured Nancy to herself, as she rose from the bedside. "But I may be too late, even now."

After quickly putting on her bonnet and shawl again, and making sure that Sikes could not interfere, Nancy left the room very quietly.

As she hurried through the back lanes and avenues leading from Spitalfields toward the wealthy West End of London, a clock struck ten. Her impatience increased. She tore along the narrow pavement, elbowing her way through the crowds, and barely escaping injury in crossing the streets.

When Nancy came close to her destination in the fashionable quarter, however, the streets were almost deserted.

The family hotel she was looking for was near Hyde Park. It was eleven o'clock when she came to the brightly lighted doorway. She hesitated for a moment or two, and then stepped into the hall and looked around uncertainly.

"Now, young woman!" said a neatly dressed maid. "What is it you want here?"

"To see a lady who is stopping in this house," answered the girl.

"A lady?—What lady?"

"Miss Maylie," said Nancy, as the other girl looked her over.

The maid called a uniformed waiter to whom Nancy repeated her request.

"What name am I to say?" asked the waiter.

"It's of no use saying any," replied Nancy.

"Come!" said the man, pushing her toward the door. "None of this! Take yourself off."

"I shall be carried out, if I go!" said the girl, fiercely. "And I can make that a job which *two* of you won't like. Isn't there anybody here that will see a simple message carried for a poor wretch like me?"

This appeal produced an effect on a kind-faced cook, who, with some of the other servants, was looking on. He stepped forward.

"Take it up for her, Joe, can't you?" said he to the waiter.

"What's the good?" was the reply. "You don't suppose Miss Maylie will see such as her, do you? We should throw her out!"

"Do what you like with me," said the girl, turning to the men again. "But do what I ask you, first. I beg you to deliver this message for God Almighty's sake."

The cook added his plea.

"Well, what's it to be?" asked the waiter, with one foot on the stairs.

"That a young woman earnestly begs to speak to Miss Maylie alone," said Nancy, "and that, if the lady will only hear the first word, she will know whether to learn her business, or to have her turned out of doors."

The man ran upstairs and soon returned, saying that the visitor would be received.

Trembling and excited, Nancy followed him to a kind of parlor where she sat down. Then he left her there to wait for Miss Maylie.

8 *Bittersweet News*

From another room, Rose Maylie soon appeared, slight and pale, but beautiful.

"It's a hard matter to get to see you, lady," declared Nancy. "If I had taken offense and gone away, you'd have had good reason to regret it one day."

"I am very sorry if anyone has been harsh with you," replied Rose. "Please forget that. Tell me why you wished to see me."

Completely surprised by the sweet voice and the gentle manner, Nancy burst into tears.

"Oh, lady, lady!" she exclaimed with difficulty, "if there was more like you, there would be fewer like me. There would—indeed!"

"Sit down," said Rose, quietly. "If you are in great need, I shall be truly glad to help you all I can. Please sit down."

"Let me—stand, lady," said the girl, still weeping, "and do not speak to me so—kindly, before you know me better. It is growing late. Is—is—that door shut—tight?"

"Yes," Rose replied, wonderingly. "Why?"

"Because," said Nancy, regaining control of herself, "I am about to put my life and the lives of others in your hands. I am the girl—that dragged little Oliver back to old

274

Fagin, on the night the poor child went out from the house in Pentonville with his package of books."

"You!" Rose Maylie was astonished.

"I, lady!" exclaimed the visitor. "*I* am the shameful creature you have heard of, that lives among thieves and that never, from the first moment I can remember, has known any better life! Do not mind shrinking openly from me, lady."

"What dreadful things you tell me!" cried Rose, backing away from her strange companion without realizing it.

"Thank heaven upon your knees, dear lady, that you had friends to care for and keep you in your childhood, and that you were protected from cold, hunger, and drunkenness; and—and—many worse things that I have known. Yes: The alley and the gutter were mine—and will be my deathbed."

"I pity you!" declared Rose, in a broken voice. "It breaks my heart to hear you!"

"Heaven bless you for your goodness!" replied Nancy. "I have slipped away from those who will surely murder me, if they learn I have been here to tell you these things. Do you know a man named Monks?"

"No," Miss Maylie answered, with surprise.

"He knows *you*—and knows you are here—for it was by hearing him name this place that I found you."

"I never heard of him!" Rose insisted.

"Then he goes by some other name amongst us," declared Nancy, "which I felt sure of before. Some time ago— soon after Oliver was put into your house on the night of the robbery, I—suspecting this man—listened to a conversation between him and Fagin in the dark. I found out then that Monks had seen the sweet lad accidentally, with two of our boys, on the day we first lost him, and had recognized him as the same child that he was watching for, though I couldn't make out why. A bargain was struck with Fagin: If Oliver was brought back, the old man should have a certain sum; and he was to have more for making the lad a thief, which Monks desired for some purpose of his own."

"Why?" asked Miss Maylie.

"He caught sight of my shadow on the wall, as I listened in the hope of finding out," said her visitor. "I had to get away quickly and so learned nothing more at that time.

"Last night Monks came again; and again he and Fagin went upstairs. Wrapping myself up, so that my shadow should not betray me, again I listened at the door. The first words I heard Monks say were: 'So the only proofs of the boy's real name lie at the bottom of the river. And the old hag that received them from the mother is rotting in her coffin.' Both men then laughed. Fagin congratulated

Monks, who then talked on and on about the boy. Becoming very excited, Monks said that, though he had got the young devil's money safely now, he'd rather have had it the *other* way. In speaking of the father's will, Monks revealed his own plot. He wanted to drive the lad through every jail in town and then have him convicted of some great crime, which Fagin could easily manage, after having made a good profit besides. And then—then the boy's neck would be stretched!"

"What *is* all this!" Rose exclaimed, pale as death.

"The truth, lady, though it comes from my lips," replied Nancy. "Then Monks said, with oaths common enough in my ears, but strange to yours, that, if he could take the boy's life without risking his own neck, he would gladly do so. Instead, Monks told Fagin he'd be on the watch for the boy at every turn in life. 'In short, Fagin,' he said, 'you never laid such traps as I'll make ready for my young brother Oliver.' "

"His *brother!*" exclaimed Rose.

"Those were his words, and more," insisted Nancy. "He spoke of you and the older lady, and said it seemed a plot by heaven or the devil, against him, that Oliver should come into your hands. Then he laughed! Yet he spoke in hard and angry earnest, if a man ever did. But it is growing late. I must get back quickly. They must not suspect me."

"But what can *I* do?" begged Rose. "What can I do without having *you* here? Why do you wish to go back to such companions? Stay with me! In half an hour I can have you made safe. Please!"

But Nancy turned her face slightly away from Rose's gaze. "I wish to go back. I *must* go back, because—because, among the men I have told you of, there is one— the most desperate of them—that I can't leave; no, not even to be saved from the life I am leading now."

"Your having interfered for dear Oliver before," said Rose, "your coming here, at so great a risk; your manner, which convinces me of the truth of what you say—all lead me to believe that you might be saved. Oh! do not turn a deaf ear to my pleadings. Let me save you for better things!"

"Sweet lady!" Nancy was deeply affected by Miss Maylie's kindness. "You are the first person that ever blessed me with such words. But it is now too late, too late!"

"It is never too late," argued Rose, "to lead a better life."

"It *is*," cried the girl, in great agony of mind. "I cannot leave that *one* man now! I could not deliberately cause *his* death."

"But how should you?" Miss Maylie demanded.

"Nothing could save him," insisted Nancy. "If I told others what I have told you, and led to the capture of those criminals, *he* would be sure to die. He is the boldest—and has been *so* cruel!"

"Is it possible that, for such a man as he, you can give up every future hope and immediate rescue? That is madness!"

"I don't know what it is." Nancy was desperate. "I only know that it is so—and with many others like me. I must go back. I am drawn back to him in spite of every suffering and ill-usage; and would go, I believe, even if I knew that I was to die by his hand at last."

"But what am *I* to do?" asked Rose. "I should not let you depart from me thus. Of what use now, after all, is the news you have brought me? This mystery must be investigated, or how will your story benefit Oliver?"

"You must surely know some kind gentleman who will hear it as a secret and advise you what to do," Nancy suggested.

"I do not seek to know where your dreadful companions live; but where can I find you when it is necessary to speak with you?" Miss Maylie could not let Nancy go without making some arrangement for seeing her again.

"Will you promise me that my secret will be strictly kept, and come alone, or with the only other honorable person that knows it; and that I shall not be watched or followed?" the frightened girl asked.

"I promise you solemnly," answered Rose.

"Every Sunday night, between eleven and twelve o'clock," said Nancy, "I will walk on London Bridge, if nothing prevents."

"Stay another moment," Rose begged, as her informer moved hurriedly toward the door. "Think once again on your own condition and the opportunity you have of escaping from it. Accept *some* money from me. Please do!"

"Not a penny! You would best serve me, sweet lady, if you could take my life at once; for I have felt more grief tonight, thinking of what I am, than I ever did before. God bless you and send as much happiness on your head as I have brought shame on mine!"

Unhappy and desperate, Nancy turned away. Then Rose Maylie, overpowered and helpless, sank into a chair and tried to collect her confused thoughts.

A moment later, the bearer of most strange news was gone.

Part 5
Penalties and Rewards

1 *Weaving the Net*

Because of her love for her young charge, Rose Maylie greatly desired to solve the mystery that surrounded Oliver's life. Besides, Nancy's story and manner had touched her heart; and she fondly wished that she could win the miserable girl back to repentance and hope.

Rose and Mrs. Maylie had brought Oliver to London for three days, to prepare for a journey of some weeks to a distant part of the coast. It was now the end of the first day. What could Miss Maylie accomplish within forty-eight hours? Or how could she postpone the journey without arousing suspicion and inviting difficult questions?

Dr. Losberne was with them and would remain for the next two days. But Rose was too well acquainted with his impulsiveness to trust him with her secret. And she had no witness. Feeling sure that Mrs. Maylie would promptly consult the doctor, Rose, therefore, hesitated to tell her. For similar reasons, she could not call in a lawyer.

And so Rose passed a sleepless and anxious night. In the morning, much against the dictates of her pride, she made the desperate decision to seek assistance from Harry.

After failing again and again even to start a proper letter to him, she was interrupted. Oliver, who had been out walking with Mr. Giles, his bodyguard, entered the room in breathless haste and plainly excited, as if there were some new cause of alarm.

"What makes you look so flurried?" asked Rose, advancing to meet him.

"I hardly know how to tell you!" cried the boy. "Oh, dear! To think—that I should see him at last, and you should be able—to know that I told you all the truth!"

"I never thought you had told us anything but the truth," said Rose, soothing him. "But what is this? Of whom do you speak?"

"I have seen the *gentleman*," replied Oliver, scarcely able to speak, "the gentleman who was so good to me— Mr. *Brownlow*, that we have so often talked about."

"Where?" asked Rose in surprise.

"Getting out of a coach," replied Oliver, shedding tears of delight, "and going into a house. I didn't speak to him— I couldn't speak to him, for he didn't see me. And I trembled so, that I was not able to go up to him. But Giles asked someone, for me, whether Mr. Brownlow lived there, and learned that he did—Look here," Oliver added, opening a scrap of paper. "Here is the address!"

Rose read the address, which was on Craven Street, in the Strand, and at once decided to put the discovery to good use.

"Quick!" she ordered. "Tell Giles to call a coach. Then be ready to go with me."

Oliver did act quickly; and they soon arrived at the Brownlow residence. Miss Maylie left Oliver in the coach, with the excuse that she was preparing the old gentleman to receive him. She handed her card to a servant, requesting to see Mr. Brownlow on very pressing business. The servant soon returned and directed Rose upstairs, where she was presented to an elderly gentleman of kindly appearance and wearing a bottle-green coat. Near him sat another old gentleman who did not look very kind.

"Mr. Brownlow?" Rose began, slightly confused.

"Yes, Miss Maylie," said the kindly old gentleman. "Please be seated. This is my friend, Mr. Grimwig. Grimwig, will you leave us for a few minutes?"

"I believe," said Rose quickly, as she sat down, "that at this point your friend need not go away. If I am correctly informed, he is familiar with the business on which I wish to speak to you."

Both gentlemen looked at Miss Maylie with puzzled expressions.

"I shall surprise you very much, no doubt," Rose continued, "but *you,* Mr. Brownlow, once showed great mercy to a very dear young friend of mine. I am sure you will be interested in hearing of him again."

"Indeed!" Mr. Brownlow exclaimed.

"You knew him as Oliver Twist," continued Rose.

Mr. Grimwig dropped a large book that he was pretending to read and, falling back in his chair, simply stared at Miss Maylie for a moment. Then he could express his amazement only in a long and deep whistle.

Mr. Brownlow, who was no less surprised, drew his chair nearer to Miss Maylie's and said: "Do me the favor, my dear young lady, of leaving out any reference to that which you call mercy. But, if you have any evidence that will alter the unfavorable opinion I was once forced to form of that poor child, in heaven's name let me know of it!"

"A bad one! I'll eat my head if he is not a bad one," growled Mr. Grimwig.

"Oliver is a child of a noble nature and a warm heart," said Rose, "and that Higher Power, which seems to have tried him beyond his years, has planted in his breast affections and feelings which would do honor to many older persons."

"I have often wondered about that, Miss Maylie," commented Mr. Brownlow, thoughtfully. "And now, will you tell me what information you may have of the poor lad. I have tried in every way to find him."

Rose, who now felt more at ease than she had at first, then related Oliver's adventures since he left Mr. Brownlow's house. But she reserved Nancy's information for that gentleman's private ear and concluded by saying that the lad's great sorrow, for some months past, had been the fact that he was unable to meet with his kind friend, Mr. Brownlow.

"Thank God!" exclaimed the booklover. "This is great happiness to me—great happiness. But you have not told me where the lad is now, Miss Maylie. Why did you not bring him with you?"

"He is waiting now in a coach at your door," replied Rose.

"At my very door!" cried Mr. Brownlow. Then he hurried out of the room and down the stairs.

Meanwhile, Mr. Grimwig rose and limped slowly back and forth at least a dozen times, finally stopping suddenly before Rose, and kissing her without the slightest warning.

"Hush!" he said, as the young lady jumped up in some alarm. "Don't be afraid. I'm old enough to be your grandfather. You're a sweet girl. I like you—Here they are!"

Just as the lame gentleman seated himself again, Mr. Brownlow entered with Oliver, whom Mr. Grimwig actually received very graciously. That pleasant scene made Miss Maylie feel quite happy and greatly relieved.

"There is somebody else who should not be forgotten, by the by," said Mr. Brownlow, ringing the bell for a servant, whom he directed to call in Mrs. Bedwin. She came as quickly as she could and stood respectfully at the door, waiting for orders.

"Why, your eyes grow dimmer every day, Bedwin," declared Mr. Brownlow.

"Well, sir," replied the old lady, "people's eyes don't improve at my age, sir."

"As if I didn't know that! But put on your glasses to see what I called you for."

The elderly lady began to search in her pocket for her spectacles. But the impatient boy rushed into her arms.

"God be good to me!" cried Mrs. Bedwin, embracing him. "It *is* my innocent boy!"

"My dear old nurse!" Oliver was overjoyed.

"He *would* come back—I knew he would!" exclaimed the kind nurse, holding him lovingly. "How well he looks, and how like a gentleman's son he is dressed again! Where have you been, this long, long while? Ah! the same sweet face, but not so pale; the same soft eyes, but not so sad." And so she went on—now holding him at arms' length, to look at him carefully; now clasping him to her bosom; and, in turn, laughing and weeping for joy.

Mr. Grimwig, now actually smiling, gathered his belongings and, mumbling his good-bye to everyone, quietly withdrew.

Leaving Mrs. Bedwin and Oliver to compare notes, Mr. Brownlow then led Rose into another room, where she told him all about her interview with Nancy. The account surprised and annoyed him. Rose also explained her reasons for not telling Dr. Losberne at once. Mr. Brownlow agreed and promised to discuss the whole matter with the worthy doctor himself. To give the booklover an early opportunity to do so, it was arranged that he should call at the hotel at eight o'clock that evening, and that, in the meantime, Mrs. Maylie should be cautiously informed of all that had occurred. Then Rose and Oliver returned to the hotel.

As Rose had predicted, the doctor could not restrain his anger when Nancy's story was unfolded to him. He spared no words in condemning and threatening her. At one point in the private conference with Mr. Brownlow, he put on his hat, intending to obtain the assistance of the police. But Mr. Brownlow stood up to him and argued until the excited doctor agreed to give up that idea.

"Then what the devil *is* to be done?" demanded Dr. Losberne, when he and Mr. Brownlow had rejoined the two ladies in nearby rooms.

"We must proceed gently and with great care," suggested Mr. Brownlow, quietly.

"Gentleness and care!" exclaimed the doctor. "I'd send them one and all to—"

"Never mind where," interrupted Mr. Brownlow. "But consider whether sending them *anywhere* is likely to gain our object: to discover Oliver's parentage and claim for him the inheritance, of which he has been robbed, if this story be true."

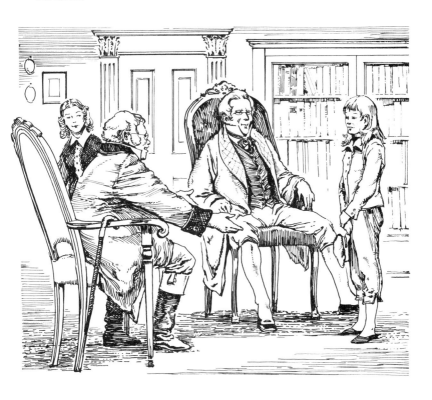

"Ah!" said Dr. Losberne, mopping his brow with his handerkerchief. "I almost forgot that."

"You see," insisted Mr. Brownlow, "placing poor Nancy entirely out of the question, and supposing it were possible to bring the scoundrels to justice without injuring her, what good could follow?"

"Hanging a few of them at least, in all probability," suggested the doctor.

"Very good," replied Mr. Brownlow, smiling, "but no doubt they will bring that about for themselves in good time. We shall indeed have great difficulty in solving this mystery, unless we can bring Monks to his knees. That can be done only by scheming to catch him alone when he is not surrounded by his criminal friends. And remember: We have no real proof against him at present. Besides, contrary to your impulses at this point, our promise to Nancy must be kept. I don't think it will in any way interfere with our plans. But, before we can decide on any course of action, we must see the girl, to learn whether she will point out Monks to us, on the understanding that he is to be dealt with by us alone, and not by the law. If she will not or cannot do that, we must get from her an account of his haunts and a description of him. Nancy cannot be seen until next Sunday night. This is Tuesday. Meantime, I would suggest that we remain perfectly quiet and keep these matters secret, even from Oliver himself."

Dr. Losberne showed his dislike of delaying action for five whole days, but finally admitted that he could offer no better safe plan, just then. And both Rose and Mrs. Maylie fully agreed with Mr. Brownlow. Therefore, his proposal was adopted.

"I should like," he said, "to call in the aid of my friend Grimwig. He is a strange creature, but a shrewd one, and might prove of real help to us. He was trained as a lawyer, but is not now active in his profession."

"I have no objection to including *your* friend, if I may call in mine," said the doctor.

Mr. Brownlow asked who he may be.

"Mrs. Maylie's son, and this young lady's—very old friend," replied Dr. Losberne, motioning toward Mrs. Maylie, and giving Rose a sly glance.

Rose blushed, but offered no objection; and all agreed that Harry Maylie should be added to the investigating group, along with Mr. Grimwig.

"We shall remain in town, of course," announced Mrs. Maylie. "I will spare neither trouble nor expense to gain the object in which we are all deeply interested. Hence, I am content to stay here, even if it be for a year, so long as you assure me that any hope remains."

"Good!" responded Mr. Brownlow. "And now, come. Supper has been announced. Call young Oliver. He has been all alone in the next room and must have begun to think that we have been plotting to cast him out. Our plans for next Sunday night must wait."

2 *Easy Money*

"Yer may thank yer lucky stars *I've* got a head! If we hadn't gone the wrong road on purpose, at first, and come back across country, yer'd have been locked up tight a week ago, my lady. And serve yer right for being a fool!" lectured Mr. Noah Claypole, as he pulled his footsore and weary companion, Charlotte, along the road. They had already passed through Highgate archway, heading toward London.

"I know I ain't as clever as you are," replied Charlotte. "But don't put all the blame on *me* and say *I* might have been locked up. *You* would have been if I had been, anyhow."

"Yer took the money from the cashbox. Yer *know* yer did!" declared Mr. Claypole.

"I took it for you—Noah, dear," put in Charlotte, smiling.

"Did I *keep* it?" asked Mr. Claypole.

"No. You trusted in me and let me carry it in this big bundle, like a dear—which you *are*," said the young lady, tickling him under the chin.

Noah had indeed trusted Charlotte to that extent, but only because, if they were pursued, Mr. Sowerberry's money might be found on her. Then Mr. Claypole could claim that he was innocent of any theft and might more easily escape.

It was the night during which Nancy had visited Miss Maylie. The two travelers had been trudging over the Great North Road, which, a long time before, had led Oliver Twist and the Artful Dodger to London. Though stronger than Charlotte, Noah was careful to see to it that he should carry a much lighter parcel of luggage than that which was now taxing her last ounces of energy.

Avoiding the main streets, they were soon among the shadows of the dark, confusing, and dirty passage ways between Gray's Inn Lane and Smithfield. Charlotte shuddered, and whispered to Noah that she was afraid.

But her companion walked on, dragging Charlotte after him; now slowing up a little to look at some small public house; and now jogging on again, as some fancied appearance made him think it was *too* public for his purpose. Finally, he stopped in front of an inn that was more humble and more dirty than any of the others he had seen. Then he announced to Charlotte his intention of putting up there for the night.

"So give us the bundle," said her manly escort, unstrapping it from the girl's aching shoulders and slinging it over his own, "and don't yer speak, except when yer spoke to. What's the name of the house—t-h-r—three what?"

"Crip—ples," whispered Charlotte.

" 'Three Cripples,' " repeated Noah, "and a very good sign, too. Now, then! Keep close at my heels!"

Then they entered the inn where Fagin and Bill Sikes often met to talk over their plots.

Just inside the rattling door, they saw nobody but a young man. With his elbows on the counter, he was reading a soiled newspaper. He was Barney, the barkeeper. After learning that Noah and Charlotte wanted some supper, and would like to sleep there that night, Barney ushered them

into a small back room next to the bar. He left them sitting at a small table, while he inquired about the prospects for supper and a night's lodging.

When Barney returned with a few cold cuts of meat, he told the weary travelers that they could be lodged there that night. Then he withdrew again.

The little eating place was a few steps lower than the bar. In a dark angle of the wall was a small curtain, which concealed a single pane of glass, through which the landlord was watching the newcomers. With his ear against the thin partition, he could hear all that was said; and, when he finally seemed satisfied, he stopped spying. By that time Barney had returned to the bar.

A few minutes later, Fagin entered the tavern. Barney told him that two young strangers from the country were in the back room and suggested that the old man might be interested in them.

"Aha!" said the crime master, quietly. "I must have a look." Then he placed himself on a stool at the spying post. He looked through the glass and turned his ear to the partition, listening attentively.

"So I mean to be a gentleman," Fagin heard Mr. Claypole declare. "No more jolly old coffins, Charlotte, but a gentleman's life for me. And, if yer like, yer shall be a lady."

"I should like that well enough, dear," agreed Charlotte; "but money boxes ain't to be emptied every day, and people to get away clear, afterward."

Pointing his finger at her, Noah announced, "There's many more things to be emptied, such as pockets, bags, houses, mailcoaches—and even banks!"

"But you can't do all that, dear," advised Charlotte.

"Ah! I shall get into company with them that can," Noah assured her. "They'll make us useful some way. Why, you yerself are worth *fifty* women. I should like to be the captain of some band, if there was good profit. And, if we could get in with the right sort of gentlemen, I say it would be cheap at that twenty-pound note you've got—especially as we don't know how to get rid of it ourselves."

After expressing this opinion, Mr. Claypole nodded wisely to Charlotte, and was thinking of another wonderful idea, when a door suddenly opened, and a stranger appeared.

The stranger was Mr. Fagin. He looked very friendly, smiling and bowing low as he advanced, and sat near the young couple. After ordering Barney to bring him something to eat, he rubbed his hands together and smiled still more sweetly.

"A pleasant night, sir, but cool for the time of year," said he to Noah. "From the country, I see, sir?"

"*How* do yer see that?" asked Mr. Claypole.

"We have not so much dust as *that* in London," replied Fagin, pointing from Noah's shoes to those of his companion, and from them to the two bundles.

"Yer a sharp feller. Ha! ha! Only hear that, Charlotte!"

"And one must be sharp in this town, my dears," Fagin informed them, in a low voice, "to empty a cashbox, or a house, or a mail coach, or a bank."

When Noah heard his own words repeated, he fell back in his chair and looked from Fagin to Charlotte with an expression of great fear on his face.

"Don't mind me, my dear," said Fagin, leaning closer to the young man. "It was lucky it was only me that heard you by chance. I'm in that way of things myself, and I like you for it."

"In *what* way?" inquired Mr. Claypole, recovering slightly.

"In that way of business," explained Fagin, "as are also the people of this house. You've hit the right spot and are safe here. There is not a safer place in all this town than The Cripples, that is, when I like to make it so, for certain people. And I have taken a fancy to you and the young woman. So I've spoken the good word for you; and you may make your minds easy."

Noah Claypole's mind might have been at ease, after this assurance, but his body certainly was not; for he shuffled about into various twisted positions, as he eyed his new friend with doubts and fears.

"I'll tell you more," said Fagin, after smilingly promising Charlotte protection. "I have a friend that can satisfy your heart's desire and put you right. You can follow whatever branch of the business you think will suit you best, at first, and be taught all the others."

"Yer speak—as if—yer were in earnest," Noah ventured.

"What would I gain otherwise?" inquired Fagin, shrugging his shoulders. "Let me have a word with you outside."

"There's no need to move," said Noah, unwinding his body gradually. Then, obeying his kingly order, Charlotte picked up the bundles and left the room.

"*Must* I hand over?" asked Noah, slapping his breeches pocket.

"It is the only way," replied Fagin, firmly.

"Twenty pound, though! You heard us talking—That's a lot of money."

"Not when it's in a note *you* can't get rid of," insisted Fagin. "Number and date taken? Payment stopped at the bank? Ah! It's not worth much even to my friend. He couldn't sell it for full value in the market."

"Um!" said Noah. "What's the wages?"

"Live like a gentleman—board and lodging free—half of all you earn, and half of all the young woman earns," Mr. Fagin explained.

Whether Noah Claypole liked it or not, he knew that he had no other choice. It was too late to back out; and he realized that he and Charlotte were now completely in

Fagin's power. For those reasons, Noah gradually yielded, saying that he thought Fagin's offer would suit him.

"But, yer see," observed the young man, "as *she* will be able to do a good deal, I should like to take something very light."

"A little fancy work?" suggested Fagin.

"Ah! something of that sort," admitted Noah. "What do you think would suit me now? Something not too trying for the strength, and not very dangerous, you know. That's the sort of thing!"

"I heard you talk of something in the spy-way upon the others, my dear," said Fagin. "My friend is much in need of somebody who would do that well."

"But that wouldn't pay by itself, would it?" queried Mr. Claypole.

"No, it might not," agreed the old criminal.

Noah watched Mr. Fagin with sharp eyes, and asked, "How about something in the sneaking-way, where it is pretty sure work, and not much more risk than being at home."

"Well, now, there's a good deal of money made in snatching old ladies' bags and parcels and running around the corner."

"Don't the old ladies holler a good deal and scratch sometimes?" inquired Noah, shaking his head. "I don't think that would answer my purpose. Ain't there any other lines open?"

"Stop!" exclaimed Fagin, laying his hand on Noah's knee.—"The kinchin lay."

"What's that?" demanded Mr. Claypole.

"The *kinchins*, my dear," explained Fagin, "is the young children that's sent on errands by their mothers, with pennies and other coins. And the *lay* is just to grab their money—they always have it ready in their hands—then trip 'em down and walk off very slow, as if there was nothing the matter but a child fallen down and hurt itself. Ha! ha! ha!"

"Ha! ha!" roared Mr. Claypole, kicking up his legs in delight. "That's the very thing!"

"To be sure! And you can have a few good beats chalked out, where they're always running errands. You can upset as many kinchins as you want, almost any hour in the day. Ha! ha! ha!" With this, Fagin poked Mr. Claypole in the side, and they joined in a loud burst of laughter.

"Well, all right!" Noah decided, when he had recovered himself, and Charlotte had returned. "When can we meet with your friend?"

"At ten in the morning," Fagin replied, adding, as Mr. Claypole nodded, "What name shall I tell my good friend?"

"Mr. Bolter," announced Noah, who had prepared himself for such an event. "Mr. Morris Bolter. This is Mrs. Bolter."

"Mrs. Bolter's humble servant," said Fagin, bowing in mock politeness. "I hope I shall know her better very shortly."

"Do you hear the gentleman, Charlotte?"

"Yes, Noah, dear!" replied "Mrs. Bolter," extending her hand.

"She calls me Noah, as a sort of fond way of talking," said "Mr. Morris Bolter," turning to Fagin. "You understand?"

"Oh, yes, I understand—perfectly. Good night!"

With many good wishes, Mr. Fagin then left the pair; and the new Mr. Bolter proceeded to enlighten Charlotte as to the arrangements he had made. His manner was proud and superior, befitting a gentleman who appreciated the importance of a special appointment on the "kinchin lay," in and near London.

3 *Jack in the Box*

"The gallows," explained Fagin next morning in his own den, after Mr. Claypole, otherwise Mr. Bolter, had arrived as planned. "The gallows, my dear, is an ugly finger post. It points out a very short and sharp turning that has stopped many a bold fellow's career on the broad highway. To keep in the *easy* road, and yet keep the gallows at a distance, is 'object number one' with you."

"Of course it is," agreed Mr. Bolter. "Why do yer talk about such things?" Clearly Mr. Bolter was finding this business of "talking things over" rather uncomfortable.

"Only to show you my meaning clearly," said the crime master, raising his eyebrows. "To be able to do that, you depend upon me. To keep my little business all snug, I depend upon you. The first is *your* number one; the second is mine. So proper care for number one holds us all together, and *must* do so, unless we would all go to pieces at one time."

"That's true," Mr. Bolter decided. "Oh! Yer a cunning old codger!"

The old crook saw with delight that this was no mere compliment, but that he had really impressed his new recruit with his genius. This was most important at the outset of their acquaintance. And Fagin followed up the blow by informing the new Mr. Bolter of the great extent of his "business." In that way, he made the beginner respect him and fear him at the same time.

"It's this trust we have in each other that consoles me

under heavy losses," said Fagin, sadly. "My best hand was taken from me yesterday morning."

"You don't mean to say he died?"

"No, no," replied Fagin. "Not so bad as that. Not quite so bad."

"I suppose he was—"

"Wanted," Fagin cut in. "Yes, he was wanted."

"Very particular?" inquired Mr. Bolter.

"No," replied Fagin, "not very. He was charged with attempting to pick a pocket, and they found a silver snuff-box on him—his own, my dear, his own, for he took snuff himself and was very fond of it. They held him for court till today, for they thought they knew the owner. Ah! The young man was worth fifty boxes; and I'd give the price of as many to have him back. You should have known the Dodger, my dear."

"Well, but I shall know him, I hope, don't yer think so?" asked Mr. Bolter.

"I'm not sure," replied Fagin, with a sigh. "If they don't get any new evidence, we may have him back again after six weeks or so. Otherwise—well, he may then be sent away for life."

At this point, the dialogue was cut short by Charley Bates, who entered with his hands in his breeches pockets, and his face twisted into a look of almost-comical woe.

"It's all up, Fagin," he announced, when he and his new companion had been made known to each other.

"What do you mean?" asked the old man, quickly.

"They've found the owner of the box. The Artful's booked for a passage out," Charley explained. "I must have a full suit of mourning, Fagin, and a hatband, to wisit him in, afore he sets out upon his travels. To think of Jack Dawkins—lummy Jack—the—Dodger—the Artful Dodger—going abroad for a common twopenny-halfpenny sneeze box!"

With this expression of feeling for his unfortunate friend, Master Charley Bates sat heavily upon the nearest chair, clearly showing how gloomy he was. Then he and Fagin discussed the situation further. Mr. Bolter listened, amazed, while Mr. Fagin twisted the real and ugly facts around to make it appear that the Dodger was a great hero, and one who should be highly honored. Indeed, for the benefit of both Bolter and Bates, the shrewd old crime master even managed to bring out several points that the boys thought were humorous angles of the Dodger's position.

"We must know how he gets on today, though, by some handy means or other—Let me think," Fagin said a little later, when he felt that the conversation could take a more serious turn.

"Shall *I* go?" asked Charley, promptly.

"Not for the world," replied Fagin. "Are you mad, my dear, that you'd walk into the very place where—no, Charley, no! One is enough to lose just now."

"You don't mean to go yourself, I suppose?" queried Charley, with a twisted grin.

"That wouldn't quite fit," declared Fagin, shaking his head very deliberately.

"Then why don't you send this new cove?" asked Charley, laying his hand on Noah's arm. "Nobody knows him."

"Why, if he didn't mind—" Fagin suggested.

"Mind!" put in Charley. "What should *he* have to mind?"

"Really nothing, my dear," said Fagin, turning to Mr. Bolter. "Really nothing."

"Oh, I dare say about that, yer know," observed Noah, backing toward the door. "No, no—none of that! It's not in my department, that ain't."

At this point, a short argument between Bates and Bolter took place, which concluded with one of Charley's outbursts of laughter. Finally, Mr. Fagin convinced Bolter that he could safely visit the police office, because he was a stranger in the city, and no news of his running away from Mr. Sowerberry's employment had appeared as yet.

Persuaded partly by such arguments, but mainly by his fear of Fagin, Mr. Bolter consented, with very bad grace, to undertake the expedition. Next, with many expressions of delight, Fagin disguised him as a farm-cart driver and coached him carefully how to act his part. Then he was escorted by young Charley through dark, winding ways to a point near the Bow Street Police Station. There, Bates gave him his final directions and left him to carry on alone.

Noah Claypole, or Morris Bolter, as the reader pleases, played his part so well that he did not have to ask any questions. And he soon found himself jostled among a crowd of people, chiefly women, who were huddled together in a dirty, frowzy room, at the end of which was a raised platform, railed off from the rest. Bolter saw the prisoners' dock on the left hand against the wall, a box for the witnesses in the middle, and the magistrates' desk on the right.

Noah looked eagerly about him for the Dodger; but he had to sit through several hearings before a prisoner appeared who, he felt sure, could be no other than the one he wanted to see.

It was indeed Mr. Jack Dawkins. He shuffled into the office with his long coat sleeves turned back as usual. The jailer led him to the dock, where he boldly demanded to know why he had been brought to such disgrace.

"Hold your tongue!" ordered the jailer.

"I'm an Englishman, ain't I?" the Dodger flared back. "Where are my priwileges?"

"You'll get your privileges soon enough—and pepper with 'em," was the jailer's retort.

"We'll see wot the secretary of state for the Home Affairs has got to say, if I don't," insisted Mr. Dawkins. "Now, then! Wot is this here business?"

A roar of laughter followed; and the jailer cried out, "Silence there!"

"Yes; *what is this?*" inquired one of the magistrates.

"A pickpocket case, your worship."

"Has the boy ever been here before?"

"He ought to have been, a-many times," replied the jailer. "He has been pretty well everywhere else. *I* know him well, your worship."

"Oh! You know me, do you?" cried Mr. Jack Dawkins. "Wery good. That's a case of deformation of character."

Another laugh and another demand for silence followed.

"Now then, where are the witnesses?" asked the clerk.

"Ah! that's right," added the Dodger. "Where are they? I should like to see 'em."

This wish was immediately fulfilled. A policeman stepped forward who had seen the prisoner taking a handkerchief from the pocket of an unknown gentleman. The officer further testified that he had seen the accused examine the handkerchief and put it back again, probably because it was old. Then the policeman declared that he had arrested the young man and, after searching him, found in his possession a silver snuffbox, on which the owner's name was engraved. The owner was present in the room and claimed the box as his property. Then that gentleman pointed to the Dodger and swore he was the thief.

Although the Artful tried all the "legal" arguments he could think of at this point, he was soon committed and led away by the jailer.

Having seen Fagin's "hero" locked up in a little cell, Noah walked rapidly back to where he had left his guide, Bates. After waiting awhile, he was joined by that young gentleman, who had been wisely hiding from public view.

Then the pair hurried to find Mr. Fagin and tell him that the Dodger was doing full justice to his bringing-up.

4 *Crossed Wires*

After her visit to Miss Maylie, Nancy reviewed daily all that she had told Rose, to make sure that she had dropped no clue which might lead to the capture of Bill Sikes. "I could have given Bill and old Fagin away easily—that's what I could have done!" she said to herself, over and over again. "But I made Miss Rose promise to keep my secret. I must trust her, for *Bill's* sake, at least."

And yet Nancy was never really at rest. Her tortured mind, even after reaching such conclusions, traveled the same old circles of doubt and fear, for she felt guilty—guilty in spite of all she had suffered through the years of her captivity. Thus that eventful week slipped by, and the girl looked pale and thin. But she was encouraged by one great hope: that her scheme would save Oliver Twist.

It was now Sunday night, and a church bell was striking the hour. Sikes and Fagin stopped talking, to listen. The girl looked up from the low seat on which she crouched and listened, too.

"An hour this side of midnight," said Sikes, raising the blind to look out for a moment. "Dark and heavy it is, too. A good night for business, this."

"Ah!" Fagin added. "What a pity, Bill, my dear, that there's none quite ready to be done."

"You're right for once," Sikes agreed, gruffly. "It *is* a pity, for I'm in the humor, too." Fagin sighed and shook his head sadly.

"We must make up for lost time when we've got things in order again. That's all I know," Sikes declared.

"That's the way to talk, my dear," Fagin remarked, patting Bill on the shoulder. "It does me good to hear you." Bill then moved out of Fagin's reach, declaring that he didn't like to feel as if he were being nabbed by the devil.

A moment later, the crime master stepped quietly up to Sikes, pulled his sleeve gently, and pointed a finger toward Nancy. While the men were talking, she had put on her bonnet and was now about to go out.

"Hello!" cried Sikes. "*Nancy!* Where's the gal going at this time of night?"

"Not far," she answered, softly.

"But I asked, *where?*" demanded Sikes.

"I don't know where," replied the girl, carelessly.

"Then *I* do," said Sikes. "*Nowhere!* Sit down!" His tone was threatening.

"I'm not well. I told you that before. I want a breath of fresh air."

"Put your head out of the winder," growled Sikes.

"There's not enough there," the girl pleaded. "I want air in the street."

"Then you won't get it," replied Sikes. He quickly locked the door, removed the key, and, pulling Nancy's bonnet from her head, flung it to the top of an old chest. "There!" bawled the ruffian. "Now stop quietly where you are, will you?"

"A bonnet makes no difference," said the girl, turning very pale. "What do you mean, Bill? Do you know what you're doing?"

"Know what I'm—Oh!" exclaimed Sikes, turning to

Fagin. "She's out of her senses, you know, or she daren't talk to me that way."

"You'll drive me on to something desperate," Nancy muttered. "Let me go this instant!"

"No!" Sikes shouted, losing his temper.

"Tell him to let me go, Fagin. He had better! Do you hear me?" Nancy stamped her foot upon the floor in anger.

"Hear you!" repeated Sikes. "Aye! And if I hear you for a half a minute longer, the dog will be at your throat. Wot has come over you?"

"Let me go," begged the girl, sitting down on the floor, before the door. "*Bill,* let me go. For only one hour—do—do!"

"Cut my limbs off one by one!" shouted Sikes, seizing Nancy roughly by the arm, "if I don't think the gal's raving mad. Get up!"

"Not till you let me go!" screamed the girl, but in vain. Mr. Sikes dragged her into a smaller room, where he threw her into a chair and held her down by force. Nancy struggled and pleaded by turns until twelve o'clock had struck. Then, weakened and bruised, she gave up the fight. After many warnings and threats, Sikes finally left her and returned to Fagin.

"Whew!" said the robber, wiping the perspiration from his face. "Wot a precious strange gal that is!"

"You may say that, indeed, Bill," Fagin agreed, thoughtfully.

"Why do you think she took it into her head to go out tonight? Come, Fagin—you should know her better than me. Wot does it mean?"

"Stubbornness: woman's obstinacy, I suppose, my dear."

"Well, it may be," growled Sikes. "I thought I had tamed her, but she's as bad as ever."

"Worse," Fagin declared, seriously. "I never knew her like this, for such a little cause."

Further discussion did not exactly solve the mystery of Nancy. But she soon reappeared, with red, swollen eyes, and swaying from side to side. Both men stared at her in surprise. Suddenly she burst into strange laughter that she seemed unable to control.

"Why, now she's on the other line!" exclaimed Sikes.

Fagin nodded to him to take no further notice just then; and in a few minutes Nancy became quiet again. Then Fagin took up his hat and prepared to leave. At the door leading to the stairs, he asked whether somebody would light him down.

"Show him a light, Nancy," Sikes commanded.

Carrying a lighted candle, she followed the old man downstairs. When they reached the passage, he laid his finger on his lips and whispered, "What is it, Nancy, dear?"

"What do you mean?" she asked in another whisper.

"The reason for all this," replied Fagin. "If Bill must be so brutal, why don't you—"

"Well?" the girl queried, as Fagin paused.

"No matter, just now. We'll talk of this again. You know I am your friend, Nance. I have the means at hand. If you want revenge, come to me. You know me of old, Nance."

"I know you well," whispered the girl, without showing any emotion, "Good night."

She drew back when Fagin was about to lay his hand on hers, but softly said good night again, in a steady voice. Answering his parting look with an understanding nod, she closed the door behind Fagin.

He walked homeward in deep thought. "The girl is weary of Sikes' treatment of her," he told himself. "She has found some new friend. It *must* be that! For her whole manner has changed. She goes out alone quite often. She does not show her old interest in us and our plans. And why did she try desperately to go out, exactly at eleven tonight? To meet someone, surely! Who? We must find out and bring that person into our little fold without delay."

There was another—a darker—thought, also. Sikes knew too much; and his ugly slurs cut Fagin deeply, though the wounds were hidden. The chief reasoned that Nancy knew she could not shake the bully and feel safe from his fury. Nor would her new friend be safe. "With a little persuasion," mumbled Fagin, "she might consent to poison Sikes? Women have done such things, and worse, before now, for the same reasons. Then the dangerous villain that I hate would be gone! Another would take his place. And my influence over the girl, with a knowledge of this crime to back it, would be unlimited."

But suppose she would not join in a plot to kill Sikes? "How," queried Fagin, as he shuffled along, "can I increase my power over her and make her do my will?"

He was near his own home when the idea came to him: "Yes, that's it! I will set a spy on Nancy, to discover who her new friend is. And then I'll threaten to tell Sikes the whole story, unless she promises to destroy him!

"*I will!*" said Fagin, in a low tone, as he turned toward a dark lane. "She dare not refuse me *then*. Not for her life! The means are ready. I shall have you yet, my dear friend Sikes!"

5 *The Creeping Shadow*

"Bolter," Fagin began, next morning, showing proper respect for the name that Noah Claypole had adopted for "business" purposes—

"Well, here I am," Noah said, interrupting the old man. "What's the matter? Don't yer ask me to do anything till I have done eating breakfast. That's a great fault in this place. Yer never get time enough over yer meals." As Fagin sat at the table opposite Bolter, that important young man quickly began a direct attack on the food in front of him.

"You can talk as you eat, can't you?" Fagin asked, without showing how much his dear young friend's greediness annoyed him. Besides, the old crook was angry because he had been up a long time before Bolter appeared for breakfast.

"Oh, yes, I can talk. I get on better when I talk," said Noah Claypole, cutting a very large slice of bread. "Where's Charlotte?"

"Out," answered Fagin. "I sent her out this morning with the other young woman, because I wanted us to be alone."

"Oh!" exclaimed Mr. Bolter. "I wish yer'd ordered her to make some buttered toast, first. Well, talk away! Yer won't stop me from eating."

308

"You did well yesterday, my dear," Fagin announced. "Beautiful! Six shillings and ninepence halfpenny on the very first day! The kinchin lay will be a fortune to you."

"Don't you forget to add three pint pots and a milk can," insisted Mr. Bolter.

"No, no, my dear. The pint pots were great strokes of genius; but the milk can was a perfect masterpiece!"

"Pretty well, I think, for a beginner," admitted Mr. Bolter, much pleased. "The pots I took off entry railings; and the milk can was standing by itself outside a public house. I thought it might get rusty with the rain, or catch cold, yer know. Eh? Ha! ha! ha!"

Fagin laughed, too, for sake of appearances; and Mr. Bolter, having at last controlled his own laughter, took several large bites of bread and butter.

"I want you, Bolter," said Fagin, leaning over the table, "to do a piece of work for me, my dear, that needs great care and caution."

"I say," rejoined Bolter, "don't yer go shoving me into danger, or sending me to any o' yer police offices. That don't suit me, that don't; and so I tell yer."

"There's not the smallest danger in it—not the very smallest," the old man assured Noah. "It's only to dodge a woman."

"An old woman?" Mr. Bolter inquired.

"A young one," replied Fagin.

"I can do that pretty well, I know," said Bolter. "I was a regular clever sneak when I was at school. What am I to spy on her for?"

"Only to tell me where she goes, who she sees, and, if possible, what she says; to remember the street, if it is a street, or the house, if it is a house; and to bring me all the information you can."

"What'll yer give me?" asked Noah.

"If you do it well, a pound, my dear."

"Who is she?" Noah inquired.

"One of us, my dear. She has found some new friends, and I must know who they are," Fagin explained.

"Yes, of course!" exclaimed Noah, eagerly. "Where is she? Where am I to wait for her?"

"All that, my dear, you shall hear from me," Fagin replied. "I'll point her out at the proper time. You keep ready and leave the rest to me."

That night, and the next, and the next again, the spy sat booted and equipped in his carter's dress, ready to go out at a word from Fagin. Six nights passed—six long, weary nights—and on each, the old man came home disappointed and simply told Noah that it was not yet time. On the seventh, however, he returned earlier than usual, plainly showing that he was delighted. It was Sunday.

"She will go out tonight," said Fagin. "She has been alone all day, and the man she is afraid of will not be back much before daybreak. Come with me. Quick!"

Noah jumped up excitedly. He and Fagin crept quietly out of the house and hurried through narrow, crisscrossing streets until they arrived at a public house. Noah remembered it as the tavern where he had slept during his first night in London.

It was about eleven o'clock. Fagin whistled softly. They entered without noise, and the door was then closed behind them.

Scarcely venturing to whisper, but substituting dumb show for words, Fagin pointed out to Noah the pane of glass in the wall, and signed to him to climb up and observe the person in the next room.

"Is that the woman?" Noah asked very softly.

Fagin nodded.

"I can't see her face well," whispered Noah. "She is looking down, and the candle is behind her."

"Stay there," whispered Fagin, signaling to Barney,

who entered the other room. Pretending to snuff the candle, Barney moved it to the required position and spoke to the girl. She looked up at him.

"I see her now," the spy said, close to Fagin's ear.

"Good! Come down quietly."

The door opened, and the girl came out. Fagin drew Noah behind a small partition that was curtained off. They were afraid to breathe as the girl passed within a few feet of them and left the tavern.

"Hist!" cried Barney. "Now."

Noah exchanged a look with Fagin and started to go out quietly.

"To the left," whispered Barney. "Take the left hand, and keep on the other side."

Noah did so. He saw the girl walking at some distance ahead of him. Then the spy moved along on the other side of the street as fast as he dared. The girl looked nervously around several times, but soon seemed to gather courage, for she moved with a steadier step. The spy, keeping at a safe distance, followed her cautiously, without losing sight of her for an instant.

6 *Danger!*

Late on that dark Sunday night, a woman who was walking very swiftly appeared on London Bridge. She seemed to be looking anxiously about her for someone she knew. In the deepest shadows back of her on the other side, and at some distance, a man advanced toward her. Whenever she stopped, he stopped also. He was careful not to gain upon her.

After crossing the bridge from the Middlesex to the Surrey shore, the woman acted as if she were disappointed, for she did not seem to find anyone she knew among her few fellow travelers. Then she suddenly turned back. But he who was sneaking behind her was not taken by surprise. Quickly he hid in a dark space at the top of one of the piers, until the woman he was spying upon passed by on the opposite pavement. When she was about the same distance ahead of him as she had been before, he slipped quietly down and trailed her again. She stopped near the middle of the bridge. The spy stopped, too.

A mist hung over the Thames River. The tower of old Saint Saviour's Church and the spire of Saint Magnus, the two faithful giant guards of the ancient bridge, were just visible in the gloom. But most of the riverboats and many buildings along the shore were hidden from view.

The girl had paced restlessly back and forth a few times—watched meanwhile by her sly observer—when the heavy bell of the great St. Paul's Cathedral in London tolled for the death of another day.

About two minutes later, a young lady and a gray-haired gentleman alighted from a carriage near the bridge and walked toward it. They had scarcely set foot upon its pavement when the lonely girl saw them and hurried to meet them.

Almost as soon as she joined the newcomers, who seemed surprised to see her, all three were surprised for another reason. Someone dressed in the rough clothes of a countryman brushed rudely against them.

"Not here," said Nancy. "I am afraid. Come down the steps yonder!"

Just then the rude countryman, who was still close enough to Nancy to hear her words, looked back and mumbled something about people who take up the whole pavement.

The steps Nancy referred to form a landing stairs from the river on the Surrey bank.

The spy, who was now moving rapidly forward, made directly for those steps, after being sure that darkness covered his movements.

The stairs are a part of the bridge, and consist of three flights. Just below the end of the second, there is a large ornamental pillar; and the lower steps widen. Hence, no one hiding around the corner can be seen from the second flight of steps. At that very spot, the spy in rough-looking clothes quickly hid himself, keeping close to the wall in the thick shadows. He hoped, however, that Nancy and her companions would not discover him by coming down to the third flight of steps to hold their conference. For the spy, the time seemed to drag on as he waited; and he had

just about decided to leave his hiding place, when his alert ears heard the sound of footsteps and voices nearby.

Scarcely breathing as he listened, the sneak heard a man speaking in soft tones:

"This is far enough. I will not let this young lady go farther down. Many people would have distrusted you for leading them here. Why have you come to such a place as this?"

"I told you before," replied Nancy, "that I was afraid to speak to you up there. I don't know why it is, but I have such a feeling of dread upon me tonight that I can hardly stand."

"A fear of what?" asked the gentleman, somewhat kindly.

"I scarcely know of what. I wish I did. Horrible thoughts of blood and death have been upon me all day."

"Imagination," the gentleman said, soothingly.

"No!" insisted Nancy in a hoarse voice. "I'll swear I saw 'coffin' printed large on every page of the book I was trying to read tonight."

There was something so uncommon in the poor girl's manner, that the spy felt chills creep up and down his spine. After all, he was a coward at heart. And so he felt great relief in hearing the sweet voice of the refined young lady, as she begged Nancy to be calm and requested her escort to speak kindly to the trembling girl.

"You were not here last Sunday night," he said gently to Nancy.

"I couldn't come. I was kept by force."

"By whom?"

"Him that I told the young lady of before."

"I hope no one suspected you of telling anyone about the matter which has brought us here tonight," said the gentleman, excitedly.

"No," Nancy assured him. "It's not very easy for me to leave *him*, unless he knows why. I couldn't have left to see this lady at first, had I not given him a drink of laudanum before I came away."

"Did he awake before you returned?" inquired the gentleman.

"No; and neither he nor any of the others suspects me."

"Good!" said the gentleman. "Now listen to me."

"I am ready," replied Nancy, as he paused for a moment.

"This young lady," the gentleman began, "has informed me, and some other friends who can be safely trusted, of all that you told her nearly two weeks ago. I confess that I had doubts, at first, whether you were to be fully trusted, but now I firmly believe you are honest."

"I am," said the girl, earnestly.

"To prove that I trust you, I will say now that we plan to frighten Monks and make him tell us his secret. But if we cannot find him or learn his secret, you must deliver up the chief of your gang."

"Fagin!" cried Nancy, in great fear. "I will not! I cannot. Oh, *devil* that he is, I will never do *that.*"

"Tell me why," the gentleman demanded.

"For one reason that the lady knows and will stand by me in. I know she will, for she promised. And also because, bad life as *he* has led, I have led a bad life, too. Many of my companions have followed the same courses together with me, and I'll not betray them."

"Then," said the gentleman, quickly, "put Monks into *my* hands, and let me deal with him."

"What if he turns against the others?"

"I promise you that, if the truth is forced from him, there the matter will rest. Surely there are circumstances in Oliver's little history which it would be painful to make public. And, if we learn the whole truth, your friends shall go free."

"Otherwise?" suggested Nancy.

"Then Fagin shall not be brought to justice without your consent."

"Have I the lady's promise for that?" asked the frightened girl.

"You have," replied Rose Maylie, "my true and faithful pledge."

"Monks would never learn how you found out?" Nancy asked.

"Never," the gentleman replied for Rose. "We should be so careful that he could never even guess."

"I have been a liar and among liars all my life," said Nancy, thoughtfully, "but I believe you."

Then, in a low voice, Nancy described the public house from which she had been followed that night, and told her new friends where it was located. She also explained how the place could be safely watched, and mentioned the night and the hour when Monks usually visited it.

"He is tall," continued Nancy, "and very strong, but not stout. He has a lurking walk, and constantly looks over his shoulder, from one side to the other. *Don't forget that.* His eyes are sunk deep. His face is dark, like his hair and eyes. He can't be more than twenty-six or twenty-eight, but he is withered and haggard. His lips are often discolored and scarred with the marks of teeth, for he has desperate fits, and sometimes even bites his hands. But, sir, why did you start?" asked the girl, stopping suddenly, as she watched the gentleman.

He replied hurriedly that he did not know he had done so, and begged her to proceed.

"Well, I don't think I can describe him more fully. But wait! Yes; I almost forgot: Upon his throat, so high that you can see part of it above his neckerchief when he turns his face, there is—"

"A broad red mark, like a burn or a scald?" asked the gentleman.

"How's this?" demanded Nancy. "You know him!"

"Yes, I think I do," said the gentleman, "according to your description. But I may be mistaken—Now, young woman, you have given us most valuable assistance. What can I do to serve *you*?"

Nancy could not restrain her tears as she replied, "You can do—nothing to help me. I am past all hope, indeed."

"Only in your own thoughts," said the gentleman, pleadingly. "The past has been dreary for you, but you *can* hope for the future. I do not say that we can give you peace of heart and mind, for that must come from within yourself. But a quiet place, either in England or in some foreign country, we could gladly provide. Even before dawn, you can escape! Come! While there is yet time, make the break from your evil associates."

"No, sir, I cannot," replied Nancy, firmly, after a little hesitation. "I am chained to my old life. I hate it, but cannot leave it. I have gone too far to turn back now—Please, sir, I am afraid to remain here any longer. I must go home, or I shall be suspected. If I have helped you and this dear lady, I am glad—But go! All I ask is that you let me go my way alone."

"It is useless," the gentleman said to Rose, with a sigh. "Probably we have kept her here too long already."

"Yes, yes!" Nancy exclaimed. "You have. But, if need be, I can find peace some night in the black water below us here!"

"Oh, no!" cried Rose. "Do not say that, please."

"You would never know, kind lady—Good night!"

"This purse," begged Miss Maylie. "Take it for my sake, that you may have some help in an hour of trouble."

"No!" insisted Nancy. "I have not served you for money. Let me have that to think of. And yet—give me something that you have worn: your gloves or a handkerchief—*anything* of yours that I can keep, sweet lady —Thanks—God bless you! Good night! And farewell!"

A moment later, the spy heard the sound of retreating footsteps.

Miss Maylie and Mr. Brownlow soon afterward appeared upon the bridge. They stopped at the head of the stairway. Nancy waited below on one of the steps and let her grief have its way in tears. Rose turned to look down; but Mr. Brownlow drew her arm through his and led her gently away.

After a time, Nancy slowly climbed up the steps, while the greatly astonished spy remained hidden. He waited at his post longer than was necessary, to play safe, before he ventured cautiously to look around him. Then, when he was sure no one else was nearby, he crept up the steps in the shadows.

After peeping out several times at the top, to make sure again that he was unobserved, Noah Claypole dashed away at full speed toward Fagin's house.

7 *Paid in Blood*

After hearing the report of Noah Claypole, the spy, Fagin was almost like a mad man. His new problems made him too desperate to think straight. Yet, he knew he had to control his anger and fears, and try to make the best possible plans to save himself.

It was about two hours before daybreak when his quick ears caught the sound of a footstep, as he sat crouched over a cold hearth in his old den.

"At last!" the gangster chief muttered to himself. Then, when the doorbell rang gently, he arose. Pulling together tightly the old coverlet in which his shivering frame was wrapped, he shuffled across the room and started up the stairs toward the street door.

Noah Claypole, the spy, remained fast asleep on a mattress. The candle, burning low in the den, cast a dim and uncertain light on his face.

Fagin was trembling and afraid. His old bones were chilled by the penetrating cold of that autumn night. He was no longer sure of himself. His carefully laid schemes were failing. He now hated Nancy beyond words for dealing with strangers. He also doubted that he could depend upon her refusal to betray him, which Noah had truthfully reported.

"Sikes may yet escape my revenge," he whispered to himself in great rage. "I will be caught, and—and—" Then he trembled more than ever.

As Fagin unchained the door, Sikes grumblingly entered, carrying a bundle. The two crooks quietly crept down the stairs to their hangout. Inside, Sikes laid the bundle on the table.

"There!" he said. "Take care of that, and do the most you can with it. Plenty of trouble getting it! I expected to return three hours ago." Then Sikes threw off his heavy coat, sat down, and scowled at Fagin.

The old man said nothing at the moment, but locked the bundle away in the cupboard and returned to his seat. He looked steadily at Sikes, and his lips quivered. His drawn, fear-marked face and his bloodshot eyes startled the robber.

"Wot now?" demanded Sikes. "Why do you stare at a man so? You look even more horrible than usual!"

But Fagin merely shook a long forefinger in the air. He seemed helpless.

"Why, he's gone mad! I must look to myself here," declared Sikes, excitedly, as one hand fumbled in a pocket to make sure his pistol was there.

"No, no!" Fagin managed to exclaim, with great effort. "You're not the one—I've no fault to find with you, Bill!"

"Oh, you haven't, haven't you?" queried Sikes, frowning at him, and boldly passing his pistol into a more convenient pocket. "That's lucky—for one of us!"

"What I have to tell you, Bill," said Fagin, drawing his chair toward Sikes, "will make you feel worse than me."

"Aye?" returned the robber, in a doubtful manner. "Tell away!—Look sharp, or Nance will think I'm lost."

"Lost!" Fagin exclaimed. "She had pretty well settled that in her own mind already."

Bill looked very much puzzled and at once became

impatient. He grabbed Fagin's coat collar in his huge hand and shook him roughly.

"Speak!" commanded Sikes, "while you have breath. In plain words, too. Out with it, you dirty old dog!"

"Suppose the lad that's sleeping there"—Fagin began—"was to give us away on his own account—not by force. Suppose he should describe us to the right people and tell how to find us—stealing out at night to meet those people, and—betray us! Do you hear me?" cried the frantic old man, his eyes flashing with rage. "Suppose he did all that—what then?"

"What then!" growled Sikes, with a wicked curse. "If he was left alive till I came, I'd grind his skull to pieces under the iron heel of my boot!"

"What if *I* did it!" Fagin almost screamed. "*I*, that know so much and could hang so many besides myself!"

"I don't know," replied Sikes, clenching his teeth and turning white at the thought of it. "Why—I'd be so strong with rage—I'd smash your head as if a heavy wagon had gone over it!"

"If it was Charley, or the Dodger, or Bet, or—"

"I don't care who," replied Bill, impatiently. "Whoever it was, I'd serve them the same."

Fagin looked hard at the robber and, motioning Sikes to be silent, shuffled over to the sleeping spy and shook him.

"Bolter, Bolter!" called Fagin. Then, looking devilishly at Sikes, and speaking slowly, he said, "He's tired—tired with watching her so long—watching *her,* Bill, my dear."

"Wot d'ye mean?" Sikes asked, drawing back.

For answer, the old criminal again stooped over the sleeper and pulled him up into a sitting position. Noah ("Bolter" to Fagin) rubbed his eyes, yawned, and looked sleepily about him.

"Tell me that again—once again, just for *him* to hear," ordered Fagin, pointing to Sikes.

"Tell yer—what?"

"That about Nancy," Fagin replied, clutching Sikes by the wrist. "You followed her?"

"Yes," the sleepy lad replied.

"To London Bridge?"

"Yes."

"Where she met two people?"

"So she did." The boy stared at Fagin, who hastily took up the story:

"A gentleman and a lady, that she had gone to of her own accord before, who asked her to give up all her pals, and Monks first, which she did—and to describe him, which she did—and to tell her what house we meet at, which she did—and where it could be best watched from, which she did—and what time the people went there, which she did. She told it all—every word—without a threat, without a murmur. She did—*did she not?*" cried Fagin, half mad with fury.

"Right," agreed Noah. "That's just how it was!"

"What did they say about *last* Sunday?"

"They asked her," Noah said, "why she didn't come last Sunday, as she promised. She said she couldn't."

"Why—why? Tell him that!" Fagin insisted.

"Because she was forcibly kept at home by Bill, the man she had told them of before," Noah replied.

"What more of him?" Fagin demanded.

"Why—that she couldn't very easily get out of doors, unless *he* knew where she was going," said Noah. "And so the first time she went to see the lady, while he was sick, she gave him a drink of laudanum."

"Hell's fire!" cried Sikes, breaking violently away from Fagin. "Let me go!"

Flinging the old man aside, Bill rushed furiously from the room and darted wildly up the stairs.

"Bill, Bill!" Fagin shouted, following him hastily. "A word—only a word!"

"Let me out!" ordered Sikes, trying to unlock the front door. "Don't speak to me. It's not safe. Let me out, I say!"

"Only hear me, Bill," begged Fagin, laying his hand upon the lock. "You won't be—too—violent, will you, Bill?"

As the old man opened the door partway, there was daylight enough for the men to see each other's faces. The fire in their eyes could not be mistaken.

"I mean," said Fagin, "not too violent for safety. Be crafty, Bill!"

Sikes made no reply; but, pulling the door wide open, dashed into the deserted street. Without pausing for a moment on the way, the robber kept to his savage course until he reached his own door. He unlocked and opened it, softly. At the top of the stairs, he entered his own room. After double-locking the door, he moved a heavy table against it.

Nancy was lying half-dressed upon the bed. He had aroused her from her sleep. She sat up suddenly, looking startled.

"Get up!" commanded Sikes.

"It *is* you, Bill!" said the girl, with a half smile of pleasure at his return.

"It is—Get up!" As she jumped quickly out of bed, Nancy saw Bill's threatening scowl.

"Bill," said the girl, in the low voice of alarm, "why do you look like that at me?"

The ruffian glared at her for a few seconds. His chest was heaving with fury. Then, grasping Nancy by the throat, he dragged her to the middle of the room.

"Bill, Bill!" gasped the frightened girl. "I—I won't scream. Hear me—speak to me—tell me what I have done!" She caught his arms in a viselike grip.

"You *know*, you she-devil! You were watched tonight. Every word you said was heard."

"Then spare *my* life, for the love of heaven, as I spared *yours*!" pleaded the frantic girl, clinging to him. "Bill, *dear* Bill, you cannot—have the heart to kill me. You *shall* have time to think! I will not loose my hold. Bill, Bill, for dear God's sake, for your own, for mine, stop before you spill my blood! I have been true to you; upon my guilty soul I have!"

The brutal man struggled violently to release his arms; but those of the girl were still clasped around his with the strength of desperation.

"Bill!" cried Nancy, in great agony, trying to lay her head upon his breast. "The gentleman and that dear lady told me tonight of a home in some foreign country where I could end my days in peace. I could have gone *then*! But let me see them again—and beg them on my knees to show *you* the same mercy. And, oh, let us both leave this dreadful place while there is time!"

Sikes freed one arm quickly and grabbed his pistol. But, even in his fury, something warned him about the sound of a shot. So he hesitated for just an instant. Then, with all his brute force, he struck her upturned face twice with the butt of the heavy weapon.

Nancy staggered and fell, nearly blinded with the blood that gushed forth. But, raising herself with difficulty on her knees, she drew from her bosom a white handkerchief that was formerly Rose Maylie's. Holding it up in her folded hands toward heaven, and gasping for breath, she offered a little prayer for mercy.

Nancy's bloody figure was a horrible sight. She moaned pitifully as her murderer staggered backward to the wall. Then Sikes dropped his pistol, seized a heavy club, and struck her down—dead!

8 *Hit–Run*

After striking Nancy with the heavy club again and again, just for "good measure," Bill Sikes stood still for a while. He breathed heavily, staring down upon the bloody scene. Bright sunlight streamed into the room to make sure that he should see every detail.

A great fear began to creep into the murderer's fury; and he suddenly began to move about. But he kept looking at the lifeless form on the floor. Was the sun ever before so radiant? He tried to shut it out, but always there were openings where sunbeams slipped through, as if to say, "We must see, too!"

Once Sikes threw a rug over the murdered woman; but it was worse to imagine that her eyes were staring at him than to see them actually glaring upward. Hence, he quickly removed the dirty covering.

He struck a light, kindled a fire on the hearth, and thrust his club into it. A strand of hair on the weapon blazed for a moment and whirled up the chimney. Even that frightened him. But he held the club until it broke and then threw the pieces on the fire.

Sikes next washed himself and rubbed his clothes; but there were spots that refused to be removed. So he cut out pieces of cloth and burned them. Blood was spattered over

326

the room! Even Bull's-eye, as he jumped about, left bloody tracks on the floor.

All this time the murderer had never once turned his back upon the corpse. Then, when preparations were completed, he moved backward toward the door, carrying Bull's-eye in one arm. After closing the door quietly behind him, he locked it, removed the key, and left the house.

Feeling relieved at being free of the room, the brutal man whistled to his dog unnecessarily and walked rapidly away.

He went through Islington to Highgate Hill. He had no clear plan, but knew he had to keep moving. So Bill Sikes, followed closely by his frightened dog, tramped along a footpath across the fields, skirted Caen Wood, and entered Hampstead Heath. Beyond the hollow by the Vale of Heath, he crossed a road and trudged through the remaining portion of the heath to the fields at North End. There he lay under a hedge and slept.

Soon he was up again, and away—not far into the country, but toward London by the highroad—then back again—then over another part of the same ground he had already covered. He wandered here and there, at times lying down to rest.

Where could the runaway murderer go, that was near and not too public, to get some meat and drink? He thought of Hendon, which was not far off. So he started toward that place, running for a while, and then loitering at a snail's pace, or stopping altogether and idly beating the hedges with his stick. But when he arrived there, all the people he met—even little children—seemed to view him with suspicion. Back he turned again, without the courage to purchase food or drink, though he was very hungry. And he lingered once more on the heath, uncertain where to go.

After wandering around aimlessly for many hours, Sikes decided to set out toward Hatfield.

It was nine o'clock at night when the weary man and the limping dog reached the quiet village. Plodding along a little street, they came to a small public house, whose dim light had attracted the ruffian. The two wanderers entered. There was a fire in the taproom, and some country laborers were drinking near it. They made room for the stranger, but he sat in a corner and ate and drank, throwing scraps of food to Bull's-eye from time to time. The workmen paid no further attention to Sikes, who, warmed and fed, was dozing off to sleep when he was aroused by the noisy entrance of a newcomer.

This was a jolly, clownish peddler, on his rounds selling razors, razor strops, harness paste, medicine for dogs and horses, cheap perfumery, and many other articles, which he carried in a case slung to his back. After exchanging jokes with the countrymen and enjoying a good supper, the comical fellow opened his box of treasures.

"And what be all that stoof? Good to eat, Harry?" asked a grinning laborer, pointing to some soaplike cakes.

"This," said the fellow, picking up one, "is the sure-thing preparation for removing all sorts of stain, rust, dirt, mildew, or spatter, from silk, satin, linen, cloth, carpet, muslin, or wool. Wine stains, fruit stains, beer stains, paint stains—any stains, all come out at one rub of this magic composition—One penny a cake. With all these powers, only one penny a cake!"

There were two buyers directly, while other listeners hesitated. So the jolly peddler talked faster: "They can't make it fast enough! Only one penny a cake! Wine stains, fruit stains, pitch stains, mud stains, blood stains!—Look! Here is a stain upon a gentleman's hat. I'll take it clean out, before he can order me a pint of ale."

"Hah!" cried Sikes, jumping up. "Give that back!"

"I'll take it clean out, sir," replied the man, winking to

the workers, "before you can come across the room to get it. Gentlemen, observe the dark stain upon this hat. Whether it is a wine stain, fruit stain, paint stain, mud stain, or blood stain—"

The peddler got no further. Sikes leaped toward him with a fearful curse, overturning the table and snatching the hat from him. Then, followed by the barking dog, the angry murderer dashed out of the tavern.

Observing that the country fellows were not chasing him, Bill hurried along up the street. Soon, in front of the post office, he recognized the mailcoach from London. Trying to act in a carefree manner, he walked up to a point where he could listen to conversation without attracting too much attention.

At the coach door stood the guard. A moment later, another man, dressed like a gamekeeper, came forward and handed him a basket.

"That's for your people," said the guard. "Now, look alive in there, Mr. Postmaster, will you? That 'ere bag warn't ready night 'fore last. This won't do, you know!"

"Anything new in town, Ben?" asked the gamekeeper.

"No; nothing that I knows on," replied the guard. "I heerd talk of a murder, down by Spitalfields, but I don't reckon much upon it."

"Oh, that's quite true," said a gentleman in the coach. "And a dreadful murder it was!"

"Really, sir?" queried the guard, touching his hat. "Man or woman?"

"A woman," replied the gentleman. "It is supposed—"

"Now, Ben!" cried the coachman, impatiently.

Just then the postmaster came running up with the mailbag. A few more words were exchanged; the horn was sounded; and the coach rattled away.

Sikes remained standing where he was for a little while, showing no signs of being upset by what he had heard. Then he started out on the road leading to St. Albans.

As he forced his aching legs along through the darkness, a great fear began to take hold of him. But even that fear did not annoy him as much as the haunting picture of Nancy's bloody corpse. He saw it plainly in the gloom, and he heard that last low moan with every breath of wind.

Strangely enough, although the ghostlike image was always behind him, he could see it just the same. At times, he turned quickly, determined to beat it off. But the horrible picture turned with him, making his blood cold with fear.

By the time Sikes came upon an old shed in a field, he was nearly desperate—Any shelter would be welcome, if only he could be rid of the ghost in restful sleep—Three poplar trees near the door swayed with the wailing wind that blew through them.

Inside the shed, Nancy's wildly staring eyes seemed to pierce the darkness. They revealed Bill's own room, with every object that he remembered in place. And the *body* was there, clearly outlined, surrounded by pools of blood. He could not stay in the shed. He rushed outside again. The image followed him. He reentered, trembling and weak. The bright eyes were there as before!

Huddled in a corner of the rude shelter, Sikes trembled in terror. Cold sweat came from every pore. He cried out, "Nance! Nance! May God help us both!"

Minutes that seemed as long as hours slipped by for the murderer. Then, suddenly upon the night wind, he heard a distant roar of shouting, mingled in alarm.

Any sound of men in that lonely place, even though they might be in search of him, would have been welcome at that moment. He regained some of his strength and energy at the prospect of personal danger, and rushed into the open air.

There he saw a light greater than that from Nancy's staring eyes. The whole sky seemed to be ablaze. Rising into the air with showers of sparks, and rolling one above the other, were sheets of flame, lighting the heavens for miles around. The shouts grew louder as new voices swelled the roar. Sikes could hear the ringing of an alarm bell. As he drew closer to the heat and confusion, it seemed that new flames twined around new obstacles and leaped aloft. The sight of the men and women who were trying to fight the fire stirred new life in the murderer. He darted onward, leaping gates and fences as madly as his dog, who barked loudly as he dashed on ahead.

Bill plunged into the crowd of half-dressed figures tearing to and fro. Some of them were dragging frightened horses from the stables, others were driving cattle away from danger. Still others were carrying heavy articles from the fire. Tongues of flame darted from all openings that were formerly windows and doorways. Women and children shrieked, and men encouraged one another with noisy shouts and cheers. The clanking of the engine pumps, and the spurting and hissing of the water as it fell upon the blaze, added to the great roar. Sikes shouted, too, and dashed to and fro with the crowd of fire fighters.

In a wild effort to forget Nancy, and blur the sharp rays of light from her eyes, he engaged in all of the struggles that were going on. The smoke choked him. The flames scorched him. But he was not actually injured, as walls and burning beams fell around him. Nor did he feel weary when morning dawned again over smoking ruins.

This mad excitement over, however, he remembered his brutal crime again, more clearly than ever. He looked suspiciously about him, for the remaining men were conversing quietly in groups, and he feared to be the subject of their talk. Bull's-eye obeyed his finger signal, and they started to leave the scene. Near a fire engine, several men were seated, eating, and they called to him to join them. He gladly accepted some bread and meat; and, a few minutes later, heard the firemen, who were from London, talking about the murder. "*He* has gone to Birmington, they say," said one. "But they'll have him yet! The scouts are out. By tomorrow night there'll be a great cry all through the country."

That was enough for Bill. He mumbled a good-bye, hurried off, and walked until he almost dropped upon the ground. Completely worn out, he lay down in a lane and had a long, but broken and uneasy sleep. Then he wandered away again, undecided as to direction, and weighed down with the fear of another solitary night.

Suddenly he made a desperate decision. He would go back to London!

"There's somebody to speak to there, at all events," he argued. "A good hiding place, too. They'll never expect to nab me there, after this country scent. Why can't I lie by for a week or so and, forcing Fagin to help, get abroad to France? That's it! I'll risk it."

Choosing roads that were seldom used, the criminal began his journey back, resolved to lie concealed within a short distance of London. He intended to enter it at dusk by a roundabout route.

The dog, though! If any descriptions were out, it would not be forgotten that the dog was missing and had probably gone with him. So Sikes resolved to drown Bull's-eye, and walked on, looking about for a pond. He picked up a heavy stone and tied it to his handkerchief as he walked.

The animal looked up into his master's face while these preparations were making. Perhaps he understood. At any rate, the dog skulked a little farther in the rear than usual and cowered as he came more slowly along. When Sikes halted at the brink of a pool and looked around to call him, he would not come forward at first.

"Do you hear me call? Come here!" cried the murderer.

Bull's-eye came up from the very force of habit; but, as Sikes stopped to attach the handkerchief to his throat, he uttered a low growl and started back.

"Come here!" growled Sikes.

The dog wagged his tail, but moved not. Sikes made a running noose and called him again.

The dog advanced, retreated, paused an instant, turned, and then leaped away at his fastest speed.

Bill whistled again and again, and sat down and waited. But no dog appeared; and at length he resumed his journey.

9 *Trapped*

Evening shadows were gathering when Mr. Brownlow stepped from a coach and knocked softly at his own door. As it opened for him, a big, strong man also left the coach. He stood aside. Another man dismounted from the box and took a position opposite the first. At a sign from Mr. Brownlow, they pulled a third man from the coach and took him quickly into the house.

Their prisoner was Monks!

They held him securely as they took him up the stairs. No one spoke. Mr. Brownlow led the way to a back room. Monks, who was by no means easily handled, stopped at the door. The two guards looked at the old gentleman, as if for instructions.

"He knows the *other* choice," said Mr. Brownlow from within. "If he makes you any trouble, drag him into the street, call the police, and turn him over to them in my name."

"How dare you say that?" asked Monks.

"How dare you force me to it?" returned Mr. Brownlow, angrily. "Are you crazy enough to leave this house? Unhand him, men! There, sir. Now you are free to go, and we to follow. But if you leave this house, I will have you arrested at once for fraud and robbery!"

"By what authority am I kidnapped in the street and brought here by these dogs?" Monks inquired.

"*By mine!*" exclaimed Mr. Brownlow. "These men are serving me. I am perfectly willing to let the law say what your liberties shall be. And you?"

Monks was now plainly doubtful and alarmed.

"Decide quickly!" commanded Mr. Brownlow. "Shall it be the law, whose penalties I cannot control, or the mercy of those you have deeply injured?"

Monks muttered something and scowled at the old gentleman.

"Is there—no middle course?" asked Monks, no longer sure of himself.

"None!"

The prisoner looked at his accuser steadily; but, reading in his expression nothing but strong determination, at last walked into the room and sat down.

"Lock the door on the outside, men!" Mr. Brownlow ordered. "And come when I ring."

His aides obeyed, and the unwilling guest and the old gentleman were left to face each other.

"This is pretty treatment, sir," Monks complained, throwing down his hat and cloak, "from my father's oldest friend."

"It is *because* I was your father's oldest friend, young man," declared Mr. Brownlow, "that I am giving you this chance. It is because the hopes of young and happy years were bound up with him, and with that fair sister of his, who died so young and left me alone. It is because he knelt with me beside his only sister's deathbed, when he was just a boy, on the morning when she was to have become my young wife. It is because my broken heart clung to him then, and through all his trials, until he died. Even now, old recollections fill my heart at the sight of you. Yes, Ed-

ward Leeford; even now—and I blush for your unworthi-
ness to bear the Leeford name."

"What has the name to do with it?" Monks challenged.
"What is the name to me?"

"*Nothing*," Mr. Brownlow answered. "Nothing to you.
But it was hers; and, even now, it brings back to me the
thrill which I once felt. I am very glad you have changed
it—*very*!"

"This is all mighty fine," said the young man, stubbornly, "but what do you want with me?"

"You have a brother," Mr. Brownlow replied. "My
whispering his name in your ear, when I came up behind
you in the street, was practically enough to make you come
with me, in wonder and alarm."

"I have no brother," Monks insisted. "You know I was
an only child. Why do you talk to me of a *brother*?"

"Attend to what *I* know, and you may learn something," Mr. Brownlow advised. "I shall interest you, by and
by—True, you were the only child of your father's first
unhappy marriage. And I know that he was only a boy of
nineteen when he was forced into that union, through his
family's pride and ambition. Besides, I know about the con-
tinual misery that the poorly mated couple suffered
through the years. Naturally, they came to hate each other
and finally separated."

"And what of it?" Monks asked, sneering.

"Your mother, who was ten years older than your
father, took you with her to Paris. There, in her gay and
frivolous life, she was soon able to forget. Your father, whose
future then offered no fair hopes, suffered from a broken
heart at home. He was then thirty-one, and you were about
eleven years old. That was fifteen years ago.

"After a while, your father changed his residence in
England, far from his old home. He made new friends. One
was a retired naval officer, whose wife had died, leaving

him with two daughters: one, a beautiful girl of nineteen; the other, a child only two or three years of age."

"What's all this to me?'" Monks was still trying to hold his ground.

Mr. Brownlow continued: "Acquaintance led to friendship. Your father, like his sister, had a fine soul and personality. Hence the old officer grew to love him. I wish it had ended there, but his daughter did the same. Her name was Agnes. The end of a year found your father solemnly engaged to that young lady. He was her first and only true love."

"Your tale is too long," observed Monks, impatiently.

"But it is a true tale of trial and sorrow," returned Mr. Brownlow. "Later, one of your father's relatives died. That rich uncle left everything to his nephew, no doubt hoping to heal old wounds with money. It was then necessary that your father should go immediately to Rome, where his uncle had sped in vain for his health. As soon as your mother learned of the inheritance, she left Paris for Rome, taking you with her. But your father, who had been stricken with a fever, died the day after her arrival. All the uncle's property fell to her and you, because his nephew had left no will."

At this point in the story, Monks held his breath and listened eagerly. When the old gentleman paused, his unwilling listener changed his position as if he were suddenly relieved.

"Before your father went abroad," continued Mr. Brownlow, "he came to me."

"I never heard of *that*," interrupted Monks.

"For safekeeping, among some other things, he left with me a portrait of Agnes, painted by himself. He was most miserable. He spoke in a wild manner of ruin and dishonor caused by himself. He told me that he intended to sell all his property, at any loss, so that he could give part of the money to his wife and you. When he told me he would then leave England, I guessed too well that he would not go alone. He promised to write—I never saw him again and received no letter!

"After learning of your father's death, I hurried off to find Agnes. I wanted to help her and give her a home. But the family had left town a week before, under cover of the night. No one knew why. No one knew where. I could not trace them."

Monks now breathed more freely and looked around with a smile of triumph.

"Much later, your *brother*," said the old gentleman, drawing nearer to Monks, "a sickly, ragged, homeless child, was cast in my way by some trick of fate. I rescued him from a life of crime and horror, without then knowing actually who he was."

"What!" cried Monks.

The narrator looked squarely at his surprised prisoner and then continued:

"I promised you my story would interest you. When the helpless lad lay recovering in my house, I was astonished to notice his strong resemblance to the picture of Agnes. And, as in a dream, I thought I saw something in his expression that reminded me of your father. Later, before I could learn all about him, he was snared away from me, as you know well—Don't try to deny it!"

"You—you—can't prove anything against *me*," stammered Monks. "I defy you!"

"We shall see," was the old gentleman's calm reply. "I lost the boy and could not trace him. I knew that you alone could solve the mystery, if anybody could. When I had last heard of you, you were on your own estate in the West Indies. You hid away there, after your mother's death. Determined to find you, I followed, only to learn that you had supposedly gone back to London long before. So I returned. Your agents had no clue as to your residence. You came and went, they said, as strangely as you had always done. But I was sure you had joined the same low company who had been your associates when you were a fierce, ungovernable boy. I wearied your agents with my inquiries. I paced the streets night and day; and, until two hours ago, I never saw you for an instant."

"And *now* you see me," Monks said, rising boldly. "What next? Fraud and robbery are broad charges! Why, you can't possibly know whether a child was born of that miserable union."

"Ah, but I *do!*" Mr. Brownlow exclaimed, rising, too. "Just within the last two weeks I have learned all. You *have* a brother and you know him. Besides, *there was a will*, which your mother destroyed, leaving the secret and the gain to you at her own death. It mentioned a child that was likely to be the result of that sad relationship. Accidentally, a year ago, you saw a boy who greatly resembled your father. You were startled—and finally located the place of his birth. There were proofs—long held back—of his parentage. *You* destroyed those proofs! And now, in your own words to Fagin, your crime partner, they *'lie at the bottom of the river.'* Yes, unworthy son, coward, liar, companion of criminals; *you*, who from your cradle brought only bitterness to your own father's heart—you, Edward Leeford, do you still defy me!"

"No, no, *no!*" the coward cried, broken at last by all the facts against him.

Showing disgust in his face, Monks' accuser went on: "Every word that has passed between you and Fagin is known to me. Remember the shadow on the wall? It caught your whispers and brought them to my ear! The sight of the suffering child gave Nancy great courage, which has cost her life. *Murder* has been done, and thanks to you!"

"No, no," Monks cut in. "I—I—know nothing of that!

340 / <small>OLIVER TWIST</small>

I was about to seek the truth of the story, when you overtook me. I didn't know the cause. I thought it was a common quarrel."

"It was not the *complete* account of your secrets," Mr. Brownlow declared. "Will you tell all?"

"Yes!" said Monks, now badly shaken.

"Will you sign a full statement of facts and repeat it before witnesses?"

"I promise."

"You must remain quietly here, until the paper is drawn up. Then will you go where I direct you, to establish the truth of the statement?"

"Yes—if you require it," the frightened man agreed.

"You must do more than that," Mr. Brownlow insisted. "You must restore the innocent child's rights. Your father left a will. You know what it provides. When you have fulfilled all your father's wishes for your brother, you may go where you please."

A few moments later, the door was hurriedly unlocked, and Dr. Losberne entered the room, greatly excited.

"The man will be taken!" he cried. "He will be taken tonight."

"The murderer?" Mr. Brownlow asked, surprised.

"Yes, yes," replied the doctor. "His dog has been seen lurking around an old haunt. It is believed that his master either is, or will be, there, under cover of darkness. Spies are watching everywhere. The men in charge tell me he cannot escape."

"Good!" exclaimed the old gentleman. "And where is Mr. Maylie?"

"Harry? As soon as he saw this villain safe in a coach with you, he hurried off to join the searching party."

"And what of Fagin?"

"When I last heard, he had not been taken; but he will be, or has been, by this time."

"Have you made up your mind, Leeford," asked Mr. Brownlow, in a low voice.

"Yes," he replied. "You—you—will be secret with me?"

"I will. Remain here until I return. It is your only hope of safety."

The two friends left the room, locking Monks in.

"What have you done?" asked the doctor in a whisper.

"All that I had desired. Coupling poor Nancy's reports with all that I had already learned, and adding what our good friend has told me as a result of his investigations, I left no loophole of escape. Write Grimwig and set the evening after tomorrow, at seven, for the meeting."

The two gentlemen hastily separated, each in a high fever of excitement.

10   *Enough Rope*

"What? You say they nabbed Fagin! When?" asked
Toby Crackit, turning to Tom Chitling. With a hardened,
runaway criminal named Kags, during the Tuesday afternoon when Monks was made prisoner, they were compar-
ing notes about all the latest news. The secret meeting was
being held in an upper room of a dirty, tumbledown house
in the old-time slums of London. That district, known as
Jacob's Island, was surrounded by a sluggish current of
filthy, muddy water called Folly Ditch, a narrow inlet from
the Thames River.

"They caught the old one at two o'clock this very afternoon," Tom replied, plainly showing that he was not feeling
very comfortable. "Charley and I slipped away up the chimney. Bolter jumped into the empty water barrel, head down.
But his long legs stuck out, so they got him. And Bet, when
she went to see the last of Nancy, just screamed and raved
and beat her head against the coffin. Now she's in the
hospital, all tied up with straps."

"And wot of young Bates?" demanded Kags.

"He hung about awhile, but he may be here afore
dark," Chitling answered. "There's nowhere else to go now,
for the people at the Cripples are all in the net."

"A complete smash!" observed Toby, biting his lips. "More than one will go with this."

"Court is sitting," said Kags. "No hope for delay and escape. And if Bolter peaches on us, as of course he will, from what he's said already, they can prove Fagin had some connection with the murder of Nancy. The trial *could* come up on Friday. Then he would swing early next week, so help us!"

"You should have heard the people howl," said Chitling. "The officers fought like devils, or the mob would have torn Long Beard away. He was down once, but the cops made a ring around him and fought their way along. You should have seen how he looked about him, all muddy and bleeding, and clinging to the police as if they were his dearest friends. I can see 'em now, not able to stand upright with the pressing mob, and dragging him along."

Even the memory of the scene frightened Chitling. He got up and paced nervously to and fro, like one in great agony.

While the other two men listened in gloomy silence to Chitling's unpleasant report, a pattering noise was heard upon the stairs, and Sikes' dog bounded into the room. Expecting to see Bill, they ran to the window, then down the stairs and into the street. Bull's-eye had jumped in at an open window. He made no attempt to follow them, nor was his master to be seen.

"What's the meaning of this?" Toby inquired, after they had closed the window and completed their search for Sikes.

"He can't be coming here, or he'd have come with the dog," said Kags, stooping down to examine the panting animal lying on the floor. "Here! Get some water for him. He has run himself faint."

"He's drunk it all up, every drop," said Chitling, after bringing a pan of water and watching the dog for a time in silence. "Covered with mud—lame—half-blind—he must have come a long way."

"But where from?" Toby asked. "He's been to the other dens, of course. Finding them filled with strangers, he came here, where he's been many a time. But where from *first;* and how comes he here without Bill?"

Chitling replied, "Sikes can't have made away with himself—What do you think, Crackit?"

Toby shook his head.

"If he had killed himself," suggested Kags, "the dog 'ud want to lead us to him. No. I think he's got out of the country and left the dog behind. Sikes must have given Bull's-eye the slip somehow, or the faithful animal wouldn't be willing to stay here, no matter what his condition might be."

Toby and Tom agreed. And the dog, creeping under a chair, coiled himself up to sleep.

By this time, darkness had fallen. One of the men closed the shutter. Another lighted a candle. The terrible events of the last two days filled all three criminals with fear. They drew their chairs closer together, jumping at every sound. They spoke little, and only in whispers.

The thoughts they dared not utter ran on, and so did the minutes and the hours. Then, suddenly breaking the silence, there came a hurried knocking on the door below.

"Young Bates!" Kags exclaimed.

The knocking came again. No, it couldn't be Bates. He never knocked like that.

Crackit went to the window. Then, shaking all over, he quickly drew in his head. His pale face in the candlelight told them who was knocking. The dog, too, was instantly on the alert and ran whining to the door.

"We must let him in," Toby said, taking up the candle with trembling hand.

"Isn't there any help for it?" Kags asked in a hoarse voice.

"None. We *must* let him in," insisted Toby, as he started down the stairs. The knocking on the door became more violent.

When Crackit returned, he was followed by a man with the lower part of his face buried in a handkerchief. Another was tied around his head, under his hat. He unmasked slowly. Like Bull's-eye, he was gasping for breath. Except for his beard of three days' growth, he resembled Sikes, but only as he might have looked in death: chalk-white face, sunken eyes, and hollow cheeks.

The murderer shuddered and glanced over his shoulder as he grabbed a chair, dragged it close to the wall, and practically fell upon the seat.

Not a word was spoken by anyone while Sikes looked closely at each of the other lawbreakers. They feared him greatly. When his hollow voice broke the spell, all three started.

"How came that dog here?" demanded the murderer.

"Alone. Three hours ago," Toby replied, almost in a whisper.

"Tonight's paper says Fagin's took. Is it true?"

"True," answered Tom. "I saw."

All were silent again for a few minutes.

"Damn you all!" Sikes exclaimed, passing his hand across his forehead. "Have you nothing to say to me?"

They all moved uneasily, but nobody spoke at the moment.

"*You* keep this house," growled Sikes, turning to Crackit. "Do you mean to *sell* me, or to let me hide here till this hunt is over?"

"You may stop here—if you think it *safe*," Toby responded, not too willingly.

More nervous than before, Sikes glanced slowly up the wall behind him. Then he muttered, "Is it—the body—is it *buried*?"

All shook their heads.

"*Why isn't it?*" he retorted, staring behind him again. "Who's that knocking?"

Crackit suggested, by a motion of his hand as he left the room, that there was nothing to fear. He soon returned with Charley Bates. Sikes was sitting opposite the door, and so, the moment the boy entered the room, he recognized the slayer of Nancy.

"Toby!" cried the boy, stepping back. "Why didn't you tell me—downstairs?"

Sadly in need of friendly company, Sikes nodded to the lad and acted as if he would shake hands with him.

"Let me go into some other room," Charley begged, retreating still farther.

"Charley!" Sikes exclaimed, stepping forward. "Don't you—don't you know me?"

"Don't come nearer me!" the boy shrieked, still retreating and looking with horror in his eyes upon the murderer's face. "You monster!"

The man stopped halfway, and the two looked at each other; but Sikes' gaze turned gradually to the floor.

"Witness, you three," Charley shouted to the others, shaking his clenched fist. "I'm not afraid of him! If they come up here after the brute, I'll give him up. I will. I'd give him up if he was to be boiled alive. If there's any pluck in any man among you three, you'll help me. Murderer! Help! Down with him!"

Pouring out these cries, and scarcely knowing what he was doing, Bates actually threw himself upon the strong man. And Charley's wild energy, and the suddenness of the surprise, brought Sikes heavily to the floor.

Amazed, the others offered no interference, and the

excited boy and the man rolled on the floor together. Charley, heedless of Sikes' blows, steadily tightened his hold with both hands in the garments about the murderer's breast and never ceased shouting for help.

But the unequal contest could not last long. Sikes soon had Bates down, with a knee on his throat. Then Crackit pulled the ruffian back, with a look of alarm, and pointed to the window. Lights flickered below. Voices in loud conversation and the tramp of hurried footsteps on a wooden bridge were heard. Several moments later, the men in the hideout knew there was no mistake about it! The crowd was gathering on the pavement below. The angry shouts filled the criminals with desperate fear. The light beams were brighter. A loud knocking on the door seemed to make the old house tremble.

"Help!" shrieked Bates. "He's here! Break down the door!"

"In the king's name!" cried the voices without.

"Break down the door!" screamed the boy, on his feet again, but still held by Sikes. "Run straight to the room where the light is. *Break down the door!*"

Heavy blows sounded upon the door and lower window shutters; and a loud cheer burst from the crowd.

"Open the door of someplace where I can lock this screeching hell-babe," cried Sikes, fiercely, as he dragged Charley across the hall. "*That* door. Quick!" he commanded Toby. Then he threw the kicking lad into the back room that was opened and locked the door—"Is the downstairs door fast?"

"Double-locked and chained," replied Crackit.

"The panels—are they strong?"

"Lined with sheet iron."

"And the windows, too?"

"Yes!"

Opening the upstairs window, the desperate murderer

then cried to the crowd below, "Curse you all! Do your worst!"

For answer, some men in the angry mob demanded that the house be burned down. Others shouted to the officers, "Shoot the beast!" Still others tried to climb up by the waterspout. But among them all, none showed such fury as a man on horseback. He roared, beneath the window, in a voice louder than all the others, "Twenty guineas to the man who brings a ladder!"

"The tide!" cried Sikes to his fellow criminals. "The tide was in as I came up. Get me a rope—a *long* rope! The mob is in front. I can drop into Folly Ditch in the rear and clear off that way. Quick! Or there will be three more murders; and I shall kill myself!"

Afraid of their lives, all three of the men helped Nancy's murderer hastily select the longest and strongest rope in the little storage bin. Then he dashed up to the tiny attic room in the rear.

Bates was imprisoned in the room below, which had only one narrow window. But, from that opening, the lad was shouting continuously to those outside, warning them to guard the back of the house. Sikes wasted no time with Charley, but climbed through a low door in the roof. In another moment, several men in the rear cried to others in the mob, "There he is! The bloody beast is on the roof!"

He fastened a board, which he had carried up with him for the purpose, firmly against the roof door, to prevent pursuers from opening it from within. Then, creeping carefully over the tiles with his rope, down to the edge, and leaning against the low wall around the roof, Sikes looked at the scene below him. The water was out. The ditch was a bed of mud!

Watching his movements, and doubtful of his purpose, the crowd stopped shouting for a while. Then they realized

that Folly Ditch would not offer him a way of escape, and a cry of triumph was raised. The news of his being cornered spread rapidly. A greater multitude than ever now gathered back of the house.

"They have him now," cried a man on the nearest bridge. "Hurrah!" And hundreds of others took up the cheer.

Then suddenly, word was passed along that the front door was forced at last. The throng rushed abruptly toward the front. Cries and shrieks of pain arose from men who were trampled down in the crushing confusion. And it therefore happened that, in the stampede, attention was directed away from the man on the housetop.

The murderer had shrunk down at the edge of the roof. The fury of the mob, and the realization that his first plan had failed, made him still more desperate. But, seeing the crowd leave the rear of the house, he sprang up, determined to make one last effort for his life by dropping into the mud and trying to escape in the darkness.

With new hope and new strength, and urged on by the threat of the loud noises that he now heard inside the house, he crept back to the chimney. Finding a safe footing there, he fastened one end of the rope tightly around the bricks and quickly made a strong running noose with the other end. His plan was to slip the noose around his body and lower himself gradually to a point within a few feet from the ground.

Holding his knife open and ready, he intended to cut the rope then and drop into Folly Ditch. But, just when Sikes had brought the loop down below his head, and was about to slip it around his body, he looked behind him on the roof. Then he suddenly threw his arms above his head and uttered a sharp yell of terror.

"Her eyes again!" he cried in a bloodcurdling screech.

Nancy's slayer staggered, lost his balance, and tumbled over the parapet. The noose he had made remained around his neck. With his weight, the knot was drawn in closely. The loop at once became tight—and tighter. Bill Sikes fell thirty-five feet, but was stopped by a sudden jerk. And there he hung! The useless knife was still clenched in his stiffening hand.

The old chimney quivered with the shock but stood firm. The murderer had escaped! His lifeless form swung against the wall. Young Bates pushed aside the body that was dangling before his little window. At the top of his voice, he screamed, "Take it away! Take it away! Let me out!"

A dog, which had lain concealed on the roof, now ran backward and forward on the parapet, howling mournfully. Collecting himself for a spring, he jumped for the dead man's shoulders. But he missed his aim and fell into the ditch; and, striking his head against a stone, dashed out his brains.

11 *Flashback*

On the following Thursday afternoon, Oliver Twist was seated in a traveling carriage, rolling fast toward his native town. With him were Mrs. Maylie, Rose, Mrs. Bedwin, and Dr. Losberne. Mr. Brownlow and another passenger rode behind them in a post chaise.

"See there, *there!*" cried Oliver, pointing eagerly out of the carriage window. "That's the stile I climbed over! There are the hedges I crept behind, for fear I should be caught and forced back. Beyond is the path across the fields, leading to the old house where I was a little child! Oh, Dick, my dear friend. If I could only see you now!"

"You will see him soon," replied Rose, gently pressing Oliver's hand. "You shall tell him how happy you are and how rich you have become. And you shall tell him that your greatest happiness is in coming back to make him happy, too."

"Yes, yes," said Oliver, "and we'll—take him away from here, and have him clothed and taught. And we'll send him to some quiet country place where he may grow strong and well—Shall we?"

Rose nodded "Yes."

There had been little conversation earlier, for Oliver's companions shared his flutter of excitement on this important journey. Mr. Brownlow had told the youth and the two ladies the main points of the confession that had been forced from Monks. The group understood that their present purpose was to complete the work which had been so well begun. The whole situation, however, was still clouded in enough mystery to keep each one in suspense. Careful planning by Mr. Brownlow and Dr. Losberne had made it possible to keep from the others the news of the recent dreadful events.

By late afternoon, they were driving through narrow streets and passing many houses, shops, and persons that Oliver Twist remembered with anything but delight. Bitter feelings arose in him as he pointed out his former prisons: Sowerberry's undertaking establishment and the horrible workhouse. The same lean porter, who tended the workhouse gate while Oliver suffered in that cruel substitute for a good home, was now standing guard as usual.

Indeed, on this return trip, the young gentleman found few things changed since he ran away from the place of his lowly birth.

They drove straight to the door of the chief hotel, at which Oliver often had stared in wonder, as if it were a mighty palace. Mr. Grimwig was there to receive them. Dinner was prepared. Their bedrooms were ready; and it seemed to Oliver that everything had been arranged by magic.

But, after the first half hour of activity, there was another period in which very little conversation took place. Mr. Brownlow did not join them at dinner, but remained in another room. After dinner, Dr. Losberne and Mr. Grimwig hurried in and out of the Maylies' sitting room with anxious faces. When the two men were present, they spoke quietly, but only to each other.

At about nine o'clock, they felt practically certain they would learn nothing more that night. Then Dr. Losberne and Mr. Grimwig entered. Mr. Brownlow followed, accompanied by a man whom Oliver almost shrieked with surprise to see. They told the lad it was his *brother*, although it was the same man he had encountered so unpleasantly at the market town. He cast an ugly look at Oliver and sat down near the door. Mr. Brownlow, with important-looking papers in his hand, walked to a table near Rose and Oliver.

"This is a painful task," said the old gentleman, "but these statements, which have been signed and witnessed in London, must be repeated now."

"Go on," Monks said, sullenly. "Quick! I have done almost enough, I think."

"This boy," said Mr. Brownlow, turning toward Oliver, "is your half brother: the illegitimate son of your father, who was my dear friend Edwin Leeford. The mother, poor young Agnes Fleming, died when the child was born—in this very town."

"In the *workhouse* of this town," said Monks, roughly. "You have the story there—in those papers."

"It must be *told* here, too!" Mr. Brownlow insisted, sharply.

"Listen, then!" Monks responded. "His father (mine, too) who was ill at Rome, was joined by *my* mother, from whom he had been long separated. She had brought me with her from Paris—to look after his property, perhaps, since she had no great affection for him, nor he for her. His senses were gone by that time; and he died the day after we arrived. Among his papers were two, dated on the first night of his illness. They were directed to you, Mr. Brownlow—and enclosed a few short personal lines to you. A note on the cover requested that the envelope was not to be delivered until after Father's death. One of those papers was a letter to Agnes; the other, a will."

"What of the letter?" asked Mr. Brownlow.

"The letter?—It was a penitent confession, with prayers that God might help her. The man she loved had convinced her that some secret mystery—to be explained later—prevented his marrying her just then. So she had gone on, trusting him patiently, but too far. She was then within a few months of Oliver's birth. His father wrote of all he had *meant* to do for her if he could have lived. He begged her not to curse his memory, after his death, although he admitted all the guilt. He reminded her of the day he had given her the little locket and the ring, engraved with her name. He implored her to keep it and wear it next her heart, as she had done before. Then he rambled wildly on, in the same manner, over and over again, as if he had gone crazy—I believe he had!"

"The will," said Mr. Brownlow for Monks, "was in the same spirit as the letter. He mentioned miseries that his wife had caused him. He described your own rebellious disposition, and your vice, malice, and bad passions. He argued that you had been trained to hate him. But he left you and your mother each an annual income of eight hundred pounds. Most of his property was to be divided into two equal portions—one for Agnes Fleming; the other for their child, if it should be born alive and ever come of age. If it were a girl, she was to inherit the money unconditionally. A son could inherit it only if, in his youth, he should never have stained his name with any public act of dishonor, meanness, cowardice, or wrong. He did this, he said, to show his confidence in the mother and express his belief that the child would share her gentle heart and noble nature. If this wish were not fulfilled, then, and only then, the money was to be yours."

"My mother," said Monks, taking up the narrative, "did what any woman should have done. She burned that will. The letter was never delivered. She kept it, with other proofs, in case anyone should ever try to lie away the disgrace. She told Agnes' father everything. Driven by shame, he took his family into a distant corner of Wales, changing his name so that his friends could not find him. He died there soon afterward. Agnes had left home secretly some weeks before. He had searched for her on foot, in every town and village near, but returned heartbroken, certain that she had destroyed herself."

"Years later," continued Mr. Brownlow, "the mother of this man, here, came to me. You had left her, *Edward* Leeford, when you were only eighteen, after robbing her of jewels and money. You had gambled, squandered, forged, and fled to London. For two years, there, you had associated with the lowest outcasts. But your mother, who had a painful, incurable disease, wished to find you before she died. For a long time, no trace of you could be found. Finally, however, her searchers located you, and your mother took you back with her to France."

"And there she died," added Monks, "after a long illness. On her deathbed, she revealed these secrets to me. She would not believe that the girl could have destroyed herself and the child, but felt sure that a boy had been born and was alive. I swore to her, that, if such were the case, and the child ever crossed my path, I would hunt it down, never let it rest—and pursue it with the bitterest hatred. And I pledged myself to drag him, if I could, to the very gallows foot—My mother was right; and the boy—*this* boy—came in my way at last. I began well. But a babbling woman spoiled all my plans!"

At this point, Monks became silent, except for muttered curses on himself. Then Mr. Brownlow turned to the terrified group and said, in bitter tones, "Yes, this villain 'began well.' He was paying Fagin, his old associate in crime, a large reward for keeping Oliver in his clutches. Fagin was expected to pay back some of that money, if the boy should be rescued. A dispute on this point had led to their visit to the country house to identify Oliver—And now, sir, what of the locket and the ring?"

"I bought them from the man and the woman I told you of, who stole them from the nurse, who stole them from the corpse," answered Monks.

"Ah, yes!" exclaimed Mr. Brownlow, nodding to Mr. Grimwig, who then left the room. He returned promptly, pushing in Mrs. Bumble and dragging her unwilling "B." after him.

"Do my hi's deceive me?" cried the heroic Mr. Bumble. "Or *is* that little Oliver? Oh, *O-li-ver!* If you know'd how I've been a-grieving for you—"

"Hold your tongue, fool!" Mrs. Bumble warned, in a whisper.

Mr. Brownlow immediately pointed to Monks and inquired of the loving couple, "Do you know that man?"

They both denied ever having seen him before.

"And you never *sold* him anything?" continued Mr. Brownlow.

"No," replied Mrs. Bumble.

"You never had, perhaps, a certain gold locket and ring?"

"Certainly not," replied the matron. "Why are we brought here to answer such nonsense questions?"

Again Mr. Brownlow nodded to Mr. Grimwig; and again that gentleman limped out. But when he next returned, he led in two tottering, palsied old women.

At once, the foremost of the pair pointed to Mrs. Bumble and said, in a shrill, trembling voice, "*You* shut the door, the night Old Sally died. But you couldn't shut in the sound, nor seal the cracks!"

"No, no," piped the other. "No, no, no!"

"We *heard* Sally try to tell you what she'd done and *saw* you take a paper from her hand. And we watched you, next day, go to the pawnbroker's shop," cackled the first, raising her shriveled hand.

"Yes," added the second, "and it was a locket and gold ring! We found out *that* and saw it given you. We were by. Oh! We were by."

"And we know even more; ha, ha, ha!" continued the first, "for she told us often how the young mother had said that, when she was taken ill, she was on her way—to die near the grave of the child's father."

"Now, Mrs. Bumble, would you like to see the pawnbroker himself?" asked Mr. Grimwig, starting toward the door.

"No!" she replied, clearly upset. "If *he*"—she pointed to Monks—"has been coward enough to confess, as I see he has, and you have sounded all the hags until you have found the right ones, I have nothing more to say. I *did* sell them; and now they're where you'll never get them. What then?"

"Nothing," replied Mr. Brownlow, "except that we will see that neither of you is employed in a situation of trust again—You may go!"

"I hope," said Mr. Bumble in broken tones, "that this —unfortunate little affair will not—deprive me of my parish office?"

"*Indeed it will!*" declared Mr. Brownlow. "You may make up your mind to that, and consider yourself lucky, besides."

"It was all *Mrs.* Bumble. She *would* do it," whined Mr. Bumble.

Mr. Brownlow explained that the law did not care about such an excuse; and Mr. Bumble expressed *his* opinion of the law. Then, seeing that his dearest was waiting for him outside, the humbled Bumble jammed on his hat and bounced after her.

Mr. Brownlow turned next to Miss Maylie, grasping her arm, and said, "Be brave a little longer—Leeford, do you know this young lady standing here?"

Monks admitted that he knew her.

"I never saw *you* before," said Rose, faintly.

"I have seen you often," Monks revealed.

"The father of the unfortunate Agnes had *two* daughters," said Mr. Brownlow. "What was the fate of the other—the child?"

"The child," answered Monks. "When her father died in a strange place, with a strange name, and without leaving any clue to his friends or relatives—the child was taken by some poor cottagers, who reared it as their own."

"Go on," ordered Mr. Brownlow, making a sign to Mrs. Maylie to approach near Rose.

"*You* couldn't find the spot where the family had located," Monks continued, "but my mother found it, after a year of steady search. And she also found the child."

"She took the little girl, did she?"

"No. Those cottagers were poor and had begun to sicken of even the little attention they were giving the child. My mother was pleased to learn that the girl was not being treated too well and, for that reason, was afraid they would not keep her longer. So Mother tried persuasion with money. They finally accepted a small sum that my mother knew would not last long. And she promised them more later, which she never meant to send.

"But, to be doubly certain of the little girl's unhappiness, my mother told the man and his wife, in harsh terms, and with changes that suited her purpose, all about the older sister's shame. She also warned them that the child came of 'bad blood,' and would surely go wrong at one time or another.

"The discontented couple believed it all, and the

younger sister dragged on a miserable existence for a long time. We were quite pleased! Then it was spoiled for us by a widow living at that time in Chester. She saw the girl one day by chance, pitied her, and took her home. We tried in every way to break the arrangement, but the girl remained there and was happy. I lost sight of her, two or three years ago, and saw her no more until recently."

"Do you see her now?" inquired Mr. Brownlow.

"Yes. Leaning on your arm."

"But none the less *my niece,*" cried Mrs. Maylie, embracing Rose lovingly. "None the less my dearest child! I would not lose her now for all the treasures of the world!"

"The dearest friend I ever had!" cried Rose, clinging to her. "My heart will burst. I cannot bear all this."

"You have borne more, but have ever shed happiness on everyone," responded Mrs. Maylie. "Come, come, my love—look who waits to clasp you in his arms, poor child!"

"Not *aunt,*" cried Oliver, throwing his arms about Rose's neck. "I'll never call her aunt, but *sister,* my own sweet sister. I have loved her dearly from the first!—Rose, darling Rose!"

The orphans, Oliver and Rose, were left alone for a long time in their happiness. Then there was a soft tap at the door. Oliver opened it; Harry Maylie entered; and Oliver withdrew quietly.

"I know it all," Harry said, taking a seat beside the beautiful lady. "Dear Rose, I am not here by accident. Can you guess that I have come to remind you of a promise?"

"Stay," said Rose. "You *do* know all?"

"All! And you gave me leave, at any time within a year, to renew the subject of our last conversation."

"I did."

"—Not to press you to alter your determination," pursued the young man, "but to hear you repeat it, if you wished. I was to lay whatever of station or fortune I might possess at your feet; and if you still held to your former decision, I pledged myself, by no word or act, to seek to change it."

"The same reasons which influenced me then, influence me now," said Rose, firmly. "If I ever owed a strict duty to her, whose goodness saved me from a life of poverty and suffering, when should I *ever* feel it as I should tonight? It is a struggle, but one I am proud to make. It is a wound, but one my heart shall bear."

Harry and Rose then referred to the history that had been disclosed during the evening. He assured Rose that the story had in no way changed his interest in her; but she insisted that the facts had not improved her position with reference to him. She felt that she was in deep disgrace. He begged her to understand how great, nevertheless, was his love for her. But, in tears, she begged him to say no more. Her tears, however, merely served to convince him that, deep in her heart, she loved him truly.

So he would not let her send him away, when she arose to signify the conference had ended. Instead, Harry Maylie pointed out how all his hopes, wishes, prospects, feelings—every thought in life except his love for her—had changed completely.

"What do you mean?" she faltered.

"I mean but this—that when I left you last, it was with a firm determination to remove all barriers that you fancied stood between yourself and me. I resolved that, if my world could not be yours, yours must be mine; that no pride of birth should curl the lip at *you*, for I would turn from it. *This I have done!* Those who have shrunk from me because of pride, have shrunk from you, and proved you so far right. Relatives of influence and rank that once smiled upon me, look coldly now—But there are smiling fields and waving trees in England's most beautiful county. Near a certain village church, there stands a rustic dwelling. It is *mine,*

Rose! Mine and yours! And you can make me prouder of it than of all the hopes I have cast aside. This is my rank and station now. Here I lay it down—at your feet—in the name of our sweet love!"

Their long embrace was their bond. Their many kisses sealed it for life.

"It's a trying thing waiting supper for lovers," said Mr. Grimwig, waking up much later in the evening. He and Mr. Brownlow were together in a large sitting room.

Finally, Mrs. Maylie, Harry, and Rose appeared, looking much pleased about something, but offering no excuses whatever for the delay.

"I had serious thoughts of eating my head tonight, for I began to think I should get nothing else," declared Mr.

Grimwig, pretending to be quite cross. Then, observing the others' smiles and the way Harry was leading Rose by the hand, he smiled broadly, saying, "But I'll take the liberty, if you'll allow me, of saluting the bride that is to be." And he did so, in spite of Rose's blushes. So did Mr. Brownlow. So did the doctor, who had just entered.

The little group was quite gay when Mr. Brownlow ordered supper to be served. Then Mr. Grimwig looked around and said, "The boy! Where is he?"

"Visiting Dick," replied Mr. Brownlow, "but he should have returned—why, there he comes now!"

"Oliver, my child," said Mrs. Maylie. "Why do you look so sad?"

"Oh!" exclaimed the lad, trying his best to control himself. "Dick—Dick is *dead*!"

12 *The Black Cap*

When the members of the jury returned to their places, and the judge banged down his gavel, the hot, crowded courtroom became as silent as death. Curious idlers who had brought their lunch even ceased eating.

"Gentlemen of the jury, have you agreed upon a verdict?" inquired the judge.

"We have, Your Honor," answered the foreman.

"What is it?"

"GUILTY!" announced the foreman, in loud, clear tones.

The building rang with tremendous shouts, and then echoed loud roars of delight from the populace outside, as hundreds of citizens greeted the news about the despised Old Fagin. The verdict seemed to cut deeply into his cruel heart. The noises, the confusion, the fury and hate of the mob all seemed to beat upon his head like heavy hammers. Fear made his hard heart feel like a block of ice within his chest. And fear, at the same time, brought forth on his forehead large drops of perspiration, which flowed in little rivulets down over his haggard face. He stared at his own lawyer, hoping for a little sign of pity. But that gentleman was looking in another direction.

The judge rapped again for "order in the court." The

364

jailer commanded Fagin to stand, but had to assist him. The noise gradually gave way to silence again. Then the judge turned toward the former crime master:

"Fagin! Have you anything to say for yourself, as to why you should not be given the sentence of death?"

Death!—Fagin was trembling from head to foot— *Death!*

The judge had to repeat the question twice before the prisoner seemed to hear. Then, in a weak, broken voice, scarcely more than a whisper, he merely muttered,

"I'm—just an—old—old man—old man!"

Then the ex-chief of gangsters was silent again.

The judge put on the black cap. Fagin watched him with bulging eyes. The judge spoke solemnly and impressively, explaining the law to the prisoner and pronouncing the sentence. It was fearful to hear. And yet, strangely enough, the old crook now stood like a marble figure, almost motionless.

His dead-white face was still thrust forward, his underjaw hanging down. And his eyes were staring when the jailer put his hand upon his arm and beckoned him away.

The officers led him through a paved room under the court, where some prisoners were waiting their turns. His guards opened the way, so that he could be seen more readily by the people who were clinging to the bars. The prisoners shouted shameful names at Fagin, and screeched and hissed. He shook his fist and was about to spit on several of them, but his conductors hurried him on through a gloomy passage into the interior of Newgate prison.

Here he was searched, that he might not have about him any means of committing suicide. Then he was led to a death cell and locked in—alone.

The fallen chieftain sat down on a stone bench—a combination seat and bedstead. Head down, his bloodshot eyes looked upon the ground. He tried to collect his

thoughts. After a while, he began to remember some fragments of what the judge had said. They gradually fell into
their proper order: "To be—hanged by—the neck—until—
you are dead." That was it! Those were the last words. He
was sentenced *to be hanged by the neck until he was
dead!*

And now, in the heavy shadows, Fagin thought of all
the men he had known who had died on the scaffold. Their
images arose in such quick succession that he could hardly
count them. He had seen many of them die—indeed had
helped bring some to that fate. And he had even joked when
he heard their last prayers—With what a rattling noise the
little trapdoor went down! How quickly the criminals then
changed from strong men to dangling racks of clothes!

Suddenly, Fagin threw himself against the door. He
tried to shout, "Light!" He tried to scream, "Light!"

At length, when his hands were badly cut from beating
against the heavy door and walls, two men appeared. One
carried a lighted candle, which he thrust into an iron
candlestick on the wall. The other dragged in a mattress
for himself. The prisoner was not to be left alone any longer.

Then came thick night—quiet and dismal. With each
hour boomed away by the church clocks, Fagin's despair
became blacker. He was being mocked, for each sound of
the big bells brought him closer to *death.*

Too quickly for the once-powerful criminal, the new
day came and slipped away into another night. He suffered
moments of weakness. There were also moments of wild,
panicky strength, during which he raved, cursed, beat upon
his body and upon the door, and tore at his hair. God-fearing
men, who came to pray beside him, were driven away by
his curses. They returned. He beat them off.

He had only one night more to live. And, as he thought
of his awful fate, another day dawned—Sunday.

It was not until the night of this last awful day, that a

withering sense of helplessness descended heavily upon Fagin's blighted soul. He had spoken little to either of the two guards who, at first, attended upon him by turns; and they were satisfied not to arouse him. He had sat there, at times, half awake, but also dreaming, when he was not jumping around in his fear and wrath. He became so terrible, at last, suffering all the tortures of his evil memories, that no man could bear to sit with him alone. So the two attendants decided to keep watch together.

The convicted Fagin had been wounded by the crowd on the day of his capture, and his head was bandaged. Some strands of his matted red hair hung down upon his ashen face. His eyes shone with a frightening light. Eight—nine—ten. Then eleven!—Time refused to stand still even for Fagin.

As Monday morning approached, the space before the prison had been cleared of little groups who wanted to be on time to "see the show." Strong barriers, painted black, had been already built across the road to break the pressure of the expected crowd, when Mr. Brownlow and Oliver appeared at the wicket. An order for admission to the prisoner, signed by one of the sheriffs, opened the gates to them.

"Is the young gentleman to come too, sir?" asked the guard on duty. "It's not a sight for young people, sir."

"It is not, indeed," replied Mr. Brownlow, "but my business with Fagin is closely connected with this lad."

The man touched his hat and glanced with curiosity at Oliver. Then the guard opened an inner gate and led them on, through dark and winding ways, toward the cells.

"This—" said their guide, stopping where a couple of workmen were making some preparations in silence. "This is the place he passes through. If you step this way, you can see the door he goes out at. Yonder, workmen are putting up the scaffold."

Farther on, a turnkey opened the door of Fagin's cell. The condemned criminal was seated on his bed, rocking himself from side to side. He looked more like a caged beast than a man. His mind was evidently wandering back to his old life, for he continued to mutter, seemingly unaware that he had visitors.

"Good boy, Charley—well done! Oliver, too, ha! ha!— Quite the gentleman now—quite the—Take that boy away to bed!"

The jailer grasped Oliver's hand and whispered, "Don't be afraid, my lad."

"Take him away to bed, some of you!" cried Fagin. "Do you hear me? He has been somehow the cause of all this— Bolter's throat, Bill; never mind the girl—Bolter's throat, as deep as you can cut. Saw his head off!"

"Fagin," said the jailer.

"That's me!" answered the prisoner. "An old man, my lord; a very old, old man!"

"Here," said the turnkey, trying to hold Fagin down. "Here's somebody wants to see you."

"Strike them all dead! What right have they to butcher me?"

As he spoke, the raving criminal saw Oliver and Mr. Brownlow. Shrinking to the farthest corner of his seat, he demanded to know what they wanted.

"Steady," said the jailer, holding him down. "Now, sir, tell him what you want. Quick, if you please! He grows worse as his time draws near."

"You have some papers," said Mr. Brownlow, "which were placed in your hands for safekeeping by a man called Monks."

"It's all a lie!" screeched Fagin. "I haven't one—not one."

"For the love of God," said Mr. Brownlow, solemnly, "do not say that now, upon the very brink of death. Tell me where they are. You know that Sikes is dead; that Monks has confessed; that there is no hope of any further gain. *Where are those papers?*"

"Oliver," cried Fagin, beckoning to him. "Come, boy! Let me whisper to you."

"I am not afraid," said Oliver, as he moved toward his former master.

"The papers," said Fagin, softly, drawing Oliver toward him, "are in a canvas bag, in a hole a little way up the chimney, in the top front room—I want to talk to you, my dear!"

"Yes, yes," returned Oliver. "Let me say a prayer. Do! Let me say one prayer. Kneel with me here, and we will talk until morning."

"Outside, outside!" the broken man cried, pushing the

boy toward the door, but clinging tightly to him. "You can get me out, if you take me just so. Now then, now then!"

"Oh! *God forgive this wretched man!*" pleaded the boy, looking up.

"That's right, that's right," said Fagin. "That'll help us on! This door first. If I tremble as we pass the gallows, don't you mind, but hurry on. Now, now, now!"

"Have you nothing else to ask, sir?" inquired the turnkey.

"No other question," replied Mr. Brownlow. "If I dared hope that we could recall him to a sense of his position—"

"Nothing will do that, sir," the jailer declared, shaking his head. "You had better leave him at once."

Then the door of the cell opened, and the guards entered a moment later.

"Press on, press on!" insisted Fagin. "Softly, but not so slow. Faster, faster!"

The men grabbed the condemned chief, disengaged him from Oliver, and held him back. He struggled wildly for an instant. Then he sent up cry upon cry, as he was forcibly taken from his cell into the open yard.

Day was dawning when Mr. Brownlow and Oliver Twist emerged from the prison. A great crowd had already assembled. All were restless and eager. There was pushing, quarreling, and joking. The whole scene told of life and action.

But all was quiet, for the moment, in the center of the large open space. Death was hovering there, above a dark cluster of objects, and was waiting as impatiently as the great human audience. All preparations had been completed. There was all the hideous apparatus: the black stage, the crossbeam, the rope with its noose—even the black hood that the hangman held ready to slip over Fagin's head, as the painless first act in the short drama.

13 *Rainbow*

Almost three months later, Rose Fleming and Harry Maylie were married in a village church which was to be the first center of the newly ordained minister's career. On their wedding day, they took possession of their new home. To their great delight, Mrs. Maylie came to make her home with them soon afterward.

All that was left of the property held by Monks was divided equally between him and Oliver. Each received a little more than three thousand pounds. According to his father's will, Oliver would have been entitled to the whole. Mr. Brownlow, however, desired that the elder son should have a fair opportunity of a new start on an honest career. Oliver heartily agreed.

Monks, still under his assumed name, left with his inheritance to a distant part of the New World. There, after quickly squandering the money, he once more followed his old courses and at last died in prison.

Mr. Brownlow adopted Oliver as his son. With old Mrs. Bedwin, they moved to a house only a mile away from the Maylies' home, thus making Oliver's dearest wish come true.

Shortly after the marriage of Rose and Harry, Dr. Los-

371

berne returned to Chertsey and promptly realized how lonely he was. He would not admit that to others, but, for two or three months, hinted that the air was beginning to disagree with him. Then, deciding secretly that his old location no longer meant much to him, he "just happened to find" a bachelor's cottage near the village where Harry was pastor. "The very place for me," the doctor told his friends, and quickly settled his practice upon his assistant. Soon afterward, Dr. Losberne moved into the little cottage. While living there, he engaged in gardening, fishing, carpentering, and various other pursuits that appealed to him. Mr. Grimwig, with whom he had formed a strong friendship, visited the doctor frequently and assisted him in his many activities. They also enjoyed reminding each other of their experiences with Oliver and his problems.

Mr. Noah Claypole, pardoned by the Crown in return for his informing against Fagin, could not decide at first how he might earn a living with the least effort. Finally, however, he went into "business" as an informer or spy for the police. With Charlotte's help, he then managed well enough.

Mr. and Mrs. Bumble, deprived of their situations, were gradually reduced to great poverty and misery. In due time, they became paupers in the same workhouse where they had once lorded it over others.

Charley Bates, thoroughly frightened by Sikes' crime and fate (to say nothing of Fagin's), carefully considered the advantages of an honest life. Deciding in favor of honesty, he turned his back upon the past and its associations, determined to make good in new ventures. He struggled hard and suffered many setbacks for some time. As farmer's drudge and as package-delivery assistant, Charley learned much about earning an honorable, simple living. He was well liked for his jolly and contented disposition. When he grew into full maturity, he was more confident of himself and became the merriest young sheep farmer in Northamptonshire.

Concerning members of Fagin's gang who are not mentioned in this chapter, further information is scarce. But those who slipped the police net for a time, or received only light punishment, probably never tried to mend their ways.

Rose Maylie, in all the bloom and grace of early womanhood, with her kind, gentle ways, was the life and joy of her family and many friends. Always happy in performing her domestic duties, she attended to them with much greater joy when she and Harry were blessed with little children. She loved them dearly and listened with delight to their merry prattle, as they clustered about her knee at the fireside. Harry viewed the peaceful, happy scene with justifiable pride; and Mrs. Maylie could have asked for no greater comfort and satisfaction in her advancing years.

Mr. Brownlow never tired of filling the mind of his adopted son with stores of knowledge, and became strongly attached to the young gentleman as his personality and character developed. When traits like those of his departed early friend were revealed in Oliver, they brought to Mr. Brownlow many old remembrances.

Rose and Oliver, having suffered greatly, knew how to love their fellow men and be merciful; but never failed to be thankful to Him who had protected and preserved them against evil.

Within the old village church, against the wall near

the altar, Oliver's loved ones placed a white marble tablet bearing the name "Agnes." If the spirits of the dead ever come back to earth, to visit shrines made sacred by the love of those they knew in life, then surely the shade of Agnes sometimes hovers close to that solemn nook. For the simple memorial is in a church; and Agnes was weak and erring.

THE END

REVIEWING YOUR READING

Part 1

CHAPTER 1

Finding the Main Idea

1. The purpose of this chapter is to
   a. introduce the parish doctor.   b. introduce Oliver.
   c. tell about workhouses.   d. tell about nurses.

Remembering Detail

2. The young mother asked
   a. to be left alone.   b. to be sent home.   c. to see her
   child.   d. to be given a meal.
3. The orphaned baby was to be sent to
   a. the workhouse.   b. his family.   c. a church.   d. a
   hospital.

Drawing Conclusions

4. When the doctor examined the mother's hand, he was
   probably looking for
   a. a gold coin.   b. a wedding ring.   c. a bandage.
   d. an injury.

THINKING IT OVER

Do you think Oliver's mother would have been kind to him if
she had lived? Explain why or why not.

CHAPTER 2

Finding the Main Idea

1. After Mr. Bumble's visit, Oliver was
   a. put to work at the workhouse.   b. adopted by a rich
   man.   c. forced to live in the street.   d. made very
   happy.

Remembering Detail

2. Oliver received his name from
   a. Mrs. Mann.   b. Mr. Bumble.   c. the doctor.   d. the
   board.
3. At mealtimes, the boys at the workhouse ate
   a. bread and butter.   b. meat and vegetables.   c. gruel.
   d. fruit.

Drawing Conclusions

4. You can guess that in Old England there were
   a. very few poor people.   b. very many poor people.
   c. laws to help poor people.   d. very few workhouses.

THINKING IT OVER

After reading this chapter, why do you think the board was horrified by Oliver's request for "more"?

CHAPTER 3

Finding the Main Idea

1. In this chapter, the board offers money to have someone
   a. take Oliver as an apprentice.   b. adopt Oliver.
   c. feed Oliver well.   d. find Oliver's family.

Remembering Detail

2. Before reading the notice about Oliver, Mr. Gamfield
   a. paid his overdue rent.   b. beat his donkey.   c. asked for directions.   d. counted his money.

3. When Mr. Gamfield appeared before the board, they offered him
   a. the full five pounds.   b. four pounds.   c. ten shillings.   d. three pound ten.

Drawing Conclusions

4. You can guess that Mr. Gamfield wanted to give Oliver
   a. easy work.   b. very hard work.   c. his own donkey.
   d. a nice place to live.

THINKING IT OVER

After reading Mr. Gamfield's description of his trade, what do you think life would have been like for his apprentice? Do you think that the work was suitable for a young boy? Explain your answers.

CHAPTER 4

Finding the Main Idea

1. Oliver finally left the workhouse to become
   a. an undertaker's apprentice.   b. a beadle's apprentice.
   c. a runaway.   d. a gentleman.

Remembering Detail

2. Oliver's luggage was wrapped in
   a. his cap. b. old cloth. c. Mr. Bumble's coat.
   d. brown paper.
3. Mrs. Sowerberry showed Oliver his bed
   a. in the kitchen. b. under the stairs. c. among the
   coffins. d. in the coal cellar.

Drawing Conclusions

4. Mrs. Sowerberry was frightened by Oliver's eating because he
   a. ate so hungrily. b. didn't like the food. c. was thin.
   d. came from the workhouse.

THINKING IT OVER

Why do you think Mrs. Sowerberry said, "I see no saving in
parish children"? Explain.

CHAPTER 5

Finding the Main Idea

1. The author used this chapter to describe
   a. how coffins are made. b. Oliver and the charity
   boys. c. Mrs. Sowerberry. d. Oliver's life with the undertaker.

Remembering Detail

2. Mr. Sowerberry thought that Oliver might make a great
   a. coffin builder. b. soldier. c. funeral attendant.
   d. charity boy.
3. The old woman asked Mr. Sowerberry to send
   a. bacon. b. bread and water. c. bread and wine.
   d. bread and cake.

Drawing Conclusions

4. In entering the dead woman's apartment, Oliver probably
   felt
   a. frightened. b. fearless. c. relaxed. d. angry.

THINKING IT OVER

What does this chapter tell you about the way orphans like
Oliver were treated in society? Explain.

CHAPTER 6

Finding the Main Idea
1. Noah made Oliver angry enough to fight when he
   a. twisted Oliver's ears. b. ate Oliver's mutton.
   c. talked about Oliver's mother. d. laughed at Charlotte.

Remembering Detail
2. Oliver believed that his mother died of
   a. a broken heart. b. too much cold. c. sickness.
   d. getting wet.
3. After the fight, Oliver was locked
   a. outside. b. in the kitchen. c. in the workshop.
   d. in the dust cellar.

Drawing Conclusions
4. Mrs. Sowerberry probably sent for Mr. Bumble because she wanted Oliver
   a. sent to jail. b. talked to. c. sent back to the workhouse. d. left alone.

THINKING IT OVER
Why do you think that Noah continued to make fun of Oliver? What made Oliver finally fight back?

CHAPTER 7

Finding the Main Idea
1. Oliver's life changes in this chapter when he
   a. goes back to the Sowerberrys. b. runs away.
   c. gets beaten by Mr. Bumble. d. makes new friends.

Remembering Detail
2. According to Mr. Bumble, Oliver was
   a. mad. b. mean. c. overfed. d. angry.
3. When he left the Sowerberrys, Oliver almost turned back because he had to pass
   a. Mr. Gamfield. b. the workhouse. c. Dick. d. Mr. Bumble.

Drawing Conclusions
4. Mr. Bumble didn't beat Oliver immediately because

a. he really was afraid of Oliver.   b. he was too angry.
c. Mrs. Sowerberry asked him not to hurt Oliver.   d. he
thought that Oliver would be good in the future.

THINKING IT OVER

After the fight at the Sowerberrys, Oliver found the courage to
run away. Why do you think he finally did so? Explain.

CHAPTER 8

Finding the Main Idea

1. The purpose of this chapter is to
   a. introduce Fagin and his criminal world.   b. show
   Oliver making friends.   c. tell about London.   d. tell
   about Oliver's travels.

Remembering Detail

2. In the country, Oliver met an old couple who
   a. sent dogs after him.   b. showed him the way to London.   c. gave him food and tea.   d. passed him by.
3. The Artful Dodger offered Oliver
   a. money.   b. lodgings.   c. a family.   d. a job.

Drawing Conclusions

4. The Artful Dodger probably thinks that Oliver is
   a. naive.   b. smart.   c. talented.   d. rich.

THINKING IT OVER

Why did Oliver consider running away from the Artful
Dodger?

CHAPTER 9

Finding the Main Idea

1. In this chapter, Oliver learns
   a. about London.   b. more about Fagin and the boys.
   c. a trade.   d. about his background.

Remembering Detail

2. Oliver pretended to be asleep while Fagin
   a. took out his treasures.   b. cooked sausages.
   c. marked handkerchiefs.   d. talked to him.

3. The Dodger and Charley brought Fagin
   a. jewelry and pocketbooks. b. snuffboxes and jewelry.
   c. pocketbooks and handkerchiefs. d. watches and
   handkerchiefs.

Drawing Conclusions
4. Fagin's pocket-picking game is meant to show Oliver
   a. that it's easy to do. b. how to become a thief.
   c. how to earn a shilling. d. how to collect watches.

THINKING IT OVER
What plans do you think Fagin has for Oliver? Explain.

CHAPTER 10

Finding the Main Idea
1. When Oliver went out with Charley and the Dodger, he
   a. went to work. b. got some fresh air. c. was
   arrested. d. picked a man's pocket.

Remembering Detail
2. The Dodger spotted an old gentleman
   a. around the corner. b. near the bookstall. c. in the
   open square. d. in an armchair.
3. Oliver was caught when
   a. he tripped. b. he was seized by the collar. c. he
   was knocked down. d. a police officer spotted him.

Drawing Conclusions
4. Oliver's reaction when he saw Dodger and Charley steal was
   a. happy. b. horrified. c. hopeful. d. angry.

THINKING IT OVER
When Oliver went out with the Artful Dodger and Charley
Bates, do you think he planned to steal?

CHAPTER 11

Finding the Main Idea
1. In this chapter, Oliver was saved from jail by
   a. Mr. Fang. b. the bookseller. c. the police officer.
   d. the Dodger.

Remembering Detail

2. Mr. Fang, the magistrate, treated Mr. Brownlow
   a. with respect. b. as if he knew him. c. very rudely.
   d. like an old friend.
3. What was Oliver's sentence for the robbery?
   a. three months with hard labor b. three months back
   at the workhouse c. six months d. three months in a
   cell

Drawing Conclusions

4. Mr. Brownlow probably took Oliver in the coach because
   a. he wanted him in jail quickly. b. he wanted to find
   Fagin. c. he wanted to help him. d. he wanted to get
   more books.

THINKING IT OVER

Why did Mr. Brownlow decide to help Oliver before he heard
the bookseller's evidence?

Part 2

CHAPTER 1

Finding the Main Idea

1. In this chapter, Oliver
   a. returned to Fagin. b. found kind, new friends.
   c. ran away again. d. met the bookseller.

Remembering Detail

2. Mrs. Bedwin gave Oliver
   a. a basin of strong broth. b. the portrait of a lady.
   c. crumbs of bread. d. some port wine.
3. Mr. Brownlow thought that Oliver's name was
   a. Tom Twist. b. Tom Oliver. c. Oliver Twist.
   d. Tom White.

Drawing Conclusions

4. You can guess that the Dodger thought that Fagin would
   be
   a. happy that Oliver was missing. b. happy about the
   robbery. c. angry that Oliver was mising. d. puzzled
   about the robbery.

THINKING IT OVER

Why was Mr. Brownlow excited about Oliver and the portrait of the lady? Explain.

CHAPTER 2

Finding the Main Idea

1. This chapter is mostly about Fagin's attempt to
   a. punish the Dodger and Charley. b. kill Bill Sikes.
   c. find out where Oliver is. d. get Nancy to dress up.

Remembering Detail

2. Bill Sikes traveled with a
   a. large door key. b. shaggy white dog. c. pewter beer pot. d. toasting fork.
3. Nancy pretended to be
   a. Oliver's mother. b. Fagin's wife. c. Oliver's sister.
   d. Oliver's friend.

Drawing Conclusions

4. Bill Sikes probably considered Fagin
   a. foolish. b. his best friend. c. his oldest friend.
   d. sneaky.

THINKING IT OVER

Do you think that Fagin and Bill Sikes like each other? Explain.

CHAPTER 3

Finding the Main Idea

1. In this chapter, the author shows how
   a. Oliver enjoys his new life. b. Mr. Brownlow dislikes Oliver. c. Mr. Grimwig likes Oliver. d. Oliver hates his new life.

Remembering Detail

2. When Oliver was well, Mr. Brownlow gave him
   a. some books. b. a new set of clothes. c. a new portrait. d. tea.
3. Mr. Grimwig's favorite saying was
   a. "A horrid boy!" b. "We shall see!" c. "I'll eat my head!" d. "Bless his sweet face!"

Drawing Conclusions

4. You can guess that Oliver was eager to go to the book-seller's because he wanted
   a. to go outside. b. five pounds. c. muffins. d. to please Mr. Brownlow.

THINKING IT OVER

Do you think that Mr. Grimwig is treating Oliver fairly? Why or why not?

CHAPTER 4

Finding the Main Idea

1. The author uses this chapter to return Oliver to
   a. Mr. Brownlow. b. the Sowerberrys. c. Fagin.
   d. Mr. Bumble.

Remembering Detail

2. What did Fagin take to share with Bill Sikes?
   a. a melting pot b. a packet of gold pieces c. a little basket d. a jug
3. On his way to the bookstall, Oliver
   a. took a wrong turn. b. stopped to talk. c. lost the books. d. met his sister.

Drawing Conclusions

4. The man who burst out of the tavern was
   a. Mr. Grimwig. b. Bill Sikes. c. a police officer.
   d. Charley.

THINKING IT OVER

After reading this chapter, do you think that Bill Sikes believes that a dog is "a man's best friend"?

CHAPTER 5

Finding the Main Idea

1. In this chapter, Oliver is brought back to Fagin to
   a. become a thief. b. be adopted. c. get lost again.
   d. go to prison.

Remembering Detail

2. The name of Sikes's dog was
   a. Bates. b. Chaps. c. To Let. d. Bull's-eye.

3. Sikes demanded that Fagin give him
   a. Oliver. b. the five pounds. c. the books. d. a club.

Drawing Conclusions
4. Nancy can best be described as
   a. completely bad. b. mostly bad. c. completely good.
   d. having both bad and good qualities.

THINKING IT OVER
Why do you think that Nancy decided to stand up for Oliver?
Do you think that Sikes and Fagin expected Nancy to behave that way?

CHAPTER 6

Finding the Main Idea
1. Mr. Bumble convinced Mr. Brownlow that Oliver was
   a. evil and ungrateful. b. a dear, gentle child.
   c. honest. d. greatly feared.

Remembering Detail
2. Before going to London, Mr. Bumble saw
   a. Oliver. b. the Artful Dodger. c. two paupers.
   d. little Dick.
3. Mr. Bumble found out about the reward for Oliver
   a. in the newspaper. b. from Mrs. Mann. c. at Pentonville. d. from Mr. Grimwig.

Drawing Conclusions
4. Mr. Brownlow believed Mr. Bumble's story about Oliver because
   a. he wanted to believe him. b. Mr. Bumble seemed so honest. c. Oliver seemed untrustworthy from the beginning. d. Mr. Bumble's story seemed reasonable.

THINKING IT OVER
If Mr. Bumble had known what Mr. Brownlow wanted to hear about Oliver, how could he have changed his story?

CHAPTER 7

Finding the Main Idea
1. In this chapter, Fagin sets out to

a. save Oliver from crime.   b. cause Oliver to become a criminal.   c. frighten Oliver.   d. make Oliver happy.

Remembering Detail

2. Fagin told Oliver about an ungrateful boy who
   a. became a magistrate.   b. was a great thief.   c. was hanged.   d. ran away.
3. The Dodger and Charley explained to Oliver that stealing
   a. was hard work.   b. was against the law.   c. was easy.   d. was fun.

Drawing Conclusions

4. Tom Chitling probably got his special "uniform"
   a. from Fagin.   b. at the workhouse.   c. in prison.
   d. from the Dodger.

THINKING IT OVER

Why didn't Fagin allow Oliver to be left alone?

CHAPTER 8

Finding the Main Idea

1. Fagin and Bill Sikes were planning
   a. to send Oliver away.   b. a big robbery.   c. to have Oliver kidnapped.   d. to send Nancy away.

Remembering Detail

2. The robbers wanted to steal
   a. silver.   b. money.   c. jewelry.   d. gold.
3. Sikes said that he only needed
   a. Crackit and the right tool.   b. a boy and a crowbar.
   c. Oliver and Crackit.   d. the right tool and a boy.

Drawing Conclusions

4. You can guess that the robbery probably will be
   a. very dangerous.   b. easy.   c. difficult.   d. enjoyable.

THINKING IT OVER

In this chapter, how does Oliver become important to Fagin and Bill Sikes?

CHAPTER 9

Finding the Main Idea

1. In this chapter, Oliver was taken to

a. Sikes's hideout. **b.** Fagin's new hideout. **c.** Tom's hideout. **d.** a robbery.

Remembering Detail

2. Fagin gave Oliver a book about
   a. London. **b.** orphaned children. **c.** great criminals. **d.** spirits.
3. What did Sikes pick up from the table?
   a. Oliver's cap. **b.** a handkerchief. **c.** a pistol. **d.** Oliver's supper.

Drawing Conclusions

4. In taking Oliver to Sikes, Nancy felt
   a. uneasy. **b.** peaceful. **c.** indifferent. **d.** happy.

THINKING IT OVER

Nancy said, "God forgive me. I never thought of this." Why do you think she decided to help Oliver again?

CHAPTER 10

Finding the Main Idea

1. This chapter is mostly about
   a. Oliver and Sikes's journey. **b.** the Coach and Horses. **c.** Oliver in London. **d.** Sikes's hideaway.

Remembering Detail

2. Sikes told the cart driver that Oliver was
   a. a runaway. **b.** a thief. **c.** his boy. **d.** a house-breaker.
3. At Chertsey Bridge, Oliver thought that Sikes would
   a. kill him. **b.** let him go. **c.** leave him. **d.** get on a horse.

Drawing Conclusions

4. During their journey, Oliver must have looked upon Sikes with
   a. admiration. **b.** fear. **c.** laughter. **d.** indifference.

THINKING IT OVER

Why do you think that Sikes used so many different means of transportation during the journey?

CHAPTER 11

Finding the Main Idea

1. In this chapter, Oliver receives
   a. a serious injury. **b.** a lot of money. **c.** bad news.
   d. a great meal.

Remembering Detail

2. What did the robbers carry when they left the house?
   a. dark lanterns and food **b.** clubs and blankets
   c. pistols and liquor **d.** dark lanterns and clubs
3. Oliver was pushed through the
   a. scullery window. **b.** kitchen window. **c.** street door.
   d. upstairs window.

Drawing Conclusions

4. The robbery was interrupted because
   a. Oliver cried out. **b.** someone in the house heard.
   c. Sikes fired his pistol. **d.** Crackit called out.

THINKING IT OVER

How would you describe Oliver's feelings during the events
that unfold in this chapter?

Part 3

CHAPTER 1

Finding the Main Idea

1. At the end of this chapter, Mrs. Corney probably thought
   of Mr. Bumble as a
   a. possible husband. **b.** good parochial officer. **c.** bad
   beadle. **d.** hard-hearted man.

Remembering Detail

2. Mrs. Corney was
   a. matron at the workhouse. **b.** upset with Mr. Bumble. **c.** afraid of Mr. Bumble. **d.** a pauper's wife.
3. Mr. Bumble went to Mrs. Corney's to deliver
   a. tea. **b.** kittens. **c.** wine. **d.** a small teapot.

Drawing Conclusions

4. In their opinions about the treatment of paupers, both

Mr. Bumble and Mrs. Corney might be described as
a. caring. b. uncaring. c. merciful. d. progressive.

THINKING IT OVER
Mrs. Corney said that Mr. Bumble might be "hard hearted." Is he? Why or why not?

CHAPTER 2

Finding the Main Idea
1. In this chapter, Mrs. Corney found out something about
   a. Oliver's birth. b. Old Sally's birth. c. an apprentice. d. Old Sally's attendant.

Remembering Detail
2. The doctor said that the patient was to have
   a. hot broth. b. some food. c. medicine. d. hot wine.
3. According to Old Sally, the young mother had said
   a. "Take pity on a poor child!" b. "Cold night!"
   c. "I shall be surprised." d. "Not long, mistress."

Drawing Conclusions
4. Old Sally probably made her confession because she
   a. felt guilty for what she had done. b. wanted to help Oliver's mother. c. wanted attention. d. wanted to be paid for her secrets.

THINKING IT OVER
Explain why Mrs. Corney seemed so concerned about what the old woman had to say.

CHAPTER 3

Finding the Main Idea
1. Fagin found out
   a. where Sikes was. b. that Oliver was missing.
   c. that the robbery was successful. d. that Toby was missing.

Remembering Detail
2. What did Toby want to do first?
   a. talk to Fagin b. eat and drink c. find Sikes
   d. talk to the Dodger

3. Where did Fagin find out the robbery failed?
   a. from the Dodger   **b.** from Tom Chitling   **c.** in the newspaper   **d.** at the police station

Drawing Conclusions

4. The mood in the old den can best be described as
   a. joyful.   **b.** tense.   **c.** cold.   **d.** playful.

THINKING IT OVER

What do you think Fagin was most worried about when he heard the news about Oliver?

CHAPTER 4

Finding the Main Idea

1. The author uses this chapter to introduce
   a. Barney.   **b.** the landlord.   **c.** Monks.   **d.** the bartender.

Remembering Detail

2. Fagin stopped at the Three Cripples to ask about
   a. Nancy.   **b.** Oliver.   **c.** Crackit.   **d.** Sikes.
3. Monks wanted Oliver
   a. to die.   **b.** made into a thief.   **c.** adopted.   **d.** to become rich.

Drawing Conclusions

4. Nancy hopes that Oliver is dead because
   a. she thinks he would be better off dead than forced to lead a criminal life.   **b.** she hates Oliver.   **c.** Oliver is a threat to Bill Sikes.   **d.** Oliver is a threat to Fagin.

THINKING IT OVER

After his conversation with Monks, do you think that Fagin will give up on finding Oliver? Explain.

CHAPTER 5

Finding the Main Idea

1. Mr. Bumble and Mrs. Corney decided to
   a. visit the undertaker's.   **b.** get married.   **c.** leave the workhouse.   **d.** visit Mr. Slout.

Remembering Detail

2. The board allowed Mrs. Corney
   a. coals, tea, and wine.   b. a peppermint mixture.
   c. tea and candles.   d. coals, candles, and a house.
3. Mrs. Corney calls Mr. Bumble
   a. a sweet beadle.   b. an irresponsible turkey.   c. an
   irreverent duckling.   d. an irresistible duck.

Drawing Conclusions

4. Mr. Bumble really wanted to marry Mrs. Corney because
   a. he loved her.   b. he wanted candles.   c. he thought
   that she had money.   d. he was lonely.

THINKING IT OVER

How is Mr. Bumble's behavior in this chapter different from
his usual behavior?

CHAPTER 6

Finding the Main Idea

1. A wounded Oliver found his way back to
   a. the scene of the robbery.   b. the town.   c. Fagin's
   hideaway.   d. the ditch.

Remembering Detail

2. Oliver, Sikes, and Toby were followed by
   a. police officers.   b. other thieves.   c. dogs.
   d. wagons.
3. Where had Sikes left Oliver?
   a. in a clay ditch   b. in a field   c. in a pond   d. in the
   road

Drawing Conclusions

4. Giles and Brittles can best be described as
   a. brave.   b. fearful.   c. resourceful.   d. loyal.

THINKING IT OVER

How do you think Oliver expected to be treated by the people
in the mansion? Explain.

CHAPTER 7

Finding the Main Idea

1. The author uses this chapter to introduce

a. Giles and Brittles. b. the Maylies. c. the cook and the maid. d. the tinker.

Remembering Detail
2. Miss Rose was
   a. mistress of the house. b. Mrs. Maylie's daughter.
   c. Mrs. Maylie's niece. d. Dr. Losberne's niece.
3. Dr. Losberne asked Mrs. Maylie and Rose to
   a. see the patient. b. leave the house. c. stay in the dining room. d. fetch something from his gig.

Drawing Conclusions
4. When the Maylies see Oliver, you can guess that they will be
   a. upset. b. angry. c. frightened. d. surprised.

THINKING IT OVER
Why hadn't Giles told everyone that Oliver was just a boy?

CHAPTER 8

Finding the Main Idea
1. The Maylies decided to
   a. send Oliver to the police. b. help Oliver. c. put Oliver out of the house. d. send Giles to the police.

Remembering Detail
2. The doctor had
   a. bound Oliver's arm in splints. b. tied Oliver's arm in a shawl. c. bound Oliver's leg in splints. d. bandaged Oliver's arm.
3. Giles said that he would never be happy again if
   a. Oliver lived. b. the robbers were caught. c. Oliver died. d. Oliver was a robber.

Drawing Conclusions
4. "This poor boy is certainly not a robber!" When Mrs. Maylie makes this statement about Oliver, she is influenced by
   a. his appearance. b. Rose's feelings. c. his words.
   d. Dr. Losberne's feelings.

THINKING IT OVER
Does the doctor confuse Giles and Brittles on purpose? Explain.

CHAPTER 9

Finding the Main Idea
 1. In this chapter, Oliver
     a. gets into more trouble. b. is cleared of trouble.
     c. loses the Maylies' trust. d. recovers from his injury.

Remembering Detail
 2. Blathers and Duff said that the robbery attempt was
     a. a professional job. b. a "put-up" job. c. a country
     hand. d. easy to solve.
 3. Rose offered the police officers
     a. tea. b. a little wine. c. something to eat. d. ale.

Drawing Conclusions
 4. The person who had the greatest influence in delaying
     the police investigation was
     a. Mrs. Maylie. b. Dr. Losberne. c. Brittles.
     d. Rose.

THINKING IT OVER
Oliver finally may have found kind friends. How do you think
he'll feel when he finds out what happened with the police?

CHAPTER 10

Finding the Main Idea
 1. Oliver and the Maylies
     a. became close friends. b. disliked each other.
     c. didn't spend time together. d. went back to town.

Remembering Detail
 2. Oliver and Dr. Losberne discovered that Mr. Brownlow
     a. had moved to London. b. had gone to the West In-
     dies. c. had moved to America. d. was still at his
     home.
 3. Every morning, Oliver
     a. studied reading and writing. b. sang and played the
     piano. c. studied the Bible. d. read aloud.

Drawing Conclusions
 4. From his actions, Dr. Losberne might be considered both

a. kind and cruel.   b. courageous and reckless.
c. wise and stupid.   d. happy and sad.

THINKING IT OVER

The disappointments at Chertsey Bridge and at Dr. Brownlow's could have made the doctor doubt Oliver's story. Do you think they did? Explain.

Part 4

CHAPTER 1

Finding the Main Idea

1. In this chapter, Rose Maylie
   a. got married.   b. became very ill.   c. left the country.
   d. became very angry.

Remembering Detail

2. Oliver went to the market town to send a letter to
   a. Harry Maylie.   b. Fagin.   c. Mr. Brownlow.   d. Dr.
   Losberne.
3. The stranger in the inn yard
   a. tried to strike Oliver.   b. ran after Oliver.   c. took
   the letter.   d. went to the Maylies.

Drawing Conclusions

4. Mrs. Maylie must have thought of Rose as
   a. just a niece.   b. a daughter.   c. ungrateful.
   d. unkind.

THINKING IT OVER

Why do you think that Oliver suppressed his own emotions during Rose's illness?

CHAPTER 2

Finding the Main Idea

1. Oliver's new life is upset when he sees
   a. Mr. Brownlow.   b. the Dodger and Fagin.   c. Fagin
   and the stranger.   d. Sikes.

Remembering Detail

2. In this chapter, Oliver meets

a. Mrs. Maylie's nephew.   b. Mrs. Maylie's son.
c. Mrs. Maylie's brother.   d. Rose's brother.
3. Dr. Losberne gave Giles a reward of
a. silver.   b. five pounds.   c. twenty-five pounds.
d. gold.

Drawing Conclusions
4. When Oliver saw Fagin, you can guess that he thought
a. that Fagin might kidnap him again.   b. that nothing
would happen.   c. that Fagin was lost.   d. of running
away.

THINKING IT OVER
Were there ever any flowers in Fagin's den or in any of the
places frequented by the other underworld characters in the
story? Would love of flowers be characteristic of Fagin, Bill
Sikes, and the other thieves? Why or why not?

CHAPTER 3

Finding the Main Idea
1. The author used this chapter to show that Rose and
Harry
a. were in love.   b. planned to marry.   c. left for
Chertsey.   d. were not friends.

Remembering Detail
2. Where did Giles go to ask about the intruders?
a. inns in the village   b. houses in the village
c. alehouses in the village   d. farms in the village
3. Rose refused to marry Harry because she
a. loved someone else.   b. had a blight on her name.
c. hadn't asked Mrs. Maylie.   d. was too rich.

Drawing Conclusions
4. Oliver called out "Fagin, Fagin!" because he
a. was happily surprised.   b. thought that Fagin was
lost.   c. was afraid.   d. wanted to return to Fagin's
den.

THINKING IT OVER
Do you think that Harry Maylie will give up trying to get Rose
to marry him? Why or why not?

CHAPTER 4

Finding the Main Idea
1. Harry makes Oliver promise to
   a. behave better. b. secretly write to him. c. talk to Rose. d. write to the doctor.

Remembering Detail
2. Harry left the country with
   a. Dr. Losberne. b. Giles. c. Rose. d. Mrs. Maylie.
3. Oliver was to write to Harry every other
   a. week. b. Wednesday. c. Monday. d. month.

Drawing Conclusions
4. You can guess that what Harry really wanted to know was
   a. had Rose become ill again. b. had Rose changed her mind about marriage. c. how Oliver liked his new home. d. had Oliver learned to write well.

THINKING IT OVER
How did Dr. Losberne account for all the inconsistencies in Harry's conduct?

CHAPTER 5

Finding the Main Idea
1. In this chapter, Mr. Bumble met
   a. Fagin. b. Monks. c. Old Sally. d. Oliver.

Remembering Detail
2. After an argument with Mrs. Bumble, Mr. Bumble
   a. frightened her. b. went for a drink. c. stayed at home. d. washed linen.
3. Monks wanted information about
   a. the workhouse. b. Oliver. c. Mrs. Bumble. d. Oliver's mother.

Drawing Conclusions
4. You can guess that Mr. Bumble and the former Mrs. Corney
   a. lived happily. b. had become richer. c. fought very often. d. knew all about Monks.

THINKING IT OVER

Do you think that Mrs. Bumble will agree to meet with Monks? Explain.

CHAPTER 6

Finding the Main Idea

1. Mrs. Bumble gave Monks
   a. a pawnbroker's ticket.   **b.** twenty-five pounds.   **c.** a gold locket.   **d.** a lantern.

Remembering Detail

2. The name engraved inside the locket was
   a. Rose.   **b.** Oliver.   **c.** Mother.   **d.** Agnes.
3. When Monks received the locket, he
   a. put it into a bag.   **b.** threw it into the stream.
   c. said he would treasure it always.   **d.** hid it.

Drawing Conclusions

4. You can guess that Monks wanted
   a. no one to find the locket.   **b.** to give the locket away.
   c. Oliver to have the locket.   **d.** to keep the locket.

THINKING IT OVER

Why do you think that Monks went to such trouble to destroy the locket?

CHAPTER 7

Finding the Main Idea

1. The author uses this chapter to show that
   a. Nancy plans to help Oliver.   **b.** Fagin had lots of money.   **c.** Monks knew Nancy.   **d.** Sikes treated Nancy well.

Remembering Detail

2. Fagin brought Bill Sikes
   a. money.   **b.** gold.   **c.** food and drink.   **d.** food and money.
3. Who did Nancy go to see in the West End of London?
   a. Monks   **b.** Oliver   **c.** Fagin   **d.** Rose

Drawing Conclusions

4. In her attitude toward Bill, Nancy can be described as
   a. loyal.   b. scornful.   c. deceitful.   d. trusting.

THINKING IT OVER

At the end of this chapter, Nancy was about to betray Fagin and his friends. What does this tell you about the kind of person Nancy really was? Explain.

CHAPTER 8

Finding the Main Idea

1. In this chapter, Rose Maylie discovers
   a. why Monks was interested in Oliver.   b. that Oliver's story was untrue.   c. that Monks was a good man.
   d. that Oliver was a real criminal.

Remembering Detail

2. Monks is Oliver's
   a. uncle.   b. father.   c. brother.   d. nephew.
3. Nancy agrees to meet Rose
   a. in the country.   b. every night.   c. on London Bridge.   d. in the morning.

Drawing Conclusions

4. The man that Nancy tells Rose she cannot leave is
   a. Fagin.   b. Charley Bates.   c. the Dodger.   d. Bill Sikes.

THINKING IT OVER

Were you surprised that Nancy did not take advantage of Rose's offer to help Nancy leave her old life and get a fresh start?

Part 5

CHAPTER 1

Finding the Main Idea

1. Oliver's friends came up with a plan to
   a. cast him out.   b. find out about his parents.   c. help Monks.   d. report Nancy to the police.

Remembering Detail

2. Oliver found out that Mr. Brownlow
   a. lived on Craven Street. b. was still in the West Indies. c. didn't want to see him. d. had left London again.
3. Mr. Brownlow suggested that Monks should be caught
   a. on London Bridge. b. with Fagin. c. alone. d. by Oliver.

Drawing Conclusions

4. Mr. Grimwig probably kissed Rose because
   a. he was upset about Oliver. b. he wanted to marry her. c. he was happy about Oliver. d. he had met Rose before.

THINKING IT OVER

Mr. Brownlow refers to Nancy as "poor" Nancy. Was he referring to her lack of money? If not, why did he use that expression?

CHAPTER 2

Finding the Main Idea

1. This chapter is mostly about
   a. the Three Cripples. b. Noah and Charlotte.
   c. Barney and Fagin. d. Barney and Noah.

Remembering Detail

2. Noah and Charlotte had stolen
   a. Mrs. Sowerberry's jewels. b. money from the Sowerberrys. c. luggage from the Sowerberrys. d. money from the workhouse.
3. Fagin decided that Noah would be good at
   a. snatching bags. b. coffin making. c. the kinchin lay. d. bank robbing.

Drawing Conclusions

4. The word that best describes Noah's attitude toward Charlotte is
   a. affectionate. b. curious. c. contemptuous.
   d. distrustful.

THINKING IT OVER

What did Noah expect the life of a thief to be?

CHAPTER 3

Finding the Main Idea
1. In this chapter, the Artful Dodger
   a. finally got caught.   b. planned a big robbery.
   c. met Noah.   d. saw Fagin.

Remembering Detail
2. The Dodger was accused of stealing
   a. handkerchiefs.   b. a lady's purse.   c. a silver snuff-box.   d. money.
3. When he went to the police station, Noah was dressed
   a. like a policeman.   b. like a farm-cart driver.   c. like a prisoner.   d. like a rich man.

Drawing Conclusions
4. You can guess that the Dodger's experience will make the other young thieves feel
   a. afraid.   b. amused.   c. pleased.   d. no different.

THINKING IT OVER
What did the Artful Dodger mean by "deformation of character"?

CHAPTER 4

Finding the Main Idea
1. Fagin realized that Nancy
   a. wantcd to kill Sikes.   b. was meeting someone.
   c. had seen Rose Maylie.   d. had told on Monks.

Remembering Detail
2. Fagin told Nancy to come to him for
   a. money.   b. safety.   c. revenge.   d. help.
3. What did Fagin decide to do about Nancy?
   a. put a spy on her   b. talk to her again   c. kidnap her
   d. tell the police

Drawing Conclusions
4. In this chapter, Nancy shows her
   a. doubts and fears.   b. trust in Bill Sikes.   c. love of Bill Sikes.   d. trust in Fagin.

THINKING IT OVER
After reading this chapter, what words would you use to describe Noah?

CHAPTER 5

Finding the Main Idea
1. In this chapter, Noah Claypole
   a. committed another robbery.   b. visited Barney.
   c. fought with Fagin.   d. followed Nancy.

Remembering Detail
2. Noah complained that Fagin never gave him time to
   a. talk.   b. eat.   c. work.   d. go out.
3. Barney told Noah to
   a. keep to the right.   b. stay on the same side.
   c. keep to the left.   d. stay close.

Drawing Conclusions
4. Instead of having one of his other boys follow Nancy, Fagin uses Noah because
   a. Nancy wouldn't recognize Noah.   b. Noah is cleverer than the other boys.   c. the other boys would probably be afraid.   d. Fagin likes Noah best.

THINKING IT OVER
Do you think that Noah is very courageous? Why or why not?

CHAPTER 6

Finding the Main Idea
1. Nancy described to Rose and Mr. Brownlow
   a. how to find Fagin.   b. what Monks looked like.
   c. Sikes's hideaway.   d. what the spy looked like.

Remembering Detail
2. Nancy thought that Monks's age was about
   a. twenty.   b. thirty.   c. twenty-six.   d. thirty-eight.
3. Nancy asks Rose
   a. to tell Oliver good-bye.   b. to give her something to keep.   c. to help her get away.   d. to forget her.

Drawing Conclusions

4. From what Nancy said, you can guess that she suspected that
   a. Rose might not come.   b. she might be followed.
   c. Rose might get hurt.   d. Mr. Brownlow lied.

THINKING IT OVER

Did Nancy wish to cause Fagin any harm? Explain.

CHAPTER 7

Finding the Main Idea

1. In this chapter, Nancy was killed by
   a. Sikes.   b. Fagin.   c. Noah.   d. Monks.

Remembering Detail

2. Fagin hated Nancy for
   a. betraying him.   b. dealing with strangers.
   c. dealing with the police.   d. betraying Sikes.
3. The weapon Sikes used to kill Nancy was
   a. a knife.   b. his hands.   c. a club.   d. a bundle.

Drawing Conclusions

4. In this chapter, Fagin loses his
   a. money.   b. self-confidence.   c. friends.   d. contacts
   in the underworld.

THINKING IT OVER

Why was Fagin worried about Sikes being violent? Explain.

CHAPTER 8

Finding the Main Idea

1. This chapter is mostly about
   a. Sikes getting caught.   b. Sikes running away.
   c. Sikes telling Fagin.   d. Sikes and his dog.

Remembering Detail

2. What did Sikes do with the murder weapon?
   a. threw it out the window   b. carried it with him
   c. hid it   d. burned it
3. The stain that the peddler saw on Sikes's hat was really
   a. wine.   b. blood.   c. dirt.   d. beer.

Drawing Conclusions

4. What did Sikes resolve to do about Bull's-eye?
   a. give him away   b. leave him in the country
   c. drown him   d. take him along

THINKING IT OVER

Do you think that Bill's actions could be explained by sorrow for Nancy's fate or by fear of being punished for what he had done?

CHAPTER 9

Finding the Main Idea

1. Mr. Brownlow forced Monks to
   a. tell the police what he had done.   b. confess all that he had done.   c. tell Oliver what he had done.   d. tell Fagin what he had done.

Remembering Detail

2. Mr. Brownlow was to be married to Oliver's
   a. mother.   b. aunt.   c. sister.   d. cousin.
3. Dr. Losberne told Mr. Brownlow that
   a. Sikes would be taken.   b. Fagin got away.
   c. Monks was frightened.   d. Sikes had escaped.

Drawing Conclusions

4. You can guess that once Monks told his secrets,
   a. Oliver would be rich.   b. Oliver would be unhappy.
   c. Oliver wouldn't care.   d. Oliver would be upset.

THINKING IT OVER

What drove Monks to do all the terrible deeds against Oliver?

CHAPTER 10

Finding the Main Idea

1. In this chapter, Sikes
   a. met his end.   b. met the police.   c. saw Fagin for the last time.   d. met Harry Maylie.

Remembering Detail

2. When Charley saw Sikes, he cried
   a. "Is it true?"   b. "A complete smash!"   c. "You monster!"   d. "Hurrah!"

3. Sikes fell off the roof when
   a. Charley pushed him.   b. he was shot.   c. he lost his balance.   d. Bull's-eye barked.

Drawing Conclusions

4. You can guess that the man on horseback was
   a. Mr. Brownlow.   b. Monks.   c. Harry Maylie.
   d. Barney.

THINKING IT OVER

Why did Charley react so badly when he saw Sikes?

CHAPTER 11

Finding the Main Idea

1. In this chapter, Oliver finds
   a. great happiness.   b. no happiness.   c. much confusion.   d. very little hope.

Remembering Detail

2. Oliver could inherit his father's money only if
   a. he never married.   b. he made up with his brother.
   c. he was an honest and brave boy.   d. he hated his brother.

3. Oliver found out that Rose was his mother's
   a. sister.   b. close friend.   c. aunt.   d. niece.

Drawing Conclusions

4. You can guess that Monks will
   a. remain with Oliver and his new family.   b. begin to care for Oliver.   c. never see Oliver again.   d. keep in touch with Oliver.

THINKING IT OVER

Reread what Oliver's father stated in his will. Did Oliver live as his father had hoped? Explain.

CHAPTER 12

Finding the Main Idea
1. The judge sentenced Fagin to
   a. life in prison.   b. death.   c. hard labor in prison.
   d. freedom.

Remembering Detail
2. Fagin yelled for someone to bring him
   a. food.   b. bells.   c. light.   d. clothes.
3. Mr. Brownlow asked Fagin to tell him where he had hidden
   a. Monks's papers.   b. money.   c. the will.
   d. treasure.

Drawing Conclusions
4. When Oliver began to pray, Mr. Brownlow probably felt
   a. angry at Oliver.   b. proud of Oliver.   c. sorry for Fagin.   d. indifferent.

THINKING IT OVER
Do you think that Fagin was sorry for his life of crime? Why or why not?

CHAPTER 13

Finding the Main Idea
1. The author uses this chapter to tell
   a. about the New World.   b. what happened to Oliver and some of his friends.   c. about prison.   d. what happened to Toby Crackit.

Remembering Detail
2. Oliver was adopted by
   a. his aunt Rose.   b. Mr. Grimwig.   c. Mr. Brownlow.
   d. Mrs. Maylie.
3. Charley Bates became a
   a. spy for the police.   b. pastor.   c. carpenter.
   d. sheep farmer.

Drawing Conclusions

4. In this chapter, it is clear that
   a. Oliver will never again suffer. b. Agnes was finally happy. c. Oliver finally had some of the happiness he deserved. d. people who live in the country are happier than those who live in the city.

THINKING IT OVER

Why do you think that the author gave Oliver's life a happy ending? Explain.